Where Old Ghosts Meet

KITTY CONWAY

ISBN: 979-8-218-56622-7

Book Cover by Kitty Conway

For Mary. . .

"On a quiet street, where old ghosts meet, I see her walking now."
On Raglan Road, Patrick Kavanagh

Part One

Chapter 1

Now

"You've dealt with crazy shit before. You'll deal with this too," I whisper, just loud enough for only me to hear.

I stand across from the funeral home, the sun long set, watching the warm glow of light streaming through its windows. Everything looks serene and peaceful. It's quiet—a sharp contrast to the hammering of my heart. I take a tentative step forward and then pause, my breath catching somewhere between my chest and throat.

"Come on, Josie. Pull it together," I mutter, urging my legs to move, but they feel cemented to the pavement. The thought of facing the people inside looms large, but it's the pain of losing Sarge, my old friend and neighbor, that clouds my fear of revisiting old ghosts. If I don't go inside, maybe I can pretend he's still alive. Instinctively, my hand moves to my belly, trying to manage my breathing—or lack thereof. I don't know who I'll find inside, and I'm not sure how I'll be received, but all that matters right now is Sarge.

I square my shoulders. "This isn't about you," I remind myself. "Breathe. You're strong. You're brave. You've dealt with crazy shit before. You'll deal with this too." I repeat the words, my mantra, the same ones I've been telling myself for years whenever I feel the walls closing in.

Drawing in a deep breath, I force myself to move, using another old trick to stave off the panic. "Name three things," I remind myself—a method that usually calms my racing heart and clears my vision.

"Car, door, tree. You're safe," I whisper until my feet, seemingly of their own accord, carry me up the steps to the entrance. "You're safe."

This is bad. I'm literally pulling out every self-help tactic I've accumulated through years of therapy and reading. I'm not sure if I'm making myself better or worse. "You're safe," I repeat as I cross the threshold of the funeral home. After offering a quick, sad smile to the man in the black suit, who nods sympathetically as he ushers me through the door, I mostly keep my eyes down. I barely glance up as I stand in line to sign the guest book. I quickly scrawl my name, my bangles jangling in the quiet, willing myself not to look at any familiar names.

Lifting my eyes, the sight of the casket hits me—along with a sudden, gut-wrenching sadness—and I rear back slightly. I was so consumed with anxiety, so focused on taming it, that I forgot I was about to face Sarge's body in a casket. I'm not prepared. I will never be prepared for this.

All my coping tricks go out the window. A wave of pure grief washes over me as my eyes land on the face of one of the few people who truly loved me. But that doesn't really matter right now. All that matters in this moment is how much I love him. He looks so peaceful, as if merely sleeping, with an American flag folded neatly in the corner of his casket. But something feels off. He doesn't quite look like Sarge. And that alone pulls the air from my lungs. I'm reminded of how long I've been gone. He seems older, thinner, less robust than I remember. Tears blur my vision as I focus on his hands—those hands that held mine through some of my darkest moments. They're still now, no Lucky Strike cigarette between his fingers. It feels wrong seeing him without one. Surely death has earned him a smoke.

After a silent prayer and the sign of the cross, I touch Sarge's hands, startled by how cold they are. I silently thank him for everything and promise that I'll keep talking to him—through the ether, if I must. I've become quite the expert at holding in my emotions, but I can't stop the tears that spill down my cheeks. I love Sarge, plain and simple, and the agony flaring inside me serves as a painful reminder of what I've lost and what I've let go.

Taking a deep breath, I gather myself and turn to face the curious glances of his family. Many of them have never met me. I've been gone too long. A petite older woman steps forward—Sarge's sister, Alice—and reaches out her hands.

"Oh, Josie. You made it. Sarge knew you would," she says, her eyes glistening with unshed tears.

"Alice!" I exclaim, my voice coming out louder than I intended as I wrap her in a hug. "I'm so sorry," I begin, but she gently cuts me off.

"Oh, hush now, dear. He had a long, good life. He wouldn't want you crying," she says with a warm, comforting smile. "You know that better than anyone. He was ready. But he made me promise you'd be here," she adds with a soft laugh. "I told him, 'William, that girl's across the ocean!' But he insisted, 'No, Alice. Josie will come.'"

A sound escapes me, something between a chuckle and a sob. Sarge knew me better than I knew myself. He believed I'd come, even when I wasn't sure. Only he could have pulled me back here, and the familiar sting of guilt creeps in for waiting until he was gone.

"How many years has it been, honey?" Alice asks, her voice gentle.

My throat tightens as I force out, "Almost fifteen."

I try to apologize again, this time for not coming back sooner, but Alice hushes me softly. "No need, love. You're here now," she whispers, glancing around before leaning in closer. "My brother left something for you. I can't explain it now, but stay awhile. Sit down. I'll find you when it's quieter," she promises with a knowing smile.

Nodding, I let her introduce me to the rest of the family. Sarge never married, never had children. That part of his life was always locked away from me, and now, only now, do I realize how strange that was. He was such a fatherly figure to me that it seemed a waste he didn't have a child or grandchild to lavish all that affection and wisdom on. After offering my condolences, I look for a corner to retreat to, but every corner buzzes with quiet conversation, despite it being the end of the viewing. My anxiety begins to spike again, and no amount of self-talk helps.

Then, as the crowd blurs into anonymity, one figure snaps into focus. One voice drowns out the rest. I'd know him anywhere—the deep timbre of his voice, the sound of his laugh, the steady energy he exudes. Even with his back to me, I feel the pull toward him. I can imagine the smile on his face as he talks with Sarge's friends—a smile that once belonged to me, a smile that once felt like sunlight warming my soul. So when Sawyer turns, mid-laugh, and our eyes meet, his smile falters and my heart sinks. And I remember what it feels like to be left out in the cold.

***

I never expected Sawyer to be happy to see me. In fact, I hoped we'd never see each other again. But I have to admit, his reaction is a bit jarring. He turns back to his conversation, excuses himself, and walks straight out the front door. Clearly, fifteen years hasn't eased the bad feelings, but frankly, I should be the one harboring them. A twinge of anger creeps up my spine. He made a decision a long time ago that didn't include me, so I upended my life to ensure we'd never see each other again. He should show a little gratitude, as far as I'm concerned.

Before returning to Maplewood, Pennsylvania, this morning, I might have obsessed over how to dodge him—my late arrival to the viewing was part of that plan. Deep down, I knew that if Sawyer was still around, I'd probably run into him—something I planned to avoid. Yet in the still, quiet moments, a profound sadness crept in at the haunting possibility that he might no longer be in Maplewood, and the unspoken disappointment at not seeing him unexpectedly began to bother me. I should be glad he walked out of the funeral home. After all, I'd put a literal ocean between us just to ensure we'd never run into each other again.

My hands are clammy, my heart thrashing in my chest, my stomach knotted. I quickly find a seat, avoiding contact with anyone who might recognize me. I certainly recognize a few people from town, but Sarge's viewing is no place for a reunion. Mrs. Miner and her brother, owners of Miner's Inn where I'm staying, sit huddled in the corner, their faces stricken with sadness. I notice a few other familiar faces from my past, mostly older now, the years etched into their features and movements. It suddenly dawns on me how long fifteen years really is.

When I reflect on those years, they seem to have gone by both quickly and slowly. The memories from when I left are as raw as they were that day, but only a long stretch of time could have changed me the way it has. The transformation I've gone through required several painful years, but the result, as far as I'm concerned, is strength—even if it was hard-fought and even if I'm not immune to panic attacks and flashbacks.

Just as I start to feel the weight of fatigue settle over me, the line of people paying respects begins to thin. Alice walks in my direction. I move to stand, but she urges me to stay seated. Planting her giant purse on the floor beside her, she sits too.

"You must be exhausted, Alice. There were so many people here."

"Oh, my brother knew everyone, didn't he, honey? He was a sort of fixture in Maplewood. A character in many people's lives." She smiles kindly and reaches for my hand again. "But he especially loved being in your life."

The tears that have been threatening to spill over all evening well up, and before I can stop them, one escapes. "I loved him. He was . . ." I shake my head, searching for the right words to measure the importance of this man in my life. But in the end, there are no sufficient words. "He was so good to me. He wasn't just a staple in Maplewood. He was—he *is* Maplewood. I loved him more than I can tell you."

"Don't think it was one-sided, sweetheart. Don't think that for even a second. You filled a hole in my brother's life that no one else could."

I shake my head and laugh. "I'm pretty sure I gave him more than he bargained for."

"Oh no, you were special. Listen, none of us know the whole story, but William wanted a family. We know that much." She pauses, her expression softening. "This life just didn't allow that for him. But you were as much a daughter to him as you could've been, and I can't tell you how grateful I am for that."

"I left." I shake my head as more tears fall. "I left everything, and I left him. And I'm so, so sorry." The guilt claws at my heart.

"Listen to me, and listen well. I haven't been around, living in Florida all these years, and I only know what Sarge told me. But I do know this—whatever happened, you needed to leave. And Sarge knew it. He often said it broke his heart that you had to go, but he also knew it was necessary."

I nod, trying to keep it together. "Alice, I really did need to go back then. But I should've come back before—before this." I can't even bring myself to say the word: *death*.

At that, she reaches into her bag and pulls out an envelope, handing it over. "This is for you."

I stare at the envelope, recognizing my name in Sarge's familiar handwriting. *A letter? He wrote me a letter?* I am overwhelmed with a mix of deep grief and excitement. The thought of never hearing from Sarge again is tearing new holes into me. Perhaps this letter will ease my broken heart. Sarge is the only one who can console me right now. And here he is—doing it from beyond the grave.

Sarge was the only person from Maplewood I had contact with over the past decade. Some conversations lasted ten minutes, others an hour. The shorter ones usually came to an abrupt end if I thought he was going to bring up old ghosts. It was only recently that I finally found myself more willing to talk. More willing to listen.

"Don't open it here. Where are you staying?"

I shake my head, rattled from my thoughts, not fully comprehending that Alice is speaking to me.

"You do have a place to stay, right, honey? If not, I can call the hotel we're staying at and see if they have a room—"

"Oh no, no. I'm sorry. Yes, I have a room. I'm staying at Miner's Inn in Maplewood. I checked in this morning, so I'm good. All settled in for the week."

"Oh, wonderful!" She leans in with a twinkle in her eye that reminds me so much of her brother. "Except for Mrs. Miner. She can be a bit dry, but her brother is lovely."

A sudden laugh bursts out of me, and I cover my mouth. "Dry is a good way to put it. But I couldn't find a place for a full week except Miner's. I guess there's a festival happening, so all the hotels nearby are booked. There was a last-minute cancellation right before I called."

"I guess that's either a blessing or a curse." She winks and stands up. I stand too and look fondly down at the much shorter Alice. "Go on now. Get some rest."

"I will. Thank you, Alice."

"No, honey. Thank you." She turns to walk away but stops short. "Oh, and I think there's an old friend of yours waiting for you outside. I spoke to him earlier. Handsome redhead."

And as if she hasn't just punched me in the gut, she walks away.

***

I exit the funeral home on shaky legs, but I'll be damned if I let Sawyer see any sign of my anxiety, so I force myself to stand tall. I scan the area for him, but he's nowhere to be found. I stand alone on the dark porch, feeling part of me suspiciously deflate. I don't want to see Sawyer, but my adrenaline kicks in, and somehow I feel ready to face him in this moment.

I immediately want to kick myself for giving him any power over my emotions. *Great, now he's the landlord of my fight-or-flight response,* I think bitterly. I don't deserve the hand I've been dealt—especially not the cards Sawyer has thrown my way.

And then, like an old, unwelcome friend, the familiar feeling of anger rises in my throat. I pace the porch, my thoughts taking off in a gallop.

He takes off like I did something wrong? Like he hasn't completely destroyed me? He has the nerve to disappear? He's a coward, just like everyone else I gave too much of myself to. And I have a right to be here.

I stomp my foot to punctuate my thoughts.

"The balls on this man," I murmur under my breath, a growl escaping my throat. It feels good to not be filled with anxiety. Even if it's anger, it's better than fear and self-doubt. Sure, I didn't do everything right, but I can't marinate in guilt when I wasn't entirely to blame. I worked hard to earn this peace.

"She lives . . ."

I jump at the familiar voice coming from the shadows, my hand flying to my chest. "Jesus!" I breathe.

I look over and see Sawyer sitting on a bench in the far corner of the porch. It's completely dark now, save for a faint porch light and the interior glow from the windows, but I still manage to make out a smirk on his face.

"You scared me," I say, hating the way my voice trembles slightly.

He stands up, a faint, unfriendly smile playing on his lips. "Funny. I should be the one scared, considering I'm the one seeing a ghost."

And here he is. The real Sawyer. Not the boy I knew years ago. This is the arrogant prick who rips hearts out and crushes them without a second thought. *Well, to hell with him!*

"Ah, clever. Such a funny guy," I reply dryly, trying to mask the swirl of emotions inside me.

"I haven't seen you in a while." Sawyer's tone holds a hint of bitterness, which really pisses me off.

It seems we're not even going to feign politeness after fifteen years. No false niceties. He's still far enough away that I can't make out his features, but I see his waves—still a little unruly. I wonder for a second if there are any grays woven through yet. What have the years seen that I didn't? I shake the sad thought and replace it with bitterness.

"Well, Sawyer, that was the plan," I say curtly.

"Was it, Josie?" And then, after a labored pause, "O."

That's a cruel reference to a familiarity we no longer share, but I'm not going to let him see me shaken, so we stand there in the darkness, saying nothing. I have no words for this man. I don't know him now, and I didn't know him then—even though I once thought I did.

I watch as he takes a deep breath, and suddenly something inside me aches at the hardness in his features, the obvious pain he's feeling. And even though I have no sympathy for Sawyer, I can understand the huge loss that is Sarge.

"I'm sorry about Sarge."

"About Sarge?" he says quietly. "Yeah, me too."

The silence between us is heavy. The years have not always been kind to me, and judging by Sawyer's tone, they might not have been kind to him either. Plus, the absence of Sarge feels like a raw, gaping wound. We are two people in obvious pain, even though I'm trying desperately to hide my side of it.

I shift uncomfortably, trying to find the right words. "It's hard to believe he's gone."

He lets out an exasperated breath, and I ready myself for battle. "Is it? Is it hard to believe when you haven't exactly been around—"

"Oh, save it, Sawyer! Save your sob story for someone who cares."

His eyes harden, and any slight sign of the boy I used to know vanishes. "And there it is! The truth! You never cared!"

"*Me?* You have no idea what I went through," I snap, my voice rising.

"Don't pretend you're the only victim here," he shoots back, stepping closer. "We both suffered."

"Because of *you*!" I shout, the anger boiling over.

His face twists with pain, anger, and confusion. "What the hell are you talking about? I'm not the one who ran off to start a new life!"

I cross my arms, trying to protect myself. "What the hell are *you* talking about? You made me!"

He steps closer, and my breath catches. I can see him now. He's stepped right under the weak porch light, and there he is. Sawyer. And my heart—if I have one—sighs. And then it twists uncomfortably, noticing the subtle signs of age, the years I've missed. And he's still so strikingly handsome. More so, in fact. Leave it to him to age well. It's cruel. But it's his eyes. The eyes I spent countless hours staring into. So full of soul and feeling and what I once believed to be love—now they seem sad, empty, tired. I wonder if he sees the same in mine.

"This isn't the place. How long are you here for?"

"A week. Why?"

He rocks back on his heels, hands in the pockets of his slacks. "A week."

I take a step back, my eyes never leaving his, realizing he's making plans. If there's one thing I've learned in fifteen years, it's the fine art of self-preservation, and I'm about to protect myself at all costs.

"I'm sorry, Sawyer," I say, lifting my hands as if to ward off the conversation. "But I have no plans to revisit the past this week. I can't go back in time, and I definitely can't go back to the past with you."

His features darken, and I find myself mourning the Sawyer I thought I knew all those years ago. I never knew him to be this serious and intense. It feels so wrong.

"Then say something to me now, Josie. Something worth saying. Something that can explain why this is the first time I'm seeing you—hearing you—in fifteen goddamn years!"

I let out an exasperated sigh, rolling my eyes. "Come on, Sawyer. You said it. This is not the place."

"Is there another time or place? Maybe twelve years ago? Ten years ago? Five years ago? You tell me when I could ask you, Josie, because you were here one day and then you were gone, and I don't know where the hell you've been!"

His hand leaves his pocket and runs through his hair in a familiar move that shows his exasperation.

"And now you're here for a week, and you can't give me five minutes of it?"

I laugh humorlessly. "Funny how five minutes can change everything, isn't it, Sawyer?"

His brows knit together, and his head tilts slightly as the lights of a car briefly illuminate him before lighting up the porch.

I hear the car door slam and footsteps approaching before a familiar Irish accent cuts through the night. "Feck it, Josie, I'm sorry. It was hell trying to get an Uber. Are you okay, love?"

I watch as Sawyer's eyes narrow, taking in Dermott as he unsuspectingly approaches me on the porch. I don't believe Sawyer deserves an introduction, but for Dermott's sake, I make an attempt.

"Sawyer, this is—"

"Yeah, I know who he is."

Dermott's familiar grin falters when he notices the tension in the air, and he puffs out a breath. "Whoa. I seem to have stepped in on something."

"No, buddy, you've stepped in on nothing." And with that, Sawyer is off the porch, walking down the darkened street toward God knows where.

I hear Dermott sigh beside me. "I take it that's Sawyer."

I don't take my eyes off his retreating shadow. "That's Sawyer."

Chapter 2

Then

It was an oppressively hot day, the kind that offered no escape from the relentless sun. Even the shade under the pavilion at the baseball field brought no relief from the stickiness.

If home hadn't been just as unbearable, I wouldn't have bothered with the game.

"Hurry up, Jason's on the mound today! You don't want to miss this," Beatrice called, heading toward the chain-link fence that enclosed the baseball field.

The heat had worn me down, and I followed slowly.

"Why the sudden interest in your brother's pitching?" I leaned against the now-cooling fence, the sun dipping below the horizon, leaving the air thick and muggy. My auburn hair, tied up in a high bun, had strands sticking to my sweaty skin. The sun seemed to soak into my reddish hair and fair skin like a sponge.

"I just need to move, or I'll stick to the bench," she said with a shrug, glancing back at the picnic table we'd just left, trying to seem casual. "Maybe he'll mess up, and I can tease him later."

I smirked, knowing neither of us wanted to see Jason fail on the field. The siblings, barely a year apart, were loyal to a fault, despite their frequent squabbles. Being close with Beatrice meant Jason felt like a brother to me too.

Jason's fastball cut through the air, landing with a satisfying thud in the catcher's mitt. The ump called a strike, and a cheer burst out of me, surprising even myself. Beatrice looked at me in disbelief before heading back to the food stand, chuckling at my sudden enthusiasm.

As the players jogged off the field, my gaze fixed on the catcher. Taller than his teammates, he removed his mask, revealing a mane of auburn waves. Some damp curls clung to his forehead, which he casually swept back with his hand as he walked to the dugout. Something about him sparked a curiosity I couldn't shake.

"Josie. Helloooo." Beatrice's voice snapped me back to the present. "Are you asleep?" she asked, laughing.

No—in fact, something I couldn't quite put my finger on had just woken up.

***

After the game, we strolled the two blocks from the field to Maplewood Corners. The warm evening air was thick with the sound of cicadas, and the orange glow of streetlights lit up the familiar path to Maple's Ice Cream Shoppe, a beloved local haunt.

"I'm so sick of my parents hassling me about finding a summer hobby," Beatrice whined in typical angsty fashion as we joined the line at the shop. "Seriously, summer vacation hasn't even started, and they're already bugging me. Like, give me a break!"

I smiled at my friend's ramblings. Once she started, she wouldn't stop.

"Anyway, I can't listen to them tomorrow. Can I come over to your house in the morning?"

Dammit. I should have seen it coming.

"Umm. Why do I feel like I'm doing something tomorrow?" I mumbled, trying to buy time to come up with an excuse.

Beatrice tilted her head. "You didn't mention anything going on this weekend?"

It was hard to lie to someone I shared everything with.

"I know. I just feel like my dad said we had plans." I laughed awkwardly, desperately searching for an excuse to keep Beatrice away from my house.

She gave me a skeptical look.

"But yeah, you can come over," I added quickly as we reached the front entrance, and she smiled. "Unless I have to do something with my parents." Her face fell, and I made a big show of looking at the menu framed on the outside of the building.

The bell above the door jingled as we stepped inside. A blast of cool air hit us, a welcome relief from the unseasonably warm day. The place buzzed with locals enjoying a sweet treat on this sweltering evening. After getting our ice cream, we walked back outside, rounding the building to the back patio. Twinkling lights draped from wooden pillars, casting a whimsical glow over the picnic tables.

"Beatrice! Come here!" a few girls from Beatrice's class called out from a table at the back. I didn't go to Maplewood Middle School like the rest of them. I attended the small Catholic school, St. Mary's, a few miles away. It might have been a short distance, but socially, it couldn't be farther away.

"You've met these girls before, right, Josie?" Beatrice asked as we approached the table. She always considered my comfort, knowing I didn't know many people outside of St. Mary's.

"I think so. I met Val and Rain before. I'm not sure about the other two."

"Hi, girls! You know my bestie, Josie?"

Val's eyes scanned me, comparing my underdeveloped thirteen-year-old body to her own. "Yeah, you've brought her around before," she said, returning to whispering and laughing with Rain.

Beatrice half rolled her eyes and introduced me to the other two girls, who seemed friendlier. "This is Abby and Molly."

I was greeting them with a smile when laughter erupted from the entrance to the patio. Jason had arrived with a few boys from the team, and my heart skipped a beat when I saw the auburn-haired catcher among them. My stomach fluttered, and I felt my pulse quicken. Thank God for the cold ice cream in my hands; I was a mess.

Jason squeezed himself between the giggling duo of Molly and Abby while snatching Beatrice's ice cream. "Hands off my ice cream, Jason!" she shouted as she snatched it back.

I laughed, momentarily distracted from the catcher until Val's voice pierced the air.

"Hey, Sawyer."

Sawyer? His name is Sawyer? My young heart could barely handle it.

Val sauntered over to him. I watched her as she confidently wove through our group while I awkwardly held my cup of ice cream.

"I waved to you earlier, but you didn't wave back," Val said.

I glanced around and saw an empty bench, quickly sitting down to avoid drawing attention, and listened to the chatting around me.

"You must not have seen me." Val popped her hip out. If there was one thing obvious here, it was that Val liked to be seen.

"I saw you," Sawyer said casually.

"You didn't wave. Rude." Val giggled, but there was a definite annoyance in her tone.

I was stirring my ice cream when I sensed someone approaching. I looked up just as Sawyer took a seat beside me.

"Hi," I said, surprised by his presence.

"Hi." He glanced into my cup. "What's in the cup?"

"Ice cream," I said softly, cursing myself for the obvious answer.

He chuckled. "What kind?"

"Cookies and cream."

"Nice. The best kind."

More silence.

"What's your name?"

"Josie. What's yours?" I asked, even though I already knew he had the coolest name ever.

"John."

I looked at him in confusion, and he laughed. Oh my God, he laughed.

"Everyone calls me Sawyer. That's my last name."

"John Sawyer," I repeated, and we shared a smile. "I'm Josie O'Driscoll."

"Wow, that's an awesome name."

"Not as awesome as Sawyer."

"Nah. Josie O. That beats Sawyer any day. So, Josie O, where did you come from?"

Beatrice joined us. "I see you met my bestie, Josie." She observed us for a second. "You both have the same color hair." I took the opportunity to observe the hair peeking out from under his baseball cap and, at the same time, stole a glance at him. His hair was darker, deeper, richer. I didn't know Sawyer, but that just felt right. Mine was a lighter shade of auburn, made lighter by the sun.

"I was just asking where she's from." He seemed to be observing me too. "You don't live around here, do you? I haven't seen you before."

Beatrice flopped down next to Sawyer, making him scoot closer to me. "Oh my God! Yes, she lives around here. Jeez, if you don't go to Maplewood schools, people act like you're from outer space. Josie goes to St. Mary's."

Sawyer frowned. "Why St. Mary's?"

I shrugged. "My mom wants me to go to Catholic school."

Val snickered nearby. I hadn't noticed she was eavesdropping on our conversation.

"What, are you joining a cult or something?" she said, her voice dripping with disdain.

Jason turned, laughing sarcastically. "Oh yeah, Val. Because Catholic school is totally a cult. Super smart of you."

Everyone burst out laughing at her expense. Val rolled her eyes and crossed her arms.

"Whatever. It's still weird," she muttered, trying to recover.

"Shut up, Val," Jason said firmly before turning back to his chat with Molly and Abby.

Sawyer turned to me. "Sorry, I didn't mean you were weird."

"No, it's okay." I took a spoon of ice cream to avoid the awkward moment and then spoke again. "My mom was raised old-school Irish, so religion is a big deal for her."

"Like, they were born there?"

Beatrice perked up. "Josie was born there too." With a big smile, she announced, "And she lives in Maplewood because of me!"

"Because of Dad, Beatrice," Jason said with a sigh. "Josie's dad and my dad work for the same company. So they moved to Maplewood."

"How long ago was that?" Sawyer asked.

I thought for a second. "Hmm. I was in first grade, so a long time ago."

Sawyer shook his head and smiled. "Then it's crazy I never met you before, Josie O'Driscoll. But I'm glad I have now."

Chapter 3

Now

After we get back to Miner's, I can't settle. The weight of everything presses heavily on me like a lead blanket. I need air, space to breathe, to escape the horrifying image of Sarge in a casket.

If the years have taught me anything, it's that I need to recognize when my mind is racing too fast or my heart is feeling too heavy. I recognize it, but that doesn't mean I'll handle any of it the way I am supposed to. My mother used to always tell me I was my own worst enemy. She wasn't wrong.

I step out into the cool night air. The chill hits my skin, and I wrap my arms around myself. The streets are bathed in a soft twilight, the hum of distant traffic the only sound breaking the silence.

If this place didn't nearly kill me, I'd think it was beautiful. I cannot believe I am back here.

I wander aimlessly, letting my feet carry me through the familiar yet distant landscape of my hometown. Fifteen years is a long time. So much has changed, but I am not the same person who left. The town, however, remains much the same, with certain places still holding echoes of my childhood.

The cute storefronts still wink at me from beneath their decorative awnings. This street is mostly filled with small businesses, the claws of corporate retail unable to fully choke the life from the moms and pops of Maplewood. Though the town has flourished, I find myself standing in front of an empty storefront, its windows dark and lifeless, the once-vibrant paint now peeling in sorrowful flakes. A wave of nostalgia washes over me as I realize where I am.

This used to be Douglas Arthur's Shoe Store. I close my eyes and let the memories flood back, the scent of leather and polish nearly tangible in my mind, mingling with my mother's faint, sweet perfume. I can see the rows of tiny shoes, perfectly aligned on wooden shelves that gleamed with fresh varnish. Part of me braces for the consequences of indulging in these memories, but I let them wash over me with reckless abandon.

I can see the old man who ran the store, always greeting us with a warm smile. His eyes crinkled at the corners, a twinkle of kindness behind his round glasses. I always assumed his name was Douglas, but it turns out that was just the name of the store. I remember my surprise when I learned his name was Frank, but my shock and slight disappointment were soon forgotten when I spotted the large tin full of pretzel rods he kept on the counter.

Frank gifted me a pretzel every time we visited. The memory of the salty crunch mixed with the excitement of a day out with my mother still lifts my heart, despite everything. I picture myself climbing up onto the small platform, feeling like a princess as I tried on new shoes, the soft cushion under my feet like a plush throne.

Frank wore brown trousers and a button-down shirt and tie. His silver hair looked as though it was perpetually tamed with one of those little black combs. I would've bet he kept one in his pocket. He measured my foot, the cool metal of the ruler sending shivers up my spine, and offered his opinions, looking to my mother for approval.

I knew what it was like to seek her approval too.

My mother's face comes into focus in my mind, her sparkling eyes and dimples lighting up her beautiful features. Her laughter was like a bell, clear and joyful, resonating with an Irish lilt that soothed my young heart. Her touch was gentle yet firm as she adjusted the straps of my shoes, the scent of her perfume enveloping me like a warm embrace. She believed it was crucial for little feet to have the best shoes, never compromising on quality. I was always taken aback by how her voice, so sweet and melodic, could turn cold and sharp in her darker moments.

But the warm memories remain as I take in the abandoned storefront. Tears well up, blurring my vision until the scene becomes a hazy reminder of what is lost. I let them fall freely, allowing myself to grieve for the beautiful, caring woman who had given me so much—and still took so much away.

I eventually walk back to Miner's. The evening is lovely, so I decide to sit on the quiet wraparound porch and take in the view of Main Street in Maplewood. When I lived here, I never noticed the beautiful little intricacies of this borough. I appreciated some things. I liked the small-town charm and recognized the camaraderie of neighbors, but I hadn't noticed how the large maple tree in Maplewood Park stands majestically in the distance, its leaves rustling softly in the evening breeze, or how the steeple of St. Mary's Church serves as a stunning backdrop to the picturesque scene.

I take a deep breath in, feeling the cool air fill my lungs, and acknowledge the butterflies that seem to flutter in my stomach since I arrived. I chalk it up to nerves, but I can't help but wonder if my body is trying to tell me something. Like there is an energy that it recognizes but I can't identify on the surface.

The gentle creak of a rocking chair nearby catches my attention. I turn to see Mrs. Miner's brother, a figure I have only ever noticed from afar, deeply engrossed in his own quiet contemplation. I never paid much attention to him, even in my youth. He seems so quiet and stoic, uninterested in the chatter of guests, but politeness outweighs my hesitation.

"I'm so sorry! I didn't see you there."

His response is somewhere between a grunt and a nod, leaving me unsure if I should say more or quietly walk away. After all, his sister—and maybe he too—owns the place.

"I didn't mean to interrupt you," I offer kindly, trying to plan a graceful exit.

He looks up with a slight nod, his face crinkling into what might be a smile or a grimace—I can't quite tell. "No harm done," he replies, his voice softer than I expected.

I smile back, unsure if that's my cue to leave or stay. "It's a nice evening, isn't it?" I gesture vaguely toward the quiet street. "There's something about Maplewood... it just sticks with you."

"Oh, it does. It certainly does. It's full of old ghosts and old stories. If these streets could talk, they'd tell you all about what could have been—if only the right words had been spoken at the right time." He sighs, a long, drawn-out breath that seems to carry the weight of years with it. "Every day, I wish I was brave enough to change things," he murmurs. "Every single day. But life . . . it doesn't give us do-overs. Just lessons."

For a moment, I'm not sure what to say. I shift uncomfortably in my chair, pulling my wrap a little tighter around my shoulders.

"I see," I manage to reply, my voice barely above a whisper. His cryptic comments about regrets and missed opportunities unnerve me more than I want to admit.

I glance over at him again; he is staring off into the distance, seemingly lost in his own world of memories. His presence, once barely noticeable, now feels overwhelmingly intense. The old man suddenly speaks again, his voice stronger this time, catching me off guard.

"People are too concerned with what others think." He stares out into the growing darkness, his eyes not meeting mine, but focused on something distant, perhaps a memory that haunts him. "It's the quiet regrets that linger the longest, the ones you can't ever speak aloud," he murmurs, as if confiding in the shadows. "They think it matters—what people say, how they judge. But it's all fleeting."

He shakes his head slowly, the rocking chair creaking under the subtle shift of his weight. "Cruelty," he continues, his voice gaining an edge, "comes from fear. Fear of what's different, fear of what they can't understand or control. And that fear, it . . . it hurts people. Deeply."

I nod, unsure how to respond to something so heavy. "That's... true," I say, fumbling slightly.

His gaze finally meets mine, piercing and sad. "Don't let the cruel ones change you or make you hide who you are. You're not responsible for their shortcomings."

The intensity of his words catches me off guard. I open my mouth to say something but think better of it and simply nod again.

After a moment, I stand, offering a small smile. "I should head inside. It's been a long day, but it was nice chatting with you."

He doesn't seem to notice my exit, lost in thought as the rocking chair creaks softly behind me. Even as I close the door, his words echo in my mind: *Don't let the cruel ones change you.*

Too late. They already have.

Chapter 4

Then

The first significant snowfall of the year wasn't a blizzard, but it was enough to coat the sidewalks and make the steps treacherous if you didn't take it easy. I bundled myself up, pulled a hat onto my head, warm socks and boots on my feet, and dug out the shovel from the small garage out back. For a moment, I debated whether to start on my front steps or Sarge's, then decided on Sarge's first.

Just as I dragged my shovel to his small front porch, a figure walked toward me with a backwash of white behind him. Sawyer's auburn curls peeked out from under his skully hat, his tall frame and striking hazel eyes giving him a presence that always seemed to draw my attention.

I hadn't really spoken to him since the haunted hallway event at Holy Redeemer, the high school I attended after graduating from St. Mary's. I'd been dressed as a witch, and he'd shown up with Jason and Beatrice. I was mortified, but after that, we didn't talk much—just brief exchanges in passing. Smiles and pleasantries, but nothing more.

The last time I actually saw him, though, was at the Maplewood Turkey Trot. I'd been helping serve coffee to spectators in the square for Mrs. Larson, who owned the bakery in the heart of town. I watched him cross the finish line, laughing and flushed from the run, and then spend the next half hour talking to Val. When they disappeared together, it tore a hole somewhere deep inside me.

I'd never felt jealousy before, and I hated the way it consumed me then. I was already broken in so many ways. That moment made me realize I didn't want to be broken anymore. I tried to move on from my innocent crush, leaving it behind with everything else I thought I'd outgrown.

It wasn't easy when Beatrice called me the day after the haunted hallway event, mostly to scold me for ditching her. I made excuses, but the truth was, I'd had to go home to take care of my mom, who was in the throes of another epic bender. Still, Beatrice also mentioned that she'd heard Sawyer tell Jason I was pretty. I'd ridden that cloud for several weeks—until the Turkey Trot.

"Are you trying to take my job, Josie O?" Sawyer's voice jolted me from my thoughts.

Stunned, I responded, "Huh?"

Sawyer came closer and nodded to my shovel. "You're taking my job."

"Oh!" I came alive and spoke a little too loudly. "You're here to shovel for Sarge."

"Nailed it," he said, pointing to his shovel. "He called me last night."

I frowned. "I told him yesterday I'd shovel for him."

Sawyer grinned. "Maybe he didn't trust you to do the job right."

I gasped, putting a hand to my chest in mock offense. "Are you saying I'm not capable because I'm a girl?"

"I didn't say that," he replied, holding up his hands in defense, though the smirk on his face said otherwise.

"You didn't have to. It was heavily implied." I spun on my heel, walking back a few steps before glancing over my shoulder at him. He was still watching, still smirking.

"Well, now you get to witness greatness," I called out with a grin. "Prepare to be amazed by my impeccable sidewalk-shoveling skills."

He chuckled as he got to work shoveling, the sound warm and easy in the cold air. I followed suit, the rhythmic scrape of our shovels filling the quiet between us. After a few minutes, he broke the silence.

"I haven't seen you in a while," he said.

I glanced at him with a playful smirk. "What are you talking about? I see you around all the time."

"I haven't *talked* to you in a while," he clarified, his gaze meeting mine for a moment before returning to his work.

"Oh, well, I saw you a couple of weeks ago at the Turkey Trot," I said, my voice trying to sound casual despite the nerves fluttering in my stomach. "I was going to say hi, but you were with Val. Then I didn't see you again after that."

My head dipped, cheeks flushing. Maybe it was the cold—or maybe it was the nerve it took to bring this up.

"Yeah, I saw you too," he said, his voice softening. "I was trying to come over and talk to you. I told Val I was going to, but she asked if I could help her find Rain first. I felt bad leaving her. She said she came to see me run, and I didn't want to be rude."

"Yeah, no. I would have done the same thing." I stumbled over my words, trying not to sound too affected. "That was nice of her. To come and see you run. Or, you know, *trot*. Or whatever turkeys do."

A laugh burst from him, warm and unrestrained, and it lit me up inside. It felt like coming in from the cold, and I wanted to stay in that moment—cozy and warm—forever.

"Did you just call me a turkey?" he asked, still grinning.

I shrugged, biting back a smile. "Hey, I don't make the rules. Turkeys trot. It's science."

"Well, I appreciate the scientific insight," he teased. "Next time, I'll make sure to save a trot for you."

I felt my cheeks grow even warmer, but this time, I didn't mind.

"Well, you deserve it after accusing me of shoveling like a girl!" I retorted, raising an eyebrow at him.

"You *are* shoveling! And you're a girl!" he shot back, his voice teasing.

We laughed easily, the sound carrying through the crisp air, and then he dropped a bomb.

"Believe me. I've noticed."

Well, shit. I had no idea how to respond to that. My mind scrambled for something clever or even remotely normal to say, but my survival instincts kicked in first.

I scooped up a handful of snow, packed it into a ball, and launched it straight at the face that had been steadily smiling at me.

"Aha! Nice catch, all-star!" I crowed, barely able to contain my own laughter.

But I didn't have long to celebrate my zinger. Sawyer dropped the shovel he'd been casually leaning on and bent quickly to start forming snowballs.

I screeched and did the same, but I wasn't fast enough for him. He started launching snowballs in my direction, and I screamed and abandoned my measly snowballs, instead looking for cover.

"Not fair! You're a baseball player!" Even in the moment, I knew he was going gentle on me. I'd seen him throw a baseball from home plate to second base from his knees like he was tossing a pebble into a stream.

"You are not getting away, Josie!" I heard his footsteps behind me and his laugh, the best sound I'd ever heard, as he gained speed. I ran along the sidewalk toward the back of Sarge's house, peals of laughter and screeching escaping me.

I was completely lacking any self-consciousness, but the sidewalks were slippery and unshoveled. As I rounded the corner, my feet went out from under me, and I felt myself lurch backward. The fall seemed to happen both in slow motion and in an instant. I hit the ground hard, landing with a jarring thud on my behind—but not before my hand shot out to catch myself. My wrist bent at an unnatural angle, the sharp twist sending a burst of pain shooting up my arm.

My laughter quickly morphed into an agonizing groan, one I definitely didn't want Sawyer to hear—but the pain overpowered any hope of self-preservation. "Shit," I hissed, cradling my wrist as I pulled it from under me and into my lap.

"Oh God, Josie. I'm sorry. Are you okay?" Sawyer's voice cracked with worry as he knelt in front of me, concern etched into his youthful features. At that moment, he looked so young—scared and guilty, all at once.

"Let me see it."

"No," I whispered, pulling my wrist closer to my chest. "I'm scared. I don't want to look at it."

"Don't be scared," he said, his voice soft but steady. "Let me see it." He tugged his gloves off quickly, the movement purposeful.

I winced as I released my hand from my lap and let him take it. "I have to take your glove off, okay?"

I nodded, biting my lip as tears welled up. The pain was sharp, and the thought of Sawyer seeing me like this made it worse. Gently, he eased the glove off, and I could feel the adrenaline surging as the throbbing intensified. His brow furrowed as he examined my wrist.

"Yeah, it's swelling up pretty fast. It looks like it could be a sprain or a break." His voice was calm, but his concern was evident.

"Does it hurt here?" he asked, gently touching a spot that made me flinch.

"Yeah," I admitted, my voice barely above a whisper.

"Okay, Josie, we shouldn't move it too much. You need to get this X-rayed." His words were firm, almost protective.

"How do you know all this stuff?"

"Sports," he said with a shrug, then added, with a sheepish smile, "and Boy Scouts."

"You're a Boy Scout?"

"*Was* a Boy Scout," he corrected, his cheeks reddening slightly.

Despite the pain, I smiled.

"I'm really sorry about this, Josie. I didn't think, and I should've known the sidewalks—"

"It's not your fault, Sawyer. It's just one of those things," I said, trying to reassure him even as my wrist throbbed.

He helped me to my feet, his arm sliding around my waist to steady me. "Let's get you inside your house—"

"No!" The word came out sharper than I intended, startling both of us. I softened my tone, cradling my wrist. "Just bring me to Sarge."

Sarge was already on his porch as we approached, as if he'd sensed the commotion. He beckoned us inside, his frown deepening as he took in my condition.

"Good Lord, Josie, what have you done to yourself?" Sarge grumbled, his voice gruff but full of concern.

Inside, the warmth of his home enveloped us, a stark contrast to the biting cold outside. He led us to the cluttered living room, where Johnny Cash crooned softly over an old record player. Clearing a pile of newspapers from the couch, he gestured for me to sit.

"Let me see that wrist," he said, pulling a stool over and settling in front of me. His calloused hands were surprisingly gentle as he examined the injury.

"It's swollen badly, Josie. We need to get this looked at," Sarge concluded. Turning to Sawyer, who lingered near the door, he added, "I'll take her to the hospital. Thanks for bringing her, son."

Sawyer hesitated. "I can go with you."

"No need for that, but thanks. I've got her."

"It's my fault. I want to make sure she's okay," Sawyer insisted, his voice firm but kind. "Or I can get her parents—"

"No," I cut in, meeting his eyes. "It's not your fault, Sawyer. I'll be fine with Sarge."

He studied me for a moment, as if sensing there was more to the story, then nodded reluctantly. "All right. But will you call Beatrice? Let her know you're okay?"

Sarge, chuckling, got up from his stool and clapped Sawyer on the shoulder. "I like this one." Turning to Sawyer, he added in a lighter tone, "Why don't you finish up that shoveling, then? I don't need any broken bones myself, eh?"

Sawyer cast one last glance at me before stepping outside. "Sorry, Josie."

"It's really not your fault, Sawyer!" I called after him, hating that he was blaming himself.

Sarge turned to me once we were alone, his expression softening. "Now, tell me honestly, kiddo, how bad's the home front? Want me to go grab your parents, or is now no good?"

Relief and fatigue washed over me, allowing me to lean back into the couch cushions. "It's bad, Sarge," I admitted, the weight of holding in the truth easing slightly with the confession. "She's bad, and he's not making it any better."

"Well, you know you're always safe here. Let's get that wrist fixed up first, though," Sarge said, grabbing his keys. "Let's not add a permanent crook to your arm to the list of worries, eh?"

As we headed out to his old pickup truck, I couldn't help but feel a wave of gratitude—for Sarge's gruff, dependable kindness and for Sawyer stepping in when I least expected it. Even in the middle of everything, it reminded me that I wasn't entirely alone. I'd been feeling that kind of loneliness for as long as I could remember.

As we pulled away, I caught sight of Sawyer in the rearview mirror, standing there in the snow, watching us drive off. Something about it made my chest ache, but I wasn't sure why.

***

Breaking my wrist was bad enough, but the aftermath? That was worse. I spent the next few weeks hiding out, doing my best to avoid Sawyer altogether. But Beatrice wasn't about to let me wallow in peace.

"Sawyer definitely likes you. It's not even a question," Beatrice said, breaking the silence as we lay on her bed, staring up at the ceiling.

I laughed sarcastically and held up my wrist, complete with cast, and pointed to it with my good hand. "Beatrice, I made the biggest ass out of myself. I literally cried."

"I don't know, Josie. He said you were pretty brave."

"He did?" My eyes were wide as I searched hers for more answers.

"He did," she confirmed, a hint of pride in her voice. "He said your wrist was scary looking. And that he couldn't believe how tough you were being."

"Hmph." I made a sound of satisfaction, looking at my cast in a new light. "I guess I am pretty brave."

"I could have told you that. You don't need someone else to make you believe it."

I could hear Beatrice shuffling. I knew she'd turned her head and was looking at me while I stared at the ceiling. "He also talked about Sarge bringing you to the hospital. And that your parents weren't around."

I swallowed around the lump in my throat.

"Josie, he said he thought he heard yelling and things breaking while you were gone."

I shut my eyes hard. Shame and embarrassment washed over me.

"Josie?" Beatrice's soft voice was soothing. "What's going on?"

I sat up in the bed, and so did Beatrice. I started to chew on the inside of my lip, thinking of what I could possibly say.

She pointed at me. "Don't you dare!"

Confused, I turned to look at her. "Don't dare what?"

"I see you biting the inside of your lip." Beatrice squinted at me, tilting her head like she was trying to solve a puzzle. "You always do that when . . . I dunno, you're cooking up some kind of excuse or hiding something."

"Hey!" I shot back, half laughing, though the truth in her words stung. "That's not—"

"Don't even try it." She shook her head, her voice softening as she reached for my hand. "Why won't you just tell me, Josie? I know something's going on. I can feel it." She sighed, her fingers fidgeting with the edge of her sleeve. "I just . . . I want you to talk to me. Don't you trust me?"

I opened my mouth, but nothing came out. She was right, and I hated that.

Beatrice leaned in closer, her eyes wide, almost pleading. "It's just . . . I hate feeling like this. Like you're keeping something big from me. We're supposed to be best friends, right? I'm on your side. Always."

I sighed. More guilt wrapped its filthy arms around my insides. Where I'd lost out in the family department, I'd won in the friend department. I knew that in my bones. I saw so many girls with their fair-weather friends. They were best friends one minute and talking the nastiest trash about each other the next. That was not Bea and me. A victory for one was a victory for the both of us. A heartbreak for one was equally unbearable for the other.

My mother was jealous of the relationship. She didn't say it as such, but I knew with the snide comments she would make. My mother didn't want our secret hell exposed, so the fewer close friendships I had, the better. But try as she might, she could not keep Beatrice and me apart.

"I do trust you. You're the only person I trust. Well, you and Sarge." I paused, hesitating before admitting the rest. "It's just . . . I'm embarrassed. I don't want you to think less of me." The words hung there, heavy with the truth I usually kept buried—the shame, the fear that I wasn't enough because of my mother and father. I was terrified that if people found out, they'd see me as some kind of fraud and turn their backs on me.

"Josie, I would *never* think less of you!" Beatrice's voice rose, her posture stiffening as she sat up straighter, like she was ready to fight anyone who dared suggest otherwise.

"I know you wouldn't—not on purpose," I said quietly, looking down at my hands. "But what if you can't help it?" My voice cracked as I straightened too, needing to meet her gaze, needing to know she really meant it.

She looked at me like I couldn't possibly be serious. I mirrored her expression.

"You honestly don't know?" I often felt like I was doing a shitty job of hiding my family's skeletons, and I knew Beatrice was far from naïve, so it would make sense if she at least knew something.

"I'm not going to lie to you." She shrugged as if the weight of what we were talking about wasn't as heavy as it was.

"So you know." It was a statement. Not a question.

"I think I know some things. Not everything. Not the truth." We stared at each other for a moment. She was waiting, hoping I would speak, and I was trying to find the words to explain my situation. I settled on the simple.

"My mom likes to drink, and things have been . . . bad." I didn't realize I wasn't making eye contact until a few beats passed. Then when I caught Beatrice's eyes, I saw the sympathy, but I also saw the knowing. "You knew that too, didn't you?"

She nodded. "My parents have known." She leaned toward me, pleading, "But don't be mad that I never said anything. I wanted you to be comfortable telling me."

"I'm not mad. Just embarrassed."

"Why are you embarrassed? You have nothing to be embarrassed about!"

I shrugged. How could you explain to someone that their life—the way their parents live and interact and care for them, showing up to baseball games and hassling them about summer plans, the whole normalcy of it all—flies in the face of your very existence? How could you explain shame like that?

How do you explain that when your dad shows up to an event, it's not to cheer you on but to bring you home so you can take care of your drunk and mentally ill mother? And not the tipsy kind of drunk. The kind of drunk that kills the drinker. The kind of drunk where an alcoholic will drink cleaning products under the sink if they can't get their booze.

The kind of alcoholic who goes into seizures when they detox. Who nearly lights the house on fire with discarded cigarettes. Who throws ashtrays at you when you beg them to stop drinking. Who tells you that you were a mistake and calls you a slut, even though you've never kissed a boy.

The kind of alcoholic who, when sober, is the most charismatic, witty, and beautiful woman in the world. The kind of mother who wants nothing but the best shoes for her little daughter's feet—yet carries a ticking time bomb on her chest.

That was Nancy O'Driscoll.

My first steps were taken on eggshells, and my first words were "I'm sorry." In my house, survival meant learning to tiptoe around the one with all the power, even before I knew how to walk.

Her moods were my moods. The slightest misstep would take the whole house of cards down. I never saw it coming—one moment, everything seemed fine, and the next, her fury would strike like a sudden storm. Maybe it was the way I looked at her, or a tone in my voice I didn't mean to use. Whatever it was, I could never pinpoint it, only feel its impact.

Her anger was a force of nature, and I was its inevitable casualty. I never questioned her, only myself. What had I done to provoke her? My mind raced, berating me for my clumsiness, my foolishness, as if I were the architect of my own downfall.

"I just never know what version of her I'm going to get," I said pensively. "And sometimes I'm scared I'm going to find her dead."

Beatrice whimpered and pulled me into a hug, being careful with my broken wrist and equally as careful with my broken spirit. "You will always have me," she swore through her tears.

I felt a weight lift off me after admitting my mother's alcoholism to Beatrice. It was as if the arms of shame released me just a little, allowing me to breathe. I was so tired of hiding. Though I wasn't ready to scream it from the rooftops, the loneliness I had felt eased. I hated lying, and now, at least, I didn't have to lie to Beatrice anymore.

In hindsight, I realized she'd probably known all along. She never got mad at me and didn't press when I dodged questions. Saying my mom was an alcoholic was simple. Anyone can picture what that might look like: images of my mother, jolly, dancing, or joking, flashed through my mind. I imagined a fun drunk or someone who drinks every night but still goes to work the next day. Someone who can't stop at just two drinks at a party. My mom was all of those and none of those.

What was hard to reconcile was the mom who existed when she was sober and the one who lived as a drunk. My mother sober was a joy, but sadly, those memories were overshadowed by the bad ones, even though I believed there were more good times than bad. The good times didn't sear themselves into my soul the way her drunken episodes did. My dad and I covered up what we could to save her reputation—or maybe our own. But in the end, we weren't saving anything.

Every time she came off a binge—shaking, embarrassed, weak, and vulnerable—she would tell me, "Never again." She promised she would never touch the stuff again, insisting it didn't help her. She swore that each time was the last, and I believed her.

Every single time.

And every single time, she went back. I'd wait for the telltale signs. The missed meals. The excuses to avoid friends. The phone calls going unanswered. The way she'd close herself off from us until, finally, the inevitable breakdown would come. Then it would be like watching someone unravel right before your eyes—like all the effort she'd put into being okay just snapped. And no one ever knew. Or at least, no one ever said anything. We lived in our house of cards, hoping the wind wouldn't blow too hard.

"I don't know how you do it," Beatrice whispered after a long silence, her voice full of genuine awe. "Like . . . I don't know how you wake up every day and just . . . act like everything's fine. I wouldn't be able to. I would've cracked ages ago."

I shook my head, unsure if I should feel proud or devastated. "I don't have a choice, Bea. I mean, what am I supposed to do? Walk around, crying, telling everyone my life's a mess? It's not like anyone can fix it." My voice wavered a little as I spoke, the frustration seeping through. "I just . . . I just have to deal with it."

Beatrice was quiet for a moment, thinking. "But that's not fair, Josie. I mean . . . you deserve better."

I let out a harsh laugh, the kind that came from a place so deep I couldn't even touch it. "Yeah, well, what's fair, right? Life isn't fair. It's just . . . life."

Beatrice frowned, her eyebrows knitting together as she reached over and squeezed my hand. "It's not supposed to be this hard. It's really not."

"I know," I said, my voice softening as I glanced down at our hands, still holding on to each other like lifelines. "But I just try to think of the future. I'll get out of all this someday."

The room fell quiet again. Beatrice lay back down on her pillow, staring at the ceiling as if she were trying to make sense of everything I had just shared. I felt a lump forming in my throat again, but this time, it wasn't shame. It wasn't even sadness. It was exhaustion. Like the weight of carrying it all, of pretending every day that everything was fine, had finally caught up to me. And now that Beatrice knew the truth, it felt like a floodgate had opened, and I wasn't sure if I could close it again.

"Do you ever think about leaving?" Beatrice asked quietly, her voice hesitant, like she wasn't sure if she should ask.

I turned my head to look at her, surprised by the question. "Leaving? Like . . . running away?"

She nodded, biting her lip as she stared up at the ceiling. "Yeah. I mean, not, like, forever or anything. Just . . . I don't know. Going somewhere. Anywhere. Just to get away from all of it."

I swallowed hard, my mind racing at the thought. Of course I had thought about it. Who wouldn't? But I couldn't. Not really. My dad needed me. My mom—really needed me. The idea of leaving them to fend for themselves felt impossible. But at the same time, I couldn't help but feel a pang of longing at the idea of escape, of freedom.

"I've dreamed about it," I admitted, my voice barely above a whisper. "But I can't. I can't leave my dad. He's . . . he's barely hanging on himself, you know? And I can't leave him to deal with her alone. And I can't leave her. She wouldn't—she would probably die."

Beatrice sighed, then her face scrunched up in frustration. "It's not fair. It's not fair that you have to take care of everyone. You're a kid, Josie. You're supposed to be able to just . . . I don't know . . . be a kid."

"Yeah, well . . . that's not my life." My voice came out more bitter than I intended, and I immediately regretted it. "Sorry. I didn't mean to sound like that. It's just . . . I'm tired."

Beatrice sat up again, her eyes full of determination. "You don't have to do this alone, okay? You have me. And Sarge. And Jason. And maybe even . . . I don't know . . . Sawyer?" She raised an eyebrow, trying to lighten the mood, but there was sincerity in her words.

I let out a soft laugh, despite myself. "Sawyer? He barely knows me."

"Yeah, but he wants to know you," Beatrice teased, nudging me with her elbow. "I see the way he looks at you. He's smitten, Josie. Whether you believe it or not."

I rolled my eyes, but a small smile tugged at the corner of my lips. "No way. But it doesn't matter anyway. My life's too much of a mess for someone like him."

"Stop that," Beatrice said firmly, her expression serious now. "You are not a mess, okay? Your parents . . . yeah, maybe they're a mess. But you? You're amazing. You're strong. And anyone who gets to know you is damn lucky."

I blinked, trying to hold back the tears that were threatening to spill over again. "Thanks, Bea. I don't know what I'd do without you."

"You'll never have to find out," she said with a grin, pulling me into a tight hug.

And for the first time in a long time, I believed her.

Chapter 5

Now

I don't sleep after Sarge's viewing, despite the bone-deep fatigue threatening to pull me under. I feel like a worn-out thread, fraying at the edges. I am raw, grieving, overwhelmed, and shaky. The funeral Mass is only a few hours away, and I need to wake up and pull myself together—for Sarge's sake. I wish I could have given Sarge the world. He did so much to keep mine spinning on its axis, and being awake and present is the least I can do.

But my mind keeps circling back to that awful interaction with Sawyer. How can I feel both furious and still have that familiar pang of heartache? How can I be so angry, yet some part of me still wants to reach out, even though I know I shouldn't? I've been afraid of many things in my life, and my greatest fears came true years ago—but this? I didn't even know I should be afraid of this.

Sawyer might have known a young, naïve girl named Josie O'Driscoll more than a decade ago, but he doesn't know me now—and he never will. I'll never let him past my walls again. I'll never let him or anyone else inflict that damage on my inner sanctum. I have to protect myself. I remind myself, over and over again, that no matter what, I cannot let my guard down. I am going back to Ireland, back to my life, my job, and my friends in less than a week, and I don't need the ghost of John Sawyer haunting my every step forward.

I throw on a T-shirt and jeans, pull my hair into a bun, and secure my chunky bangles around my wrist—the same ones I never leave without. I don't care who sees me. I just need caffeine before I can think about how this day will play out. Dermott is just waking up when I tell him I'm going to grab some coffee. He grunts appreciatively as he makes his way to the bathroom and shuts the door.

There's a continental breakfast in the lobby of Miner's, but I need more than a small cup of weak coffee. So I politely wave to Mrs. Miner and scurry out before she can corner me with questions or level me with her judgmental glare. She always has a look of disapproval on her face that I don't want directed at me. Lord knows I've spent enough of my life with the rays of criticism beating down on me.

I step out into the bright, unforgiving sunshine, taking my first real look at my hometown in the light since I left more than a decade ago.

Am I really that awful for leaving?

Sawyer's words about me being a ghost tear something open inside me. *But wasn't I the one who was haunted? Wasn't I the one who lived in terror?*

I would have faced it. I would have fought it. I would have overcome any-thing—for him. *With* him. He was my person. Until he wasn't.

Still, a gnawing feeling stirs inside me, an unwelcome echo of my old in-securities. *Did I really have to leave everything behind? Was there anyone—or anything—from my former life that I should have held onto?*

These questions swirl around my head as I quicken my pace toward Larson's Bakery. I used to work for Mrs. Larson on and off through high school. This place served as one of my safe reprieves, and to this day, the smell of fresh-baked bread and coffee settles me down better than any Xanax ever could. I fear I might see familiar and curious faces, but my need for caffeine outweighs my need for isolation, so I continue down the street toward my drug of choice.

"Josie? Josie, is that you?"

I freeze at the familiar voice behind me. My heart races, caught between fear and hope.

"It *is* you!" Her voice quivers with disbelief and emotion, the years of separa-tion etched into every word.

Hands trembling, I turn around. I left this place at barely eighteen, growing into a woman in the years since, but in my mind, the people I left behind remain frozen in time. Maybe my anger toward Sawyer helped me maintain some composure last night, but seeing Beatrice standing here, fifteen years older than the last time I saw her, is like a punch to the gut.

"Bea?" I manage to whisper before the sobs overtake me.

Before I can wonder how she'll receive me, she rushes toward me, just like she would have all those years ago, and wraps her arms around me. We cling to each other, both crying, as if no time has passed at all. Her embrace immediately grounds me. The racing thoughts and anxiety tamp down under the weighted blanket that is Beatrice.

I don't know how long we stand there on the sidewalk, locked in an embrace that feels like a salve to my frayed nerves. Each time I whisper an apology, she shushes me with soothing murmurs, her grip tightening, settling me. Just as she always did when I was scared in the past. What have I done for her in return? I left without the courage to explain why, disappearing off the grid for all these years.

As we finally step back, her eyes search mine, and she takes a deep breath. "I heard you were here. I was on my way to Miner's to find you."

I am stunned. I shake my head in disbelief. "I can't believe that after everything, you wanted to find me."

She grabs both of my hands and squeezes, biting her lip. "I've been wanting to find you for years—and then Sawyer came by last night and told me he saw you. He was sort of a mess, so I couldn't get all the details, but I must have left the funeral home right before you got there."

A mess? I get caught on that for just a second before the pain written all over Beatrice's face causes a new wave of guilt to wash over me. I begin to apologize again, but she stops me.

"Look at you." She smiles, her eyes softening as she touches my hair. "You're still so beautiful. No grays in that ginger hair." She laughs nervously. "I'm so happy you are literally standing in front of me right now. I don't think anyone expected you to come back ever. I held out hope for a while, but after so much time, I never expected to see you again."

I want to spill everything. I want to explain what happened and why I disappeared, but my God, it is all too heavy, and I don't have the strength to carry it right now.

"I really need coffee," I blurt, feeling a rush of relief when Beatrice lets out a soft laugh.

"Can I come with you, Josie? For coffee?" The look on her face is hopeful, yet afraid—as if I would tell her no.

I squeeze her hands in mine. "God, there is literally nothing in the world I want more."

Only now do I fully take in my beautiful friend. Beatrice is still petite and full of energy, with golden-blonde hair that seems to catch the sunlight just right. Her bright, expressive eyes still sparkle with mischief and kindness all at once. Her smile is still infectious, wide and genuine, and capable of lifting my spirits. The passage of time is subtle. Her cheeks have lost the roundness of youth, and her big, bright eyes have new creases around them—but it all manages to make her better, more herself.

"You're so beautiful and grown-up, Bea."

"Okay, okay, I forgive you," she jokes, and I laugh, surprised at how easy this moment is, knowing if we continue talking, it won't stay easy. "Let's walk." She jerks her head in the direction of the bakery.

Beatrice was always a little spitfire, and I can see that she still has that in her. We were the same height until around freshman year, when I joked that she was shrinking while I was getting taller. She still moves with an effortless grace, a dancer's poise mixed with a touch of tomboy roughness that always made her so relatable and down-to-earth. She never took shit from anyone. I admired that so much growing up. She was never afraid to speak her mind or stand up for what she believed in—and often what she believed in was me.

But despite the sunshine that seems to live inside her, as we continue walking, the air between us fills with a heavier silence, one that speaks of years and changes. Beatrice glances over at me, her expression tinged with a mix of relief and old pain, like she still can't believe I'm here.

"I'm really sorry about Sarge."

I nod, fighting to dissolve the lump in my throat.

"Were you in touch with him?" The way she says it feels like she's asking if there's anyone I haven't discarded.

"We stayed in touch." Her eyes widen, and I catch the brief flash of hurt before she looks away. "But it was a few years after I left. He, umm, he found me through my aunt and got in touch. And then we talked every couple of weeks."

Beatrice shakes her head, disbelief and frustration etched across her face. "I tried everything to find you. I can't believe Sarge was able to." She pauses, reconsidering her words. "I can't believe he didn't tell us."

I get stuck on the word *us*—still not sure why Sawyer is factoring into this equation.

"How's Jason?" I change the subject.

"Good! Reeling from the news that you're back—like the rest of us." There it is again. *Us.*

"Josie, when you left, it was like you vanished into thin air," she starts, her voice soft but carrying a sharp edge of old hurt. "I didn't just lose my best friend; it felt like I'd lost a part of my family."

I keep my eyes fixed on the sidewalk ahead, the cracks and fallen leaves blurring together. "I know," I murmur, the words barely above a whisper. "I know I left without a word, and it was wrong. I just . . . couldn't handle everything back then."

Beatrice stops walking, turning to face me fully. "I was so worried, Josie. I didn't understand why you'd just disappear. I was afraid you were dead. I had to convince myself you weren't." Her voice cracks slightly, laden with the weight of years spent in confusion and concern.

But she can't know how right she is. I was dead in some ways. Maybe in most ways—for a while.

Feeling the sting of tears, I stop too, meeting her gaze. "I was broken, Beatrice." I pause, the words catching in my throat as I skirt around the full truth of that night—the night that changed everything for me—and the unbearable time that followed.

She reaches out, taking my hand, her grip firm and warm. "I know what happened wrecked you. I wanted to be there for you. Prove that we were your family. But after so much time, we mourned you, in a way. And all this time, I've just hoped you were out there somewhere, getting better, finding some peace."

"I'm so sorry. I've missed you so much," I say, the admission feeling like breaking through the surface after being underwater for too long. "I thought I was doing the right thing by staying away. I don't know if I'll ever be able to explain it." I'm not sure I even want to. I don't know how.

She looks at me sheepishly. "I hope that we have time to catch up?" It's a question. "How long are you around for?"

I wince, and so does she. "Less than a week." Knowing it's not enough time.

We step into the soft hum of the bakery. I am relieved to not know anyone—and a little sad too. The girl behind the counter is young. She would have been a child before I left. So much has changed, and yet, feeling Beatrice's presence beside me, I can admit that some things feel the same.

"Is Mrs. Larson . . . ?" I don't want to finish the question.

"Hmm?" Beatrice pauses for a second, clearly reading my thoughts. "Oh! Yes—she's fine. Mostly retired but alive and well." I breathe a sigh of relief at her words, not sure I have a right to but doing it all the same.

"What are you having?" I glance at the menu board above the register.

"I'll have an Americano, but please, let me treat you."

A laugh bursts out of me. "No way. I took off for over a decade, and you're going to buy me a coffee? Hell no." We argue back and forth for a moment, but I win.

I order our coffees, temporarily forgetting about Dermott at Miner's, and shuffle around in my oversized bag for my wallet. My hands land on the envelope Alice gave me the night before. "Oh shit."

"Oh shit, what?"

I pull the envelope out, with Sarge's familiar scrawl of my name adorning the front, and hold it up for Beatrice to see.

"What's that?"

"A letter from Sarge," I say slowly, fully aware of the enormity of what I'm saying.

Beatrice's eyes widen, her hand instinctively reaching out to touch the envelope. "He wrote you a letter?"

"Yeah," I say, my voice trembling slightly. "Alice gave it to me last night. I forgot about it until right now."

She nods, her eyes softening with understanding. "Sarge always had a way of reaching out when you needed it most."

I take a deep breath, feeling the weight of the envelope in my hands. I can't believe the letter slipped my mind, but the mix of fatigue, jet lag, grief, and Sawyer has dulled my ability to fire on all cylinders.

We find a small table in the corner, the cozy atmosphere of the bakery wrapping around us like a warm embrace. The scent of freshly brewed coffee and baked goods is comforting. Beatrice sits across from me, her presence a steadying force as I contemplate the letter.

"Do you want to open it now?" she asks gently, her eyes filled with concern and curiosity.

"Jesus. I don't know." I stare at the envelope, unsure of what to do. We both laugh for a moment at my indecisiveness and the absolute craziness of this situation.

"Will it bother you too much to wait until after the funeral? You might need some time to digest it, and I'd hate to see you rush through it when you're not ready."

"You're right. I still have to go back to Miner's and get ready, and I don't want to be late for the funeral and—" I pause, remembering Dermott back at Miner's. "Shit. I have to bring Dermott coffee. Jesus, I almost forgot. Oh, he'd murder me if I forgot."

"Dermott?" Beatrice says the name slowly, cautiously, curiosity piqued—but I don't catch her assumption right away. I'm too busy staring at the envelope as if willing it to speak.

"Yeah, he's a beast without coffee. He'd probably suffocate me in my sleep if I came back without an Americano for him." I look up to see the horror on my friend's face. "What?" I realize she has no idea who I'm talking about. "Dermott, my cousin? You met him years ago when we were kids. He came over to visit when we were maybe ten years old."

She visibly relaxes. "Ah, of course, your cousin."

"Yeah, I just made him sound like a total asshole, but he's not. He would be if I made him go to a funeral without coffee or a muffin, though."

"Your *cousin*," Beatrice repeats with a smile. "Put a pin in that. We'll come back to that later." She starts gathering her things. "But I'll just say I'm actually scared to find out what happens when we pull on this thread."

I shake my head, half laughing. "Oh, now we're speaking in riddles, as if things aren't messed up enough?" I'm confused but don't have time to ask any questions. I head back to the counter to order Dermott's coffee and figure we just added to the list of topics to cover.

Chapter 6

Then

That spring of my freshman year, I went on my first date, a funny memory now, considering I wasn't even that interested in the kid. How could I be when all my thoughts revolved around Sawyer?

Ricky was in some of my classes at Holy Redeemer, and we whispered to each other during Sister Honor's endless stories about her idyllic and moral upbringing in upstate New York. He was funny and cute, and apparently, he thought I was funny and cute too, because when the whispers of the spring freshman formal started echoing through the halls, he asked if I would go with him.

If I said that I hadn't imagined for a second going to the formal with Sawyer as my date, I'd be lying. But Ricky was nice, and we went to the same school, making him seem like a safe and sensible choice. Besides, my self-esteem wasn't strong enough to believe that someone like Sawyer would ever consider me. Not when he was surrounded by girls like Val, who seemed so far out of my league.

I went home after school, relieved that my mom seemed to be in a good mood. Things were going well, and I allowed myself to imagine what it would be like if it stayed this way. Not pushing my luck meant I was extra vigilant. I didn't want to upset her in any way, but I feared going to a dance with a boy would be like a stick of dynamite in my fragile little world.

I lifted my hand in a wave and gave her an over-the-top smile as I climbed the stairs, trying to figure out how to tell her a boy had asked me to a dance. I was sure other girls didn't have to worry about their mothers' reactions to these sorts of things, but I walked on eggshells and broken glass every day.

"Josie, love, where are you going? Come here and talk to me. How was your day?" she asked, her voice carrying that melodic Irish lilt that held the history of who she was and where we'd come from. I inwardly winced and came back down the steps toward her.

I hesitated in the doorway of the kitchen, adjusting the straps on my backpack. "Good!" I said a little too brightly. Forcing myself to seem relaxed, I stepped closer. "Actually, something funny happened today at school," I began, my voice tingling with a mix of nerves and excitement.

She paused, her hands stilling as she wiped down the counter. "Oh? What's that, then?"

Taking a deep breath, I finally blurted out, "I was asked to the spring formal." I laughed awkwardly, making a face like it was the craziest thing in the world.

Her brow furrowed slightly in confusion. "The spring formal?"

"It's like a dance for freshmen," I explained quickly, watching as she slowly nodded, her expression still a mask of curiosity.

"And who asked you to go?" Her tone was light but carried an undercurrent of scrutiny that wasn't lost on me.

"His name's Ricky McGrath." I hoped the Irish last name would help. "He's in some of my classes at Holy Redeemer," I replied, trying to sound casual yet confident that this was a totally normal conversation.

"Mmm," she hummed, turning back to the counter and continuing to clean. "Ricky, is it? You don't want to go to a silly dance, right?" The way she cleaned seemed almost interrogative, each wipe of the surface a silent question.

I shrugged, not wanting to give too much of myself away. "Everyone else is going, and yes, I want to go too," I rushed, eager to convince her, perhaps more than was necessary, and also hoping Ricky's name wouldn't come up again.

"Is this Ricky a decent boy?" she asked, her tone softening. "Will there be chaperones?" Her question hung in the air. Why did I feel like I was telling her I was pregnant or something?

"Yes, of course, the teachers will be there," I assured her, and she seemed satisfied with that, her hands pausing to brush a lock of hair from her face. "And the nuns." That should do it.

"Well then, I suppose we'll need to find you a lovely dress, won't we?" Her change in demeanor would give you whiplash if you weren't used to it. It would do more damage if you were. A smile spread broadly across my face and only got bigger when I saw the same smile mirrored on hers. I saw the mother who used to bring me shoe shopping when I was a little girl, and I wanted to reach out and hold on to her so tight that she would never slip away again.

"Can we go shopping?" I ventured, the idea of a mother-daughter day appealing to me more than I expected.

"Yes, let me finish up here and call your father, and we'll go," she agreed, her smile genuine. "We'll find you something beautiful to wear."

"Thank you," I squealed, feeling a weight lift from my shoulders as she moved around the counter to give me a quick hug.

"Of course, love. But remember," she added, pulling back to look me in the eyes with a playful sternness only she could manage, "you'll always be my little girl. No matter how fancy the dress."

Her words, warm and teasing, carried a hint of the deep care beneath them—and maybe a warning too. As we discussed colors and styles, I couldn't help but feel grateful for these moments of normalcy, so sharply contrasted against the unpredictable shadows of our lives.

***

As promised, my mom and I went shopping. We went to the mall, but my mom said if we had more time, we would have gone to a mall she liked right outside of New York City. She didn't like the idea of anyone possibly having the same dress as her daughter. "Nothing cheap," she had said. And although she didn't completely mean money-wise, she meant class-wise. One thing Nancy O'Driscoll wanted to make clear on the outside was that she wasn't some poor immigrant. Another thing I realized years later.

We were deep in a sea of satin and sequins when I spotted Sawyer. He seemed detached, scanning the crowd until his gaze landed on me. His tall frame stood out even in the busy mall, his auburn curls peeking out from under a backward Maplewood Mariners baseball cap. His hazel eyes, always shifting between green and brown, seemed to find mine with an intensity that made my heart skip a beat.

"Josie, look at this one," my mom said, holding up a vibrant blue gown that sparkled under the store lights.

"That's a nice one, Mom," I replied, but my attention was split as I watched Sawyer make his way over to us, his approach hesitant but determined. My heart pounded in my chest—like someone plugged a charger into it and it suddenly came alive.

"Hey, Josie," he said, a gentle smile playing on his lips as he reached us. My mom, sizing him up with a quick, discerning glance, nodded politely before turning her attention back to the dress and then walking away to another display.

"Hey!" I said, a little overly friendly and wincing at my awkwardness.

"How's your wrist?"

I followed his gaze to my wrist and bent it back and forth. "Well, the doctor said you better watch your ass because I'll be throwing snowballs like a champ by next winter." He laughed, and it felt like a jolt of electricity coursing through me.

"Noted," he joked.

Sawyer took in our surroundings. "There are a lot of sequins." His gaze dropped to the blue gown my mom had set aside and then to my face—a question in his expression.

I smiled and clasped my hands together. "Well, yours truly is going to the spring formal, and it turns out my usual attire of jeans and hoodies is not going to cut it."

I loved his smile, especially when I was the one who managed to coax it out of him. But just as I was basking in my success, his expression shifted, his eyes locking on mine with a look that made my breath catch.

"You're beautiful, Josie," he said, his voice steady, his gaze unwavering. "It doesn't matter if it's jeans, a ball gown, or anything in between—you just are."

The sincerity in his words hit me like a tidal wave, leaving me breathless.

The moment stretched between us, neither of us knowing where to go from here, until it was abruptly pierced by my mother's voice calling from a few racks away. "Josie, do you know what color tie your date is wearing?"

Caught off guard by her question and the sudden intrusion into the bubble that had formed around Sawyer and me, I felt my cheeks warm with a blush. "Uh, I think Ricky said he'd match whatever I wear," I managed to reply, my voice a bit higher than usual.

Sawyer's expression shifted slightly, a subtle mix of disappointment and understanding crossing his features as he nodded. "Blue's a good choice," he said quietly, forcing a smile that didn't quite reach his eyes as before.

The air around us changed, and I felt a twinge of sadness for the brief connection that was now retreating. The bubble we were in burst completely when I heard a familiar high-pitched voice slicing through the hum of the mall.

"There you are!" Val's voice, sharp and intrusive, found its way to us. As she approached, her eyes gave me a calculated once-over, her gaze scrutinizing every inch of me with barely concealed judgment.

"Oh, hi, Josie." The sneer in her voice didn't go unnoticed.

"Hi, Val," I replied, striving to keep my voice neutral despite the irritation prickling at the back of my neck.

Val was one of those girls who, from a distance, seemed effortlessly beautiful, the kind of girl who turned heads and drew admiring glances. But up close, the illusion began to fade. Her makeup, heavy and meticulously applied, masked homeliness that was buried under layers of foundation and powder. Her lashes, thick with mascara, clumped together in a way that seemed almost deliberate, while her lips, painted a vivid red, had a hint of garishness that felt out of place in the bright lighting of the mall. Her hair was bleached blonde, and the dark roots were beginning to show. There was something cheap about her appearance, a veneer that didn't quite match the polished image she tried to project.

But she had the body. She was developed in ways I was not, and she owned every inch of it with the way she carried herself. Where eyes on me made me turn inward, eyes on her made her fully charged.

She glanced around, noting the racks of dresses. "Dress shopping?" she asked, her tone suggesting she found the activity trivial.

I nodded. "Spring formal."

"That's cute." Her words dripped with condescension. Then, as if considering me nothing more than a minor inconvenience, she hooked her arm firmly through Sawyer's. "Come on. The movie is starting, and I want you to buy me popcorn first."

It felt like my heart splintered right then and there.

Sawyer gave me a soft, apologetic smile, clearly uncomfortable. "Have fun at the dance, Josie," he said, his voice low and sincere.

Then Val tugged him away, but not before I caught Sawyer's lingering glance. As they retreated into the crowd, I saw him look back at me again, his eyes holding something like regret before he disappeared from view, swallowed by the mall's bustling activity.

Left standing amid a sea of dresses, the echo of his farewell and the sight of him walking away with Val settled heavily in my chest. I suddenly had no interest in these dresses, but when I turned and saw my mom looking at me curiously, I forced a smile, hiding the ache behind it. I had learned long ago how to make everything look fine, even when it wasn't.

***

The spring formal was more eventful for others than for me. Ricky, it turned out, had a fleeting crush on me, but his heart belonged to Julia Hilton. They confessed their feelings on the dance floor and disappeared under the stage for the rest of the evening.

I was unbothered, to be honest. Ricky was a nice guy, but after spending five minutes with him, it was clear how unlike Sawyer he was—and that left no space for him in my thoughts. To say my heart wasn't feeling a bit bruised wouldn't be true. As much as I tried to stop myself, my thoughts kept going back to Val pulling Sawyer away to go to the movies. I didn't have the experience Val did, and I may have been more sheltered than others my age, but I was not stupid. I knew by the way she touched him that they shared other touches in the dark. It was enough to make me sick, but not enough to stop wishing I was the girl he was bringing to the movies.

I nonchalantly brought up the whole awkward exchange to Beatrice, who, by now, was fully aware of my budding crush and was completely scandalized by the news that Sawyer and Val were dating. She roped in Jason to stealthily probe Sawyer about Val, under strict instructions to keep my name out of it. Under absolutely no circumstances was my name or the incident at the mall to make its way into the conversation. Jason was simply going to find a way to ask Sawyer if he was fooling around with Val.

One lazy afternoon, as Beatrice and I lay sprawled on her bed, staring at the ceiling and listening to music, Jason burst in without knocking.

"Knock, Jason!" Beatrice screamed.

"Who's there?" Jason smirked, intentionally trying to piss his sister off.

"Ugh, you're an idiot," Beatrice groaned.

"Okay, whatever. So I told Sawyer that Josie wanted to know if he was dating Val, and he said no."

We both shot up from the bed in unison, shrieking, "Jason!" Our panic spiraled into a frenzy of disbelief and name-calling. At some point, I curled into the fetal position and cried that I was never going to leave my house again. Beatrice called him "the world's shittiest detective."

Jason looked genuinely perplexed. "What? You wanted to know, and he said no."

"You weren't supposed to say I wanted to know!" I cried, mortified.

He paused, a smug smile creeping onto his face. "Well, he seemed awfully curious about why you were asking."

"Wait. What do you mean?" I pressed.

Jason shrugged. "He asked why you wanted to know."

I was in his face in less than a second, so close it was borderline invasive. I leaned in, my voice a frantic whisper. "Okay, but *how* did he ask? Was it like, 'Ugh, why does she care?' or more like, 'Huh, why does she care?' with a little sparkle of intrigue? Be honest—did his eyebrow do *the thing*?"

"Oh my God, Josie." Jason recoiled, his eyes wide with mock horror as he took an exaggerated step back. "*The thing*? Are you serious? Do you want me to draw you a diagram next time or maybe record it for analysis? Or do you want me to ask him again and take notes this time?"

"No!" Beatrice and I screamed in unison before Jason mumbled that we were crazy and left the room.

As the door closed behind him, Beatrice turned to me, her eyes filled with frustration and amusement. "We need a new plan," she said, shaking her head.

"No. No new plan," I groaned, slumping onto the nearest chair. The embarrassment of the whole situation felt like a weight pressing down on me. "Let's just let it go. All of it."

Beatrice raised an eyebrow, smirking. "Let go of what? Sawyer or the idea that Jason could ever be a competent spy?"

I let out a dramatic whimper, burying my face in my hands. "Both. Definitely both. Maybe throw me into the mix too while we're at it. I'm a lost cause."

Beatrice laughed, nudging my foot with hers. "Oh, stop it. You're ridiculous, but you're not *that* hopeless."

Chapter 7

Now

The funeral Mass for Sarge takes place in St. Mary's Church, an old brick structure with a steeple that overlooked my childhood. This church was a constant, the backdrop to my early years. Here, I confessed my sins to middle-aged priests and wore a white dress, resembling a miniature bride, for my First Holy Communion. I remember my mother's pride as she snapped photos with her disposable camera while my father fidgeted in his suit jacket.

Dermott and I walk into the church, my eyes roaming the familiar interior adorned with stained glass and elaborate paintings of birth and crucifixion. The old guilt of an Irish Catholic upbringing rises in my throat as I admit to myself just how long it has been since I last entered a church. The wooden pews hold dozens of mourners, and despite the attendance, I am acutely aware of everyone around me. My eyes instinctively search for Sawyer, just as they did in crowded rooms years ago, but he is nowhere to be seen.

I parted ways with Beatrice in front of Miner's, promising to meet again at the funeral. Dermott and I enter the pews, genuflect, and kneel to pray. Throughout my childhood, I knelt here, often unable to muster a prayer. My mind always wandered, and today is no different. I try to reel it back in, attempting to pray, but I can't bring myself to recite the old incantations that never made any sense to me.

Instead, I ask God to take care of Sarge, to let him know I love him and am thankful for him. Then I question why I can't just tell him myself. Can he hear my thoughts, floating somewhere in the ether? If he could, he'd hear me saying sorry, again and again. I've lost years, not just with Sarge and Beatrice, but even with Sawyer—though those years might have been lost regardless. Realizing this places a heavy fear in my heart, rendering me immobile. The guilt often makes me hate myself, and the perceived weakness wreaks havoc. I start to feel the clutches of anxiety. *You've dealt with crazy shit before. You'll deal with this too.* I'm not sure God would approve of this prayer. I remind myself that I am strong. I am resilient. Didn't my childhood train me for this?

Dermott shifts beside me, and I turn to him with a weak smile. "I'm sorry I've been the worst travel companion."

He rolls his eyes, sarcasm evident. "Sure, everyone dreams of visiting the States to attend funerals and witness their cousin's brooding ex-lover nearly combust on a funeral home porch."

I glance around, stifling a laugh. "Shh, someone might hear you."

"Pfft, these people don't understand a feckin' word coming out of my mouth," he whispers, his thick southern Irish brogue adding a layer of truth. He's probably right; it takes a moment to adjust to the rapid-fire rhythm of his speech.

I shake my head, feeling a bit deflated. Dermott notices immediately. "What's going on in that head of yours?"

I blow out a frustrated breath. "I can't seem to focus on Sarge. I'm overwhelmed. Every time I turn around, there's another memory, another loose end, another heartbreak. I can't seem to absorb the loss."

Dermott turns fully toward me. "That last bit you said is a big part of what's wrong with you."

My jaw drops. "Wow, Dermott. What a way to put it," I whisper.

He shakes his head. "Seriously, you shouldn't be absorbing more sadness, Josie. You've had your fill. You don't need to absorb the loss and definitely don't need to feel guilty for not feeling guilty enough. That's really fucking Irish of you, by the way."

I start to protest, but Dermott cuts me off, a mischievous glint in his eye. "And I know you're going to say..." His voice shifts, adopting an exaggerated American accent. "'No, Dermott, I didn't mean absorb *literally*.'" I purse my lips, unimpressed by his attempt at imitating me. "But I know what you meant. I know you better than you know yourself right now. You need to work on that."

"Thanks. I'll bring it up in therapy," I say dryly. Dermott just smiles.

"I should start charging for these therapy sessions, Josephine." He loves using my given name in jest.

I smirk, glancing around again, still not seeing Sawyer. Just then, Beatrice clicks up the aisle and slides into the pew beside me.

"Hi," she whispers.

"Hi."

Leaning over, she extends her hand to Dermott. "I'm Beatrice. I think we met once before."

Dermott shakes her hand. "Ah yes, I remember. We must have been around ten. Even if we hadn't met, Josie's talked about you so much over the years, I feel like I know you."

Beatrice's eyes soften as she looks at me, not missing the implication that while I may have left her, she has never really left me.

The solemn notes of the organ begin, setting a reverent tone. The vibrations transform the atmosphere into a hallowed space as the pallbearers lift Sarge's coffin. There, of course, is Sawyer. He carries the weight with steady hands, the coffin resting on his strong shoulder. Because that's Sawyer—steady, safe, and strong, always there to hold you up when you need it most. I would know. He held me steady so many times, carried me when I couldn't find my own footing, and then practically threw me off a cliff.

I can't help but stare, transfixed by his profile—somber and solid, heavy with responsibility. I know Sawyer would call it an honor. He probably teared up alone after being asked to carry Sarge's casket, but he'd never do it in front of anyone. Not because of ill-placed masculinity or fear of perception, but because he cares so deeply about those around him. He wouldn't want anyone to feel scared or insecure. He'd bear the weight alone, making it look effortless—but I know Sawyer. Even after all these years, I can see in his face and the way he carries himself that his heart is aching. Sarge was his too.

I eventually tear my gaze from him, but throughout the Mass, I steal glances at him. He stands, solemn and respectful, his quiet dignity more pronounced now as a man, though it had been evident even as a boy. The Mass proceeds with traditional rites, hymns, and prayers. I participate mechanically, my responses automatic, but my mind and eyes wander to memories I have packed away in a box labeled "Past."

As the time approaches for Sarge's casket to be carried out, I try to keep my eyes on the altar. I almost succeed, but when Sawyer walks past, our eyes meet. Something in his look takes my breath away—a blend of sorrow, regret, and a depth of feeling I can't quite grasp. Last night, he seemed angry. Today, he seems sad. Grief can unsettle anyone, even the steadfast Sawyer I once knew.

The casket is carried out of the church into the bright afternoon light. The honor guard has prepared an area outside for Sarge's final military honors. I have never attended a funeral with military honors, so I'm not sure what to expect. Alice, Sarge's sister, walks ahead of the procession, her head held high with pride for her older brother.

We gather in the designated area as Sawyer and the other pallbearers place Sarge's casket into the hearse and step aside. The military honor guard assembles with precise movements. The rifle party, standing in formation, raise their rifles.

"What are they doing?" I whisper to Dermott.

"Hell if I know," he mutters, scratching the back of his neck.

Out of the corner of my eye, I notice Beatrice pressing her fingers to her ears. Before I can figure out why, the first crack of the three-volley salute rings out like a cannon.

"Jesus!" I yelp, clutching my chest.

"Fuck it!" Dermott bellows, flinging his hands in the air like someone just pulled a gun on him.

Dozens of heads swivel in our direction. My face burns as I grab Dermott's hand, squeezing it like I can somehow mortify him into silence.

"Christ almighty, warn a fella next time," he mutters, glaring at the honor guard as if they've wronged him personally.

Beatrice is biting her lip so hard she looks like she might pop a blood vessel, her shoulders shaking as she tries not to laugh. I shoot her a desperate, wide-eyed look.

Then, the second shot rings out.

"Mother of God!" Dermott shouts, jumping a full inch off the ground.

"Dermott!" I hiss, slapping a hand over my mouth to stifle my own shriek. I glance at Beatrice again, who has now turned away entirely, her body vibrating with suppressed laughter.

Just then, I feel someone lean in close behind me, and Sawyer's low voice brushes against my ear. "There's one more, Josie O."

The third shot fires before I have a chance to process Sawyer's words. I leap backward with all the grace of a startled cat, colliding straight into his chest. His hand grips my arm to steady me as I flail, my heart pounding in my ears.

"Aye, Jaysus!" Dermott cries, clutching his chest like a man on the brink. "For fuck's sake, are there any more? Or are we safe now?"

Every nerve in my body is on high alert—Sawyer's cologne wrapping around me, the solid warmth of his hand grounding me, the deep calm of his presence. My head tilts back slightly, as if it has a mind of its own, and for one irrational moment, I want to lean into him, to stay there.

"That's all of them, Josie," Sawyer whispers in my ear, his voice low and steady, sending an electric charge through my already frayed nerves.

And then, just as quickly as he appeared, he's gone. Back to the hearse, moving with the same quiet certainty that has always undone me.

I stare after him, my pulse still racing like I've run a marathon, while Dermott mutters something about "military ambushes at a funeral." Beatrice finally loses the battle with her composure, letting out an uncontrollable snort of laughter that sets me off, too.

In the midst of the absurdity, I swear I can almost hear Sarge's warm chuckle echoing somewhere in the breeze, as though he's laughing along with us from beyond the grave.

But when the casket is loaded into the hearse, it's over. There's no blessing at the cemetery, no funeral luncheon. That's it.

"Alice says he wants us to let him go," Beatrice murmurs softly beside me, "and carry on with our lives."

I nod, but a lump rises in my throat. Sarge has always been my anchor, the one constant I could never imagine losing. And even though he's gone now, his letter tucked into my pocket reminds me that, for now, I don't have to let him go entirely. Not yet.

***

Beatrice and I agree to meet for a walk along the river, eager to bridge the fifteen-year gap since we last met. I'm curious about every aspect of her life—her parents, her brother, her job—everything. It feels impossible to cram more than a decade into a single week, but I'm hopeful we'll make the most of the time we have while I'm in Maplewood.

Dermott went back to Miner's for a nap, still fighting off jet lag, while I'm too wired to even think about sleep. When I arrive at the trailhead, I spot Beatrice waiting for me, her vibrant smile a beacon of familiarity amidst the changing scenery.

"Josie!" she calls, waving me over.

I jog the last few steps to meet her, a grin spreading across my face. For a moment, neither of us says anything, just taking each other in like we still can't quite believe this reunion is real.

She nudges my shoulder playfully, her smile widening. "Come on. Let's go."

We fall into step together, the sound of the river a soothing backdrop to our conversation.

As we walk along the trail, the rustling leaves and distant bird calls create a peaceful ambiance. Beatrice occasionally bends down to touch a wildflower or admire a particularly lush patch of greenery, but the weight of lost time lingers between us.

"So," we both start, then laugh at the synchronicity.

"Where do we even begin?" Beatrice asks, her eyes sparkling with curiosity and nostalgia.

"I want to know everything, Beatrice. Everything. Don't leave anything out. Where's Jason? How are your parents? Do you have a boyfriend? Where do you work? Are you happy and healthy?"

Her expression softens at my flood of questions. "Mom and Dad are good, fully retired now and lovingly driving each other crazy. They became snowbirds—moved to Florida three years ago—just like everyone else who retires in this town. And Jason? He's doing great, settled in Chicago."

My mouth drops open. Another reminder that life in Maplewood hasn't frozen in time while I've been gone. "Chicago?" I say, still stunned. "Jason is the definition of Maplewood for me." I picture him in his Maplewood Mariners baseball uniform, a symbol of the life we lived here.

"Yes, it's crazy. He actually followed a girl out there. I only met her a few times. It didn't work out with her, but he loved the city, got a great job, and decided to stay. We don't see each other as much as we used to. The trips he used to take home are split between here and Florida now. But we talk and text all the time."

A strange blend of pride and sadness washes over me. "I'm really happy for him. I'm sad I won't see him, but I'm happy he's doing so well." We walk quietly for a few more moments. "On another note, how about you? Do I have to compete with anyone for your time this week?"

Beatrice rolls her eyes dramatically. "Ha! Hardly. I'm planning on keeping it that way." She pauses, raising her water bottle for a sip before crouching to examine a delicate fern unfurling along the trail. She hesitates for a moment. "I'm actually divorced."

The words shock me more than a crack of thunder on a clear day. I choke on my breath, coughing as I try to process the news. "Beatrice, I'm so sorry—"

She stands, waving off my concern with a laugh. "Don't be. I married a complete asshat and divorced him three years later. I deserve congratulations more than sympathy."

I'm not convinced, even with her intentionally light tone. I left this town and, foolishly, wanted to believe that everything I cherished had remained unchanged, frozen in time. But here is a clear example of how life marches on, with joys and sorrows that didn't stop just because I disappeared.

"Well, in that case, I'm not sorry that you divorced an asshat, but I wish I'd been here for you when you went through it," I admit, my voice tinged with regret. We start walking again. "Who was it? Do I know him?"

"I married Sawyer," she says nonchalantly.

I freeze and choke again, gasping for breath.

"Just kidding!" she says with a laugh, enjoying my reaction.

"Wait—you didn't marry him?"

"Ha ha, no! That would be the biggest violation of girl code on the planet. But I was curious if you'd have a reaction to him after all these years, and well, there's my answer!"

"That was cruel," I manage to say, half joking.

"You deserve it. Leaving without a trace. But I won't punish you anymore." Her joke is lighthearted, but I don't miss the hurt in her eyes.

I look at my beautiful best friend in front of me. She will always hold that space in my heart, although I am sure my place in her life has been long since filled. I can't blame her for that. And this strong woman standing before me, having lived a whole life in my absence, still has the grace to spend time with me after I abandoned her—after all she has done for me. I don't deserve it. I don't deserve this grace—even if she doesn't know the whole truth.

The words burst from me. "Why are you talking to me, Beatrice? Why didn't you tell me to go to hell when you saw me? I deserve that from you."

She doesn't flinch. She just sighs and slows her pace as if she expected the question. "Truthfully? I don't know." She's quiet for a moment and I wonder if she will say any more.

After a beat, she finds the words she seems to be looking for. "I've thought of you coming back, and I've pictured myself being mad. And I was mad. Believe me, I was mad. But after that wore off, I was just so heartbroken. And I knew. I *knew* that the agony you were feeling was your own, and I couldn't take it away even if I wanted to. And that's what killed me. That I couldn't love your pain away. And then I'd get mad that you didn't give me the chance, and it would start the cycle again."

How many times can I say I am sorry? I wish there were another word. Another way to express the regret that has nestled so securely inside me it has become an organ next to my heart. All I can do is apologize again and again.

"I'm sorry. I know it seems like I just left and didn't look back. That's not what happened."

She is quiet for a moment before chancing a glance in my direction. "What *did* happen?"

"Ugh, Bea, that is such a big question I just don't know how to start an explanation on that now."

She looks disappointed, and that makes the regret throb inside me, but despite the gnawing guilt, I just can't get into it now.

"Tell me someday?" she asks innocently, as if the story will be simple.

I wonder if Beatrice knows that a heart can become so broken that when there is no space left for it to break, the shattering will move to your mind. I suspect and hope that she doesn't. I am broken enough for the both of us.

"I'm sure my promises mean nothing to you after what happened, but I promise I will tell you everything. It's just a lot. More importantly, I really want to know about you and the world's biggest douchebag and where I can find him to kick his ass."

A laugh bubbles out of her. "I am definitely not wasting my precious time with you talking about the world's biggest douchebag." She looks at me with mirth dancing in her eyes. "His name is Dash. I should've freaking known."

"Dash?" I say with exaggerated disgust. I draw out the name. "*Daaaaaash?* What the hell?"

"Very appropriate name, in fact." She chuckles. "When shit got tough, he dashed right out the door."

I open my mouth to begin a line of questioning, but she lifts her hand. "Not wasting our time, though."

As we continue to walk, the background noise of the river and the rustling leaves fades into a comforting buzz. It feels like no time has passed at all, and yet the weight of the years is ever-present, filled with stories waiting to be told. She tells me she opened a floral shop, which is so perfectly Beatrice. In fact, the flowers for Sarge's funeral and viewing were done by her and her staff. My girl Beatrice has staff. I am blooming with pride.

I tell her I am an ESL teacher in Dublin, having moved from southern Ireland to the capital city six years before.

She tries valiantly to bring up Sawyer, but I shake my head, cutting her off before she can get too far. "I'm not ready for that conversation yet," I say softly. I can't promise I'll ever be ready to talk about him.

Instead, I reach into my purse and pull out Sarge's letter, letting it rest in my hands for a moment before holding it up.

"You ready?" I ask, my voice barely above a whisper.

Beatrice tilts her head, thoughtful. "Do you think he meant for you to read it alone?"

I shake my head, resolute. "Sarge wasn't big on me being alone when my heart was hurting. He wouldn't have made that a condition."

She studies me for a moment, then nods knowingly. "You're right. Well then." She smiles, gesturing toward the letter. "Open it."

We find a bench along the path and sit. I tear open the envelope, the familiar aroma of Sarge's Lucky Strikes wafting up. As I unfold the paper, tears blur my vision, turning the words into a jumbled mess. I blink them away, take a deep breath, and begin to read, trying to make sense of his final message.

***

My Josie girl,

Well, kid, if you're reading this, I've kicked the bucket. I've had one foot on a banana peel and the other in a grave for some time now, so I started writing you these letters because I need you to tie up some loose ends I've left dangling.

I need you to know something. I've never met anyone who has as much heart as you. I know you don't think that's a good thing. Sometimes when you have all that heart you think you are prone to breaking. But, honey, you never broke. You were forged in flames. I've seen it all. I fought in the jungle. I've watched people get blown apart, put back together, and blown apart again, but you—you stood in the heat for so long it damn near killed me to watch. I know grown men who couldn't do it.

You've been gone a long time, but I knew you had your reasons. I'm proud of you for doing what you needed to become whole again, but I'm also proud of you for coming back. It proves you're not afraid to face old ghosts. We all have 'em, but now it's time you take yours out to dance.

Now do me a favor. Head to the baseball fields the day of my funeral at 4:00 p.m. on the dot. I don't want any silly funeral luncheon, so no excuses. Why there? 'Cause it's where I spent countless evenings as a young man, not just watching baseball games but thinking about my special person before I stood in my own fire. Yeah, that's a surprise, right? That place was our little slice of heaven, even if the hot dogs were lousy and Vietnam was about to take me away.

There's a big tree behind the left field gate. Look at the markings and then go to the food stand. I've figured out a way to have your next clue taped under the picnic table closest to the counter.

Remember this, Josie girl—sometimes we put down our own roots. The choice is ours.

Catch you later,
Sarge

Chapter 8

Then

I spent the summer before my sophomore year in Ireland, but not before finding myself drawn to the baseball field, my eyes often seeking out the catcher. There was something about the way Sawyer commanded the space behind the plate—his stance wide and sure, helmet slightly tilted as he signaled to the pitcher with a subtle, practiced flick of his fingers. His gear, marked by scuffs and dirt, told the story of countless games and unwavering dedication. Watching him bat was no less intriguing. Even from the food stand, I could sense the intensity in his gaze, a fierce concentration that never wavered. But more than anything, I loved watching him catch.

When the batter popped the ball straight up, Sawyer sprang from his crouch, sliding his mask atop his head and exposing a mess of auburn curls. My breath hitched. My pulse quickened, and for a second, everything around me faded—the chatter of the crowd, the smell of popcorn, even the distant hum of the game. It was just him, calm and composed, like he had the entire field under his control. I swallowed hard, my chest tightening with the familiar ache that reminded me how far out of reach he really was.

Before the game ended—another victory for Maplewood High—I made my way back to the food stand just as a rush of spectators started lining up for food and drinks. Peeking behind, I saw Beatrice's mom and another woman struggling to keep up with the crowd of customers. Beatrice had sauntered off to a group of kids—the social butterfly she was. Mrs. Knight, relieved to see me, looked up from the register.

"Oh, Josie, thank God. Can you come back here and help us? We usually have three more moms, but they all flaked on us."

I looked around, pointing at myself. "Me?"

"Yes, yes! Come in here now. You can man the slushie machine."

Mrs. Knight looked exasperated, so I didn't question her again. I rounded the little building and entered through the side door. She beckoned me over to the slushie machine.

"Four pumps of whatever flavor or color they want. Then, put the cup under here and pull the nozzle. It comes out fast, so push the nozzle back in a second before you think you need to. Got it?"

"Got it," I said decisively, though I was pretty sure I didn't get anything.

"Lids and straws are here." She pointed to a stack of supplies and then to another woman shuffling around behind a small case with a few fries and mozzarella sticks. "That's Lizzy. She's working the fryer."

I waved at Lizzy just as she shouted to seemingly no one that fries were up.

Is this a food stand or a freaking diner? I had no idea what I was in for.

Before I could think, Mrs. Knight shouted to the line of people, "If you're ordering a slushie, line up here!" She turned to me and physically stationed me at one side of the counter. "Stand here. They'll come to you." And come to me they did.

As I fumbled with the slushie machine, my eyes drifted back to Sawyer, and I didn't even realize the cup had overflowed until bright-red syrup started dripping onto my hand. I snapped back to reality, wiping the sticky mess with a napkin, my cheeks burning as I hoped no one noticed. I thought I saw his eyes flick up from the field for just a moment, catching mine before I hurried to clean up. My heart thudded against my ribs, betraying me.

My first few slushies were less than stellar—some too watery, others too icy. But soon enough, I got the hang of it, managing to produce perfectly blended icy treats that made the kids at the counter beam with anticipation.

Behind me, the fryer station was a nonstop whirlwind of activity. Lizzy, the woman manning it, was nothing short of a force of nature. With her rich, boisterous laugh and easygoing charm, she handled the flood of orders like a seasoned chef at a five-star restaurant. Despite the relentless pace, she moved with the grace of a dancer, her hands a blur as they shifted from frying basket to serving tray. I wondered who her kid was and what it must be like to have her as a mom. She was everything.

"Josie, darling," she called out over the din of sizzling oil and chattering customers, "once you're done crafting those slushie masterpieces, would you mind running these onion rings to the folks over by the picnic tables?"

With a smile, I grabbed the tray piled high with golden-brown rings and navigated through the sea of people, delivering the food with a flair that earned me appreciative smiles from the waiting fans. Returning to the stand, I slid back into the rhythm of pouring and mixing slushies, the sweet, tangy aroma of syrup filling the air.

Lizzy, watching me dart back and forth with a tray in one hand and a slushie cup in the other, let out a musical laugh. "Look at you go, girl! You're handling this better than some of the veterans I've seen!"

Her compliment, shouted over the noise, was filled with warm amusement. It felt good to receive praise from Lizzy. Though I'd only known her for a short time, when she looked at you, it felt like she was seeking out the good—not the bad. She stood tall, strikingly beautiful, and somehow handsome. She struck me as someone who could have been a supermodel in the nineties. Her presence was steady. She drew me in.

"It's all in the wrist!" I joked back, demonstrating an exaggerated twist of the slushie machine handle, sending us both into a fit of laughter. "We're lucky these slushies are even drinkable. I broke my wrist before Christmas, so it's a miracle they're awesome."

Lizzy paused, looking at me with a new expression, as though noticing me for the first time. "Wait! You're Josie? My son is Johnny!"

I tried to figure out if I knew a Johnny, but before I could, she laughed again, understanding my confusion. "I mean Sawyer. I don't call him that because—well, it's our last name. I'm Lizzy Sawyer."

Before I could register this, she looked over my shoulder and smiled. "There he is!"

I turned to see Sawyer smirking, leaning up against the counter as the crowd began to thin. His ball cap hung loosely in his hand, his hair damp with sweat from the game. The final inning must have wrapped up amid the rush of fried foods and slushies, but instead of heading off with his team, he was here, his eyes focused on me. My heart thudded painfully in my chest as I watched a bead of water roll down his temple.

"Did my mom seriously put you to work?"

I was both stunned that Lizzy was Sawyer's mom and somehow not surprised. I glanced back at her—tall, statuesque, with chestnut hair cascading in waves. Her steady presence and confident grace made it all so clear now. This was the woman who made Sawyer who he was.

"No, I did, though!" Mrs. Knight called out playfully as she reached past me for a stack of napkins. "And you better be careful, or I'll put you to work too. My own daughter disappeared when she saw all hell breaking loose!"

I laughed. "Your mom is awesome."

He nodded. "I'll admit it. She is."

"You had a good game," I said, just loud enough for only the two of us to hear.

"You were watching?" His eyes met mine, and for a moment, I sensed vulnerability. His voice was quiet, like he didn't expect me to care.

"Of course, until I was kidnapped and forced to work."

"Well, thank you." He smiled, and I melted.

"Can I interest you in a slushie?" I joked, never expecting him to order.

Just then, Val came up behind Sawyer and leaned against him. His cool demeanor didn't fully mask his annoyance.

"Eww, slushies? Sawyer, will you buy me a—" She glanced around, her nose wrinkling in distaste. "Ugh, all this stuff is gross. I'll just take a Diet Coke."

Sawyer kept a straight face. "You can get whatever you want, but I can't buy anything for you."

"Why not?" she asked, laughing in disbelief. He stepped back from the counter and gestured to his uniform, indicating he didn't have his wallet. As he moved away from Val, our eyes met, and I caught a flicker of relief—like he was glad for the excuse.

With a sigh, Val slapped a dollar on the counter. "Diet Coke," she said, her tone sharp, as if I were the one inconveniencing her.

"Diet Coke coming right up," I replied, barely hiding my satisfaction. I grabbed her dollar and returned with the drink. "Here you go."

She took it, but her eyes flicked to the crowd for a brief second—searching. It was quick, almost too fast to notice, but there it was, that fleeting flash of hesitation. Insecurity? I wasn't sure, but it disappeared as fast as it had come. She took a sip, her lips pressing into a tight, dissatisfied line.

"You coming?" she asked Sawyer, her voice rising with forced confidence.

"Nah," he replied casually.

Her eyes narrowed in frustration. "Why not?"

"I'm staying here," Sawyer said. His eyes met mine, holding my gaze a beat longer than necessary. "I want to help Josie clean up."

Val's eyes locked on me. It was as if she was noticing a bug or some sort of nuisance for the first time. It wasn't the first time, though. I knew what it was like to be on the receiving end of her ire. She looked back to Sawyer before her gaze shifted to me again, sharp and calculating, but this time, it felt like she was trying to remind herself who she was supposed to be—the Val everyone expected. I could almost see the mask slipping back into place as she stomped away, the vulnerable moment erased, replaced by the haughty façade she wore so well.

I couldn't dwell on her attitude for long. A line of customers pulled me away, and as another wave of spectators crowded around the stand, the atmosphere buzzed with a fresh flurry of activity. Amid the chaos, I was busy wrestling with the slushie machine when Sawyer suddenly vaulted over the counter, landing beside me with a grin. "Can I help?"

Before I could respond, Mrs. Knight appeared. "Sawyer, if you're staying, let's switch things up. I'll take over the slushies and drinks. Josie, handle the money. Sawyer, you take care of the food orders. We'll finish quicker this way."

As the rush of customers slowed and the last few slushies were handed out, Lizzy wiped her hands on a towel and shot a knowing glance at her son, a mischievous smile playing on her lips.

"Sawyer, you planning to stick around and keep helping out, or are you just here to flirt with Josie?" she teased, her voice light but full of warmth.

Sawyer rolled his eyes good-naturedly, but there was an unmistakable affection in the way he looked at her. "Mom," he groaned, though he didn't deny it.

Lizzy laughed, the sound rich and full of life. "Well, if you're going to stay, make yourself useful. I don't have all day to watch you pretend to be busy." She winked at me, and I couldn't help but smile.

Sawyer's cheeks reddened ever so slightly, and he grabbed a nearby towel, swiping it across the counter. "I'm helping," he muttered, his eyes flicking briefly to mine, as if checking to see if I was watching.

I was.

Lizzy gave him one last playful shove before turning back to the fryer. "Good boy. You always know how to show up when it matters."

And with that, we were off again, caught up in the final surge of business.

The rest of the shift flew by in a whirlwind of flavors and laughter, the stress tempered by the thrill of being so close to Sawyer. The stand, with its sticky counters and air thick with the scent of fried food and syrup, couldn't have been a better backdrop for our interactions.

We fell into a rhythm, him passing me the orders, me handling the transactions. Every so often, our hands brushed, and I found myself stealing glances at him. The memories of all our past interactions played back vividly.

As I handed over the change to the next customer, I felt the warmth of Sawyer's arm brush against mine. It wasn't much, just a brief touch, but it sent a current through me. I glanced up, half expecting him to pull away, but he didn't. He stayed close, our shoulders nearly touching as we worked side by side, and the space between us seemed smaller than ever.

Sawyer caught me looking, his eyes meeting mine for just a second longer than I expected. A flicker of something crossed his face—amusement? Curiosity? Whatever it was, it came with a small, almost secretive smile that sent my heart into a freefall.

"I think I had more fun back here with you than I did out there," he said, nodding toward the field as he wiped his hands on a towel.

I blinked, caught off guard. "You mean you prefer slinging hot dogs to playing baseball and socializing with your adoring fans? Somehow, I doubt that."

His smile widened, slow and easy, like it was just for me. "Who says I have fans?"

"Oh, please," I said, rolling my eyes. "You don't think I noticed all the grandmas circling the stand, giggling every time you handed out ketchup packets?"

He leaned an elbow on the counter, tilting his head, his grin deepening. "Jealous?"

The word hit like a lightning bolt, and I sputtered out a laugh, my cheeks burning. "Of *ketchup packets*? Okay, first of all, I *love* ketchup, so tread carefully. But no, I'm not jealous." An image of Val unbidden flashed through my mind. "A little scared of the grandmas, maybe."

Sawyer let out a laugh, shaking his head as if I were an impossible puzzle he didn't mind figuring out. "You're something else, Josie," he said, his voice softer now, almost thoughtful.

Feeling the air shift between us, I fumbled to steer things back to safer ground. "Well, thank you for staying. I mean, for helping."

"Wouldn't want to be anywhere else," he said, his gaze holding mine for a moment that felt both too long and not long enough.

My stomach fluttered, and I busied myself with a napkin, suddenly aware of how small the space behind the counter felt with him standing there. His words from the mall came rushing back: *You're beautiful.*

For just a second, I let myself imagine a world where Sawyer wasn't just a friend helping out—where he was mine.

Chapter 9

Now

As the baseball complex comes into view, the weight of memories feels heavier on my heart, like stepping back through years in just a few steps. The field is quieter now, the usual roar of cheering crowds replaced by a soft early evening breeze that rustles through the leaves. The sun is low, casting long, melancholy shadows across the diamond, making the place look deserted and steeped in nostalgia.

Beatrice offered to accompany me to the baseball field, sensing the pressure of Sarge's request. However, she had to return to her shop for a bit, leaving me to face this part of the journey alone. I assured her it was okay, promising to catch up with her later for an update. This is something I need to do alone, after all.

When I get to the field, my eyes immediately go to the empty stands, where I felt moments of pure happiness in an otherwise dark and dysfunctional youth. And of course, my thoughts go to Sawyer.

Even though I try to convince myself that my heart is healed, I feel it thud painfully inside my chest, reminding me of how broken it once was. I close my eyes, breathing in the fall air. It's so different from the springtime and early summer evenings I spent here. But as I try to find a moment of serenity, Sawyer's face appears in my mind's eye.

I picture him here, his auburn hair peeking out from under a baseball cap that catches the light with every turn of his head. He had a boyish charm that belied a deeper intensity in his gaze. I remember that gaze meeting mine behind the food stand. His eyes, a vibrant mix of green and brown, conveyed warmth and mischievousness. His smile was soft and friendly, easily drawing people in. He moved with a confident, relaxed grace, the kind of natural ease that made it seem like he was perpetually surrounded by a soft spotlight.

And I hate him for being so perfect, for haunting my memory all these years later. What I believed him to be and what he became is the ultimate betrayal. I didn't trust my own judgment for years, and I blame it on that smile.

Shaking off the thoughts, I look in the direction of left field. I walk toward the tree, imagining a young Sarge here, laughing about the lousy hot dogs before Vietnam claimed him. Sarge rarely spoke of that time in his life, a subject too painful to broach, I assume.

Reaching the big tree he mentioned, I pause, looking at the carvings on its trunk. A set of initials tries to tell me a story, a whisper of the past that lingers in the grooves of the bark. I trace these marks with my fingers, feeling the "WB + RP" underneath my fingertips and wondering what it means. I know Sarge as Sarge, simple as that. But the name he was born with—William Baker—was the name given to a baby who had no dreams of being a sergeant.

This unexpected mystery adds a layer of depth to the man I thought I knew. Sarge had always been a fixture of my childhood, a grandfather figure, sturdy and reliable like this very tree. Yet here is a hint of his past, a love perhaps, wrapped in secrecy and now exposed by the passage of time. It makes me wonder about the stories he never told, the names and faces that were significant to him yet remain unknown to those he left behind.

This discovery, this "RP," is a puzzle piece from a part of his life that has remained hidden, tucked away like the letter he said was tucked under the picnic table. As I stand there, the wind rustling through the leaves above, I feel a renewed connection to Sarge—not just as a memory, but as a person who lived and loved, with mysteries of his own.

Following Sarge's instructions, I move next to the food stand, which is shut down for the season. The shutters hide the inner workings of its magic. It stands as a silent witness to countless afternoons of shared snacks and laughter. I know it's the backdrop to my own youth, but I never considered Sarge as having a youth of his own.

Under the picnic table closest to the counter, just as he described, I find my next clue—an envelope, sealed and taped firmly underneath. Peeling it off feels like unearthing a secret, one that Sarge has left specifically for me to find.

As I peel the envelope from its hiding place, a familiar voice startles me from my reverie. "Find anything interesting, Josie?"

I spin around, my heart pounding—not from fear but from a rush of unresolved anger. There he is—Sawyer, leaning nonchalantly against the fence, his auburn hair tousled as if he has just removed a baseball cap. The low sun casts sharp shadows across his features, highlighting the lines and signs of the fifteen years that I couldn't quite catch last night on the porch of the funeral home.

"What are you doing here?" I ask, my voice tight, every word laced with years of pent-up frustration.

He pushes off the fence and walks toward me and the picnic table, his movements unhurried, like he's been here a thousand times before. He doesn't answer right away. Instead, he lets his gaze drift around the field, lingering on the empty stands, the food stand, the tree beyond left field. It's like he's soaking in the place, as if it holds some unspoken comfort for him.

"I come here sometimes," he says finally, his tone casual, but there's a weight to it, like an admission of something deeper. "It's quiet. A good place to think."

There's something about the way he says it—like this field is a part of him. It makes my chest tighten. I wonder how many times he's stood here, working through his own demons while I stayed away, avoiding mine.

But then he reaches into his back pocket and reveals his own sheet of paper that looks suspiciously like a letter.

I narrow my eyes at the paper just as he places it back in his pocket. "What the hell is that?" I demand.

"Well, I'm assuming by the look on your face you got one too?"

"A letter from Sarge?"

"It would seem so."

I puff out an angry breath. I feel a sharp twinge of betrayal—how could Sarge have involved him? The idea that Sarge has tricked me into a reunion does nothing to ease the tension simmering just beneath the surface. And I can't even say anything to him because he's dead—and then the guilt settles again, like a weighted vest over my heart.

"Well, he didn't mention you in my letter," I say pointedly.

Sawyer's eyebrows lift slightly, a challenge flickering in his eyes. "Yeah, he didn't mention you in mine either. Guess Sarge had his reasons for keeping us in the dark."

I look at the new letter in my hand and notice the writing scrawled across the front in Sarge's familiar handwriting.

Josie and Sawyer

It feels strange seeing our names written together like this.

"Before I open this, did your letter tell you to go to the tree behind left field?"

Sawyer nods. "It did, but I saw you over here going to the picnic table, so I stopped here first."

I take a moment, trying to decide what to do next. Sarge obviously had a plan or a game or something he wanted to accomplish by having us meet here, and after everything Sarge did for me, I am not going to let him down.

"You should see the tree. I'll walk with you," I say matter-of-factly, not allowing even a hint of kindness to seep into my tone. This is Sawyer, the person who pulverized my heart. I won't give him any more time than I have to.

Sawyer studies me for a moment, a mix of old pain and something else—perhaps a trace of relief—at my offer to walk together. He reaches back to his other back pocket where he has stuffed an old baseball cap. Tugging it back onto his head, he nods once, his movements sharp but effortless, carrying a confidence I remember all too well.

We walk in silence, the short distance to the tree feeling longer under the burden of our shared history. The field is quiet, the noise of distant traffic barely a murmur compared to the loud, tumultuous rush of thoughts swirling through my mind.

Reaching the tree, Sawyer stops and looks at the carvings. His eyes scan the weathered bark, finally resting on the "WB + RP" inscription I found earlier. He traces the letters lightly with his finger, a gesture so familiar it tugs at something deep within me.

"This was him, huh?" Sawyer's voice is low, almost reflective. "Sarge had his secrets too."

Secrets. I know Sawyer has his.

"I suppose so. It feels like he's airing everything now. I'm not sure why. And I really don't know why he'd put us in this awkward position together." I cross my arms and stare out toward the baseball field.

"Yeah, it doesn't seem right. Especially with your boyfriend here. What's his name? Dermott?" I catch the sneer in his tone.

I recoil. "Whoa, what?"

Sawyer's hands go up in a sarcastic gesture of apology. "Oh, so sorry. Husband? Fiancé? Whatever he is."

"Try cousin, you asshole." My glare is icy. "You're way out of line." I turn to storm off, but Sawyer, looking completely dumbfounded, quickly recovers from his shock just as I head toward the stand.

"Josie! Josie! Wait!"

"Go to hell, Sawyer!" My shout echoes off the empty stands, a harsh soundtrack to our fractured past.

"That guy's your cousin?" He is catching up with me.

"I already told you that," I say, continuing to stomp away, fury painting my features.

"No, you didn't, Josie. You didn't tell me anything about Dermott being your cousin!" Sawyer's voice is strained, tinged with desperation as he hurries to keep pace with me.

I stop abruptly, spinning around to face him, my anger boiling over. "What the hell ever made you think he wasn't my cousin? Because I show up to Sarge's funeral with a guy you think you have the right to question me? Sawyer, it has been fifteen years! Fifteen years! Who's to say I'm not married with six kids right now? It's actually none of your goddamn business." I storm off again, Sawyer following. "I mean, you're probably married at this point—"

"I'm not," he interjects quickly, seemingly only picking up on my last words.

I scoff, slicing through the air with a dismissive hand. "Well, I don't care if you are."

"Josie, can we talk?"

Laughter, sharp and bitter, bursts from me before I can temper it. "You think you're entitled to a conversation now?"

He is persistent, trailing behind me as I make my way through the empty complex, his voice laced with urgency. "Josie! Please, just wait!"

"I didn't come here to see you, Sawyer! There is nothing to say."

Sawyer stops, the lines of confusion softening into something that looks like remorse. "Josie, I didn't know. I swear, I—"

I stop and bore into his eyes with an anger I thought I had long quenched. "Save it," I cut him off, the coldness in my voice sharper because of the old warmth we once shared. "What does it matter anyway? I'm not here to soothe your conscience or clear up your mistakes. I've healed. I've moved on. I don't need your apologies, and I definitely don't owe you anything."

Feeling redeemed, I begin to walk away again, this time sure I am done with Sawyer completely.

"The letter!" he calls after me, and I stop, groaning in defeat. "Let's at least read Sarge's next letter."

The mention of Sarge, the reminder of the man who has been more of a family to me than my own, pauses my retreat. I hold the letter in my hand, my anger simmering as I meet Sawyer's gaze. "I'm only here for Sarge. This doesn't change anything between us. Understand?"

Sawyer nods. "Understood."

I tear open the envelope, my fingers trembling with a cocktail of rage and painful curiosity. Whatever Sarge's reasons, I know that walking away won't make me feel better in the long run. As I unfold the letter, my eyes flick up to Sawyer's face—one last glare to fortify my resolve.

"Let's get this over with," I mutter, stepping back to put distance between us once more, every step heavy with a reluctant commitment to uncovering whatever truths Sarge has left for us to find.

And then I read Sarge's words out loud.

***

Hiya kids,

If you're reading this together, I reckon you're probably pretty steamed at me right now. Maybe that's better than being steamed at each other. I hope you made it through the dust of the old ball field without a brawl.

You know, I've spent a lot of time thinking about that old tree at the edge of the field. Its roots dig in deep, holding steady no matter how hard the wind blows or the ground shakes. Makes me wish I'd planted my own roots that solid. Wish I'd had the guts to stand firm and live life the way I really wanted to. Instead, I made some calls that weren't so great. Umps aren't the only ones who make bad calls—you know I did too.

Regret is a stubborn thing. It settles in your bones and makes itself at home, especially when you know you've let something precious slip through your fingers. I've lived with my fair share of regrets, carrying them around like old, worn-out luggage. But you two—you're my chance to tie up some of those loose ends, to make right what once went wrong.

Now it's time to head down to Maple's Ice Cream Shoppe. That joint's seen more of my brooding hours than any barstool. I grappled with life's tough calls there—hang on or let go? Guess you know how my choices shook out.

Find yourselves the second table on the left by the window. Look under it—you'll find your next piece of this puzzle stuck there. There's an old picture nearby with some old ghosts looking into the camera.

Remember, it's the bitter that makes the sweet worth tasting, and the paths we dodge can haunt us more than the ones we take.

Catch you later,

Sarge

Chapter 10

Then

I couldn't convince my parents to let me transfer to Maplewood High, so I started my sophomore year at Holy Redeemer. But in a strange twist of fate, my mother's bad decisions worked in my favor for once. During one of her alcoholic rages, she locked my father and me out of the house, and that changed everything.

It wasn't the first time. She had done this before when I was in elementary school, and because my dad enabled her behavior, we wouldn't break in or call EMS to check on her. She'd berate us if we did. So I slept in a hotel room and missed a lot of school until my dad quietly called the church to ask for a spare uniform, since mine was locked in the house. Of course, as soon as that call was made, my mother opened the door. I remember being disappointed. I really liked the hotel.

When we returned from Ireland at the end of the summer, my mom went on another bender that continued into the school year. I refused to endure the embarrassment again. Years of pent-up anger and resentment came pouring out one afternoon on the back porch.

We tried getting in, seeing her shadow and the lit cigarette through the window as she moved around like a ghost, ignoring us. People call alcoholism a disease, but in those moments, it felt like sheer selfishness. Instead of school shopping or planning classes, my mom wallowed in her misery, missing her family in Ireland, and coming up with every excuse to drink herself into oblivion.

And I loved my dad. He put up with more than any man should have, but he made his bed, and I had to sleep in it. I was constantly worried that a misstep might trigger a bender, and that the bender would lead to death. I never worried that it would be my fault—I knew it would be my fault. That knowledge was as ingrained in me as my own DNA. I bore a responsibility to do whatever it took to keep my mother alive. But what scarred my heart the most was how my dad played the victim too. He was the poor suffering husband, and yet neither of my parents seemed to think about how horribly wrong it was that I was sick with worry and couldn't even get into my house to get my damn school uniform.

But anytime I asked to transfer to the public school, my mom met the idea with utter disgust. My mother associated a certain prestige with sending me to Catholic schools, but I began to realize it was more about paying for appearances. She liked to flaunt the fact that they could afford the tuition, lest she be considered a poor immigrant. In reality, she was trying to buy herself a pass to make poor choices without facing judgment. That was the Catholic way, after all, though we would never admit it. I had the tuition thrown in my face more times than I could count. If I grew frustrated with her drinking or cried from her cruelty, she would remind me that she was kind enough to pay for my education. I'm sure my dad would have liked to see that tuition payment go away, because the truth was we were in debt up to our eyeballs. But he would never dare argue with his wife over it.

I felt invisible, and that was sometimes better than being noticed. Sarge noticed me, though. It was impossible to hide from him. The day we got locked out, he came around, pretending not to know what was happening, offering help like he didn't understand the situation. And God love my dad, he acted the martyr immediately. I don't remember how he opened the conversation, but I remember him saying how hard he was working and how my mom was having a really hard time adjusting after coming home from being with her family for the summer. He failed to mention how drunk she'd been there too. It was getting worse—the times between the binges were getting shorter, and the binges were getting longer.

Sarge pulled my dad aside, speaking in short, clipped tones, his eyes flicking over to me every so often. My dad just kept shrugging, shaking his head in defeat. It was ironic—Sarge was trying to protect me by pulling my dad away, but I'd never been protected from anything. My whole life, I'd been placed right in the middle of the chaos—deliberately, intentionally, without a second thought. Still, I appreciated Sarge's judgment. It validated how I felt. I was just shy of sixteen, but I knew this was bullshit. Adults were supposed to make better choices, and mine had failed miserably.

I used to dream of escaping, leaving it all behind. But deep down, I knew that no matter how angry I was, I'd never truly leave. I'd keep picking her up, cleaning her face when she fell into walls. I'd make the calls to therapists and rehabs, even though she'd refuse to go. I'd take her insults, let her call me names, and degrade me when she was drunk. I'd duck as ashtrays were hurled at my head, crying to my dad, who'd just shake his head and say we had to help her. I'd even give her sips of alcohol to stop her from seizing during detox. And every time, I'd believe her when she promised it would never happen again.

My mom had a pattern: sober, drunk, guilty, and then angry at everyone but herself. And who did she take it out on? Me. The cycle never broke. I was paying for sins that weren't mine.

Eventually, my dad came over, his head down, while Sarge pretended to inspect his backyard. "We're going to have to call the cops, Josie," he said, resignation thick in his voice. I nodded, knowing it would unleash my mom's wrath but seeing no other option. Her binges were longer, the sober intervals shorter. She needed help. We needed help.

She'd been drunk for four straight weeks with no sign of stopping. I'd already torn through the house, hunting for her stashes—thinking I'd gotten them all—only to find more hidden in places I'd never think of. She pulled out boards in walls and hid bottles behind them. Liquor in the water tank of the toilet. In drawers, boxes, any space she could find. I poured out more alcohol than most people see in a lifetime. I took her car keys to stop her from driving, and when she hid them, I let the air out of her tires. But she always found a way—she'd call taxis to buy her booze, and soon enough, even the taxi drivers were dropping it off at the door. It was humiliating, but at least she wasn't wandering the streets like a drunken lunatic.

My dad would cry because he had to go to work, and sometimes I had to stay home from school to "watch" her. But it wasn't watching. It was restraining. I'd skip school just to physically restrain my mother, to stop her from hurting or killing herself. And now we were calling the cops—another layer of humiliation. She'd get an involuntary hold, which never lasted long enough, and then she'd be released, furious. She'd turn on me like a caged animal let loose.

I knew the drill. I hated it. But I always hoped that maybe this time something would change. That she'd finally see what she was doing to herself, to us. I was so naïve.

I nodded to my dad, steeling myself for what was to come. I wondered who would show up this time. Would it be the cops who were patient, or the ones who looked at me like I was part of the problem? Would they see my mom as a threat and call for restraints, or would I need to fight for signatures from indifferent social workers who didn't care if she lived or died?

Once, a social worker looked right into my tired young face and said, "It's not illegal to commit suicide," as if that justified doing nothing.

I agreed to call the cops from Sarge's house, and as I turned to leave, something unexpected happened—my dad surprised me.

"You're not going back to Holy Redeemer," he said. "I'll support your transfer to Maplewood High."

I stopped, turning back toward him, stunned. "What did you just say?"

"I'll make the arrangements tomorrow," my dad continued. "You can't keep missing school for this." Sarge grunted in approval. A glimmer of hope pierced the darkness. I was going to Maplewood High—and Sarge would be right there beside me for the fallout.

Sarge followed me as I entered his house. "Hold on, Josie," he said, just as I reached for the phone. "I'll make the call."

"What?"

He reached into his pocket, pulled out a few bills, and handed them to me.

"No, Sarge, I don't need money."

"I know you don't, honey, but you can't get into your house right now. I want you to take this and get out of here."

I frowned. "I can't leave. I have to call the cops. You heard my dad—"

"Yes, I heard your dad," Sarge interrupted, "but you need to hear me now. I'm friends with a lot of these officers. I served with some of their fathers in Nam. I'll make the calls, and I'll get them out here to take your mom to the hospital. I don't want you here when that happens."

I smiled at his kindness, mistaking it for naïveté. "Oh, Sarge, thank you, but it's okay. I'm used to this—"

"I know you are, and dammit, you shouldn't be, Josie!" he snapped, his voice rising in anger. It was rare to see Sarge like that, and I stepped back, startled, putting the phone down. Silence hung between us. I wasn't afraid—I just felt a deep sadness, guilt that my mess of a life had spilled into his. I didn't want him to be upset because of me. I opened my mouth to apologize, but Sarge cut me off.

"Don't you dare say sorry, Josie girl." He softened his tone. "I should've caught on to how bad this was sooner. This isn't something a kid should handle, and certainly not a daughter. Take the money, go find your girlfriend, and get some ice cream or something."

"Beatrice is out of town, and my dad—"

"I'll take care of your dad. Now go. Out the side door so he won't see you." His voice was gentler now, laced with regret, but firm. He knew I wouldn't leave easily, and he didn't have time to coax me.

"Josie, I said go. Now."

And I did as Sarge told me, slipping out the side door.

***

After exiting Sarge's house, I lingered close by for a few minutes, unsure of what to do. I didn't actually trust anyone to handle this job. I was the expert when it came to getting my mom a 302, the code for an involuntary psychiatric hold. But I also knew I couldn't go back now. I paced back and forth for a bit before resigning myself to the fact that I had no job in this scenario.

As I walked down the serene, peaceful, tree-lined street of my hometown, I knew it was in stark contrast to what was about to unfold at my house. Despite my frustration with my dad, I felt awful leaving him alone. I could be mad at my dad when tensions were high, but there was also a big part of me that knew we were the only two people who truly understood what our world was like, and I felt an overwhelming need to protect him. I halted for a moment, just before reaching the corner that would lead me to the main street. I couldn't shake the feeling that I was abandoning him, so I turned back.

Just then, Sawyer rounded the same corner quickly, almost slamming into me but catching me at the last minute, his hands grabbing my shoulders to steady me.

"Shit, Josie. I'm sorry." His big hazel eyes under the brim of his baseball cap scanned my face, and I saw concern form a small line between his brows. "What's wrong? Are you okay?"

I realized then that I must have been crying. I bit the inside of my lip for a second, trying to think of how I could turn this around.

"Hey, Sawyer! I'm fine. Just—uh—going for a walk. You?" Inside, I was dying at my awkwardness, but it was overshadowed by what I knew was happening at home.

He looked over my shoulder down the street toward my house, but we were far enough away that there was nothing for him to see.

"I'm going for a walk too," he said.

"You looked like you were power walking."

"I wasn't power walking," he said with a grin.

"Like those ladies in walking groups where they somehow walk faster than people who are actually running."

He shook his head, laughing quietly. "You are something else, Josie O."

The sirens pierced the air, a striking difference to the quiet street around us. My body tensed instinctively, my shoulders drawing up as though bracing for impact. The sound of sirens always did this to me—triggering a memory of every emergency, every time my mom had been carted away, drunk and angry. My breaths came faster, shorter, as the weight of the past settled in my chest.

Sawyer heard them too. His head came up, and he caught my eyes just as they started to well up with new tears. Then an uncomfortable realization dawned on me. Sawyer had seemed to be in a rush until he saw me, and the direction he was heading led only to a few houses, including Sarge's and mine. My shoulders dropped in defeat and shame.

"Sarge called you, didn't he?"

"Yes," Sawyer said quickly, like he had been found out.

Mortified, I shook my head and looked down at my feet as a few defiant tears escaped my eyes.

"He shouldn't have done that."

Sawyer reached out and grabbed my hand, and if I wasn't in such a shitty headspace, I would have been left gazing heartsick into his eyes.

"He didn't give me details. He just told me you were alone and that something was happening that you couldn't be home for."

The sound of the sirens got closer, their blaring matching the pounding in my head.

"Are those—?"

"Yep." I kicked some imaginary dirt on the ground while a cop car flew past, with an ambulance following shortly behind. I noted that sometimes the police would come with sirens blaring; other times, they would come with the sirens off. The response was as unpredictable as my mom's moods. The sirens quieted in the distance, likely arriving at my house.

"They're for my mom."

He nodded, not pushing.

"Beatrice?"

I sighed. "She's gone to New York for the weekend with her aunt. They're seeing a show."

"Want to go for a walk with me?"

"Sawyer, I'm so sorry. You don't have to waste your day on me."

At that, he scoffed. "There's nothing I'd rather do than spend the day with the coolest girl I know."

I tilted my head, ready to fire back with a playful retort, but something stopped me. When I really looked at him, I caught the subtle shift—a flicker in his gaze as his eyes dropped for just a second before meeting mine again, a faint blush creeping up his cheeks. He looked almost nervous, like he'd let something slip. The vulnerability in that moment caught me off guard, making my heart tighten just a little.

"What do you say? Come for a walk with me?" He asked.

"Actually," I started, noticing how Sawyer's face fell a little at the thought I might turn him down, "Sarge directed me to go eat ice cream with a girlfriend, and since Beatrice is away and I don't want to disobey Sarge, I was wondering if you'd have ice cream with me?"

A smile broke across his face. "But I'm not a girl, Josie O."

I felt brave in the moment. "I've noticed." A blush crept up my face.

He grinned. "Well, if we can bend the rules, it would make my day to have ice cream with you."

***

While the police and EMTs were at my house dealing with my mother—who turned into the bionic woman when she drank—I sat in an ice cream shop with Sawyer. The juxtaposition was jarring: chaos at home, while here I was, sharing a moment of normalcy I didn't feel entitled to. Staring down at my cookies and cream, I felt a deep sense of guilt, like I was betraying my dad by allowing myself this small break. I wasn't hiding my worry as well as I thought.

"Are you okay?" Sawyer's voice was gentle, his eyes searching mine for signs of the pain I was working so hard to mask.

I managed a nod, scooping up another mouthful of ice cream. How could I explain that I wasn't really okay, that I hadn't been okay for a long time? Maybe ever?

"Is your mom sick?" he asked tentatively, his voice soft.

I sighed, the weight of years of secrecy pressing down on me. This was the part I dreaded—the inquiries, the pity, the awkwardness. I wasn't ready to mix the little joy I could find with the bitter reality that awaited me at home.

"I don't know how to answer that," I admitted. "You could say she's sick, yeah."

"You don't have to tell me anything, Josie," Sawyer said quickly, his tone earnest. "But just know, you're my friend. You can talk to me about anything, whenever you're ready."

I tried to smile through the anxiety churning in my stomach. Sharing this part of my life with anyone was always difficult, but doing so with the guy I had the biggest crush on felt unbearable. I felt exposed and embarrassed, struggling to process the moment. It was yet another thing my mother had robbed me of—the dignity of a first date, even though I knew this wasn't one. And then, as if on cue, the dam broke. Tears streamed down my cheeks, no longer held back by the feeble gates of my composure.

"I'm sorry," I stammered, grabbing a handful of napkins from the dispenser, desperately trying to stem the flow.

Before I could retreat further into myself, Sawyer moved to sit beside me, his arm wrapping around my shoulders in a gesture so natural and comforting that it only made me cry harder. Here, in this little ice cream shop, under the fluorescent lights and the gazes of a few curious onlookers, I felt a glimmer of safety, wrapped in the simple kindness of a boy who might just accept the chaos of my world.

"Don't be sorry," he whispered. "Does Beatrice know?"

"She knows about my mom, but not about this incident happening now. She's in—"

"New York," he finished my sentence, proving he had been listening. He paused, and I could tell he was measuring his words.

"I heard the yelling and stuff after Sarge brought you to the hospital when you broke your wrist."

I winced at the memory, feeling a flush of embarrassment.

"It's so humiliating."

"No, Josie. It's really not a big deal. Everyone's got their own stuff, you know? But I figured if you knew I get it—and like, I've got my own stuff too—maybe it wouldn't feel so heavy." His eyes met mine as he tenderly tucked a loose strand of hair behind my ear. "It doesn't change how awesome you are. It doesn't change the way I see you."

The way he saw me? My heart fluttered with a cocktail of emotions, tinged with confusion.

He shook himself out of a trance, looking at me. "But right now, you need a friend. Please, let me be your friend."

I nodded, smiling through my tears.

Sawyer echoed my nod. "Let's finish our ice cream, and then you're coming with me."

We tossed our empty ice cream bowls and stepped out into the cool evening air, which carried the distant sounds of cheering and the high school band playing. As we walked toward the school, the familiar hum of the game and the crowd wrapped around us, feeling oddly comforting.

"The football game?" I asked. The bright lights of the stadium shone like a beacon in the dark evening, guiding us to a place that promised the oblivion of normalcy, if only for a few hours.

"Yeah, the football game," Sawyer replied, a warm smile spreading across his face. "It's a chance for me to show off that the coolest girl in Maplewood doesn't mind hanging around with me."

I felt a blush creeping up my cheeks, and I giggled but quickly recovered to tease him a little. "Oof. I don't know if my reputation could take the hit."

Sawyer laughed, the sound easy and genuine. "Yes, but my reputation will only soar."

"All right," I agreed with a grin. "But if I get there and somehow end up behind a snack stand slinging slushies, I am out of here!"

He roared with laughter, making me beam with pride. "I promise." He lifted one hand in oath.

"Scout's honor?" I could barely contain my laughter.

He grabbed me and pulled me close, pretending to mess up my hair and sending my heart into overdrive. "I am not a Boy Scout. You are a menace." We both laughed as we entered the stadium.

The bleachers were packed with people, their faces alight with excitement and team spirit. We found a spot high up where the noise was a little less overwhelming. Sitting there, surrounded by people yet isolated in our bubble, I felt a weird mix of being part of something yet distinctly apart.

"Thanks for bringing me here," I said, turning to Sawyer, who was watching the game with the kind of focus that came naturally, like he was completely at ease in his element.

He glanced at me, a soft smile spreading across his face. "Nowhere else I'd rather be."

As the night went on and the evening air grew chillier, I couldn't help but shiver. I had left my house so quickly, and I hadn't planned to be gone this long. I hadn't planned for anything at all. Especially not this. Noticing my discomfort, Sawyer slipped off his hoodie and draped it over my shoulders. Its warmth was immediate, and the faint scent of his cologne was strangely comforting.

"Thanks," I murmured, pulling the hoodie over my head.

"No problem," he replied, flashing a quick smile before turning his attention back to the game.

As halftime rolled around, Sawyer nudged me gently. "Come on."

With the sound of the school band filling the evening air, we approached the snack stand. "Ohhh no, buddy," I joked.

He took my hand. "I promise I won't put you to work, Josie O."

At the stand, Sawyer ordered a hot chocolate, and as we waited, I nodded toward the approaching crowd of his friends, letting him know they were headed our way. Jason was among them.

"Hold up! Is that Josie O'Driscoll in a social setting without my sister? I never thought I'd see the day," he teased.

I laughed, acknowledging the truth. It was a little strange being out in the wild without Beatrice.

"Hey, Sawyer! Didn't expect to see you here—whoa, is that hot chocolate?" One of his friends laughed as they reached for the cup, but Sawyer swatted his hand away.

Then Val stepped forward, and a cold sweat crept up my neck. Her gaze crawled over me, lingering on the hoodie I was still wearing—Sawyer's hoodie. I squirmed under her scrutiny, hating how exposed I felt. She glanced between Sawyer and me.

"Wow, Josie, I didn't take you for the football type."

Before I could respond, Jason jumped in to defend me. "Oh, come on, Val. Like you know the first thing about football."

Rolling her eyes, Val moved closer to Sawyer as if to stake her claim, but he subtly shifted away, handing me the steaming cup. "Do you want anything else?" he asked.

"No, thank you for this," I said, offering a grateful smile. He nodded in return, and though I hadn't asked for the hot chocolate, somehow he knew it was exactly what I needed.

Val's eyes narrowed as she noticed the shift between us. Sensing the tension, Sawyer subtly positioned himself in front of me, shielding me. His friends, some pretending not to notice the awkwardness, quickly redirected the conversation to the ongoing game. Jason asked if we wanted to join them in the student section, but Sawyer declined with a grin, saying he wouldn't be able to hear my "expert commentary" over their noise.

I snickered, appreciating the humor he was weaving into the evening to keep things light. I could feel Val's eyes still on me, but I refused to meet her gaze. I sipped my hot chocolate—it wasn't the best I'd ever had, but in that moment, standing under the stadium lights with Sawyer by my side, it felt perfect.

With the brief encounter with Val behind us, we settled back into our quiet corner of the stands to watch the game. The players were back on the field, and the crowd's energy surged as the second half kicked off. Sawyer's commentary—filled with exaggerated gestures and mock seriousness—drew laughter from me, lightening my spirits with each playful quip.

As the game unfolded, I found myself getting more involved, cheering and groaning along with the rest of the crowd. The initial discomfort began to fade, replaced by a surprising sense of ease. For the first time in a long while, I felt genuinely present, enjoying the moment. Sawyer's presence—steady, supportive—made the evening feel almost perfect, despite its rocky start.

"See? Who needs the student section when we have VIP seats right here?" Sawyer joked during a particularly exciting play, gesturing grandly to our humble spot on the bleachers.

"You're right," I said, laughing. "This is much better."

The game ended with a narrow victory for our team, and the stands erupted into cheers. As people began to file out, Sawyer glanced over at me with a smile.

"So, game's over. What now?"

I hesitated, wanting nothing more than for the night to stretch on a little longer. But that gnawing feeling hadn't left me, despite the fun I'd had. I needed to check in—either with my dad or Sarge. My cell was locked in my house with my mom, and my dad was probably ready to murder me for leaving him to pick up the pieces of my mother's alcoholic binge alone.

I didn't think I'd ever felt so disappointed as I did when I told him I probably should go home.

"Are you sure? Is anyone there?"

I shrugged. "I don't know. I don't have my phone with me."

As we made our way out of the stadium, he handed me his phone. "You can use mine."

"It's okay. I'll just walk home and see what's happening." My eyes caught his group of friends beckoning us over. Val was lingering near them, watching our every move.

One of the guys called out, "C'mon, let's go to the diner."

"Go with your friends. I promise I'm fine."

Sawyer let out a disbelieving laugh. "You are out of your mind if you think I'm going to just let you walk home alone."

"It's fine." I waved him off.

He turned, his eyes locking onto mine with an intensity that made my heart skip. "No, it's not. And I don't want to go to the diner. I want to walk with you." Then, without another word, he took my hand in his, the gesture natural, like we'd done it a hundred times before. Together, we walked away from the bright lights of the stadium and into the quieter streets of Maplewood, heading toward my home. But even as we left, I couldn't shake the feeling of Val's gaze, watching me the entire time.

***

When we reached my house, Sarge was sitting on his front porch, a Lucky Strike in hand and Johnny Cash playing softly from his old cassette player. The sight of him caused a wave of guilt to wash over me, and I started to stammer an apology, trying to explain that I should've called. But Sarge just chuckled, his eyes crinkling in that familiar way.

"You think I was worried about you with that young fella there? Best there is. You wouldn't be safer with anyone else." He looked to Sawyer and nodded, who was standing with his hands in his pockets.

I looked to my house and saw that the lights were on. Sarge tracked my movements.

"Door's open, but nobody's home. You can come on in and stay here with me until your dad gets home."

I nodded, knowing that my dad would be at the ER until all hours. They'd keep her there until her blood alcohol level came down, and then she'd sign herself out and probably go on a bigger binge just to spite us.

I smiled. "I'm okay. Thank you." I spun to look at Sawyer. "Thank you both. And, Sarge, I know you're right here if I need you."

Sawyer smoothly pulled his phone from his pocket and handed it to me. "Mind putting your number in?" His tone was casual, but the slight anticipation in his eyes betrayed him.

Trying to match his nonchalance, I took the phone, my fingers lightly tapping as I entered my number. *This is normal. Totally normal,* I reassured myself. Handing it back, I tried to keep my composure.

"I'll text you so you have mine too," he said, locking the contact. He glanced over at Sarge and gave a quick wave. "Sarge, catch you later!" Then, as he started to walk away, he paused and turned back to me with a grin that could have lit up the darkening evening.

"Oh, and Josie," he said, his voice dropping a little, "today was—I mean, I know it wasn't easy for you, but honestly . . . I'd take any excuse to hang out with you. Doesn't matter what's going on." His smile was easy, but there was something behind it that made my heart skip a beat.

With that, he turned and walked away, leaving me frozen in place.

I was pulled from my trance by Sarge's chuckling voice as he rose from his porch chair, saying, "Keep an eye on that one, Josie—he's going places, but I reckon he'd like to take you along for the ride."

And then, Sarge was gone too.

Chapter 11

Now

After the baseball field conundrum, I need to get back to Dermott, and I still want to pop into Beatrice's shop. Sawyer and I parted ways at the baseball field after making plans to meet at Maple's Ice Cream Shoppe tomorrow. I had planned on lingering at the field for a bit, but Sawyer mumbled goodbye, and I watched as he walked over to the empty dugout and sat down. So I left.

As I stroll toward Miner's Inn, my mind keeps returning to the moments before Sawyer and I parted ways, pondering Sarge's cryptic letter and its implications. After I finished reading it, we stood there quietly for a moment. I wanted so badly to start unpacking everything right then and there. I longed for Sawyer and me to pull every word apart, trying to piece together Sarge's scattered puzzle. But I can't bring myself to trust him like that—not after everything. I can't let him into my thoughts, my heart, or any corner of my soul that holds even the slightest vulnerability.

Sarge mentioned wishing he'd had more courage. To me, there was no braver man than Sarge. He didn't talk much about his past, but I know he fought in Vietnam, and I suspect he didn't come back unscathed. His letters are beginning to hint at truths I might not be ready to face. I naïvely thought being a medic meant staying behind in hospital tents, tending to wounded soldiers. It wasn't until high school that I began to understand the true gravity of his experience.

One afternoon during lunch, my friend Ellen, whose grandfather was a regular at the VFW, told me stories about Sarge. Ellen's voice dropped to a conspiratorial whisper as she relayed what her grandfather had shared.

"Did you know Sarge was a badass? He was in the thick of it in Vietnam—not just a medic, but the kind who went into firefights to drag soldiers back. He saved a lot of lives."

I remember feeling a mix of awe and disbelief. The man who helped me fix my bike and spent afternoons teaching me how to plant tomatoes had been through hell and back. It was hard to reconcile the gentle, patient Sarge with the image of a battlefield hero, braving bullets and explosions to pull the wounded to safety.

In my mind, I tried to picture it. The Sarge I knew, kneeling in a muddy, smoke-filled jungle, bullets whizzing past his head, explosions shaking the earth. I imagined him, his face streaked with dirt and sweat, running through gunfire to reach soldiers who were screaming for help. Blood staining his hands as he worked to patch wounds, his heart pounding but his hands steady. The heat, the chaos, the smell of burning flesh and fear hanging thick in the air—all the things that marked the battlefield in ways I could never fully comprehend. The noise of helicopters overhead, the relentless rat-a-tat of machine guns, the cries of the wounded—it must have been unbearable. And yet, he did it. Over and over again. A quiet man, facing hell on earth, dragging his comrades back to safety, only to come home and never speak of it.

Later, I asked Sawyer if he knew this about our old friend. He did. Mr. Johnson, another veteran from our town who had his grass cut by Sawyer, had mentioned that Sarge had received several commendations for his service. I learned that Sarge had been more than just a medic; he was a sergeant, leading other medics and sometimes even taking command when things got rough. Mr. Johnson said Sarge never liked to talk about it, that the war left scars deeper than the eye could see, but that he was the kind of person everyone trusted with their lives. That made sense to me. I trusted Sarge with mine.

It made sense why Sarge rarely spoke of his past. The few times he did, his eyes glazed over, staring into a distant memory. He'd say things like, "War changes a man, Josie. It takes something you never get back." And then he'd always steer the conversation to lighter topics, like sharing a tale about his tomatoes or asking about my school projects.

I wonder now, what did it take from him? How many ghosts did he carry silently while tending to his garden or laughing with me over something trivial? The image of him, standing tall, unshaken by the small bumps in life, belied the truth of what lay beneath—the years of pain he tucked away, too deep for anyone to reach. It breaks my heart to think of what he might have gone through, the courage he had to muster each time he put his life on the line for someone else, only to come home to a world that couldn't begin to understand what he'd seen.

It strikes me now that Sarge never married. I used to wonder about that when I was younger, imagining that someone so kind and strong would have found someone to share his life with. But now, I wonder if maybe he chose to be alone. Maybe he went through so much that letting someone in—truly letting them see the scars that war had left on him—was too painful. How could you ever share that kind of burden? How could you ask someone to understand the things you couldn't even put into words? Maybe it was easier for him to be alone, to keep those memories locked away, only letting them out in pieces.

I can't help but feel a pang of regret. Maybe if I had been more curious, more insistent, he might have shared more of his story with me. But Sarge was always about the here and now, about making the best of what we had. He spent his life quietly helping others, using his skills and wisdom to heal—not just physical wounds, but the invisible ones as well. He certainly took care of me. I thought I knew him, but it turns out he was a mystery all along.

More than just questions about Sarge are swirling around in my head. There is the matter of Sawyer. Why, after fifteen years, did he look so absolutely bitter at the thought that I might possibly have a partner? He ensured our relationship was destroyed beyond repair. What makes him think he has any right to question my life now? The more I think about it, the angrier I get. I want to go back to the baseball field and lay into him all over again, this time prepared with more clever insults and jabs.

My anger doesn't stop my thoughts from hopping on a runaway train, though. I can't help but wonder about his life. What job does he have? What are his days like? Has he stayed in Maplewood all this time, or has he moved away? How is his mom? I could have checked social media over the years, followed digital breadcrumbs, and found my answers, but the truth is I've been hiding myself, not wanting to be found. In some ways, I was afraid to find out a truth online that would hurt me, so I shut myself away.

Yet one question lingers relentlessly, haunting the corners of my mind. He mentioned he isn't married. *But how long did he stay with her?*

The pain I have tried so hard to bury is threatening to resurface. I feel frustrated and anxious. I am trying to employ my standby mindfulness tricks as I walk into the lobby of Miner's, where I find Dermott sitting with a big smile.

"Well, hello there, Josephine! I have some delightful news." He looks like the cat who swallowed the canary. I watch my cousin in amusement as he effortlessly charms the old innkeeper, Mrs. Miner, who sits primly beside him, clearly captivated by his friendly demeanor.

Dermott continues, "My room has opened up, and I can move my cot out of yours!"

"Wow! I didn't think there was another room available until tomorrow."

"Well, it turns out Mrs. Miner and I started chatting, and she has family near where my father's brother-in-law's niece's neighbor has family."

I nod slowly, figuring out Dermott's angle.

Mrs. Miner claps her hands together. "We're practically related!"

My smile is tight, feeling a twinge of defensiveness for Mrs. Miner. "Is that right?"

Dermott must see my annoyance because he pops up from his chair. "Well, thank you again, Mrs. Miner. I'm just going to move my things from my dear cousin's room. Lovely chatting with you!"

"I'll help you!" I call, a little louder than necessary, and then we both head in the direction of the hall toward the rooms.

"Dermott!" I whisper-yell through gritted teeth.

"What?" he whisper-yells back.

"Don't lead poor Mrs. Miner on! You are not related to any of her people. You just wheedled your way into someone else's reservation. She probably kicked someone out for you!"

He looks at me in mock offense. "You feel bad for her? I'm the one who had to sit there for over a feckin' hour and listen to her go on about her family tree! I deserve a suite after that! She wrecked my head," he says, rubbing at his temples. "She asked me if I knew the Kellys in Dublin, Josie. For fuck's sake."

I take him by the elbow and pull him down the hall. "Shh."

"The poor old man in the library looked like he was going to keel over listening to her go on and on and feckin' on."

I snicker. "Oh my God, that's Mrs. Miner's brother." My mind wanders momentarily, snagging on the odd conversation we had the night before.

"Well, if he were her husband, she'd have him driven demented."

"Oh, come on, Dermott, she's not that bad."

"Says you! I'm afraid to leave my room again. I took a nap and came out to find a cup of tea or something, and she got me. All kinds of questions about you too. You should be thanking me! I let her go on about her family tree to keep her off of you!"

Dermott's antics, however misguided, do lighten the mood a bit. "Let's get your stuff out of my room and go out for a while."

"Suits me fine!"

After we hastily move his belongings from my room and into his well-earned one, we decide to head out. The encounter with Dermott in the lobby, while amusing, only added to my stress. I glance at my watch, realizing time is slipping by.

"I need to stop by Beatrice's floral shop before it closes," I murmur, more to myself than to Dermott.

"Lead the way!"

And away we go, into the little town that could very well swallow me whole, its memories waiting like shadows to pull me under.

***

Dermott and I stroll through the quaint, familiar streets of Maplewood, the crisp autumn air nipping at our cheeks as we make our way to Beatrice's flower shop. The town is adorned in its fall best, with golden leaves fluttering gently to the cobblestone pathways and festive decorations beginning to sprout in anticipation of the season's events. When I lived here, I didn't appreciate how stunning this little borough was. It takes leaving and coming back to appreciate the simpler things.

As we turn the corner, my heart swells with pride at the sight of Beatrice's shop, aptly named Blossom & Briar. I remember it as an abandoned storefront with broken windows and the skeleton of an awning when we were kids. Now, the charming storefront is a picturesque vision of rustic elegance, nestled perfectly among the other small businesses that line the street. The exterior is painted a warm, inviting sage green, with large clear windows displaying an array of vibrant floral arrangements. A vintage wooden sign hangs above the door, its elegant script a testament to Beatrice's attention to detail.

The window displays are a riot of color, with pumpkins and gourds interspersed among arrangements of chrysanthemums, dahlias, and marigolds, all echoing the rich palette of fall. Twinkling fairy lights frame the windows, casting a magical glow that beckons the passersby to stop and admire.

Stepping inside Blossom & Briar, we are enveloped by the soothing scent of fresh earth and blossoms. The interior is a cozy, welcoming space, with wooden floors that creak softly underfoot and shelves lined with artisanal vases and gardening books. The center of the shop features a large rustic worktable where Beatrice crafts her masterpieces, surrounded by buckets brimming with fresh-cut flowers in every hue.

Delicate garlands of dried flowers hang from the ceiling, and small potted plants add a touch of green to every corner, making the entire shop feel like a secret garden tucked away in the heart of Maplewood. It's clear that Beatrice has poured her heart and soul into every detail, creating not just a store but a sanctuary for all who enter. As I take it all in, my admiration for her dedication and creativity only deepens, reaffirming the sense of pride I feel for her achievements.

I don't realize my mouth is hanging open in awe until Beatrice steps out from a back room and starts laughing.

"Beatrice, I have no words."

Dermott is taking it all in beside me. "Holy Jesus. This is extraordinary."

"Thank you," she says, curtsying with dramatic flair. She looks around. "It is pretty nice, isn't it?"

"Nice? Beatrice, this is heaven!"

"Well, I went through hell to get it looking like this, but I'm really happy with it, so it was worth it." She wipes her hands on her apron. "And then I'll tear it all down and start on the next season. But enough about me. I'm hungry, and I want to know what happened with the letter, but I have to finish this last thing first."

I begin to recount the day's events but pause as I watch Beatrice in fascination. She makes her way to the center table, pulling a small flowerpot toward her. A delicate chrysanthemum with bright-yellow petals, not unlike the ones in the window display, is waiting to be transplanted. She moves with the same care she always has, gently loosening the soil and pressing the flower into a larger pot. It's such a simple, soothing action, and I find myself getting lost in the rhythm of her hands as they work the earth.

I watch her in quiet contemplation, my thoughts wandering before I realize I've spoken aloud. "Do you think it hurts the flower to be moved like that?" My voice is soft, almost an absent-minded question. "I mean . . . does it remember where it came from?"

Beatrice pauses mid-movement, her hands stilling over the soil as she looks up at me. There's a moment of silence between us, heavy with something unspoken.

"I don't know," she says quietly, her voice carrying a weight that surprises me. "Does it?"

I don't say anything out loud this time, but the chatter picks up in my brain. It does hurt—not like a sharp, sudden pain, but a dull ache, a longing. It's the agony of losing something you never really had and don't know how to find. And in the midst of all that aching, you try to protect yourself, covering up old roots with fresh soil, hoping no one notices the scars beneath. I shake off the thought and, in a pure show of avoidance, drop the biggest bomb from my earlier conversation with Sawyer—anything to quiet the noise in my mind.

"So, Sawyer thought Dermott was my boyfriend."

Dermott, oblivious to the moment, gasps in surprise.

"Oh wait! It gets worse. He actually had the nerve to be angry about it."

"Well, I don't know if anger is justified, but I'd understand a certain element of disgust since we are related, Josephine."

I roll my eyes. "Dermott, no! He didn't know you're my cousin."

Beatrice makes a little "humph" sound and seems oddly unsurprised by this revelation as she continues working with her chrysanthemum. It's almost as if she expected this reaction from Sawyer. I file her expression away for later and continue diving into the story of how Sawyer and I are now entangled in following Sarge's meticulously planned clues.

"It turns out Sarge suffered some heartbreak. The letter led us to the tree out by left field. He had his initials carved alongside a certain mysterious RP."

This detail seems to particularly catch Beatrice's attention.

"Sarge had a lady?" she exclaims, her eyes widening in surprise.

"It would seem so," I reply, the mystery deepening.

Beatrice finishes her work and cleans up, ready to call it a night. As we prepare to leave, Beatrice suggests, "Let's grab some dinner," offering a temporary escape from the day's revelations. Yet as we head toward the door, she adds, "And I might have some insight into why Sawyer mistook Dermott for your boyfriend."

Dermott groans audibly. "Christ, I need a drink for this."

Chapter 12

Then

Maplewood High School's annual career fair was a bustling hub of students from all grades, each buzzing with dreams and plans for their futures. In the whirlwind of college brochures and recruitment posters, the most venomous snake saw her opportunity to strike.

I had settled into Maplewood High School relatively easily, thanks to Beatrice and Jason, who had become my steadfast allies. The real challenge was getting used to seeing Sawyer every day. The football game had felt like a date, though I never let myself believe it. But it didn't matter now—six months had passed. When I recounted every detail to Beatrice, she squealed with delight, insisting I was crazy not to see that Sawyer liked me as more than a friend. I had spent so much of my life being disappointed that I refused to acknowledge Sawyer's interest, terrified I'd gotten it all wrong. I couldn't bear to be crushed again.

Now, attending Maplewood High, I was sure that if he'd had any interest in me, it had faded. I was no longer the intriguing girl from another school. Instead, I was just another student, with all my dysfunction laid bare for everyone to see. I had a serious case of imposter syndrome to go with my low self-esteem, but I worked hard to hide it.

Sawyer, with his steady charm and easygoing nature, remained the kind and decent person I'd always known him to be—even if I was firmly in the "friend zone." His boyish grin would light up his face whenever he spotted me, and his warmth was unmistakable in the hallways, where he'd call out a cheerful "Josie O!" across the crowd. My heart always fluttered when I heard it. Despite being a year ahead of me, he made an effort to walk me to class whenever he could, making me feel like I truly belonged. He was a good friend.

Val, on the other hand, was far from thrilled about my presence. Her glares and thinly veiled jabs grew sharper as the year went on. Even with Beatrice by my side and the added protection of Jason, my insecurities grew. I could feel Val's eyes on me, her icy stare cutting through me every time we passed in the halls. She seemed to take pleasure in making me feel small, whispering and giggling with her friends whenever I was nearby. Any sense of security or inclusion I gained from others was quickly undercut by Val's venomous looks and snide comments. The only saving grace was that she was a year older, which lessened the chances of crossing paths too often.

The auditorium buzzed with energy during the career fair, packed with students set loose for a class period. Amid the chaos, I quickly lost track of Beatrice and the friends I'd come with. But I didn't mind. It wasn't long before I found myself absorbed in the various tables and programs, content to wander and consider the possibilities. I dreamed of running away, though I knew that wasn't a real plan. Most days, I couldn't see beyond tomorrow or my mother's next binge. But as I approached the Penn State table, I let myself imagine, just for a moment, a future filled with success and independence—bright, and mine for the taking.

As I stood examining a pamphlet, Val sauntered over, her sinister smile curling like smoke. My stomach dropped. The table was crowded, buzzing with students laughing and chatting, making her approach all the more unsettling. She was never alone—her clique followed, flanking her like a pack of wolves.

"Thinking about your future, Josie?" Val's voice rang out, cutting through the noise and drawing attention. She leaned casually against the table, her body language relaxed but her tone razor-sharp.

I forced myself to look at her. "Yeah, just looking," I managed, though my voice sounded thin and weak to my own ears.

Val smirked, tilting her head as if she were genuinely interested. "That's so brave of you, considering . . ." Her eyes sparkled with cruel delight as she trailed off.

Her clique snickered, their gazes darting between Val and me like they were waiting for the punchline. My palms grew damp as I clutched the pamphlet tighter.

"Oh, speaking of futures," Val said, her voice taking on that sickly-sweet tone I knew all too well, "I've been thinking about nursing school. You know, my mom's a nurse. Actually," she paused dramatically, her gaze locking onto mine, "my mom mentioned your mom. She had her as a patient."

My stomach clenched so tightly I thought I might be sick. I felt every pair of eyes around us shift toward me, the curious buzz of conversation dimming as the crowd tuned in.

Val's smirk widened as she leaned in slightly, her voice dripping with mock concern. "She said your mom was . . . unforgettable. Said her reputation really precedes her. Apparently, she was a nightmare patient when she was detoxing. Something about throwing up all over the nurses? Charming."

Laughter rippled through her group, and my vision blurred as I tried to keep my expression neutral.

"She also said," Val continued, her voice rising slightly, "that it's a real Irish thing, isn't it? All that drinking. Must run in the family, huh, Josie? Gotta be careful with that."

The blood roared in my ears, drowning out the low murmur of the crowd. Students nearby had gone quiet, their attention now fully on the spectacle.

Val's smile widened as she delivered the final blow. "You know what they say: the apple doesn't fall far from the tree."

Her clique erupted into laughter. I glanced around, desperate for an escape, but all I saw were faces—some amused, some pitying, some frozen in awkward discomfort. And then my eyes landed on Sawyer. He stood just a few feet away, his expression shifting from surprise to something harder, angrier.

Val's gaze followed mine, and her smirk deepened. "It's just . . . so sad, Josie. But hey, maybe you can write about it in your college essay? 'Overcoming adversity' is super inspiring, you know."

The murmurs around us grew louder, a mix of uncomfortable whispers and muffled laughter. Val stood there, basking in the attention, her victory sealed by my silence. Before I could fully process the humiliation washing over me, Jason stepped forward, planting himself firmly between Val and me.

"Val, tell me," he said, his tone dripping with feigned compassion, "is it hard not having your mom around because she's banging a different guy every night?" His words were loud enough for everyone to hear. "Or is it not a big deal because you're doing the same thing? Apples not falling too far from trees and all."

Jason's words echoed through the auditorium, enveloping the crowd in a momentary stunned silence. It was as if everyone collectively held their breath, waiting to see what would happen next. From the back of the room, a slow clap started. But Jason wasn't done.

Val's face turned a furious shade of red that clashed with her heavy lipstick, her usual air of superiority crumbling under the weight of public humiliation. Jason leaned closer, his gaze unwavering, his voice now a sharp edge, but low enough for only the nearest people to hear.

"And another thing, Val. If you ever try to throw something in Josie's face again, remember this. We all have skeletons, and I'm pretty good at digging. So back off, or next time I won't be this polite."

"Fuck you, Jason!" Val spat, her voice cracking.

"In your dreams, Val!" he retorted, following it with an exaggerated gag, causing laughter to erupt around him.

Val, defeated and humiliated, retreated with her friends trailing behind like a shadow of shame.

Beatrice pushed through the crowd to my side as the tension broke, her face alight with a mix of relief and amusement. "Damn, Jason!"

"Don't get used to this knight-in-shining-armor thing. I hate Val more than I love you, Josie!" Jason gave me a quick, mischievous wink before he turned to leave. But his humor didn't bring me comfort. The tears I'd been fighting back threatened to spill, and I bolted, weaving through the crowd, losing Beatrice, as the walls of the room closed in around me.

***

My legs moved mechanically, carrying me through the halls, past the bright, bustling common areas, and into one of the quieter corridors. My heart was racing as I found the nearest bathroom, tucked away in a far corner of the school—one that few students used, especially at the end of the day.

I pushed open the door, the metallic echo ringing in the empty space. The fluorescent lights buzzed faintly above, casting their harsh glow on the pale tile walls. I barely reached the sink before the nausea hit, doubling me over as my stomach twisted painfully.

I gripped the edge of the sink, my knuckles white, fighting to steady myself as tears blurred my vision. My breath came in short, ragged gasps, the weight of everything—Val's insults, the whispers, the cruel glances—crashing over me. The humiliation from her words clung to me, heavy and suffocating.

The knots in my stomach tightened as my thoughts spiraled, each one sharper than the last. My chest ached, my throat tight. I squeezed my eyes shut, desperate to escape—to disappear into nothingness, to be anywhere but here.

I let out a shaky breath, wiping my mouth with the back of my hand as I straightened up. My reflection in the mirror stared back at me—pale, shaken, and teetering on the edge of falling apart. I splashed some cold water on my face, the shock of it momentarily breaking through the haze of nausea and panic.

How long would I be Val's target? The thought looped endlessly as I tried to steady my breathing. My mom wasn't perfect, but she didn't deserve this—neither did I. Still, Val's words clung to me, sharp and unrelenting, making it impossible to forget how much I didn't belong.

I leaned against the cool tile wall, forcing deep breaths as the emotions churned inside me. A part of me wanted to scream, to fight back, but instead, I felt hollow, defeated. Shame, anger, and sadness twisted together, tightening like a spring ready to snap.

Eventually, I sank to the floor, hugging my knees as the tears came. In the silence of the empty bathroom, I let myself feel it all—the sting, the weight, the exhaustion. With each sob, the tension eased slightly, but the hurt remained, raw and unyielding.

I wiped my face with a tissue and stood, shaky but determined to keep going. Then I heard footsteps echo faintly in the hallway, and my momentary calm dissolved. My heart raced as I quickly left the bathroom, slipping into the main hall unnoticed.

All I wanted was to go home, to bury myself under my covers and disappear. Jason's rescue had been kind, but it couldn't erase the damage. Val's words about my mother were etched into the consciousness of my peers, and the humiliation was suffocating.

As I neared my locker, my legs felt heavy with exhaustion, but I forced myself to keep moving. Without warning, I felt a harsh shove from behind. My body slammed against the cold metal with a resounding clang. Whirling around, I came face-to-face with Val, her eyes burning with malice.

"You think you can just waltz into our school and ruin everything?" Val's voice was low and menacing. "Go back to where you came from, stupid bitch!" She shoved me again, harder this time. "Sawyer is mine!"

I had no idea what was happening. My heart hammered against my ribs, fear mingling with confusion.

"Look at me, you deranged little leprechaun," Val hissed, her face inches from mine. "I will ruin your life. I will *ruin* it. No matter what it takes. Remember that." And then she was gone, leaving me leaning against my locker, breathing heavily, panicking.

I could still feel the lingering sting of Val's words as I made my way to the school exit. The halls seemed emptier now, as if everyone had already disappeared, leaving just me and my thudding heart behind. My body was still trembling, the adrenaline from the locker shove making my hands shake. Val's threats, her venomous words—it was all too much.

But when I saw Sawyer heading toward me, his casual stride and familiar reassuring presence cutting through the tension, my instinct was to bury it. *Hide the hurt. Pretend like nothing had happened. He doesn't need to know. No one needs to know.*

"Hey," he said, his voice laced with concern as he came up beside me, his eyes scanning my face. I could tell immediately that he knew something was wrong. His gaze was too sharp, too focused. "You okay?"

I plastered on a smile, one that felt too tight on my face. "I'm fine! Good. Everything's good."

The lie was shaky at best, but I was banking on Sawyer not pushing too hard. I didn't want him to see how close I was to unraveling. I didn't want him to know that Val's words had cut deep or that her shove had left me feeling more fragile than ever. The last thing I wanted was to appear weak in front of him.

But as soon as the words left my mouth, I saw the way his eyes narrowed, not buying it for a second. He stepped closer, his arm brushing mine, his touch gentle but grounding.

"Josie, you don't have to pretend with me. We're friends, right?" His voice was low, steady—like he was trying to coax the truth out of me without pushing too hard.

I swallowed, the lump in my throat growing tighter. *Friends.* The word clattered around in my mind. It didn't feel like enough. Not with Sawyer. My heart ached with the weight of it, but my instinct to protect myself was stronger than the urge to open up. I couldn't let him in. I couldn't let him see all the ugly pieces of me.

"Yeah, we're friends," I said, my voice quieter now, more fragile than I intended. I wanted to believe it, wanted to feel like I could just lean on him for a second, let him be the person who saw the real me. But I couldn't shake the fear—the gnawing worry that if I let him see too much, he'd pull away. Or worse, he'd pity me.

I saw his gaze flicker, searching my face like he could sense the tug-of-war going on inside me. For a second, I thought about telling him everything—the confrontation with Val, how she'd shoved me into the locker, how her threats lingered in my mind like a dark cloud, ready to pour. I wanted to tell him about the fear tormenting me, the doubt that clung to every thought.

But then, the voice in my head—the one that had always told me to stay quiet, to not show weakness—took over. It whispered that if I told Sawyer, he'd see me differently. He'd see what I've tried to hide, the mess, and maybe he wouldn't want to stick around anymore.

So I swallowed back the words, burying them deep inside, and forced another smile. "Really, Sawyer. I'm fine. Just . . . a long day."

The warmth in his eyes only made him more handsome, but I quickly looked away, blinking back the tears threatening to fall. I wasn't ready for this—not yet.

He stared at me for a second, like he was trying to find words. "Josie, I'm sorry. I heard her say those things to you and I froze. I couldn't believe what she was saying, and by the time I started moving toward you, Jason was already there."

I laughed it off, not wanting Sawyer to feel guilty. "Well, Jason has known me for years, and he is well trained. I'm actually surprised Beatrice didn't get there first and throw herself on Val like a spider monkey." My smile faded when I thought of the possibilities. "Surprised and relieved, actually."

Sawyer smiled and wrapped an arm around my shoulders, pulling me close. "I'm still sorry."

As we walked toward the school exit, Sawyer's easy presence by my side helped me feel anchored, like the world wasn't spinning out of control, even after everything that had happened. His arm brushed against mine, a comforting, grounding presence.

Just as we reached the lobby of the school, Sawyer suddenly stopped, and I turned to look at him, surprised by the flush of red creeping up his neck and settling on his cheeks. He wasn't looking at me, though. His eyes were fixed on the floor, like he was trying to gather himself.

"What?" I laughed, momentarily thrown by his change in demeanor. "Sawyer, I promise—it's okay."

He winced slightly, rubbing the back of his neck, his gaze flickering to mine and then quickly darting away again. His usual confidence seemed to falter. He shoved his hands deep into his pockets, shifting from one foot to the other like he was trying to muster the courage to say something important.

"I'm bad at this," he muttered, his voice quieter than usual.

"At what?" I asked, crossing my arms with a playful grin, though inside, I could feel my pulse quicken, sensing something was different.

He bit his bottom lip, glancing up at me before looking away again and then back down at the floor. "Josie . . ." His voice trailed off like he was searching for the right words, his hands still buried deep in his pockets, his shoulders slightly hunched.

Finally, he let out a breath and looked me square in the eyes, though his voice still wavered slightly. "Josie, will you go out with me tomorrow?"

The words tumbled out in a rush, like he was afraid he might lose the nerve if he waited too long. His hands remained in his pockets, his shoulders tense, and for a second I thought I saw his jaw clench, like he was bracing himself for rejection.

"You . . . want to go somewhere with *me*?" I asked, completely caught off guard, pointing to myself as if I needed clarification.

His cheeks darkened and he laughed, though it was a nervous, almost disbelieving sound. "God, how could you be so smart and have literally no idea?"

"What's that supposed to mean?" I tried to keep up the playful banter, crossing my arms again as if I was insulted, but my smile gave me away.

He pulled one hand out of his pocket, running it through his hair as his nervous energy seemed to build. "It means you're smart . . . and you're funny . . ." He trailed off again, his gaze locking onto mine, this time with a gravity that made my breath catch in my throat. "You're beautiful. I like you—a lot."

For a second, everything else fell away. I watched him fidget, his hand running through his hair again, as if he wasn't sure what to do with himself. He was trying so hard to play it cool, but the slight tremor in his voice and the way he shifted on his feet gave him away. He was nervous—genuinely nervous. And somehow, that made the moment feel even more real, more important.

I couldn't believe it—the worst day was somehow morphing into the best.

And then, because I'm me, I did the most ridiculous thing possible: I burst out laughing.

His eyes widened in shock, his whole body tensing up as if I had just crushed his heart in my hands. "Oh God," he groaned, shaking his head as a sheepish smile tugged at the corner of his lips. "You're laughing at me. That's just . . . perfect."

Before he could retreat further, I grabbed his arm, still laughing, but this time with warmth and affection. "I'm not laughing at you," I reassured him quickly, my voice softening as I caught my breath. "I just . . . I didn't expect this. I thought . . ." My own nerves kicked in, and I looked down for a second. "I thought you just saw me as a friend."

Sawyer stepped closer, his hand hovering near mine, as if he wanted to take it but wasn't sure if he should. He leaned in slightly, his voice barely above a whisper. "Go on a date with me, Josie," he said, the insecurity in his voice tugging at my heart. His hazel eyes held mine, waiting, hoping.

I pretended to consider it, biting my lip to hide the smile tugging at my own mouth. "Okay," I finally said, trying not to let my excitement show too much, though I was sure my cheeks were betraying me.

His entire face lit up, that familiar boyish grin finally returning as he let out a breath he seemed to have been holding for hours. He reached out, wrapping his arm around me and pulling me closer, his body relaxing into mine with relief.

But just as we stepped into the lobby, my body went cold. I stopped short, my laughter dying in my throat as I caught sight of her.

Val.

She was lingering just inside the doors, leaning casually against the wall with her arms crossed, her eyes narrowing into slits the moment she saw us. Her gaze zeroed in on Sawyer's arm around me, her lips curling into a smirk that sent a shiver of dread down my spine.

My heart sank. A wave of nausea roiled in my stomach, and I felt like I had been punched in the gut. My pulse accelerated, a cold sweat prickling at the back of my neck as all the confidence I'd built up with Sawyer evaporated in an instant.

She had heard everything.

Chapter 13

Now

The low rumble of conversation and laughter fills the Maplewood Bar and Grill, a staple in the small town where everyone somehow knows your name—or at least your face. The setting sun throws stripes of orange and pink through the large front windows, bathing the room in a warm, welcoming light. The scent of grilled burgers and fries wafts through the air, mingling with the faint woody smell of the worn wooden bar.

I step in alongside Dermott and Beatrice, feeling the familiar yet distant buzz of the place seep into my bones. It has been over a decade since I last crossed this threshold, yet little seems to have changed—the weathered bar still manages to gleam under the overhead lights, and the walls are still decked with old sports memorabilia and faded photographs of local heroes. My chest aches when my eyes find the older framed photo of Maplewood High's baseball team, Jason and Sawyer with proud, wide smiles, having won the championship that year.

"Quite the cozy spot," Dermott remarks, taking in the scene with an appreciative eye. His presence next to me is both comforting and a stark reminder of how much life has shifted. He has always been a protective force in my life—he and his parents took me in when I first arrived in Ireland without my parents, badly broken. He refused to let me come here from Ireland alone for Sarge's funeral, not wanting me to be by myself while inevitably facing the ghosts that haunt me here.

We make our way to a booth by the window, the chatter around us blending with the clinks of glasses and the occasional burst of laughter from the bar. Dermott slides in across from Beatrice and me, his curiosity about my hometown evident.

"So this was the hangout spot, huh?"

"Still is, it seems," I reply, a smile tugging at my lips despite the nerves fluttering in my stomach. I glance around, half expecting familiar faces from my past to suddenly appear.

"Definitely still the hot spot," Beatrice comments. "I come here way more than I should. It's like I don't have a kitchen in my house," she jokes as she scans the menu.

Just then, the waitress appears, taking our orders. When she leaves, Beatrice doesn't waste any time launching into a whirlwind of words.

"Okay, we have to cover a few things because we have a lot to talk about. How much does Dermott know?" She waves her hand in his direction.

"Dermott knows everything," I assure her with a deep breath, bracing myself for the emotional unpacking that is to come.

"Everything?" she confirms.

"Everything. He probably knows more than you do." I wince as soon as the words leave my mouth, immediately recognizing how they would make Beatrice feel.

"Noted." I don't miss the hurt in her voice.

"Beatrice. I'm sorry."

She waves off my apology with a gentle smile. "It's okay. It's going to hurt, but we will heal. We *will* heal," she reassures, grasping my hands firmly.

"But that aside," she continues, her tone shifting as she leans in closer, "Sawyer has been walking around with a stick up his ass for fifteen years thinking you took off and played house with Dermott."

"My cousin?" I cry as Dermott fake gags across the table. I clench my fists, feeling the heat of frustration rising within me. Even though I know this from

Sawyer's admission at the baseball field, I still cannot wrap my head around the ridiculousness of the situation. "I just can't understand this stupidity!"

"This is what I meant when I said I was afraid of what would happen when we pulled on this string," Beatrice muses.

"When has Sawyer even seen Dermott?"

"In a picture," Beatrice answers decisively.

"Dermott and I have a thousand pictures together," I counter, my voice rising.

"Val," Beatrice says simply, and the temperature in the room seems to drop.

The mention of Val sends a shiver of dread through me, reviving the sharp edges of betrayal and hurt that I have worked so hard to dull. The memories of Val, woven deeply into the darkest chapters of my past, are reminders of countless hours spent trying to heal. It is as if her face, taunting me, has been branded on my soul.

Beatrice takes a deep breath, her normally bright expression grave as she prepares to unravel what she thinks is just a tangled web of misunderstandings that have kept Sawyer and me apart for years.

"It was after you left," she begins, but I raise a hand to stop her.

"I don't know if I can do this," I admit, the old wounds too raw, too near the surface.

Dermott frowns, his protective instincts for me flaring up. "That bitch again?" Knowing my suffering firsthand, recognizing Val's name from the stories I entrusted to him, Dermott tries to open the safety latch. "Jesus, Josie, I don't know if we should be going there."

Not fully grasping the depth of my past trauma, Beatrice continues. "She planned it, Josie. She had a photo of you and Dermott that she found online somewhere. You were at the beach."

I nod and look at Dermott. "Probably Ballybunion." I shrug. "We went there a lot."

Dermott nervously taps the coaster on the table. "I don't like what this could bring up for you, Josie."

"Anyway, Val showed Sawyer the photo and spun a tale about how you'd moved on, that you were living a new life in Ireland with another man."

I sigh. "Beatrice, that's ridiculous. Why would he even believe that? We were—" I swallow around the lump in my throat. I can't say it. I can't say out loud that we were in love. It sounds so petty and cliché now. So naïve.

"He didn't. He basically told her to go to hell. But she kept following him, showing up at parties he was at, just relentless. So when the phone calls stopped and you didn't come back, I started to believe it myself. You disappeared. I just assumed maybe it was true. I couldn't call you to ask—I didn't know where you were. I couldn't find you on social media. You became a ghost."

I shake my head, desperate to defend myself. "No. I came back." I lock eyes with Dermott, finding a well of knowing sympathy. "And then I became a ghost."

Not hearing me, Beatrice continues, her voice tinged with sadness. "So after a while, Sawyer grew more sullen. He sank pretty low, became angrier, bitter . . . and then he just shut down completely." She sighs, reflecting on the drastic change. "You were only supposed to be gone for a few months."

I nod, feeling the weight of those months like a heavy cloak draped over my shoulders. "Exactly. But despite everything that happened here with my parents—" I pause, the air thickening around me as the painful memories of my parents intrude. "Despite it all, I wanted to be with Sawyer. So I came back."

The confusion is evident on Beatrice's face. "Wait. Did you just say you came back?"

I glance at Dermott, who gives me a supportive nod. "I wanted to surprise him on his birthday." As I speak, a single tear breaks free and trickles down my cheek. I quickly brush it away, gathering my composure. "It's been a long time, and I've put a lot of effort into moving past—everything." My voice falters slightly, betraying the lingering pain beneath my words.

Beatrice's eyebrows slam together as she obviously tries to make sense of what she is hearing. Then she sits back and covers her mouth in shock before saying, "Oh shit. I think I know what happened."

The conversation has grown too heavy, and I can feel myself teetering on the edge of a breakdown. I glance up, meeting Beatrice's concerned eyes. "Can we change the subject for a bit?" I ask.

I know Beatrice is eager to dive deeper, her mind swirling with theories, but I recognize the familiar warning signs within myself. If there is anything I have learned over the years, it's the importance of being gentle with my mental health. I don't always follow the rules I have set to take care of myself, but this is one of those moments I know I have to. I have to take a step back and separate myself from that trauma, even if I know I'll have to face it sooner rather than later.

When the food arrives, I find myself unable to eat. The burger and fries sit heavy and uninviting before me. I just push the food around on my plate, lost in a tumult of emotions. Returning to Maplewood feels like stepping into a viper's den. The thought of meeting Sawyer tomorrow looms large over me. Despite the years, the anger is still there, but so are the remnants of love I once felt for him. Falling out of love hadn't been a choice; it was something I had to painstakingly engineer, rewiring my brain and reshaping my life to envision a future without him. Coupling that with dealing with my parents' fate places me in a headspace I desperately wish to escape but am inevitably bound to revisit.

Throughout the meal, I manage small nods and smiles, acknowledging the flow of conversation and chuckling at Dermott's occasional quips. I answer questions about my life in broad strokes, yet my mind is elsewhere, gripped by the anticipation of confronting some of my most painful memories. Mostly, I push food around on my plate, letting Dermott steer the bulk of our discussion.

Suddenly, amidst the casual chatter, I find myself blurting out, "Is she still around here? Val?"

Dermott and Beatrice freeze, the sudden shift in the conversation striking.

"Is there any risk of me running into her?" I ask, the urgency in my voice cutting through the previously lighthearted atmosphere.

Beatrice sets her fork down gently and shakes her head. "I haven't seen her in years, Josie. I really have no idea what became of her, but she's not in Maplewood."

"Good," I reply, relief washing over me as I finally take a bite of my food. The confirmation that Val is no longer a local threat allows me to relax slightly. I can feel Beatrice staring at me and know she has so much she wants to say, but I avert my eyes, sending a clear message. I do not want to talk about it anymore.

I try, for my companions' sake, not to be poor company for the rest of dinner, and once I realize I won't bump into Val over the next week, I mostly succeed. But I have to consciously try to shake the memory of those dark weeks over and over again. So despite my smile and conversation, I feel a chain wrap itself around my heart and lock into place.

***

After dinner, I head back to Miner's alone, leaving Dermott and Beatrice to linger at the bar. I am happy to see them getting along so well. They are deep in conversation with a few locals who have dropped by, the laughter and stories flowing easily. I exchange warm greetings with several familiar faces, feeling the pull of nostalgia with each hello. Yet as the questions begin to drift too close to personal territory, I excuse myself, keen to avoid a night of explanations. I encourage Dermott to soak in the lively atmosphere, assuring him I'll text as soon as I reach the safety and solitude of Miner's. I want him to enjoy at least a little of his time in America.

The cool night air is so different from the warmth of the bar, and I wrap my sweater tighter around me as I walk. The crunch of gravel under my feet is the only sound as I approach the front porch of Miner's. The faint smell of wood smoke and the distant hoot of an owl add a sense of calm, though I know it will be another sleepless night.

As I near the porch, I notice Mrs. Miner's brother sitting there, his silhouette bathed in the soft glow of the porch light. This must be his time of night to sit and ponder. I definitely don't plan on interrupting him again. He stares straight ahead as I climb the stairs to the porch and toward the front door. Trying not to be rude, I smile and say hello but walk quickly by.

Just as I reach for the door, his voice, low and gravelly, stops me. "People think they know," he mutters, not really looking at me. "They think they understand, but they don't. That's what weakens them, you know. Makes them scared."

I turn slightly, caught off guard by his sudden speech. "I'm sorry, what did you say?" I ask, curious despite myself.

"Fear, that's what it is. Makes people run from the truth," he continues, still not meeting my eyes. His gaze seems fixed on some distant point in the dark, far beyond the porch. "They don't want to face reality. Don't want to do the hard work."

His words echo in my mind, pulling me into an uneasy silence. I can't quite place why, but something about his tone and the cryptic nature of his comments makes me stop and listen. It reminds me of Sarge's letters, full of hints and half-spoken truths that I am still trying to piece together.

"Facing danger is one thing. Facing yourself, now that's a whole different battle," he says, his voice trailing off into the night air.

As I stand there, his words hang in the air, sending a shiver down my spine, intertwining with my thoughts about Sarge. The idea of running from the truth, not wanting to face reality and do the hard work—it all seems to resonate deeply. Sarge was always a pillar of strength for me, yet now I am beginning to see that his courage wasn't just about the battlefield, but about the silent battles he fought within himself. What are his letters trying to tell me about him?

And then I wonder what the letters are trying to tell me about myself. It seems like Mrs. Miner's brother can see right through me, without looking at me at all. The idea of running from the truth and avoiding the hard work of facing reality strikes a chord. Is he talking about me? No one is more afraid than I am, and no one has run farther away. I can't shake the feeling that his words are a signal, a nudge I'm not ready to acknowledge. My thoughts are jumbled, filled with uncertainty.

I don't know what more to say, so I simply nod and murmur a quiet good night, slipping into Miner's with a head full of questions and a heart full of conflicting emotions. This man, odd and unfriendly yet strangely insightful, has only added another layer to this bizarre mystery. I know there is more to his story, just as there is more to Sarge's, and I can't shake the feeling that, somehow, they are both guiding me toward an understanding I'm not yet ready to face.

Chapter 14

Then

I had never been on a date before, and I wasn't sure what to expect. Listening to the other girls at school talk about their weekend escapades felt like overhearing stories from a different universe. I wasn't judging them; I just couldn't fathom how they were all so experienced while I hadn't even kissed a boy yet. Unless I counted that awkward peck with Max McNulty behind the basketball court at St. Mary's when we were eleven, convinced the ground would swallow us into the bowels of hell. My thoughts drifted to how many girls Sawyer had kissed, but I quickly shoved that thought away.

He texted to say he'd pick me up that evening, but there was no way I was letting him come near my house. My parents' moods were too unpredictable, especially my mom's, and this wasn't a risk I was willing to take. So I asked him to meet me at the park instead. He didn't question it, which I appreciated; he just agreed and promised he wouldn't be late. "I don't want you waiting by yourself," he said, and somehow, I think he understood a bit about my family's chaos without me having to explain.

I told my mom, who was sober, that I was going to Beatrice's house. If I told her I was going on a date, it would have resulted in an extremely awkward exchange that would have left me feeling dirty or wrong—or it could have resulted in her simply saying no. I couldn't risk either.

I made my way to Maplewood Park and found Sawyer sitting on the bench under the large maple tree.

"Hey! I thought I'd get here first!" I said, walking toward him with a giant smile stretched across my face.

He stood, matching my huge grin. "I told you I didn't want you waiting for me." His eyes roamed over me. "You always look so beautiful."

I burst out laughing, looking down at my soft jeans and long-sleeved T-shirt. "You're easy to impress."

He shook his head. "No. You are the prettiest girl I ever saw." My cheeks turned pink with embarrassment. "But I won't make you feel weird. I just thought you should know." He stepped closer to me and leaned down to place a soft kiss on my forehead. Something inside me melted—or came alive.

"Well, thank you. You're not so bad yourself."

He grinned and then reached out, taking me by the hand. "Come with me. I have my mom's car, so don't judge me for the little hula lady she has on the dash, okay?"

"It's okay to admit she's your hula lady, Sawyer."

He laughed, the sound warm in the cool evening air. "Maybe I like the way she dances," he joked as we walked toward the street.

The park was quietly beautiful, the setting sun painting the sky in hues of pink and orange. As we approached his mom's car, I could see the hula lady perched on the dashboard, her grass skirt poised for motion.

Sawyer held the passenger door open for me, a gesture so charmingly old-fashioned that it made me smile. "Thank you," I said, sliding into the seat.

"No problem," he replied, closing the door gently behind me before walking around to the driver's side.

As he started the car, the hula lady began her dance, swaying back and forth to the hum of the engine. I couldn't help but giggle, the tension of the day easing slightly.

"So, where are we headed?" I asked, curious about what he had planned.

Sawyer put the car in gear, pulling away from the curb. "Have you ever been to Foley's Family Fun Park?"

I clasped my hands together and squealed. "Not in years!"

"Well, it's your lucky day, because you get to watch me die a slow and painful death on the miniature golf course because I have no skills."

"Yes!" I pumped my fist in the air while Sawyer threw his head back and laughed.

"But first, I'll feed you. It's not five-star cuisine, but Foley's has the best snack bar—hands down."

"Better than the baseball field food stand?" I asked in mock surprise.

"Most of the time, unless there's a cute Irish girl working the slushie machine. Then it's the baseball field for me." He winked at me, and there was that melting again. This guy was going to ruin me.

We arrived as the sky began to tinge with the gold and purple hues of the setting sun, adding a magical backdrop to our evening. The park was bustling with families and couples, the air filled with the sounds of laughter and the clinking of golf clubs hitting balls.

Sawyer led the way to a picnic table tucked beneath another sprawling maple, its branches alive with the soft, glowing colors of spring. He dropped a tray heavy with hot dogs and fries on the table, the smell of fried food cutting through the crisp air.

We settled into our seats. Sawyer tossed me a ketchup packet with a playful grin. "Go wild," he said, his voice tinged with laughter.

I drenched the fries in ketchup and took a greedy bite, savoring the perfect salty crunch. Sawyer watched, delight flickering in his eyes before he took a thoughtful bite of his hot dog. The comfortable silence stretched between us, filled only by distant laughter and the metallic ping of golf balls.

"Did you come here a lot as a kid?"

He nodded while he chewed. After a moment, he spoke. "My mom would bring me and my older brother here. I used to go to the batting cages when I was probably too young to be in there." He laughed.

"You have an older brother?"

"Yeah, he's eight years older. He lives in Harrisburg. He got a really good job in marketing, so he moved a few years ago."

I noticed he didn't mention a dad, but he had mentioned his mom, and I of course met her and worked with her at the baseball food stand. "Is it just you and your mom?"

He was quiet for a second. "Yeah."

"I'm sorry. I'm being nosy. You didn't have to answer that."

"No, I want to answer. I do. I just haven't said anything about my father out loud in a while."

"It's okay." I shook my head and gave my attention back to the fries, inwardly scolding myself for asking too many questions.

"He took off when I was three and Joey, my older brother, was eleven."

My head popped up; I was surprised at his easy admission but sad to see a hint of pain in his expression. "I'm sorry."

"Don't be. My mom is awesome." He laughed. Sawyer could hide things too, it seemed. "I think I was sort of a surprise. Joey is so much older. They thought they were out of the woods. My father thought it would start to get easier, and then *boom*, along comes baby Johnny." He was joking, making light of a clearly difficult situation. He popped a fry in his mouth. "Anyway, he stuck it out for a few years and then took off. For a long time, I wondered if I did something wrong to make him leave. I wouldn't know him if he was sitting next to me."

The idea that anyone, especially someone as warm and caring as Sawyer, could believe he wasn't enough made my chest tighten. What kind of person could walk away from him? I couldn't fathom someone abandoning a kid like Sawyer, who went out of his way to make me feel safe, who laughed easily, and who treated me with more kindness than I knew what to do with. The idea that someone—his own father, no less—could leave him behind was appalling.

"He doesn't live around here?" I asked.

"No." He shook his head, his features momentarily darkening. "This place was too simple for him. I guess he wanted more excitement. More adventure. His family wasn't thrilling enough."

A surge of defensiveness flared up inside me. The thought of Sawyer as a child, wondering why his father left him, twisted in my chest. "Well, his loss, because his son is one of the best people I know—and I feel like the luckiest person every time he talks to me."

Sawyer blinked once, almost like he was surprised by how much my words meant to him. For a brief moment, his gaze held mine, and I swear I saw something flicker there—something unspoken but full of meaning. Like he wasn't used to hearing someone say they cared.

He cleared his throat, but the corners of his lips still tugged up, betraying him. "Thanks, Josie O. You don't even know." His voice was huskier than usual, like he was trying to rein in something bigger.

My heart fluttered in my chest, skipping a beat at the way he looked at me. No one had ever looked at me like that before—like I was something rare, something worth admiring. And for the first time, I felt a tiny thrill at the idea that maybe I could be.

Sawyer's hand brushed mine, just barely, but it sent a spark through me. His touch was so light, almost hesitant, but it left me wondering if he felt the same pull I did—this invisible thread tugging us closer together.

"Your mom is pretty cool," I blurted out, a little unnerved by the intensity of the moment.

"Yeah, she really is," Sawyer agreed, a warm smile spreading across his face. "Honestly, I've never felt like I was missing out by not having a dad around. It was always my mom and Joey tossing baseballs with me in the backyard. She comes to every single one of my games too, even though I've told her a thousand times she doesn't have to." He shrugged. "It's not like she doesn't kick my ass sometimes, and she gets on my case about stuff all the time, but she works really hard and always made sure I had enough money to play baseball. That's why I started cutting grass and shoveling snow as soon as I was old enough."

Listening to Sawyer talk about his mother, who stepped up in every way imaginable, left a bittersweet pang in my chest. My own mother, with her unpredictable alcoholic tendencies, and my father, ever the enabler, seemed so far removed from the nurturing care Sawyer described. My parents' orbit was one of chaos, a never-ending cycle that sucked in happiness and spat out turmoil, leaving me perpetually on edge. Where Sawyer had stability and unwavering support, I navigated a labyrinth of mood swings and neglect, always bracing for the next outburst or disappointment.

This conversation was sharpening the budding feelings I harbored for him, making them feel both precious and terrifying. The simplicity and depth of his family bonds highlighted what I had missed, igniting a yearning for something I'd never known but desperately wanted. As these emotions swirled within me, they added to my growing weakness for Sawyer, transforming it into something profound and slightly frightening. His presence, his laughter, even the way he shared his fries with me became laden with meaning, stoking a fire of affection and fear—fear because to feel this deeply could only mean one thing: there was so much more to lose.

I glanced at Sawyer, feeling a question bubble up that I'd been too afraid to ask. Trying to sound casual, I said, "So, is there anything going on between you and Val?"

Sawyer's features eased into a smile, and he shook his head slightly. "If there was anything going on with Val, I wouldn't be here with you, Josie." He looked me in the eyes, his sincerity clear. "Trust me on that."

Relief washed over me, mingling with the warmth his words had sparked. "Okay," I said softly, squeezing his hand.

We shared a long look, where our mutual admiration was fully on the surface. Sawyer glanced at his watch then at me, a hopeful look in his eyes. "Well, if I haven't scared you off by being a momma's boy, maybe I can scare you off with my awful mini golf skills."

I giggled, feeling a lightness rise within me, so different from the heavy emotions that had just passed between us. "I think I can handle your mini golf skills," I teased, grateful for the shift to a lighter mood. The warmth from his hand lingered even as he pulled away.

As we stood to throw away our trash and head toward the mini golf course, I felt a new ease between us. He grabbed my hand again as we walked the short distance to get our clubs and golf balls.

***

The game of mini golf was a delightful mess of laughter and playful teasing. Sawyer was true to his word—his mini golf skills were hilariously awful, but his enthusiasm and the way his laughter rang out under the canopy of stars made my heart flutter uncontrollably. Every miss was met with a grin, and each successful putt was celebrated like a major victory. Our hands seemed to find each other naturally between holes, our fingers intertwining with an ease that felt like slipping into a dream. I couldn't remember the last time I'd felt so genuinely happy, so carefree. As he helped me line up a particularly tricky shot, his hands guiding mine, I caught myself hoping the night would never end.

When the game finished, and with a mock-serious declaration from Sawyer that I was the mini golf champion, we headed back to the car. Sawyer wanted to drive me home and walk me to the door, but I asked him not to, promising that I would explain more one day. He didn't push, and I was so grateful for that kindness.

When we pulled up to Maplewood Park, he asked if I had time to sit with him for a bit. Sitting down on the same bench, now under a sky sprinkled with stars and the giant maple tree, there was a moment of peaceful reflection. The soft glow of the streetlamps painted shadows across his face, highlighting the gentle earnestness in his eyes.

"Thank you, Sawyer," I said quietly.

"For what?"

I shrugged. "For everything. For seeing me. For making me feel like I'm special."

He sighed, like he was trying to hold back, like he was trying to gather restraint. "Josie, I could sit here and tell you all the lines in the world to make you feel special—but the truth is nothing can explain how I see you."

I swallowed, getting lost in his hazel eyes as he continued speaking.

"When I see you, I have to tell myself to breathe. The sound of your laugh, the way some of your words have a faint Irish accent, your smile." His eyes landed on my lips as he spoke.

Sawyer's eyes shifted to mine, his voice a little softer, more careful now. "Your eyes are the coolest shade of green I've ever seen. They have these little gold flecks." His gaze dipped to my lips again for a moment. "And your freckles across your nose. Your hair. The way you smell. The fact that you live in jeans and T-shirts. Your lips. I just want to—"

My heart was pounding in my chest, my breath hitching in my throat as he spoke. His words were tumbling out in a rush, and I could feel the tension thickening between us, the air charged with something electric. He leaned in just a little, and suddenly the space between us felt almost too small, too intimate.

I had never been this close to someone in this way before. *What if I did it wrong? What if he could tell I'd never done this before?* A surge of panic flashed through me. My palms felt clammy, and I realized I was holding my breath.

"I've never kissed anyone before," I blurted out, my voice barely a whisper, as if saying it out loud made it too real, too vulnerable.

Sawyer's eyes grew gentle, and he smiled, his hand coming up to softly cup my cheek. "Can I be *anyone*?" he asked, his voice low, almost breathless.

I felt the words catch in my throat, a sudden wave of fear mingling with the desire bubbling up inside me. *What if I wasn't what he expected? What if this changed everything?*

But the look in his eyes, that steady, patient gaze, melted away some of the fear. He wasn't rushing me. He wasn't pushing. He was just there, waiting. Waiting for me.

I nodded slowly, trying to speak, but the words wouldn't come. Instead, I just leaned in, closing the gap between us.

Before I could second-guess myself, his lips brushed against mine, so soft at first I wasn't sure if it was really happening. The world seemed to pause in that moment—my nerves, the noise of the park, everything faded away except for the feel of his mouth on mine. My breath hitched again, but this time it wasn't out of fear. My mouth opened so slightly, and that's all it took for him to kiss me until I was out of breath, with a tenderness that drew a sigh from deep within me.

We shifted and moved, trying to get closer to each other. Hands were everywhere. My hands on him. His hands on me. Hair was being grabbed, and by the time I came to my senses, I was practically on his lap on the bench. When we both pulled away, we were out of breath, looking at each other with surprise and some new level of intrigue before we dove into each other again.

I didn't know what was happening, I just knew I wanted it to keep happening—over and over again, every day, forever into eternity. Nothing to this point in my life had been better.

"I could kiss you here all night," he whispered, his forehead resting against mine as we breathed heavily, sharing the electrically charged air.

"Do you think you might want to have more dates so we can kiss again?"

His eyes crinkled when he smiled. "How about we make this a habit?"

"Okay," I agreed quickly, and we leaned in, taking each other's breath away again . . .

Chapter 15

Now

The sweet aroma of waffle cones combined with nostalgic décor makes me smile, but does little to ease the tension knotted in my stomach as I step into Maple's Ice Cream Shoppe. I look for the table Sarge mentioned in his letter, intending to sit and wait for Sawyer, but my smile drops when I see him already there, his hazel eyes locking onto mine.

"You're here," I state flatly, stripping any warmth from my greeting.

Sawyer's eyes flicker with surprise, but he recovers quickly. "Nice to see you too," he responds, a hint of sarcasm in his tone.

I approach the table, my response icy. "I never said it was nice to see you." I drop my purse beside me, taking a seat with a deliberate thud.

Sawyer's face tightens for a split second before he looks away, his fingers tapping lightly on the table. It's brief, but I catch it—like my words hit harder than he's willing to admit. He turns his gaze back to me, but there's something guarded in his eyes now, a wall going up. "Right," he says quietly, his voice losing some of its earlier sarcasm.

I roll my eyes at his reaction and meet his gaze with a directness that borders on confrontational. "Shall we?" I prompt, eager to get this over with.

"You're in rare form today, aren't you?" he remarks, though there's less bite to his words now, as if he's trying to gauge the situation, figure out how much he can push back.

"What the hell is that supposed to mean?" I snap back.

Sawyer holds up his hands, a gesture of peace. "Come on, Josie, I don't want to fight," he says, his voice lowering, carrying a thread of sincerity that almost catches me off guard. "We never used to fight." He's not looking at me now, his eyes drifting to the table between us, like he's searching for something in the past that he can't quite find.

His words hang in the air, reminding me of our shared past—a past filled with better days, now overshadowed by the pain of our separation. I feel the sting of his words but refuse to let them land.

"Yeah, well—I can remember a fight or two. You have a convenient memory," I retort sharply, my words clipped. "Anyway, that was a long time ago, and I'm not the same."

Sawyer's eyes lift back to mine, and for a moment, I see something—a flicker of regret, maybe. But it's gone almost as soon as it appears, replaced by a resigned sadness. He presses his lips together and nods, accepting my words without protest.

"Let's just get to why we're here," I say. "We need to follow what Sarge planned for us, and that's all."

Sawyer nods slowly, like he's still processing everything, but recognizing the need to move on. "Okay. Let me see the letter again."

I reach into my bag and pull out the letter we found taped under the picnic table at the baseball field the day before, handing it over. Sawyer's eyes scan the page. He reads a section of the letter out loud.

"'Find yourselves the second table on the left by the window. Look under it—you'll find your next piece of this puzzle stuck there. There's an old picture nearby with some old ghosts looking into the camera.'"

We both glance around at the pictures on the wall, but one hanging behind Sawyer catches my eye.

I gesture to the picture just over his shoulder. "That one. Could it be that one?"

Sawyer turns, following my gaze to the aged photograph framed against the nostalgic wallpaper of the ice cream shop. The photo, a black-and-white image, shows a group of young people, carefree and smiling, captured in a moment of youthful exuberance. Among them, a young man with a familiar posture and a striking resemblance to Sarge stands out, his arm draped casually around a girl.

"Is that . . . ?" Sawyer trails off, squinting slightly as he tries to bridge the decades that separate the youthful faces from their present-day counterparts.

Before I can respond, the door chimes, and a group of teenagers strolls in, laughing and jostling one another as they make their way toward the counter. One of the boys looks over and grins. "Hey, Mr. Sawyer!" he calls out, giving a casual wave.

Sawyer lifts his hand in acknowledgment. "Hey, guys," he replies, his voice easy, familiar.

I blink, surprised by the interaction. *Mr. Sawyer?* I file it away, curiosity tugging at me, but I push the thought aside. *Focus, Josie.* I turn my attention back to the photograph, though the new layer of intrigue lingers in the back of my mind.

I move over to Sawyer's side of the table; the excitement of finding the picture makes me forget myself as I crowd into his space. I'm standing over him, trying to get a good look, when I feel him stiffen beside me.

"I'm sorry," I say quickly, moving away.

"No, it's okay," he responds, but his voice falters slightly. "It's just . . . nothing. Never mind."

"What?" I ask, feeling self-conscious and suspicious.

Sawyer hesitates, his eyes dropping briefly before he answers. "You smell the same. Same perfume." His words hang in the air, unexpectedly intimate. It's subtle, but it's there. A moment of softness that makes the air between us feel heavier, more charged.

I feel a flush rise in my cheeks, a mixture of surprise and the stirring of old memories. He's right. I may have changed, but my perfume never does. I always find myself drawn back to the same scent.

Sawyer shakes his head, a faint smile tugging at the corner of his mouth as if he's caught in the unexpected closeness our quest has brought about. "Sorry, it just took me back for a second," he admits, his voice softer, less guarded than before. "Better days."

He's trying to play it off, but I catch the way his fingers brush lightly over the edge of the table, like he's steadying himself, as if that small memory stirred something deeper than he wants to admit.

I take a deep breath and pull my eyes from him, trying to refocus on the photograph, though part of my mind lingers on his comment. I wonder what's wrong with his days now. I shake it off. "Well, we should probably keep looking at this," I say, gesturing back to the picture, eager to steer our interaction back to safer, less personal territory.

"Yes, of course," he agrees, though I think I feel his eyes regarding me a bit longer.

We turn our attention back to the photograph, scrutinizing the other figures now with renewed intensity. The young woman is laughing, her head thrown back in a moment of joy, standing next to the young Sarge, who is unmistakably the center of this group.

"I wonder who she is," I muse, half to myself. "Look at them," I point out, tracing the outline of their bodies with my finger on the glass. "They look like they were really close. More than just friends, maybe?"

Sawyer leans in closer, his earlier hesitation forgotten as curiosity takes over. "That's definitely a young Sarge. Before he was Sarge." Pointing to the girl, he adds, "This is crazy, but I think that's Mrs. Miner."

I gasp loudly, causing Sawyer to laugh. "No way!" I try to edge closer to the picture.

"Any closer, Josie, and you'll be in the photo."

"I can't imagine Mrs. Miner being anything other than—other than—" I struggle with my words, trying not to sound mean.

"Old?" Sawyer asks, amused.

"Exactly. Old and serious."

We both study the photo a bit longer, my eyes tracing the outlines of the other figures, all captured in a moment of carefree youth. My finger hovers over a figure in the background—a man with a tilted hat. "And what about him? He seems . . . out of place, somehow."

Sawyer leans in again, squinting slightly. "Yeah, he's not mingling like the others. He's sort of on the fringe. Could be shy, or maybe he's just an observer."

"Or maybe he's keeping an eye on things," I suggest, the enigma of the unknown figure weaving another layer of intrigue into our quest. "Sarge must have included this picture for a reason. Oh! What if he's Mr. Miner?" My eyes widen with the thrill of the possibility as I turn to face Sawyer. His expression is warm, tinged with amusement. "I never met Mr. Miner."

"Me neither. I assume he passed away young." His words hang between us, prompting us both to turn our gazes back to the photograph, almost expecting the figures captured in time to reveal their secrets.

Sawyer clears his throat. "For now, let's figure out the next step in Sarge's letter. He mentioned something taped under the table, right?"

"Right," I confirm, glancing around to ensure we aren't drawing too much attention. We both stoop slightly, checking under our table until my fingers graze something slightly adhesive. "Got it!" I exclaim, pulling out another envelope.

As we sit back down to open the new envelope, things start to feel more natural between us. I don't feel anything but curiosity in that moment, my anger toward Sawyer temporarily thwarted. I open the letter, reading Sarge's words out loud.

***

Hey kids,

If you're squinting at that old photo, trying to figure out what it's whispering, you're exactly where I wanted you to be. Not everything's as it seems, and the truth? Well, it's usually hiding in plain sight. People, too—just like Roberta Miner, all bright smiles and laughs back in her salad days. She had a lot more going on than folks realized.

Now, before you go charging off, don't even think about leaving that ice cream shop without grabbing a cone. I know you two might be tempted to tell me to pound sand, but trust me, nobody sets foot in that place without tasting the best dang ice cream you'll ever have. Don't let me down, all right?

Your next stop's at my special set of bleachers over at Maplewood High's football field. That place has seen more secrets than you can count. It's where I said goodbye to the love of my life. Didn't know it at the time, but it's also where I said goodbye to the man I used to be before Vietnam. William left, and Sarge took his place—a stranger even to myself.

Y'all know how much I love Johnny Cash, right? I've been thinkin' about him and June Carter lately. Johnny said once that June was his lighthouse, guiding him through the dark. She saw the deepest, roughest parts of him and still loved him, storms and all. Some folks get that—the kind of love that fights through every battle. Others? Well, they end up saying goodbye under a set of bleachers, wondering if they'll ever find their way back. Funny thing is, sometimes that journey away is the one that shows you who you really are.

Now, under those bleachers, you'll find another letter. One's for you, the other goes to Miner's Inn. I've told you before, I've got some loose ends to tie up. Life's truths are simple sometimes, like an old set of bleachers or a familiar face. But it takes guts to look past what you think you know and really see what's there.

This ain't just a stroll down memory lane. It's about finding the parts of yourself that got buried along the way. I couldn't do that for myself, but I'm hoping you can help me now. As you dig through my past, you might just find pieces of your own truth too.

Catch ya later,

Sarge

PS: Remember, the deepest answers are often hiding in plain sight.

Chapter 16

Then

The street was slick with a thin layer of ice as I waited outside my house, bundled up against the chill of the December evening. The festive glow from neighboring houses, adorned with Christmas lights, did little to ease the flutter of nerves in my stomach. It was Christmas Eve, and though excitement thrummed through my veins at the prospect of spending it with Sawyer and his family, anxiety buzzed just beneath the surface about him possibly meeting my parents under unpredictable circumstances.

My mom had been sober for a few months now—a miraculous streak by any standard in our household—and it brought an unexpected lightness to my junior year. But the unpredictability of her sobriety, especially around the holidays, had left a residue of caution in how I introduced her to parts of my life, including Sawyer. I wasn't ready to risk it tonight.

"What the hell are you doing out here in the cold, Josie girl?" Sarge called from his front porch.

I giggled. "I should be asking you the same question!"

"Just waiting for the baby Jesus," he joked, holding up his Lucky Strike, "and having a smoke."

"Are you doing anything tonight?"

"I'm heading over to a party at the VFW in a bit. What about you?"

I smiled, excitement lighting me up. "Sawyer invited me over for Christmas Eve."

Sarge chuckled, his breath forming a misty cloud in the crisp evening air. "Ah, spending time with that young man of yours, eh? He's a good one, Josie."

"Yeah, he really is," I admitted, feeling a warm flush of pride at the affirmation.

"He's got a nice family too. Good people," Sarge added, nodding approvingly. "Make sure you give them my best."

"I will, Sarge. You know, I'm a bit nervous, though," I confessed, tucking a loose strand of hair behind my ear.

Sarge's face softened under the glow of his porch light. "Don't you worry, kiddo. Just be yourself. They're gonna love you. You've got a good head on your shoulders—no thanks to your old man, or that whirlwind of a mother."

I laughed, a bit of tension easing from my shoulders, but I glanced back at my house to make sure my mother hadn't heard him. "Thanks, Sarge. It means a lot."

Headlights pierced the early evening's dim as Sawyer's car turned onto my street, its familiar hum a comforting sound in the crisp air.

Sarge nodded in the direction of the oncoming car. "Now go on, get out of this cold before you freeze your toes off. And, Josie?" Sarge called out as I started down my front porch steps.

I turned back. "Yeah?"

"Merry Christmas, kid. Enjoy your evening."

"Merry Christmas, Sarge!" I called back, smiling over my shoulder before jogging to the car.

I darted from the porch, my boots crunching over the frosted grass, making it to the passenger-side door just as Sawyer reached over to open it from the inside.

"Merry Christmas Eve," Sawyer greeted with his irresistible smile, the warmth in his eyes making me momentarily forget the cold. "I was going to get out and open the door for you, but you ran out of there like there was a fire."

"Merry Christmas Eve," I echoed, sliding into the seat and quickly closing the door behind me. The warmth of the car enveloped me immediately, a stark difference from the frigid air outside. "I'm just excited to see you."

Sawyer leaned across the console, and I met him there for a kiss. "Hi, beautiful girl," he whispered. I smiled against his lips, and he kissed me again before leaning back into his seat.

As Sawyer pulled away from the curb, he glanced over, a question lingering in his expression. "Everything okay? You really did rush out like there was a fire."

I forced a smile, turning to him with a slight shrug. "Just didn't want to keep you waiting in the cold," I said, skirting around the full truth. "Plus, my mom's having one of her quieter nights. Best not to stir things up."

He nodded, understanding flashing across his face without needing further explanation. Sawyer had become familiar with the careful dance around my home life. "Got it. Well, my family is excited to meet you, and I'm sort of afraid they'll scare you away."

A laugh burst out of me. "Scare me away? Do you have any idea where I come from?" I joked as he reached for my hand and squeezed.

The drive was filled with the sound of holiday music from the car's radio, creating a bubble of Christmas cheer that eased the tension that seemed to always exist when I was home. Sawyer's hand continued to hold mine across the center console, his fingers interlocking with mine in a reassuring grip. I leaned back in my seat, allowing the melodies and his presence to calm the whirlwind of thoughts, focusing instead on the joy of our first Christmas Eve together. I'd never had this before, and I never wanted to give it up now that I had.

When we arrived at his house, there were cars parked all over his driveway and down the street. "Oh my God, Sawyer. Who's all here?"

"Well, my mom and my brother." He took in the cars as he parked his own. "My two aunts and their families. My uncle and his family. I have a few older cousins with their families. Probably my mom's best friend and her family . . ." He trailed off, throwing the car in park and looking at me. "Are you okay?"

"Yes. Just really nervous." My eyes were the size of saucers as I looked at the house and imagined the throngs of people inside.

Sawyer smiled gently, turning off the car and facing me. "Hey, they're going to love you," he reassured me, his eyes warm and steady. "And if it gets overwhelming, just give me a signal, and we'll find a quiet corner or take a walk, just the two of us."

I nodded, feeling a wave of gratitude for his understanding and support. "Okay, that sounds perfect. Thank you, Sawyer." I took a deep breath, trying to calm the flutter of nerves in my stomach.

"Ready?" he asked, his hand still holding mine.

"Ready as I'll ever be," I replied with a nervous chuckle. We exited the car and walked up to the brightly lit house together. Christmas lights twinkled around the windows and eaves, casting a cheerful glow that felt both inviting and daunting.

As we stepped onto the porch, the sound of laughter and music seeped through the door, hinting at the festive chaos inside. Just before Sawyer could push it open, I tugged gently on his hand, pausing him. "Thank you. I always wanted to have big family Christmas gatherings, and I've never had any, so—thank you," I managed to say just as someone from inside flung the door open, and we were instantly enveloped in the warmth of his family home, scented with pine and freshly baked treats.

The room was bustling with energy, filled with people of all ages, their voices mingling in a lively cacophony. Sawyer wasted no time; he wrapped an arm around my shoulders, leading me into the heart of the gathering, introducing me with clear pride.

"This is my girlfriend, Josie," he announced to a group of his relatives, who turned to greet us with smiles that were both open and inviting.

"Welcome, Josie!" one of his aunts exclaimed, pulling me into a hug that was surprisingly comforting. "We've heard so much about you! Oh my God, Sawyer, she's stunning! Sawyer told us you were gorgeous, but my God, look at you!"

Her words felt like a warm embrace, yet a small twinge of discomfort accompanied them. I wasn't used to being noticed this way—being welcomed so openly. I managed a small, appreciative smile, but inside, it was hard to shake the feeling that I didn't quite belong. "Thank you," I said, though the words felt foreign in my mouth. My cheeks flushed, and I glanced at Sawyer, who was grinning as if to reassure me that everything was okay.

As we moved through the house, I noticed the wine glasses in people's hands. Sawyer's aunts and uncles clinked glasses, laughter bubbling up as they toasted the evening. It was strange—at home, drinking meant tension, a thin line between calm and chaos. But here, the drinks were part of the celebration. They sipped wine with easy smiles, leaning on each other, sharing stories. It was different. Light. Safe. Here, there was nothing to fear.

Sawyer's mother came up to me and wrapped me in a hug. "There she is!" And then she brought me around to introduce me to more people. Looking over at Sawyer, who was watching me with a tender expression, I began to feel a profound sense of belonging.

His older brother, Joey, stepped up next. "Whooo, Johnny boy, not to sound like a creep, but you did good," he teased with a wink before shaking my hand. "It's my duty to terrorize him. Sorry if I made you uncomfortable."

Before I could respond, Sawyer's arm snaked around my waist and pulled me away as I laughed.

Dinner with Sawyer's family was a lively affair, full of hearty laughter and delicious food that seemed to never end. The dining room table groaned under dishes of roast turkey, honey-glazed ham, and all the trimmings. Conversation flowed as easily as the wine, which made itself evident when a few of Sawyer's aunts got a little tipsy, and I found myself swept up in the cheerful spirit. Sawyer's relatives were storytellers, each one with a tale more entertaining than the last, making the meal pass in a blur of enjoyment.

As the evening rolled on, Sawyer took my hand, a mischievous twinkle in his eye. "Come with me," he whispered, leading me away from the diminishing bustle. As we started ascending the stairs, his mom called out, "Door open, John!"

I giggled as he groaned. "Yep, Mom!" And then we scurried up the stairs, down the hall to his bedroom. "She never misses anything," he muttered. My eyes opened in wonder as we entered his room. I had never been here before. It was a window into a part of his world that I had never seen.

Inside Sawyer's bedroom, the walls were adorned with posters of baseball legends and photographs of high school triumphs—a glimpse into the passions and memories that had shaped him. The room was neat, with a sense of ordered chaos in the stacks of books and trophies lining the shelves. As I took it all in, Sawyer closed the door, though he left it slightly ajar, respecting his mother's rule.

He looked around the room as if taking it in for the first time. He seemed so much bigger than it. A young man in a boy's room in some ways. "I've had these posters up for years."

I walked along the room, taking it all in. I scanned the posters and the pictures. I noticed the sound of Christmas music from downstairs was still audible from his room as my eyes landed on his bed, and I felt a flush creep up my neck.

"I have something for you." He went over to his dresser and pulled out a small, beautifully wrapped box. The anticipation built in me as he turned around, his expression a mix of nerves and excitement. "I wanted to give you something special," he said, handing me the box with a gentle smile.

"Sawyer, I didn't bring your present. We said—"

"No, Josie. This is about you."

I smiled softly at him, feeling my heart swell. I opened it carefully, and inside, nestled on a bed of soft velvet, was a claddagh necklace.

I gasped just as Sawyer started rambling. "I know this is probably incredibly cheesy. I mean—you are probably more Irish than that necklace, and you probably already have one—or maybe two—but when I saw it and I read the story about it—I had to buy it for you."

I knew what this necklace meant. The traditional Irish symbol of two hands clasping a heart topped with a crown—representing love, loyalty, and friendship—gleamed in the soft light of his room. I traced the delicate craftsmanship with a fingertip, overwhelmed by the thoughtfulness of the gift.

"I don't have one," I managed to choke out, my voice thick with emotion. "Sawyer . . . this is beautiful. What made you think of this?"

He took the necklace from the box, stepping closer to fasten it around my neck. His fingers brushed lightly against my skin, sending a shiver down my spine. "Because," he started, his eyes locking with mine in the mirror as the necklace settled into place, "it represents what I feel for you. We have all these things, Josie. Friendship—because you are my best friend. Loyalty—because we would never betray each other." He slowly turned me around so I could face him, and as I looked up into his eyes, he said the words I never could have dreamed would come from his mouth to my ears. "And love—because I love you."

Tears welled up in my eyes as I looked at him in awe, the necklace pressing gently against my skin, its cool touch a steady reminder of the moment's significance. "I can't believe you're mine," I said, reaching up to touch the pendant again.

"I'm yours, Josie. Always." His voice was earnest, his gaze intense.

I threw my arms around him, the necklace between us a new link in the chain of our growing bond. "I love you too, Sawyer. So much," I murmured into his shoulder. He rubbed my back as I held on to him, never wanting to let go. Finally, I pulled back just enough to look into his eyes.

We hadn't gone beyond kissing. I knew we both wanted to, but I was scared, and Sawyer was patient. At this moment, there was nothing I wanted more than to be fused to Sawyer in every way, but the reminder of his mother downstairs came barreling back when I heard her laughter mixing with his family's. The reminder of my own mother was never far away either.

I searched his eyes, wondering if he was feeling the same way, and then his lips crashed into mine. Sawyer would often kiss me softly, lovingly, but this—this had a hint of desperation. The world fell away as the space between us disappeared. I could feel the heat rising, a quiet intensity growing with every moment. His hand gently tangled in my hair, and a soft sound escaped me. It was all we needed—a spark igniting something deeper, something we weren't ready to name. But instead of pushing further, we held on to the closeness, letting it say what words couldn't.

We found ourselves on his small twin bed, my heart racing with the closeness of the moment. But a quiet voice of caution, or the Irish Catholic guilt, threaded through the excitement, reminding me of the line between what felt right and what might be too much too soon. Alone together in his room, the temptation to let go completely hung in the air, but I knew we weren't ready to cross that line just yet.

Breathing heavily, we parted, our foreheads resting against each other, our breath mingling in the charged air. "Sawyer," I managed to say, my voice a whisper of both desire and restraint.

He nodded, understanding without needing more words, his eyes reflecting the same whirl of emotions. "I know," he whispered back. His thumb caressed my cheek softly, a silent promise of respect and patience. "We have all the time in the world, Josie. I'm not going anywhere."

The moment hung between us. "We should probably talk about how this—how we—when we—" I stumbled over my words, my heart thrashing around my chest.

Sawyer's smile was gentle, reassuring. "Josie, we'll figure it out together, okay? We'll take it step by step, no hurry."

I nodded, feeling a rush of gratitude for his understanding and patience. "Thank you," I whispered, "for being you, for being patient."

He pulled me into another hug, warm and secure. "Always," he murmured into my hair. "Especially when it comes to you."

We stayed like that for a moment longer, wrapped in each other's arms, the world outside momentarily forgotten. Then, taking a deep breath, I sat up, feeling a bit more composed. "We should get back," I said, my voice steadier now.

"Yeah, they'll be wondering where we've disappeared to," he agreed, a playful glint returning to his eyes. He got off of the bed and then held out his hand, and I took it, feeling the strength of his grip as he pulled me to my feet.

"I love you," Sawyer whispered.

I grinned, feeling a warmth bloom in my chest. "I love you too."

A slow, mischievous smile spread across his face. "I love you." He said it again, this time with a playful lilt, like he was testing the waters.

I laughed softly. "I *just* said that I love you too."

"I know, but . . . I love *you*," he repeated, now leaning in, his voice softer but with a teasing edge.

I raised an eyebrow, catching on to his game. "Oh? You love *me*?"

"Yeah, I love you," he shot back, his grin widening.

"Well, I love *you*," I countered, poking him lightly in the ribs.

He chuckled, then leaned in closer, our noses nearly touching. "I love you."

"I love you."

"I love you."

"I love you."

We dissolved into laughter, the words bouncing between us like a Ping-Pong match, growing sillier each time but never losing their meaning. And with each "I love you," the novelty and joy of finally saying those words made my heart feel impossibly light.

Finally, he pulled me close, eyes sparkling. "Okay, okay, I love you. Winner. Done."

I smirked. "Oh no, I definitely love you more."

He shook his head, smiling. "Not possible."

We laughed as we descended the stairs. I touched the necklace hanging around my neck, and the sounds of merriment and conversation welcomed us back, grounding us in the present. The warmth of the house enveloped us as we entered the living room, where his family continued to celebrate, oblivious to the shift that had just occurred in the quiet sanctuary of Sawyer's room.

Chapter 17

Now

I place my hand over my heart when I finish reading, the tears temporarily blinding me. I reach for the napkin dispenser and dab at my eyes, trying to stop them, conscious of Sawyer sitting across from me.

"Are you okay?" Sawyer's voice cuts through my haze of emotion, soft but cautious.

"I'm fine." I wave him off, trying to suppress the flood of emotions rising inside me. "I'm just picturing Sarge before he was Sarge. I never thought about how the war could have changed him, or how much pain he was in."

"No, he kept those stories close to his chest," Sawyer agrees quietly, the weight of shared memories sitting between us.

"Yeah." I sigh, leaning back in the chair, my mind drifting to places I've buried for years. The memories—unspoken, unresolved—begin to churn inside me. Sarge's war changed him, and my own battles—the chaos of my mother's alcoholism, years spent trying to hold my family together, and the heartbreak that made me leave—have left scars. Scars I've hidden so well, even from myself. I wonder if Sawyer sees any of that in me now. If he can sense that beneath the layers of who I am now, there's still a broken girl trying to find her way.

"You sure you're okay?" Sawyer asks again, his eyes searching mine, concern creasing his brow.

"I suppose I'm as okay as I can be," I murmur, unsure if this is a conversation I'm ready to have with him, of all people. The air between us hums with too much history, too much hurt, thick enough to choke on.

I glance at him, and the realization lands hard—he was the one behind so much of this pain. *Why am I here with him, sorting through the debris of my past?*

"It feels strange being back here," I add, my voice barely above a whisper, deflecting.

"Hasn't changed much," Sawyer replies, his tone neutral, but there's something in his eyes. Sadness? Pain? I can't quite tell, but it's there, just under the surface. *Has he been hiding his own scars all these years?* The steady, familiar calm he projects is just a front, I realize. There's a storm under there too.

"Not on the surface, but it has," I say, trying to keep the moment light. "I mean—Sarge not sitting on his porch waiting for me, smoking his Lucky Strikes. Can it get any different than that?" I force a laugh, trying to break the heaviness.

Sawyer smiles at the memory, and I feel a sharp pang in my chest when I see it. "Ha! No, it can't. I remember my mom accusing me of smoking when I came back from his house one day. I made her call him to confirm I was just cutting the grass and not smoking his cigarettes."

I laugh lightly, but the sound feels foreign, forced. For a moment, I consider asking him about his life, just to distract myself from my own swirling thoughts. "How is your mom?" I ask cautiously, watching for his reaction.

Sawyer's eyes widen slightly, as if the question caught him off guard. His hesitation makes my heart race—what if something's wrong? I sit up a little straighter, tension squeezing my core.

"She's good, actually," Sawyer says, his smirk revealing slight amusement, as if he's caught me caring. "She got married a few years ago."

"What? Shut up! She did?"

"Yeah. It's a funny story, actually. She ran into this guy she went to day camp with as a kid. He was in town for a wedding or something. Anyway, they start talking, and next thing I know, I'm a grown man with a new stepdad." He chuckles, the fondness clear in his voice. "Ken's a great guy, and my mom is really happy."

"That's amazing. Tell her I said hi." The words leave my mouth before I can stop them. I freeze, realizing what I've just said. "Or . . . maybe don't. I don't want to make it weird."

"It's already weird," he jokes, but there's a tightness behind his smile.

"I loved your mom," I say, more quietly this time.

"She loved you," he replies, his voice soft.

His mom. His family. His house. Everything that was so warm and safe for me at a time when my own world was chaos. The memories press in on me, but I force myself to focus. "Sarge's words keep rattling around in my head. Trying to figure out who he was before life changed him. Before trauma changed him." I glance at Sawyer, and there's a quiet understanding in his gaze. "It kills me that he felt that way, but I think we both know Sarge is getting at something else."

Sawyer nods slowly, his expression contemplative. "Yeah, there's a story here. He wants us to figure it out, obviously."

The silence stretches between us, thick and uncomfortable, before he turns his attention back to the faded photo on the wall. "Mrs. Miner in her salad days. Haven't heard that one before."

"Why wouldn't they get back together after he came back from Vietnam?" I ask, curiosity gnawing at me.

"Maybe she was already married?" Sawyer offers with a shrug.

"Maybe," I say, frowning. "But that's kinda a shitty move, right? Moving on when Sarge was in the jungle."

"Or maybe," Sawyer adds, his voice quiet but pointed, "she didn't love him the way he loved her." His words cling to the air between us, thick with meaning. They cut deeper than they should, hitting too close to home.

I feel the familiar stir of old emotions rising—pain, resentment, longing—but I push it down. Not now. Not here. I take a deep breath, doing my best to center myself. "Or maybe he really did change," I whisper.

Beatrice comes to mind, and panic claws at me as I think about what she might have gone through. The thought of Sarge's possible heartbreak leads me to hers, and I can't shake the worry that the worst has happened to her. Was she abused? Broken? The pain in my heart refuses to subside.

Sawyer glances over at me, sensing the shift in the air. "You've got something you want to ask," he says softly, his eyes following the nervous twist of my hands around the napkin.

I look up, startled. "Why do you say that?"

"You've always done that," he says, nodding to the napkin in my hands. "Twist it around when you're nervous."

I bite my lip, knowing I can't hide anything from him now. "Beatrice told me she's divorced," I say quietly, testing the waters.

Sawyer nods, his expression thoughtful. "Yeah. A few years now."

"She's okay?"

"Did you ask her?"

"Yeah," I admit, "but she didn't want to talk about it."

"She's strong," Sawyer says, a note of pride in his voice. "But no, he didn't hurt her—not like that. He just . . . didn't put her first."

I nod, absorbing his words. "I feel awful that I lost touch with her. I should have tried harder. After—" I catch myself and let the sentence hang in the air.

"After?" he prompts gently, but I can't finish. I'm not ready to go there. I simply shake my head and fix my gaze on a point behind his shoulder, willing myself to keep my emotions in check. The silence stretches between us, far more bearable than digging into a conversation I'm not prepared to have.

Sawyer sighs, a sound of defeat and resignation. "Listen, I know that things are incredibly awkward with us—but Sarge demanded we have ice cream."

A faint laugh slips out of me, the sound a small but necessary release. "I can't not have ice cream here. When we left, I was going to wait until you were out of sight and then come back and order."

"My God, you are ridiculous," he says with a soft laugh, the strain between us easing slightly as he stands up and walks to the counter.

I start to get up, but he holds his hand up, stopping me in my tracks. "Please, Josie. Just wait here."

I don't know why I listen. Maybe it's because I don't want to fight him. Maybe part of me just wants to be here—with him—but I don't want to admit that to myself. I'm not the same weak girl who left here, riddled with guilt that wasn't my own. I'm stronger now. I'm brave and courageous, and I have worked damn hard to make sure nobody will break me the way I was broken when I left this town so many years ago. At least that's what I tell myself most mornings in the mirror.

His back is to me, allowing me to observe him unnoticed. The years have treated him well—he's taller and broader than I remember, his shoulders have widened, and he carries more weight, but it suits him, giving him a presence that is undeniably solid and reassuring. He has matured into the potential he showed early on, filling out into a man who moves with an easy confidence that is both new and familiar. It isn't fair how good he looks. It isn't fair that I can look at him and have to acknowledge to myself why no other man has ever compared. He isn't wearing his baseball cap today. His hair, still wavy, is tidier now, suggesting regular visits to a barber rather than the unruly tousles of his youth—hair that I have run my fingers through so many times before.

I think about his hands, the way they used to cup my face so gently. It's strange, seeing those same hands now, older, rougher, and I can't help but wonder if they are still capable of tenderness.

Never married. A pang of something sharp and unidentifiable shoots through me. Could there have been someone else who held more of his heart than I did? There must have been. Was there a woman—or many women—in those lost years? *Her.* The thought stirs something bitter inside me as I twist my bangles, the familiar metal cool against my skin, steadying me in the moment.

When he returns with the ice cream, he hands me a cup. "Cookies and cream," he says with a small smile.

"Thank you," I murmur, the simple familiarity of the flavor momentarily bridging the gap between past and present.

He nods toward the door, holding it open for me as I step out into the crisp air. He follows, his own ice cream in hand, and we make our way around to the back of the building where picnic tables and heat lamps are set up on a quiet outdoor patio.

"This is where I talked to you for the first time," he says as we settle into our seats, scooping up a bite of ice cream.

"How do you even remember that?" I ask, surprised.

"Josie, how could I forget?" His voice is soft, almost reverent.

I take a spoonful of ice cream, letting the sweet, creamy texture remind me of some of the better days of my past. "Oh my God, this is so good. I missed this."

"Believe it or not, I haven't been here in a while myself."

"Really?" I dig in for another spoonful. "I don't know how you could resist."

"Yeah, well." He shrugs but doesn't explain further.

"I'm sure you have a busy life. What is John Sawyer doing these days?" The question slips out as I allow myself the luxury of curiosity.

"I'm a teacher," he reveals simply, and my expression must register shock because he laughs. "What? Is that surprising?"

"No. No, actually, it's perfect, really." I shake my head, grinning. "Mr. Sawyer. What do you teach?"

"History. Ninth grade."

I wince. "Freshmen. That's tough."

"Nah. It's not that bad, really. And I coach baseball in the spring."

"So those kids were—"

"My students."

I blow out a breath, impressed. "That's really awesome, Sawyer." I pause awkwardly. "So how are you here, then? Why aren't you working?" I ask, my curiosity deepening. "Why weren't they in school?"

"It's Saturday, for one," he replies, amusement flickering across his face.

"Shit, is it?" I laugh, a little embarrassed.

"And I took a few days off for the funeral and whatnot."

"Makes sense." I let that information settle in for a few more moments. "So you still love baseball?"

Sawyer shrugs. "It's a part of me. I coach it. But I don't play. Haven't in a long time."

I don't know why, but that admission makes me incredibly sad.

"How about you? What do you do with your days?" he asks.

"Oh. I'm a teacher too, actually." His eyebrows shoot up in surprise. "Not high school. I teach ESL, English as a second language. To adults."

"Don't they speak English in Ireland?"

"In the cities, there are a lot of other nationalities—like everywhere else. So there are probably loads of Polish people walking around Dublin with a Maplewood, Pennsylvania, accent." I laugh at myself. When I don't hear him join in, I look up from my ice cream to see a gentle smile directed at me.

A wave of emotion forms in my throat, followed by a surge of fear. Fear that this is too much. Too much emotion for me to handle safely. So I do what I have taken to doing when I'm uncomfortable—I keep talking. "I moved to Dublin a few years ago. I never thought I would. I'm not really a big-city person, but that's where I could get work. And then I just sort of stayed."

"Where were you before that?"

"The country. More rural. County Kerry. With my aunt and uncle."

"Are you happy there?" he asks, his voice carrying a weight that demands honesty.

I still, the spoon nearly to my lips before I place it down. How do I answer that? How do I say that I'm okay, but not happy? How do I say that happiness stopped being my goal once I realized it was not achievable? I'm alive. I survived. I have an apartment with decent furniture. I have friends. I even had a boyfriend for two years. I have Dermott and my aunt and uncle, who love me in ways my parents never could or would.

But I live easy. I quit while I'm ahead. I leave the table while I'm still winning. I leave well enough alone. I basically never put myself in a position to get hurt—and that means I stay well inside the lines. That, for me, is living. Feeling? That is too close to dying.

I bite the inside of my lip, and Sawyer chuckles. "You're about to dodge the question." I look at him inquisitively, and he points at me with his spoon. "You bit the inside of your lip. It's one of your signature moves."

I tilt my head and roll my eyes. "If you must know—I'm not unhappy."

"See. Dodged it."

"What? I'm not unhappy!"

"Are you *happy*?"

"I'm okay," I answer quickly. "And that's better than—better than a lot of things." I'm temporarily satisfied with my answer. "How about you? Are you happy?"

"I haven't been happy in fifteen years, Josie."

His answer is so sudden and unexpected and blunt that I don't know how to react. I don't know how to bow out gracefully from this conversation. I don't know how to leave on a high note. I freeze and then fumble.

"Well, you seem to be doing okay—"

"*Okay* was never the goal for me."

"Yeah, well, what was your goal?" I feel the anger brewing, the pain opening, and the red lava creeping up through my chest.

"You. Anything as long as it was with you. That was the goal. That was happy. Okay was never the goal."

"Well, sometimes okay is all we've got."

"Yeah, I guess so," he concedes, his gaze drifting away for a moment before returning to meet mine.

I try to will my heart to slow down to a normal pace. I try to stop the sadness from rising in my throat. See, this is why. This is why I keep myself in a safe little box. Because these feelings are enough to obliterate me where I sit, and I cannot go through it again.

We sit in silence for a moment longer, the tension between us thick and unbearable. I try to think of something to say, something to ease the ache in my chest, but the words won't come.

Finally, I stand. "We should focus on what Sarge wanted us to do. It's safer." As soon as I say it, I flinch. I shouldn't have said safer.

"Safer?" he questions, a hint of challenge in his tone.

"Yes, Sawyer, better off. Okay? We had an understanding. I let my guard down for a second, and I shouldn't have." I feel the anxiety creeping in and start counting the things around me, hoping he doesn't notice. He takes me in for a moment, like he is deciding what to pursue and what to leave behind.

"You're right." He nods, and that's when I know he sees me counting.

After a moment, we edge onto somewhat safer ground, so I sit back down.

"Mrs. Miner, though? I can't picture it," Sawyer says.

"Roberta? That's the R in RP." The words come out in relief, and I feel my anxiety begin to subside.

"I wonder what her maiden name was?" Sawyer muses.

"I'm staying at Miner's, and Dermott has gotten to be friends with her, so I could probably get the scoop."

And with the mention of Dermott, the air becomes charged.

A heavy sigh escapes Sawyer. "Josie, I am so sorry about the whole thing with Dermott. I'm at a loss here. This is tearing me apart."

A spark of frustration flares within me. I just got off the precipice of an anxiety attack, and I'm tired. "Sawyer, please, I can't rehash this right now. It's too much."

"I know," he pleads, his voice raw, "but I am begging you. I know it doesn't matter to you. I know I don't matter to you, but I have not slept. My mind has been racing, trying to figure out this mess in my head. I can't put the pieces together."

And I snap.

"Because that dirty little skank you were so fond of tricked you into thinking my cousin was my boyfriend. Here's an idea. Maybe you should have asked me?" And I am off to the races, my words laced with sarcasm.

Sawyer runs a hand over his face. "That's not the way it happened, Josie."

"Ah, so you admit something happened."

He looks genuinely perplexed. "What? No. What are you—"

"Spare me the details, Sawyer. It has been fifteen years. We've both moved on."

"I haven't moved on," he says quietly, and the raw sincerity in his voice nearly knocks the wind out of me. It would be a lie to say that it doesn't touch a raw, tender part of my heart. But along with that tenderness comes a resurgence of anger.

"Well, I have." My voice is flat, resolute.

He nods slowly, accepting those words. "I never believed you left me for another guy."

"Well, Sawyer, I'm glad you know I didn't leave you for my cousin." My voice drips with disdain, even though the bitterness in my chest makes it hard to breathe.

Sawyer rubs his face, exasperation clear. "I didn't know he was your cousin. And when you didn't come back . . . it was the easiest story to tell myself."

I roll my eyes. "This again?" I throw my hands up, feeling the familiar anger bubble up. "I did come back! You, of all people, know this! Or did you expect me to come back twice?"

A puzzled look crosses Sawyer's face. "You didn't come back."

I shake my head, letting out a dry laugh. "Oh, right. I guess you were too busy with your little pleasure fest to notice." I don't bother to hide my disgust. "But I came back, Sawyer. You know I did. Ask your girlfriend."

And with that, I am out of my seat and gathering my bag. I toss the rest of my ice cream in the trash nearby and then turn back to him. "But regardless of how I feel about you, I owe everything to Sarge, and I'm going to see this through for him." Sawyer looks stricken.

I start toward the exit, looking back at a stunned Sawyer. "So the football field tomorrow. See you there. Same time," I say, trying to hide the memories Sawyer and I have there ourselves.

"Tomorrow." He nods.

I take a breath as I step onto the sidewalk, the cold air biting at my skin. It's only after I start down the street that I realize my hands are shaking.

Chapter 18

Then

The fluorescent lights of the Maplewood High auditorium buzzed faintly overhead as students and parents filled the rows of cushioned seats. The air was thick with the hum of anticipation, a mixture of whispers and the faint rustle of programs as people fidgeted, waiting for Awards Night to begin.

It was nearing the end of my junior year, and this ceremony was one of the precursors to the larger awards events, meant to recognize achievements in individual subjects for underclassmen. I suspected it was held separately to keep the senior honors ceremony from running too long. I was being honored for the publication of an essay I had written on children's mental health in *The Adolescent Wellness Review*—a national quarterly journal geared toward young academics.

The only person who even knew my essay had been accepted for publication was my psychology teacher, so when Sawyer and Beatrice found out, they were dumbfounded. Not because they didn't think I was capable, but because I had never mentioned it. As it turns out, it was a pretty big deal.

I glanced around nervously, searching for any sign of Sawyer in the crowd. I knew he would be late. I hadn't actually expected him to come because he had a baseball game, but he'd insisted he would never miss this. The past year had been a whirlwind with him by my side, but tonight felt different. More intense.

More significant. The school year was winding down, that magical cusp of spring turning into summer, and I had finally decided it was safe for Sawyer to meet my mom. This seemed like a safe place to do it.

Mom sat beside me, stiff and unnaturally quiet. She looked good—too good, really, with her hair perfectly curled and makeup applied with precision, entirely different from the woman who, when drunk, looked like she'd crawled out of a cave. But her composure had a sharp edge to it, a tension I could feel radiating off her. I was so hyperaware of her moods that it was hard to breathe.

I knew she was brooding, simmering just beneath the surface. When I told her about the award, she was smugly proud. Of course, her daughter was being recognized. She should get credit for my outstanding achievements because, without her, I'd never have had the opportunities or education to accomplish this. Naturally, it must have come from my Catholic schooling. She was still bitter that I was attending public school. But she'd walked in here, head held high, because her daughter was important tonight.

But when we walked in and I was immediately greeted by Sarge, who had come just to see me receive the award, and she saw the Knights congratulating me warmly, also there for me, I could feel her mood shift. When she saw me smiling and laughing, receiving praise, I felt her body stiffen beside me. I can only think she felt like an outsider—because she was. They were making a big deal of me and my achievement—and I don't think my mom even knew what I had done to earn the recognition. I must have taken something from her in that moment without even realizing it. So I found myself fawning over her. Trying to bring her into the loop. Trying to make her happy and comfortable. Pointing out things in the school I thought she'd like or find interesting. Trying to include her in conversations in the lobby. But nothing worked. I could see the look in her eyes. Everything I did was wrong. Everything I said was wrong. And to make it worse, Sawyer would be meeting her in this state of mind.

Dad had managed to escape this one. A sudden business trip, he'd claimed, though we both knew it was a convenient excuse. So it was just me, Mom, and this uncomfortable social setting.

Mrs. Knight had been a good friend of my mom's when we first moved to Maplewood. I vaguely remembered her coming over with a mini Beatrice in tow, spending time at our house. I'd found pictures of those days, discarded in a plastic bin in the attic. I'm sure my mother would've destroyed them if she remembered they were there. I asked my dad what happened once, and he just sighed and said, "What always happens." As I got older, I saw the pattern. My mom would make a friend, they'd get too close, see too much, and she'd inevitably find some character flaw in the friend and push them away. If she couldn't ghost them, she'd fight with them. I was grateful the Knights had allowed her to ghost them, because if there had been an outward fight, it would've made my friendship with Beatrice more difficult.

Mom might've been seething with rage when we arrived in the lobby and saw my little support system—but she'd never show it on the outside. I would get the brunt of it later. Still, I watched her closely, hoping for any sign of pride, joy, or happiness. I was always hopeful.

When we first arrived, Mom's charm was on full display. "Sarge! Always a pleasure to see you." Now I knew she was full of shit because, like the Knights, my mom was fully aware that Sarge knew her secret and didn't consider her a victim. She kept her distance from "that nosy old man," as she called him. She resented our friendship.

There were times when I reflected on how the people who loved and supported me—Sarge, Beatrice, and her parents—were disliked by my mother. It spoke volumes, but I always turned the noise down. It was too loud. But now I worried about how long it would take before she turned on Sawyer too. A twinge of anxiety twisted inside me as I wondered how Sawyer's close relationship with Sarge would color her opinion of him. In truth, my mom did nothing to warrant her opinion meaning so much to me—but it did. I wanted her approval so badly.

Sarge chuckled. "You have a wonderful daughter there, Nancy."

"Oh, I don't know about that." She laughed again. "No, I do. I do." She wrapped an arm around me and smiled. Even though I wasn't sure of her authenticity in this moment, I chose to believe it was real.

My mom's mood shifted as soon as we sat down, with Sarge and the Knights a few rows behind us.

As the principal took the stage and began the ceremony, I spotted Sawyer making his way down the aisle, his tall frame standing out among the other attendees. He held a small bouquet of wildflowers, plucked from the roadside, and when he caught my eye, he gave me a quick, reassuring smile.

"You're on the program, love," Mom said, flipping through it as though the words were of little consequence. "Let's get this over with. I need a cigarette," she muttered under her breath.

I bristled but said nothing. There was no point in starting something now, especially not here. I just wanted to get through the night without incident.

Sawyer arrived at our row, offering a polite nod to my mother. "Mrs. O'Driscoll," he greeted her, holding out the flowers with a gentle smile. "These are for you."

Her eyes flicked from the flowers to him, a fleeting look of surprise crossing her face. "Thank you," she said, accepting them with a tight-lipped smile that didn't quite reach her eyes. "Very thoughtful."

I could feel the tension crackling between them, but Sawyer, ever the optimist, seemed unfazed. He slid into the seat next to me, his hand brushing mine in a gesture of quiet support. I exhaled, grateful for his presence, even as my stomach churned with nerves.

The ceremony dragged on, name after name being called to the stage. My mother shifted in her seat every few minutes, checking her watch or sighing impatiently. I knew she hated events like this. She hated anything that required her to play the part of the dutiful parent, and it was only a matter of time before her mask slipped.

Finally, the principal called my name, glancing down at an index card like he was seeing it for the first time. Clearing his throat, he began to read, his tone betraying a hint of surprise.

"Josephine O'Driscoll, a junior at Maplewood High School, is being recognized for her contributions to a nationally recognized publication focused on issues affecting teenagers and young adults, particularly in the fields of mental and emotional health, education, and social development."

He paused, his brow furrowing slightly as if weighing the significance of the words. When he continued, there was an almost reluctant admiration in his voice, like he hadn't expected to be impressed.

"The journal seeks to amplify the voices of young writers, educators, and healthcare professionals, providing a platform for innovative ideas and personal stories. Its mission is to raise awareness around adolescent mental health and wellness, offering practical advice, research insights, and personal essays from a variety of perspectives."

By the time he finished, his gaze lifted briefly from the card to meet mine, a trace of acknowledgment in his expression that sent a murmur through the crowd. I stood, feeling a flush creep up my neck as the applause washed over me. Sawyer squeezed my hand before I made my way to the stage.

As I accepted my certificate, I scanned the audience. My eyes landed on my mother. She was clapping, but it looked robotic, as if the action was purely for show. She caught my gaze and gave me a tight smile. There was no pride there, only obligation, and maybe even a hint of jealousy.

Sawyer was standing, clapping, beaming up at me, his smile wide and genuine. His pride was palpable, and it made something inside me ache. I caught the smiles of Sarge and the Knights. This was what it was supposed to feel like—unconditional support. The contrast between them and my mom was glaring, and I suddenly felt a surge of anger toward her.

As I returned to my seat, I caught the tail end of a whispered exchange between my mom and Sawyer.

"She's incredible," Sawyer said, his voice calm but firm, as if daring her to disagree.

Mom just nodded, not meeting his gaze. "Yes, well . . . she's been given a lot of opportunities."

My jaw clenched as I sat down. The comment stung, a veiled jab that hit harder than I expected. I wanted to say something to defend myself, but I couldn't. Not here. Not now. I knew better. Instead, I forced a smile, trying to focus on the ceremony as it continued, though my heart wasn't in it anymore.

Sawyer leaned over, his voice low. "You okay?"

I nodded, though I wasn't sure if it was true. "I just . . . I'm ready for this to be over," I whispered back, my voice tight with the emotion I was trying to hold in.

The ceremony finally came to an end, and as people began to file out, I stood quickly, eager to escape the heavy atmosphere that clung to the night. Mom, ever the performer, bid a few polite goodbyes to other parents as we made our way to the exit, but I could see the strain in her expression.

I assumed she was bringing me home, but as I was saying my goodbyes to the Knights, she got in the car and drove away—leaving me standing on the sidewalk. The abruptness of her departure left me frozen, feeling hollow and deflated.

Sawyer hadn't left yet. He approached and slipped his arm around me, pulling me close. "You are amazing," he said softly, his voice steady and comforting. "Don't let her ruin this for you. I've got you. I'll bring you home."

"She left them under her seat."

His brow furrowed slightly. "What did she leave under her seat?"

I looked into his eyes, feeling the burn of unshed tears. "Your flowers. She didn't even take them."

Sawyer's expression shifted, a hint of pain on my behalf flickering across his face. "Josie," he said gently, like I was being too hard on myself. "It's okay. I don't care about that."

"I do."

He sighed softly, pulling me closer. "I know. But all I care about right now is you. Okay?" He ducked his head a little, searching my eyes. "Okay?"

I nodded, leaning into his warmth, but the weight of my mother's indifference still pressed down on me. As we walked toward Sawyer's car, I couldn't shake the feeling that no matter how much I accomplished, no matter how well I did, it would never be enough for her.

Sawyer didn't bring me straight home. Instead, we made our way to our special bench under the maple tree in the park. We sat quietly for a while. I was having a hard time pretending that I wasn't crushed by my mother's brush-off.

Sawyer's eyes were on me, his presence anchoring me as the quiet of the park wrapped around us. The stillness was such a contrast to the storm swirling in my head. He waited, not pushing, just letting me sit with my thoughts until I was ready.

"You've been really quiet," he said softly, his voice careful, like he didn't want to shatter the fragile moment. "Do you want to talk about it?"

I shrugged, my gaze fixed on the ground beneath my feet. "I don't even know what to say. I guess . . . I knew she'd do something like this, but it still hurts."

Sawyer shifted closer, his arm tightening around my shoulders. "There's nothing I hate more than seeing you hurt. I wish I could take it all away."

Usually, I'd force a smile, brush it off like I always did. I'd bury it deep down so no one, especially Sawyer, would have to sit with the discomfort I'd grown so used to. I'd been protecting everyone from this part of me for so long. But tonight . . . I just didn't have it in me.

I sighed, the tension in my chest loosening just a little. "I don't know why it still gets to me. I should be used to it by now, right?"

Sawyer squeezed me a little tighter, his voice firm. "No. No, Josie. I don't ever want you to get used to being treated like that. You deserve so much more."

His words were like a balm, soothing the ache inside me. But at the same time, they stung because I wasn't sure I believed him. My voice came out small. "It's just . . . no matter what I do, it's never enough. I could win every award, do everything right, and it still wouldn't change anything."

Sawyer turned slightly, lifting my chin gently so I'd look at him. His eyes were filled with something deeper than I could even put into words—love, yes, but also this unshakable belief in me. "Listen to me, Josie. You are more than enough. You always have been. Your mom . . . she doesn't see it, but that's on her. It doesn't change who you are. You are so strong, so brilliant, and the way you keep going despite everything? That's incredible."

My chest tightened again, but this time it wasn't from pain. It was something else—something lighter, like a flicker of hope I didn't want to acknowledge yet.

"I don't feel that strong right now," I whispered, my voice breaking a little.

He leaned his forehead against mine, his voice gentle but filled with conviction. "You don't have to feel it all the time for it to be true. You are strong, Josie. Even in the moments you doubt it, I see it. And one day, you're going to see it too. I promise."

His words wrapped around me, and for the first time that night, I let myself believe—just for a second—that maybe, just maybe, things could be different. That I could be different. That I didn't have to let her hold this power over me.

Sawyer's fingers brushed my cheek, wiping away a tear I didn't realize had fallen. "I love you, Josie. And I'm not going anywhere. You're going to rise above this. You've already started."

"Thank you. You are—you are so special to me."

"Oh, Josie, if you only knew how much I think about you and wonder what the hell a girl like you is doing with me."

A sudden burst of laughter escaped my lips, shifting the dynamic. "You're crazy, but you're awesome."

"You are."

"Which one? Crazy or awesome?" I giggled.

"Both." Sawyer bopped me on the nose, and we laughed together, sharing an adorable moment in the midst of the drama of the day.

"Did you figure out what day you leave for Ireland?" Sawyer asked, hesitation in his voice, like he was dreading the answer. It was typical for me to be gone for eight to ten weeks in the summer.

I smiled, remembering I hadn't told him yet. "August."

"August?" he asked in disbelief. "But—"

"I'm not going for the whole summer this year. Just two weeks." I squealed. "What a first-world problem to have." I snapped my fingers and made a mock-disappointed face. "I'm not spending the whole summer in Ireland."

"I am so happy you are forced to spend most of your summer in this tiny, uneventful borough in Pennsylvania," Sawyer joked as he held me close. I could feel the steady beat of his heart against mine, reassuring and strong.

"Me too," I replied, my words muffled against his chest. The scent of him—soap and a hint of cologne—filled my senses, rooting me in the moment.

Sawyer leaned back, his hands framing my face, his eyes searching mine. "Two weeks is still too long, but I guess I can handle it if it means you'll come back to me."

"I'll always come back to you," I promised, the sincerity in my voice mirroring the depth of my feelings. "I love you," I said, my heart swelling with affection for this boy who made everything seem so simple, so right. "And maybe, one day, you'll come to Ireland with me?" It was a question. A sure signal that I hoped he would want to come with me one day.

Sawyer's grin widened. "I love you too. And I promise one day I will go to Ireland with you." We settled together on the bench. "Tell me what we would do. What would you show me?"

I found myself eagerly sharing tales of my second home across the sea. As I toyed with the claddagh necklace around my neck, I described the unique scent of turf mingling with fresh morning rain, a smell that evoked memories of my childhood. I reminisced about the lush fields where I'd spent countless hours running freely, and I chattered happily about my favorite Irish chocolates, candies, and crisps that were nowhere to be found here. I told him about my family, my favorite places to go, and where I liked to sit on my uncle's farm and think.

Sawyer listened with rapt attention, his eyes alight with wonder. I suspected his fascination was sparked more by my enthusiasm than by the quaint details of the little country I spoke of. Imagining him by my side there one day, exploring the rolling green landscapes and sharing those beloved treats, filled me with an exhilarating sense of possibility.

"I want more than anything to go there with you." He kissed my lips softly. "Because I don't feel like I could ever really know you without knowing that part of you too."

And yet, he seemed to know me so well already. But what he couldn't have known, what no one could have known, was that when I got home that night, my mother was drunk.

Chapter 19

Now

The days are slipping away, and a nagging worry that Sarge's loose ends might take more time than I have begins to weigh on me. After leaving Sawyer at the ice cream shop, I find myself wandering through the familiar streets of Maplewood, lost in a haze of nostalgia and uncertainty. I walk around the track at Holy Redeemer, through the old cemetery behind St. Mary's, and down the quiet neighborhood streets that were the backdrop of my youth. I go almost everywhere familiar—almost.

Eventually, I return to Miner's Inn, reminding myself to keep my composure if I encounter Mrs. Miner. I am still waiting for more clues from Sarge, which feels odd—relying on hints from someone who isn't around anymore. His letters have become a lifeline, guiding me through this tangled web of memories and unresolved feelings.

Pausing outside Miner's, I take a moment to really look at it. It was always part of the backdrop of my youth, but now it's quickly becoming central to my story. Miner's, with its gabled roof and large, inviting windows, stands prominently on Maplewood's main drag. I find myself wondering how Mrs. Miner ended up owning it and what part Sarge played in its history.

This time, instead of hurrying to my room, I walk in with the intention of really seeing the place. There's a cozy room off to the side, with a wall full of books, a couple of comfy chairs, and an ottoman by the window. Mrs. Miner's brother is there, sitting and staring out the window, his gaze distant. I decide to quietly slink away, not wanting to bother him and also avoiding any confusing banter.

My mind keeps going back to Sarge's letters. My heart breaks at the thought of him having unfinished business that he needed Sawyer and me to handle—that he felt like he had failed at something while he was alive. I know Sarge wanted to throw the two of us together and saw an opportunity. But it doesn't change the fact that something gnawed at him for most of his life—something he couldn't face while he was alive.

I can still picture the day I sat in his cluttered kitchen, trying to hold it together after one of my mother's episodes. Sarge didn't press for details. He never did. Instead, he set a cup of tea in front of me and said, "Josie, sometimes it's the ones we love that hurt us the most. But you've got a choice—let them drown you or let them show you how strong you are." His gaze was steady, full of understanding that didn't require any explanation. I felt seen in a way that few people ever made me feel. He didn't fix things, but he always made me believe I could. And right now, I wish I had him sitting here across from me, guiding me through all of this chaos the way he used to.

I shake my head, trying to clear the swirling thoughts. "Mrs. Miner, eh? She must have been one hell of a lady in her salad days after all," I murmur to myself, glancing around the inn. In fairness, the feat she must have undertaken to run Miner's for as long as she did—and as successfully—couldn't have come easily. It's clear she has a lot of help now, given her advancing age and her small but attentive staff, but she must have been a force to be reckoned with if she developed this place into the thriving business it is as a widow.

The front desk is empty at the moment, with a small bell neatly placed for anyone needing assistance. On the other side is a little dining room that looks like it could seat everyone staying in the inn's ten or so rooms. I figure the kitchen is through the door on the other side of the dining area. The lobby, with a beautiful Oriental rug and some chairs, feels welcoming—a homey spot right in the center of the inn. Off to the left, a hallway leads to five rooms, with likely more upstairs.

On the other side is a lovely patio that I give only a passing glance to at this point. I just don't have the time. Miner's is indeed quaint, a small but charming haven in the heart of Maplewood.

I walk down the quiet hallway and knock on Dermott's door but get no response. I figure he's probably out exploring our picturesque little town, and here I am, possibly the worst travel companion ever. With a sigh, I head back to my room to regroup.

Alone with my thoughts, I ponder everything that has been said—and left unsaid—between Sawyer and me. Do I really want to delve into what Val did? How did she manage to convince Sawyer that I'd left him for another man and jetted across the globe when nothing in our relationship had ever suggested such a betrayal? Where did it all go so wrong? And does it even matter anymore?

The words from Sarge's letter echo in my mind: *Not everything is as it seems, and the truth often hides in plain sight.* I shudder at the thought that tries to push its way to the forefront of my mind. It couldn't be more straightforward, I think bitterly—Val smirking at me as my life burst into flames around me.

Back then, I made it through to the other side of that pain, and I'm not eager to revisit it. Yet there's a part of me—the young girl who loved Sawyer too much, who saw him as her safe harbor and was shattered because of it—that craves those answers. She deserves to know. But that girl has also seen too much death, come too close to her own demise. She crossed a bridge to a place from which she can't return without risking everything. To go back would be to jeopardize her survival.

I watch from the window of my room as the wind picks up outside, rustling the trees. Something about the stark, restless scene takes me back—back to my father. Thomas O'Driscoll, or Tommy, as everyone in Ireland called him. He was once my rock in a sea of chaos, the funny, vibrant soul that lit up every room he entered. People in Ireland still speak of him fondly, their eyes twinkling with the memories of a man full of life and laughter.

When I was a child, he used to lift me up high, showing me off to his family in Ireland like a prized possession. "Look at my Josie," he'd say with pride, his Irish accent making every word sound like a melody. "She's the light of my life." I remember those trips vividly, the way he'd take me by the hand and lead me through the bustling streets, introducing me to distant relatives and old friends.

They all adored him—Tommy, the boy who'd left for America with dreams of striking gold and making it big.

In those early years, before my mother's alcoholism consumed our lives, my dad was my hero. He had a spirit that couldn't be contained, always eager to take on the world with a smile and a laugh. But as the years went by, that spirit dimmed, crushed under the weight of my mother's addiction and the endless cycle of enabling and martyrdom he had fallen into.

My father loved my mother fiercely, even as her drinking spiraled out of control. At first, he was always trying to protect me from the worst of her tirades, shielding me with his love and loyalty. And he was strangely loyal, in some ways, standing by her even when it meant sacrificing his own happiness and dreams. I loved him for it—for the way he never gave up on her, on us, even when the world seemed to be falling apart.

I shake my head, trying to clear the fog of the past, but it lingers. The memories always come back when I least expect them. When things got bad, when my mother's rages became too much to bear, my father would whisk me away to the relative safety of another room, whispering soothing words, telling me stories of his youth in Ireland, of the dreams he once had. "Don't worry, Josie," he'd say, his voice a soft comfort in the storm. "We'll get through this, together. Your mother will be just fine. She's just merry right now."

"Mary?" I'd asked, confusing *merry* with another woman's name.

"Yes, merry." He would smile, trying to choose a softer word than *drunk*. But in my innocent mind, I believed that "Merry" was an actual person—a mean, nasty woman named Mary who had temporarily replaced my mother. I eagerly waited for Mary to leave so that Nancy, the mother I loved, could return. To me, they were two separate beings—one could not exist with the other.

But even as my dad tried to protect me from Mary, I saw the toll it took on him. The way he became a shell of the man he once was, trapped in a cycle of enabling my mother's behavior, always hoping that things would get better, that she would change. His love for her was like a vise, squeezing the life out of him until there was nothing left but a man who had given up everything.

Eventually, my dad tired of the relentless battle, and the weight of my mother's addiction grew too heavy for him to bear alone. He stopped protecting me, and in a painful twist, began to use me as a shield against her. By the time I was ten, I was no longer the protected; I was thrust into the role of enabler, forced to shoulder responsibilities no child should ever have to bear. Babysitting my mother so he could "work," but never really knowing where he was or what he was doing—and never wanting to ask. I didn't want to know the answers, but I imagined his loyalty had its limits.

I actively concealed the reality of our life, crafting lies for teachers and friends to explain away the absences from school, the slurred way my mother would answer the phone, or why the police lights were shining outside my house. Without even realizing it, I slipped into the role of enabler, becoming the one thread holding our fractured home together. I was an expert at navigating the storm of my mother's rages and the hollow spaces left by my father's frequent absences. The weight of it all pressed down on me, heavier than my mother's addiction. It wasn't just the torment of living with an alcoholic mother; it was the deep, searing betrayal of knowing that my dad—the one person who should have shielded me—had left me time and again to face the very danger he was meant to protect me from. To him, as long as I was fed and breathing, everything was fine. If the wounds weren't visible, they didn't matter. But no one could see the bruises on my heart, the fractures forming in my mind. I became the one tasked with ensuring our survival, struggling to guard the shattered remnants of our lives with no tools, no guidance—because my father wouldn't take up the mantle, and my mother refused to clean herself up.

I close my eyes for a moment, trying to picture him as he was before her drinking took over—before the bright, hopeful man who came to America to make it big became a shadow of himself. Those fleeting glimpses of the man he once was, the Tommy who was full of hope and aspirations, always stayed with me. I clung to them, even as I watched him slowly lose himself in the struggle to prop my mother up. I sometimes wonder why that was even the goal.

When I left fifteen years ago, I promised myself that I would never let someone hold my heart so tightly that they'd squeeze the life out of me, like my mother had done to him. I didn't want to turn out like my dad, a man who had given so much of himself that there was nothing left of him. Whatever life I had left after all the trauma, I vowed to protect it fiercely, to never let anyone take that from me. But just as strongly, I knew I couldn't end up with someone like my father—someone who would abandon me when the darkness closed in.

Yet here I am, back in the place that holds so many memories, so many echoes of the past. The girl who left with a broken heart and a shattered spirit is still inside me, yearning for answers. She deserves to know why everything went so wrong, why the love that seemed so strong with Sawyer fell apart. But the fear of letting love destroy me has added more bricks to the wall I've built around myself. That girl might never find out why. Protecting her means I can't seek the truth, even if that's exactly what Sarge wants me to do.

Exhausted, I throw myself onto the bed and lie there motionless, allowing myself a rare moment to simply feel—to truly acknowledge the weight of the anguish pressing on my heart. It is terrifyingly profound. My hand instinctively finds its way to my chest, resting just above my heart as the tears begin to flow. They come first as quiet whimpers, then grow into wild, uncontrollable sobs until sleep mercifully sweeps me away.

***

A few hours later, a sharp knock on my door jolts me awake. "Josie, are you in there?" Dermott's voice carries a hint of concern, piercing through the fog of my sleep.

Groggily, I reply, "Coming!" as I scramble to my feet. The exhaustion from travel, the weight of profound grief, and the emotional toll of confronting my past have finally caught up with me, knocking me flat.

I open the door to find Dermott stepping past me with an urgency that speaks volumes. "For fuck's sake! I've been ringing you for hours," Dermott says, his tone somewhere between exasperation and concern. "Jesus Christ! My nerves!"

"I must have fallen asleep. What time is it?" I ask, my voice thick with sleep. My stomach growls loudly, a painful reminder of how I've neglected even the basic need for food.

"It's already half six, and the festival's about to kick off. If we don't get moving, we'll miss all the fun, and I'm not waiting till the last of the stalls is packing up," Dermott says, a spark of excitement lighting his face.

"Oh my God, that's right. The Harvest Festival." Memories surge through my mind, unbidden and vivid. There was the year my dad thwarted my attempt to go with Sawyer, insisting I stay home for a family dinner—but really, I had to make sure my mother didn't throw up in her sleep or light the house on fire. But there was another year, when I snuggled up to Sawyer, our hands wrapped around steaming cups of hot cider as he whispered sweet words into my ear. The Maplewood Harvest Festival had always been a cherished event, a beacon of warmth and joy in the chill of autumn.

"Fancy a stroll down there, then? Could be good to stretch our legs and take it all in," Dermott says, his eyes twinkling as he waits for my response. "I heard there's a band too."

"Yes, and I'm starving. If it's anything like it used to be, there'll be some awesome food there." My face lights up with a memory, a fleeting joy piercing through the melancholy. "Oh! I wonder if they still have that veggie chili? It was so good." I'm already looking through my clothes for a cardigan.

"Oh dear. Cousin Josephine is famished. Let's get her fed before she gets a headache," Dermott teases, a playful smile softening his features. "Get yourself ready. I'll meet you out front in ten minutes."

As Dermott leaves, I quickly begin pulling myself together, my earlier grogginess giving way to a mix of anticipation and sadness. The thought of wandering through the festival, experiencing the sights and sounds that once filled me with so much joy, is almost too much to bear. I remember how Sawyer and I traversed the booths my junior year, hand in hand, laughing and tasting everything in sight. Why did it all have to go from so good to so terribly wrong?

A tightness grips my chest, a familiar ache that reminds me of the fragility of my healing journey. I fear that this trip back to Maplewood will set me back years, reopening wounds that have only just begun to scar over. But it's too late now. I'm here, and there is no turning back. I have to face whatever lies ahead, even if it means confronting the ghosts of my past. But I'll do it carefully.

***

After eating our way through all the food vendors, we find ourselves beneath the beer tent—undoubtedly one of the festival's top attractions, and one I never got to experience during my time living here. Returning as an adult certainly has its perks. Although I'm not much of a drinker for obvious reasons, I do enjoy a drink in social settings, which usually means only with Dermott if there's a rare chance we meet up in Dublin. The truth is, playing it safe has turned me into something of an introvert.

We settle at a high-top table, soaking in the lively atmosphere, when I notice Dermott watching me closely over the rim of his pint glass.

"What?" I ask.

"You've been crying. Your eyes are puffy."

"How do you know it's not from being absolutely exhausted?" I say, drawing out the last words.

"Because I know you."

I drop my shoulders, admitting defeat. There is no point in lying to Dermott. "Seeing Sawyer is—" I search for a word to describe it and come up short. "Hard."

He nods, knowing better than anyone how bone-deep my grief goes. "I was afraid of this but also expected it. But I didn't expect you'd have to go on a scavenger hunt with the fucking man or learn that some little slut had him convinced I wasn't your cousin."

I shake my head. "No. That timeline doesn't work. Even if he thought I'd moved on with someone else, it wouldn't have been until after." I take a sip of my drink.

"After what?"

I roll my eyes because the answer is obvious. "After his birthday."

Dermott taps a beer coaster on the table, clearly trying to piece it all together. "Seems Beatrice has an idea of what happened."

I tilt my head, curious. "And?"

"I was worried about you, of course. *Am* worried about you. So I popped into the flower shop today to see what the craic was."

I know Beatrice has her theories. She mentioned them the night before at the Maplewood Bar and Grill, but I didn't entertain them. Beatrice doesn't know everything about what happened—only Dermott does, to be fair. But I suppose

I could've asked her thoughts, though the mention of Val sets off a response in me I'm not prepared for.

"She really had no idea you came back before now," he says, looking sad on her behalf.

I digest that for a second. "Neither did Sawyer, apparently."

Dermott's mouth drops. "How is that possible?"

"It's *not* possible. But it doesn't matter, does it? I was basically a kid. I'm not the same. He's not the same."

"Are you trying to convince me or yourself?"

"Dermott, you know what happened to me after. Entertaining anything other than getting the hell out of here in—what day is it now? Four days? Entertaining anything else is risky."

"Josie," he says, leaning in, "that won't happen again. And you can't be living in fear that it will. It was a perfect storm, and you were just a child in the middle of it. You were reared to believe things about yourself that weren't true. You've done all the hard work. Now, would you ever stop living like the storm is coming? It's not. It's over."

"But other storms—"

"Ah, for fuck's sake, life is full of them! Would you ever cop on? There's no one stronger than you. I wish you could see what I do. What everyone sees, Josie." He shakes his head. "You see yourself as weak when you're the strongest person I know." I look down, knowing he's right, practically, but never able to fully believe it. "Look, I'm only saying you have the right to get the story—or the excuse, whatever it is. You owe it to yourself. Or at least to the young woman who came to Ireland all those years ago."

We sit quietly for a while as I absorb his words. Dermott may hide behind his jokes, but beneath it all, he's one of the most thoughtful people I've ever known. He's proven it time and time again, especially in moments like this, when his words reveal just how deeply he understands me. On some level, I know he's right, but when you're constantly afraid, it's hard to expose yourself. Vulnerability can be a deadly flaw, and here I am, swimming in it.

"You're right. I know you are." I go into the details of the day with Sawyer at the ice cream shop, Sarge's letter, Mrs. Miner, and the exchange with Sawyer that left me reeling.

Dermott listens, like always. "Talk to Beatrice. Hell, talk to Sawyer. Then decide what to do with the information. No one expects you to move back to Maplewood and live happily ever after—but you might live a little happier in Dublin with this shit sorted. Don't let this life haunt you anymore."

Suddenly, a little ball of sunshine in the form of Beatrice appears. "Hey, you guys!" She pulls her petite body onto the open stool at our high-top. "Fancy seeing you here."

As crappy as I'm feeling, Beatrice's energy is contagious. "Yay! You're here!" I find myself celebrating.

Dermott chuckles beside me. "Ah no, Josie. While you've been out gallivanting on your scavenger hunt, Beatrice has been minding me. She's here as my friend tonight."

I gasp. "Never! You can't have her. She's mine."

The night takes an unexpectedly jovial turn. The band starts playing a series of the best eighties sing-along songs, sending Dermott into another galaxy altogether. For the next couple of hours, Beatrice and I cling to each other, laughing while Dermott guzzles pints and sings at the top of his lungs—terribly.

I'm relieved that the tears I'm wiping from my eyes are from laughter and not pain for once. But, my heart sinks into my legs when I spot Sawyer at the bar nearby. I know he sees me, but we both look away, pretending we didn't catch each other staring. When his back is turned, I nod in his direction so Beatrice can see he's there. She looks over and frowns, clearly feeling awkward. I lean in, speaking over the music and Dermott's impromptu karaoke. "Bea, you could go sit with him. I won't be offended."

She waves me off. "It's okay!" she shouts over the music as she hops off her stool. "I'll just bring him over here."

Beatrice makes a beeline for Sawyer before I can protest, and a knot tightens in my stomach as I watch her chatting with him at the bar. *What is she doing?* This isn't like her. Beatrice doesn't usually push this hard. Maybe she thinks dragging him over will force me to confront something I'm not ready to face.

But as they walk back together, I catch the glint in her eye. This isn't just playful—she's testing something, watching us both carefully, waiting to see what happens. I want to tell her to stop, to let things stay buried where they belong. But a part of me—the one still aching from seeing Sawyer earlier—wonders if maybe she's right. Maybe it's time to face this, whether I like it or not.

Meanwhile, Dermott is still harmonizing with an older lady at the next table, his voice loud and carefree. Suddenly, he turns to me and shouts over the quieting music, "Josie, remember when you nearly got engaged to that eejit from Kildare? The lad loved this feckin' song, and now I have to hate it!"

I groan, burying my face in my hands, half laughing, half mortified. When I finally lower my hands, Sawyer is there, and he doesn't look impressed.

I notice the way his jaw tightens the second Dermott brings up my past relationship. His eyes are glued to the table, his knuckles turning white around the glass in his hand. He's trying to look composed, but every little movement screams discomfort.

Beatrice, always the instigator, leans in closer, her eyes sparkling with curiosity. "Who were you engaged to?"

Her tone is light, almost teasing, but I can see the sharpness in her smile. She's pushing this for a reason. *Is she trying to get me to crack in front of Sawyer, or does she really think this is the way to help?* I can't tell. My eyes flick between her and Sawyer, and I suddenly feel like I'm caught in the middle of a game I didn't sign up for—a game Beatrice is controlling without me even realizing it.

"Bea, what are you doing?" I whisper under my breath, but she just shrugs, feigning innocence. She knows exactly what she's doing.

Sawyer's reaction is subtle but telling. His eyes meet mine for a brief second, sharp and questioning. I see his throat bob as he swallows, like he's forcing something down, and I can practically feel the tension rolling off him.

"I was not engaged," I say quickly, hoping to kill the conversation before it spirals out of control.

But Dermott, still laughing with the older woman, catches my eye again just as Sawyer's lips press into a thin line. He's watching, even through the haze of drinks, and I know he's gauging the situation.

Then, leaning in, Dermott says with a grin, "Practically. He lived with you!" He mock gags. "I hated him. He was boring as hell. Like a block of ice in a meat locker. What was his name? Philip? Stuffy bollocks!"

"Dermott!" I gasp, horrified, just as he turns and finally locks eyes with Sawyer.

A slow smile spreads across Dermott's face, looking far too satisfied with the tension he's caused. "Ah, there he is. Sawyer, so nice to finally meet you."

Dermott's playing his role—the drunken joker, the guy who keeps things light when they threaten to spiral. But I know better. Beneath the jokes, Dermott is always watching, waiting to see if I need him to step in. He's not just being a dick—he's got my back in his own strange, protective way.

Beatrice narrows her eyes at me, seemingly forgetting she dragged Sawyer over here. "I told you I was divorced, and you didn't mention you were engaged!"

"That's because I was not engaged." My eyes flick up to Sawyer, who looks both uncomfortable and angry. For a moment, I wonder if I should have pretended I was engaged just to see his reaction, but I remind myself that I don't care enough for that. And truthfully, I feel bad for him in this moment.

"How long were you with the guy?" Beatrice presses, and that's when I know with certainty she's doing this on purpose, trying to gauge Sawyer's reaction.

I shrug. "A little over two years. It was a while ago."

"What happened?" She leans in, like this is the juiciest news she's heard all year.

"Nothing. He was a good guy. It's not like he cheated on me or anything." I look to Sawyer at that moment, but his expression, although stern, is unreadable. "But he wanted to settle down, and I just wasn't on the same page."

Dermott jumps back into the conversation. "He was feckin' obsessed with you. If you told him to bend over and bray like a donkey, I swear he'd do it."

"Dermott!" I gasp again, trying to suppress a laugh.

Beatrice laughs, but still manages another question. "But you lived together?"

I wish I didn't care that the tension rippled through him, or that the way he shifted on his feet made me think he was seconds away from storming out. But I did care—more than I wanted to admit.

I twist my lips in thought. "I wouldn't say we lived together. He stayed over a lot."

Sawyer moves quickly, mumbling an excuse that he's meeting someone at the bar, and then he's swallowed up by the crowd. I feel an ache inside me at his departure and notice my hands are shaking. I look up at Beatrice, shocked, but she just winks at me.

"He'll be okay. I like lighting fires under people's asses." Then her face pales at what she's said. "God, Josie, I am so sorry."

"Oh my God, Bea, stop! You can say 'fire' without me crumbling into a ball." She visibly relaxes, and I reach over and grab her hand. "But that was not nice. What you did to Sawyer."

She shakes her head and takes a sip. "Nah. I like seeing a little life in the guy, even if it's like that. He was like the walking dead for so long. It feels good to see him getting a little irritated. I have to keep him on his toes. It's all in friendship and love."

The music drifts into the background until the familiar opening notes of Johnny Cash's "I Walk the Line" pull me back. Memories wrap themselves around my heart as the melody washes over me. I instinctively glance back toward the bar. Sawyer's back is to me, but I notice it right away—his posture shifts at the first notes of the song, like the music struck a nerve. He doesn't move at first, just stands there, listening, absorbing. But then, slowly, he turns, and his eyes find mine.

Time seems to stop.

He doesn't look away this time. Neither do I.

The lyrics hang in the air, heavy with meaning. And I wonder if he's thinking the same thing I am. But before I can figure it out, his expression hardens—just slightly, but enough for me to notice. He breaks eye contact, turning away again, his back to me once more. I watch as he runs his hands through his hair, grabs the back of his neck, and then leaves. I don't see him again for the rest of the night, and I hate the traitorous disappointment that colors the rest of my evening.

Chapter 20

Then

The days leading up to Sawyer's prom were a whirlwind of excitement and anticipation. I had spent weeks imagining how the night would go—the dance, the photos, the laughter. For once, everything seemed perfect. Sawyer had planned out every detail with me, right down to the flowers he'd be bringing. I had already pictured us dancing together under the dim lights of the ballroom, surrounded by our friends, all of us dressed in our finest.

I felt so lucky to be a part of Sawyer's big night. This was *his* prom, and more than anything, I wanted it to be memorable for him. He deserved it—his senior year, his last dance in high school. Years from now, when he looked back, I wanted him to remember this night as something special, something magical. And somehow, I wanted to be part of that magic for him.

My mom, surprisingly present and supportive, had helped me pick out the perfect dress—a shimmering dark-green gown that made me feel like a star from old Hollywood. The moment I saw it in the shop, I knew it was the dress. Its deep emerald hue set off my auburn hair beautifully, the contrast making me feel radiant. When I twirled in front of the mirror, the soft waves of my hair caught the light, glistening like fire against the green fabric. It was as though I had stepped out of a dream. I could already imagine the way Sawyer's eyes would widen when he saw me.

Slipping money into my hand as I left to get my hair and makeup done, my mom said, "Just because you look all grown-up and gorgeous doesn't mean you aren't my little girl." Her smile had been genuine, her words meaningful. It gave me hope. Maybe this time she really would be different. Maybe tonight we'd share one of those mother-daughter moments that I'd been craving for years.

Beatrice came with me to the salon, even though she wasn't going to the dance. Her excitement was contagious as stylists twirled and teased my hair into elegant curls and makeup artists painted my face with soft, flattering colors. I watched as they worked, feeling like I was in a dream. I wasn't the girl with a messy life or the one constantly stressed about what was happening at home. Tonight, I could just be Josie. And tonight, I could make everything feel perfect for Sawyer.

"Josie, you are—" Beatrice breathed, leaning over to snap another picture on her phone. "You are absolutely stunning. And you don't even have your dress on yet! Sawyer is going to *die* when he sees you."

Her words made me laugh, but I blushed at my reflection. Even I had to admit I looked the best I ever had. My auburn curls, glossy and soft, had been swept up into an elegant updo, with a few tendrils falling perfectly around my face. The makeup brought out my eyes in a way that made them seem to glow. For once, I felt confident.

It felt like everything was falling into place. I imagined stepping into the night with Sawyer, seeing his eyes light up when he saw me in that dress. I pictured us slow dancing, our friends laughing beside us—a night filled with the kind of joy I'd only ever seen in movies. The promise of a perfect evening swelled in my chest, bringing with it a hope so big it felt like I might burst.

Bubbling with joy, I returned home, eager to step into my dress with my mother's help. Seeing her happy filled me with a thrill I couldn't contain. For once, it felt as though she was truly proud of me. It might have been silly, but it meant everything.

In the fitting room, when she saw me in the dress, there had been a spark in her eyes—a glimpse of the mother I'd always longed for. One who saw me. One who was proud. Naïve, perhaps, but I let myself believe that tonight, of all nights, she would share in my joy.

Sawyer was coming over, and she'd promised to take pictures of us. She'd even planned to put out snacks and had been on the phone with her friends in Ireland, raving about the dress we'd bought. I couldn't wait for her to acknowledge how perfect it all was—how worthy I was.

All I wanted was for her to see me and be proud.

But the moment I opened the door, a suffocating darkness greeted me. The silence was broken only by the sound of my own heart sinking.

"Mom? Dad?" My voice trembled, slicing through the quiet.

My dad appeared from the shadows, his face a mask of despair that sent a chill down my spine. That's when the sharp tang of alcohol hit me. My heart plummeted.

How? How could she do this to me?

But what really upset me was how I could let myself believe that she wouldn't. My mother was an alcoholic. I knew that much. But beyond that, she was angry, resentful, and bitter—but I didn't know why. I wasn't even sure there was a why. But her bitterness often came out when the attention was off her, when she felt like someone was getting something she didn't get, when she felt slighted. And as I stood there with my hair and makeup done, I felt like such a fool because I should have known that her resentment would be directed toward me. Did I think there was a part of my mother that wanted to lift me up and place me above herself? Yes—but that version never won out. And neither did I.

"She's drunk again," my dad said, throwing up his hands. "What could I do? What am I supposed to do?"

"Where is she?" I said, my sadness turning into rage, as I pushed past him.

From the darkness, the sound of a body hitting the wall; then my mother emerged, barely upright, a lit cigarette dangling from her lips.

"Jesus Christ, what did she drink? I've only been gone a few hours!"

"I didn't drink anything!" she slurred. "I'm just tired. I'm just so tired."

That was the thing about my mother. I never saw her drink openly. She wasn't one to go to bars or socialize at events. All her drinking was done in secret, a solitary, shadowy affair, even though the effects were far from hidden.

"Dammit, Mom, why? Why can't you just let me have this?" I cried out, my voice cracking under the strain of heartbreak and fury.

"Josie," my father warned, a feeble attempt to stem the tide of chaos.

"Look at the abuse I take, Thomas," she hissed, her words slurring into a venomous spit as her eyes, glassy and unfocused, locked on mine. "See the gratitude I get for paying for that thankless pup's hair?" She took a drag from her cigarette, her sneer deepening. "Looks cheap. Where did you go to get it done? I want my money back."

I bolted upstairs, tears streaming down my face as I threw my belongings into a bag. My beautiful dress, my shoes, my hopes for the evening—all thrown haphazardly into a duffel. I couldn't let Sawyer see this, see the chaos that was my life. There was no way I could let him pick me up here as planned.

I heard my mother's unsteady footsteps as she made her way up the stairs. The old wood creaked under her weight, each step a painful reminder of the state she was in. My father's pleading voice followed, a desperate whisper trying to halt her drunken ascent. "Nancy, please, not tonight. Let her have this one night."

Ignoring him, she continued her clumsy climb, her voice slurring but loud enough to pierce through the closed door of my room. "Josie! You think you're so much better than me, don't you? Going to your fancy dance with your fancy friends."

My heart was pounding and my hands were shaking. I had to get out of there. I knew what she was capable of and I couldn't let her ruin this night.

"Mom, *please*," I called out, my voice steadier than I felt. "You know I can't talk right now."

She burst into my room, her eyes wild and unfocused. The smell of alcohol was overwhelming, mixing with the scent of stale smoke that clung to her clothes. "Talk? Like you talk to all those boys? Thinking you're going to leave this place and forget where you came from? Going with that cheap piece of shit who tried to give me flowers he picked up off the side of the road? Who do you take me for? A *fool*!"

I backed away, my heart pounding in my chest. She scoffed, staggering slightly as she pointed a shaky finger at me, the cigarette between her fingers trailing a faint curl of smoke.

"I paid for you to be painted up like a clown."

She lunged forward, her free hand snapping out to grab a fistful of my hair, pulling hard enough that the delicate pins holding my updo snapped, sending strands spilling around my face. "You think you're so much better than me? That you deserve this dance with your friends?" she hissed, her breath foul as she yanked my head back.

The pain was sharp, and tears sprang to my eyes, more from the shock and betrayal than the physical hurt. "Mom, stop! You're hurting me!" I sobbed, reaching up to try to loosen her grip. "Dad! *Dad!* Help!" I cried out for my father, who lingered outside the room. "Dad! Why aren't you helping me?"

Her hold only tightened, her other hand—still holding the lit cigarette—gestured wildly as she continued to berate me. "You're just like your father—always wanting what you can't have, always reaching for more than you deserve."

Finally, my dad appeared in the doorway. "Nancy, let her go!" he demanded, crossing the room quickly to intervene.

With a bitter laugh she released me, pushing me away so forcefully I stumbled against the bed. "See the abuse I get, Thomas?" She turned her glassy eyes on him. "See the thanks I get for trying to make her *decent*?"

I rubbed my scalp where she had pulled, tears streaming down my cheeks. My beautifully styled hair was a mess, half up and half down, a symbol of how quickly things could fall apart.

She pointed at me again. "You're not going anywhere."

The fury was building inside me—a slow, simmering rage that had been buried for years, waiting for the right moment to surface. For years, I'd let her words beat me down, let her reduce me to nothing with just a look or a sneer.

But not tonight.

"You are nothing but a no-good drunk." My voice trembled at first, but I steadied it, each word landing like a punch. "You can't stop me."

I dodged past them both, grabbing my things and heading for the door. Behind me, my mother's taunts continued, but they were muffled by the pounding of my own heart as I fled the house, desperate for safety and sanity. As soon as I got outside, I saw Sarge coming toward my house.

"Honey, I thought I heard you calling for help."

"Sarge! Sarge! Can I come to your house, please?" I cried, nearly hyperventilating. He didn't hesitate; his face was a mask of concern as he nodded vigorously and led me away from my own personal hell.

***

Once inside Sarge's comforting home, he guided me to his living room, a sanctuary of calm, with its walls lined with books and the soft crackle of a record player in the background. He steered me toward a cozy armchair and sat across from me, his wise eyes watching me intently.

"You sit here and catch your breath, Josie. I'll get you some water," Sarge said, his voice gentle, grounding.

I took out my phone, my hands trembling as I typed a message to Beatrice first and then Sawyer. My heart raced, not just from the panic of the situation but from the fear of what this could do to his night. This was his senior prom—his night. I couldn't let my family's chaos ruin that for him. He deserved better than to see the mess that was unfolding at my house.

I stared at the screen, my vision blurred by tears as I texted him: *Can you pick me up at Sarge's instead of my house?* I hesitated, my thumb hovering over the send button. What if he asked why? What if he pressed me for details? I couldn't bear for him to know what was happening right now. I couldn't let him see the ugliness of my life.

But I sent it, praying he wouldn't ask questions, hoping I could keep him sheltered from this.

He responded immediately: *No problem.* No questions. No hesitation. He probably already had an idea, and that made my heart ache even more.

When Sarge returned, he handed me the glass of water and sat down across from me, his eyes reflecting concern and something firmer—maybe anger on my behalf. He waited for me to take a sip before he spoke, his voice even and thoughtful.

"Josie, life's going to throw a lot at you—sometimes more than you think you can handle," he began, folding his hands in his lap. "And sometimes it's the people closest to you who will hurt you the most."

I nodded, clutching the glass tighter, feeling the coolness seep into my palms. As I looked down, I saw a drop of red land on my hand. Startled, I wiped it away, only to feel a sting on my scalp. Sarge's brow furrowed as he leaned in closer.

"Hold still a minute, Josie." His gentle fingers brushed through my hair, revealing a small cut where my mother had ripped out the pins. Blood trickled down, barely noticeable amidst the tangle of curls, but enough to make me wince.

"I didn't even realize," I whispered, more to myself than to him. The pain, both physical and emotional, was so tangled up inside me that I hadn't noticed one over the other.

Sarge rose from his chair, moving quietly to grab a first aid kit from a cabinet. He returned and knelt beside me, carefully cleaning the wound with a cotton swab, his touch tender and deliberate. "Your mom might have hurt you, Josie, but you've got people who care about you," he said as he worked, his voice soft but steady. "You can't let her tear you down."

I swallowed hard, feeling the sting of the antiseptic and the weight of his words. "How do I not let it affect me, Sarge?"

Sarge leaned forward slightly, his expression earnest. "By remembering who you are, Josie. By knowing that you are not your mother, and you are not defined by her actions or her words. You are your own person, with your own strengths and your own worth. When someone's cruel, remember that it's a reflection of them, not you."

I blinked back tears. "I don't want her to ruin tonight. This is Sawyer's prom. I just—I just want him to have a perfect night. I'll do anything to make sure he doesn't see the mess I come from."

"It's not bleeding now. All cleaned up." Sarge finished cleaning the cut and sat back down, his wise eyes meeting mine. "Tonight, you go to that prom not as the daughter of anyone but as Josie—bright, brave, and beautiful. Don't give anyone the power to dim your light, especially not those who can't find their own."

His words, simple yet profound, felt like a balm to the raw edges of my spirit. "Thank you, Sarge," I managed to say, my voice thick with emotion.

"Now, you take your time. When you're ready, go ahead into the spare room there and get yourself dolled up."

Before I could respond, a knock came at the door. Sarge stood up, glancing at me before heading to answer it. When he opened the door, there stood Beatrice, makeup kit and hair products packed into her old trusty Caboodle, her face pale with worry.

"Is she okay?" she asked breathlessly, her eyes scanning the room until they found me sitting in the chair.

"Come in, honey," Sarge said gently, stepping aside.

"That was fast," I breathed, amazed at how quickly Bea had gotten there.

Beatrice rushed toward me, her eyes wide, clearly upset but trying to hold it together. "I grabbed my stuff and got here as fast as I could."

I moved into the guest room, taking my dress and bag with me to try to pull everything back together. Beatrice was right on my heels. I sat on the bed and exhaled a shaky breath. Her Caboodle landed on the floor with a thud as she knelt beside me, her hands trembling slightly before she placed them on mine. "Are you okay?"

I swallowed the lump in my throat and nodded, though I could see the relief in her eyes as she squeezed my hands.

"I'm fine, Bea. Really."

Sarge watched quietly for a few moments from the doorway as Beatrice opened her Caboodle, pulling out makeup brushes and hair products like a woman on a mission. Her hands still shook a little, but her determination to make me feel better, to make sure I looked beautiful, was obvious.

Beatrice smoothed my hair back, her face pinched with concentration. "We're going to fix everything, okay? You're going to look incredible. Sawyer won't even notice what happened. He'll just see how stunning you are."

I wanted to say something, to reassure her, but the truth was, her presence alone was doing more for me than words could. She cared so much, and she wasn't going to let me leave this night feeling anything less than wonderful. Beatrice always knew how to make things better.

I nodded, blinking back tears as Beatrice worked on fixing my hair and makeup, her hands steadying as she focused on her task. She knew how much this night meant to me, and as she transformed me, bit by bit, I could feel myself coming back together.

"I'm going to make sure Sawyer sees the girl he's always seen in you," Beatrice said, her tone fierce, as if willing everything to be okay. "No more tears, no more worrying about your mom. Tonight is about you and him."

I squared my shoulders, knowing that with Beatrice by my side, I wouldn't crumble tonight. I couldn't. I wouldn't let anything ruin this night for Sawyer or for me.

When I finally stepped out of the guest room, Sarge was waiting in the hallway. His eyes lit up when he saw me, and his warm smile made me feel a rush of affection and gratitude.

"There you are!" he exclaimed, his voice full of pride. "Look at you, Josie! All set to turn heads at the prom. I must say, you look absolutely stunning."

I couldn't help but smile, his words healing more than he could know. "Thank you, Sarge. It means a lot to me that you think so."

He approached and took my hands in his, giving them a gentle squeeze. "I'm proud of you, Josie. Not just for how you look tonight, but for the strength you're showing. You're a remarkable young woman, and don't you ever forget it."

His affirmation filled a void I didn't realize was so deep. "I won't," I promised, feeling a newfound resolve stir within me.

Not long after, Beatrice left, and Sawyer arrived to collect me, holding a stunning bouquet of flowers that somehow paled in comparison to his dashing appearance. Dressed impeccably, he looked every bit the heartthrob I knew him to be. When he caught sight of me, his usual eloquence faltered, his words tripping over themselves in a display of awe.

"Holy shit." He blew out a breath and then looked apologetically at Sarge. "I'm sorry. I'm sorry. I meant wow! You look like—you look like a goddess."

"Thank you. You look very handsome."

Sarge chuckled and turned toward the kitchen. "Have a good night, kids."

When Sawyer was just out of earshot, Sarge paused and glanced back at me. "Just remember, kiddo," he added with a soft smile, "the best revenge is living well. Go out there and shine—for yourself."

As Sawyer and I drove away, I caught a glimpse of Sarge in the side mirror, heading toward my house, his steady steps full of quiet determination—like a man who wasn't going to let them get away with this.

***

As we entered the prom venue, the doors swung open to a world bathed in soft multicolored lights and the sound of a lively jazz band. It felt like stepping into a dream. The hall was decorated with sparkling fairy lights that hung from the ceiling, casting a magical glow over everything. Students turned to look as we walked in, and it wasn't just the décor that was stunning—Sawyer and I felt every bit the part of a fairy-tale couple.

Sawyer kept close, his hand finding mine, interlocking our fingers. He leaned in, whispering, "I can't stop looking at you," his breath warm against my ear, making me blush.

We mingled, laughing and talking with classmates, the night unfolding with a perfect blend of music and laughter. My mind occasionally wandered to my mother, but Sarge's words strengthened me, and I allowed myself to enjoy the evening with Sawyer and his friends.

The dance floor was alive with the energy of our peers, the music a pulsing heartbeat that kept us moving. Sawyer led me to the dance floor, his confidence infectious, and we danced with abandon, our laughter blending with the rhythms of the night.

As the DJ shifted the music to a slower, softer melody, Sawyer pulled me close. The lights dimmed, and under the gentle glow of the disco ball, it felt as if we were alone in the universe. His hands were gentle on my back, his eyes locked on mine with an intensity that made my heart flutter.

"Do you want to talk about why I had to pick you up at Sarge's house?"

"Absolutely not." I laughed at my own response. "Not right now, anyway."

He hummed in acknowledgment, and then we swayed back and forth silently for a few beats.

"You know," he murmured, his voice barely above the music, "I never in a million years thought I'd be so lucky to have you as my prom date, let alone my girlfriend."

"Ha! C'mon, Sawyer," I teased, though I couldn't ignore the way my heart swelled.

He pulled back slightly to look at me, his eyes filled with sincerity. "No, I'm serious. You were so far out of my league. Still are, as far as I'm concerned. I used to watch you from across the room, and you were like . . . this untouchable goddess. Strong, smart, wickedly funny—and don't get me started on how beautiful you are." He grinned, but there was no teasing in his eyes.

I felt a blush creep up my neck. "You're exaggerating," I muttered, shaking my head.

"I'm not. I've never met anyone like you, Josie. You've got this way about you—this red-haired, sharp-witted, old-soul magic. It's like you stepped out of a story, some kind of Celtic goddess or something." He paused, his fingers brushing a strand of my hair. "And what gets me the most is how you don't even know it."

I felt my throat tighten as I searched his face. How could he think that? I was a mess most of the time—constantly second-guessing myself, never feeling like I was good enough. How could he see anything else?

"You're genuine," he continued, his voice soft. "You care about people in a way no one else does. You've got this kindness that's so rare. You don't pretend to be anything other than who you are, and I swear, that's what makes you stand out. You're not like anyone else."

I rested my head against his chest, overwhelmed by the depth of his words. "That's hard to believe," I whispered.

"I'll spend every day reminding you, until you finally believe it. I love you."

I lifted myself onto my toes and kissed him, hoping he knew how much I loved him because I wasn't sure my words would convey it.

But our beautiful moment was soon shattered. When the song ended, Val was there, standing on the edge of the dance floor with a poisonous look on her face.

Her dress was striking—a bold red that demanded attention. But it was too tight, clinging in all the wrong places, like she was trying too hard to fit into something she had no business wearing. From far away, she probably looked like a hot blonde, someone who could turn heads. But up close, it was impossible to miss how her features looked harsh under the heavy makeup, her skin stretched too tight. Her bleached hair was overstyled, stiff from too much product, and there was something almost desperate in the way she carried herself, like she was grasping at some version of herself she couldn't quite achieve. She looked older than she should have at our age, and though she smiled, there was something sharp and hollow about it.

"Josie, you look . . . different," Val said, her voice dripping with sugary sweetness that couldn't hide the venom underneath. She tilted her head slightly, her eyes scanning me up and down. It wasn't a compliment—it was an appraisal, a judgment.

Sawyer's arm tensed around me, his posture subtly shifting as if to shield me from her words. But he didn't say anything. He didn't move. I felt his hand around mine, but the pressure wasn't reassuring. It was stiff. Uncomfortable.

"I suppose I'm just happy to be here with my boyfriend," I replied, trying to keep my voice steady, refusing to let her see how her presence affected me. I hoped Sawyer would say something, do something—anything. But he stayed quiet. Still.

Val's smile tightened, her eyes flickering with something sharp before she regained her composure. "Well, I just wanted to wish you a memorable night," she said, her tone heavy with implication.

"Thank you, Val. I hope your night is as pleasant as you are," I responded, forcing a smile. Sawyer squeezed my hand, but I could feel the undercurrent of tension in the air. My pulse quickened. Something was coming. I could feel it. And still—Sawyer said nothing.

"Oh, and I hope your dress doesn't have too many buttons. Sawyer doesn't like trying to get those off." Her voice dropped to a purr, and her gaze flicked to Sawyer with calculated malice. "I'm still mad about how you broke the buttons on my favorite dress when you were tearing it off of me." She let the words hang in the air like poison, her smirk widening. "Remember that, Sawyer? That was a fun night."

The ground beneath me disappeared. My stomach twisted, and I could feel the blood drain from my face. I searched Sawyer's eyes for a denial, for anything to make this not true, but his face was frozen in shock. He didn't move. He didn't say a word.

Do something, I silently begged. *Say something, Sawyer. Please.*

But he just stood there, letting the silence grow, letting the moment stretch into something unbearable.

He didn't stop her. He didn't defend me. He didn't deny it. And with each second that passed, my heart broke a little more.

Val's cold, mocking laugh echoed as she turned and sauntered off, satisfied with the chaos she'd caused. She had been waiting for this. The entire night, she'd been circling, watching, waiting for the right moment to strike—and she had delivered her blow with precision.

A thousand thoughts raced through my mind. *How long had she been waiting to drop that bomb? Was this all a game to her, some sick pleasure in watching me unravel?*

But worse than Val's words was Sawyer's inaction. His hand, still wrapped around mine, felt suddenly foreign—like it didn't belong to the boy I trusted. Like it had been someone else's hand all along. The shock in his eyes didn't feel like enough. I had opened myself to him, made myself vulnerable in ways I hadn't with anyone else. And now . . . now it was all laid bare for Val to tear apart, and he had just let it happen.

Moments later, I burst through the exit doors of the Hilton, the cool air slapping my tear-streaked face. It was oddly pleasant compared to the figurative slap I'd taken inside.

"Josie!" I heard Sawyer rush through the exit behind me.

I pulled my shoes from my feet and started running, my adrenaline pushing me forward.

"Josie, wait!"

I didn't know where I was going. I couldn't go home, and I couldn't go back inside. So I ran to a lawn adjacent to the parking lot. Sawyer was still calling my name as he reached me, breathless.

"Sawyer," I begged through my tears. "Please, just leave me alone!" I wasn't trying to play games. I just wanted to be alone in my devastation, even if it was in a patch of grass next to a parking lot. It was the only safe place I had in that moment.

"Josie, please, listen to me." He was shouting now, his voice ragged, desperate. I turned to look at him, pain streaking across his face, and waited. I waited for him to tell me it wasn't true, that Val had made it all up. But instead, he just looked at me, anguish written all over his features.

My hand covered my mouth. "Oh God."

Sawyer stepped forward, his hands trembling as if he wanted to reach for me but didn't dare. "No, no, Josie. I didn't cheat on you. I would never."

"But—" I searched his eyes, desperate for answers that made sense. How had I been so stupid to trust him? To believe I could be a part of something perfect?

"Before you. Before us," he stammered, his voice breaking.

I turned away, bile rising in my throat. "My God, Sawyer, I figured you hooked up with her—but you—you tore her dress off of her?" I turned back to him, fury burning through my veins. "You are disgusting! Anyone who had their hands all over her will never have their hands on me."

I wanted to make a dramatic exit, to leave in a blaze of glory, but instead, I covered my face with my hands and sank to the grass. My chest felt tight, and I could barely hear the words coming out of Sawyer's mouth.

"It meant nothing—I swear, Josie." His voice cracked as he ran his fingers through his hair.

I reached into my clutch and pulled out my phone, dialing Beatrice. She answered on the first ring. "Can you come get me? Now?" She was already jogging to her car when we hung up.

I looked up to see Sawyer, his back turned to me, crouching down as if the weight of everything had physically broken him. Then he got up and paced, running his hands through his hair again. I felt like such a fool. Maybe my mom was right. Maybe I was a clown. Maybe I didn't deserve this dance.

But then a small voice in the back of my mind whispered, *You don't deserve this either.*

Chapter 21

Now

When I reach the football field and see Sawyer sitting on the bleachers, his head down, it feels like I've been scraped from the inside out. I'm torn between running toward him and running away. He looks so sad, and I know it shouldn't twist my insides the way it does—but I feel gutted all the same.

I approach quietly. "Hey. I thought I'd get here first," I say softly, trying to shed the sharpness that's tainted our recent encounters.

He looks up abruptly, his eyes meeting mine as I stop in front of him. Hesitation roots me to the spot before I shift uncomfortably. His gaze is weary and worn, with a frailty I didn't expect to see. It strikes me how deeply all of this—us—is weighing on him. I'd convinced myself that Sawyer had moved on long before I even realized it was time to let go. But the man looking back at me seems stuck somewhere—suffering—and that disorients me, hurts me in ways I didn't expect.

"I didn't want you waiting," he murmurs softly, his voice a gentle echo against the sounds of the Harvest Festival starting its second day nearby.

"Do you mind if I sit?"

"No, please, sit," he says, snapping out of what seems like a deep reverie.

I climb the bleachers and settle next to him, taking a deep breath. "I'm sorry about last night. I know it was a little . . . weird."

Sawyer stays quiet for a moment, and I start to wonder if he's going to say anything at all. Finally, he speaks. "It was weird, but I think I made it that way."

I want to tell him no, to make him feel better. But maybe it was weird. The fact that he was triggered by the idea of me being in a relationship . . . I don't want to think about what that means. I feel too raw, too exposed. His emotions are like a brush burn on my skin. And yet, seeing him like this—so sad—hurts me more than it should. But what could we expect after fifteen years? We both would have moved on.

I try to reset, absorbing the familiar sight of the football field. My mind drifts, uninvited, to the first time Sawyer brought me here—when Sarge sent him to rescue me. I chuckle inwardly at the thought. There were so many times after that. I loved football season with Sawyer. The chill in the air, sharing his hoodie, snuggling so close I could smell his deodorant and shampoo. The band's celebratory music filling the air, the rush of a Maplewood High victory. It was magical. And sneaking away under the bleachers to steal kisses? That was the closest thing to pure happiness I knew. For a girl with the upbringing I had, those simple moments were the greatest gift I could ever receive.

"It's been a long time since I've been here," I say with a sigh, letting my gaze drift before settling on him.

"Obviously," he says, a hint of resentment creeping into his voice.

My good intentions crumble with that single word—obviously. I take a deep breath, frustration rising. He has a way of igniting something in me lately, something that simmers just below the surface. I try to stay calm, but it's slipping.

"Here we go again," I murmur, then look at him pointedly.

"Well, it's true."

"Can we just read the next letter before you start this again?"

Sawyer exhales dramatically, frustration radiating from him. "Come on, then," he says, nodding toward the underside of the bleachers.

I follow Sawyer down, each step reverberating through the metal, the familiar clanking sound pulling me into a memory I didn't expect. My boots feel heavy against the echoing steps, and suddenly I'm no longer here but back in high school. Back when everything was different with him—simpler, easier.

I hadn't thought about those moments in years, but now it feels like they're waiting for me in the shadows under the bleachers. Places hold memories, even when you're not ready to face them.

We used to sneak under these very bleachers after games. The cold metal frame always felt like ice against my back, but it didn't matter. Sawyer would pull me into his hoodie, the fabric soft and warm, smelling like him—something fresh and clean, with a hint of pine. The crisp autumn air bit at my cheeks, and the scent of the football field—freshly mowed grass mixed with popcorn and distant smoke from the bonfire—filled the air.

I remember how the lights from the field cast long, dancing shadows around us, the roar of the crowd above muffled by the structure. I'd rest my head against his chest, feeling his heartbeat, a steady rhythm that matched the drums from the band. There was something magical about those nights—everything felt right, untouched by the messiness of my world.

Sawyer would wrap his arms around me, his breath warm against my hair, and whisper something that made me laugh. We'd steal moments like this—away from everyone else, as if we were the only two people who existed. His touch, his presence, was all that mattered. It was simple. It was enough.

The familiar smell of grass and the faint echo of the festival nearby should bring back warmth, but instead, it just reminds me of everything that's changed. We're not those teenagers under the bleachers anymore. There's too much history, too much pain.

We come to a stop under the row in the bleachers Sarge led us to, and Sawyer reaches up, tugging something from beneath the bleachers. His hands reemerge holding two envelopes. He hands me one, marked with the initials RP—clearly meant for Mrs. Miner.

"Can you keep this safe?" Sawyer asks, his voice low. I move closer as he hands me the letter, and our fingers brush—just for a second—but it's enough to send a shockwave through me. I tuck the letter into my small sling bag, my breath catching as the air between us thickens.

For a moment, neither of us moves. His eyes lock onto mine, and suddenly we're back there again—under these same bleachers—teenagers, stealing kisses in the shadows. I remember the way his lips felt, how he'd pull me close, leaving me breathless. The same electric pull hums between us now, dangerous and undeniable.

I try to focus on the other envelope in his hand, the one with our names written across it in Sarge's familiar scrawl. But all I can think about is how close we are, the warmth of his body, and how easily we used to give in to this magnetic force between us. I can see the memory flash in his eyes too—the way he used to lean in, like he couldn't help himself.

I feel the pull again, like gravity drawing us closer. My heart hammers in my chest as his eyes drop to my lips, just for a second, before flicking back to meet mine. The space between us feels fragile, like it could shatter at any moment.

His breath falters, and I know he's thinking about it too—how easy it would be to close the distance like we used to. For a heartbeat, I think we will. His face is so close to mine, I can feel the warmth of his breath, and I swear time stops.

But then he pulls back, blinking hard. "It's too dark. I won't be able to read the letter under here," he murmurs, but I know it's not the darkness he's running from. It's the weight of everything we used to be.

I nod, forcing myself to step away from the edge of that memory, though my pulse is still racing. We both know what almost happened. We both remember what it felt like when we didn't fight it.

I walk toward the sunlight, leaving the tension that still buzzes between us behind. He follows, and I can't help but feel like we've left something unfinished, like those old moments are still lurking in the shadows.

I stop and turn to him, shoving down the swirl of emotions rising inside me. "Go ahead," I say softly, gesturing to the envelope. My voice feels distant, like it belongs to someone else. I notice the way his eyes search mine, as if he's trying to find something I'm hiding.

I feel the weight of his gaze—the way he's noticing, really noticing, that the mask I've been wearing is slipping. The wall I've built, the anger I've clung to like armor, is cracking, and for the first time, I can't hide it from him.

"Josie . . ." His voice is low, uncertain, like he wants to ask something but doesn't know if he should. I swallow hard, refusing to look at him, because I know if I do, he'll see everything I've been fighting to keep buried. But despite my best efforts, I give in, allowing our eyes to meet.

Sawyer holds my eyes for a long moment, weighing something, before finally nodding. He turns back to the letter, his expression unreadable, and begins to read aloud.

***

Hey kids,

Well, if you're reading this, you've probably figured out by now this ain't just about my past. It's about facing some of those messy truths we've all tried to sweep under the rug. Life's got a funny way of kicking you in the teeth with lessons you never asked for, doesn't it?

That letter you're holding—the one marked "RP"—it's tied to a chapter of my life I don't talk about much. It's about love, regret, and a whole lot of mistakes. I loved someone, but I let people steer me in the wrong direction, and in the end, I hurt the one person who mattered most. That letter? It's my chance to say what should've been said years ago.

See, we're all real good at telling ourselves stories to make sense of our screwups. Problem is, those stories can trap you if you're not careful. You get stuck in your own head, believing the version of events that hurts a little less. But that's no way to live, kids.

When you deliver this letter, don't think of it as just doing me a favor. It's more than that. It's a step toward setting things right—not just for me, but for you two too. The truth? Yeah, it stings like hell, but it's the only way to find peace. I want you both to have the guts to be honest—with yourselves, and with each other. Even if it means facing the stuff you'd rather avoid, it's better than living behind a wall of lies.

I'm counting on you. The truth has a funny way of sorting things out, even if it takes time. It'll catch up to you, so it's better to meet it head-on before it steamrolls you.

Take care of yourselves. The truth might hurt, but trust me—it's a whole lot lighter to carry than a lifetime of regrets.

Catch ya later,

Sarge

***

When Sawyer finishes reading, he carefully folds the letter and hands it back to me, his movements slow, deliberate. He doesn't say anything right away, but I can see the tension in his shoulders—the way he's holding something back.

We stand in silence for a while before I walk toward the field, leaning against the chain-link fence that separates the bleachers from the sidelines. Sawyer follows, positioning himself beside me. He seems hesitant, his posture awkward and unsure in a way I'm not used to seeing from him.

"Do they still hold graduations here?" I ask, keeping my eyes forward, searching for something familiar to anchor myself to.

"As long as the weather holds, yeah," he replies.

"The last time I was here was for your graduation." I feel his head turn sharply toward me. His reaction is immediate, like my words hit harder than I expected. "I didn't come to any football games during my senior year. Just Penn State—obviously." I glance sideways at him, emphasizing the word. "And—well, we both know I didn't make it to my own graduation."

Sawyer exhales beside me. He rubs the back of his neck, a gesture I've come to recognize as discomfort, maybe even guilt. "I'm sorry, Josie. I've been an asshole," he murmurs, his voice softer than usual, like he's struggling to say the words out loud.

I shake my head and hold up the letter between us. "No, Sarge said it best. I'm facing the stuff I avoid. Kinda a big deal for me."

Sawyer's jaw tightens, his eyes flicking to the letter and then back to me, but he doesn't say anything. It's as if he's waiting for permission to speak, unsure of how to start.

"Why didn't you come to any football games during senior year?" His voice sounds strained, not just curious, but like he's afraid of the answer. "I don't think I ever knew that."

"You didn't." I look down. "You were starting college, trying to find your way. I didn't want to add to your stress. My mom was . . . difficult back then. I didn't have the time or energy to come to games, let alone socialize."

My words hang heavy in the air. Needing to break the tension, I turn and look up at the bleachers.

"I wish I could've taken all that away from you," Sawyer says after a moment. He looks down at the ground, and for a second, I catch a glimpse of something fragile in him—a reflection of burdens he's carried for far too long. "Sometimes, when I think about what you went through . . . it kills me."

His words create a jolt that sends a shiver through my chest. "When you think about it?" I ask. "When do you think about it?"

"All the time." His eyes meet mine, and I can see the longing, the regret etched into his expression.

But anger rises inside me. He wanted to take away my pain—when he caused so much of it. I push it down, force myself to keep moving forward. "It's water under the bridge," I say, managing a small, forced smile. I don't want to go back to that place.

Sawyer looks like he wants to say more, but whatever it is, he swallows it down. His jaw clenches, his gaze drifting back to the field as if he's trying to avoid the truth that's right in front of him.

"And this letter," I say, eager to change the subject before things get more complicated. "Why did Sarge live like this? Why didn't he try to fix things with Mrs. Miner when she's practically just a few blocks away?"

Sawyer runs a hand through his hair, the confident boy I once knew replaced by someone uncertain. "He probably thought he hurt her too much. Maybe he figured it was a lost cause."

I ponder this for a moment. "Is anything worth fighting for ever really a lost cause?" Deep down, I already know the answer when it comes to us: Yes. We were a lost cause long ago.

Sawyer looks away, staring out at the field. After a moment, he says, "I was with Sarge a lot after you left."

I don't know why that stings the way it does—him having time with Sarge that I didn't. But I made my choice, and still, the feeling simmers beneath my skin.

"I feel bad, you know? That Sarge was going through all of this while he was dealing with me," Sawyer adds.

I look at him, confused. "What do you mean?"

He sighs and clarifies. "Sarge saw me pretty broken up for a long time."

I freeze. His words hit harder than I expect. I was broken too—probably more than anyone knows. But I can't let him off the hook that easily. "Because of me?" I ask, incredulity creeping into my voice.

He laughs, but it's humorless. "Yeah, Josie. You leaving? It gutted me."

I blow out a breath, trying to keep my emotions in check. "I didn't come out of this unscathed, Sawyer." It feels like he's completely ignoring the damage he did.

"We obviously have different versions of what happened."

"Different versions?" I stare at him, disbelief turning into a deep sadness. "Sawyer, who are you? I know I don't know you anymore, but I thought I knew you better than this. I never pegged you for a gaslighter." My voice trembles as old wounds rip open.

"What? No, I—"

"Holy shit." I feel like I'm going to explode. Sawyer's bewildered expression only makes it worse. "This isn't me telling myself a fake story. I know what happened."

Sawyer throws his hands up, frustrated. "Jesus Christ, Josie! What happened? Are you ever going to tell me? Don't I deserve to know?"

The audacity of his words fuels my fury. He wants me to say it? He wants me to relive it when he's the one who threw me away? "I don't owe you anything, Sawyer! Not an explanation, not a damn thing." I turn to leave, needing to get away before I lose control.

"Go ahead, Josie! Keep running, like you always do," he shouts after me.

I stop dead in my tracks, something breaking inside me. Slowly, I turn back toward him. "What did you say?"

"You heard me."

"I didn't run away, you asshole. You THREW me away!" I march toward him, toe to toe, my voice seething. Sawyer meets my gaze, fire blazing in his eyes, but he doesn't say a word. "And if it weren't for Sarge, I'd be thrilled—*thrilled*—to never see your traitorous face again."

His face crumples, and for a moment, I see the boy I once knew—the boy who loved me.

"Josie," he murmurs, but the fire in his voice is gone. I've won, but it feels hollow. There's no victory here.

I turn on my heel, heading for the stadium exit. Without looking back, I call over my shoulder, "I'm delivering this letter—with or without you."

I hear Sawyer's footfalls behind me. I walk slightly ahead, but Sawyer quickly catches up, his steps matching mine as we move across the field in tense silence. I feel his presence beside me, familiar yet distant, pulling at something deep inside me.

Before I can figure out what to say next, a couple of voices call out from across the field.

"Coach! Mr. Sawyer!" Two teenagers, boys from Maplewood High, are heading our way, waving as they approach. Sawyer straightens, his posture shifting into something more comfortable—more natural. The vulnerable man I had just confronted fades, replaced by the teacher and coach these kids know and respect.

"Hey, guys," Sawyer says, his voice calm but carrying an edge of distraction. He glances at me—probably worried I'll start yelling at him again—but we both know I wouldn't do that, especially not in front of them. I'm mad as hell, but I'm not an asshole.

"Coach, where have you been? You coming back tomorrow?" one of the boys asks, glancing between us.

Sawyer clears his throat. "A few more days, guys. Just need to take care of some things," he says.

"Class is brutal without you," one of the boys says, shaking his head.

"Yeah," the other chimes in, "the sub is totally lost. Complete disaster."

Sawyer winces but forces a chuckle. "You better respect the substitute, or there'll be hell to pay when I get back." His tone is light, but his expression tells a different story.

"We know your rules, Coach." The boys glance curiously in my direction, clearly wondering who I am.

Sawyer hesitates, obviously unsure what to say, so I step in. I extend my hand to the boys. "I'm Josie. I went to high school with your coach here."

Their eyes light up, and their animated reaction pulls an unexpected laugh from both Sawyer and me.

"You have stories, then?" one of them asks, eager for some inside scoop.

"Oh, I have stories," I tease, a mischievous grin spreading across my face.

Sawyer lets out a good-natured laugh, but he's probably terrified inside. "All right, that's enough. You guys behave. I'll see you soon."

As we walk off, I catch a smile tugging at the corner of Sawyer's mouth, and for a brief moment, the tension between us seems to ease.

But as soon as they're out of earshot, I catch the way Sawyer's shoulders sag, just slightly—like the weight of pretending had taken more out of him than he'd let on. The sight stirs something in me, and I open my mouth to say something, anything, but before the words can form, Beatrice's voice slices through the air.

"Josie! Sawyer!" Her call comes from the direction of Miner's, sharp with urgency.

Neither of us hesitates. Without a word or a glance, we take off running toward the inn—side by side, our footsteps in sync, but with miles of unsaid words stretching between us.

Chapter 22

Then

Sawyer's graduation was a mix of emotions. Standing in the crowd at Maplewood High School's football stadium, I clapped when they called his name. But I wasn't there for him—I stood with Beatrice and her parents, cheering for Jason. Sawyer and I hadn't spoken since prom, two weeks before the graduation. He'd called and texted, but I just couldn't bring myself to respond, even though I knew I eventually would.

His future had been decided long before that disastrous prom night. He'd had his pick of scholarships and had chosen Penn State University—just over an hour away. He'd had offers from as far away as California. Knowing he'd be close should've been a comfort, but the knowledge that Val would also be enrolling at Penn State made me sick with jealousy.

She wasn't just some girl. She was dirty and nasty, a walking representation of everything that was wrong in the world. I couldn't imagine anyone, least of all Sawyer, touching her. Just the thought of her smug face, the way she'd flaunted her past with him, made me feel like I was choking on bile. She was evil. And knowing she'd be there—so close to him, to his new life—gnawed at me in a way that I couldn't shake.

The weeks following graduation blurred together. I spent most of my time taking care of my mother. The other rare moments were spent with Beatrice and Jason, trying to distract myself from Sawyer's looming departure. But each time my phone buzzed with a message from Sawyer, guilt and longing washed over me. I wanted to respond. I wanted to talk to him, but the memory of prom night, of Val's words, haunted me.

Eventually, his persistence broke through my silence. One afternoon, as I lay on my bed staring at the ceiling, my phone rang. His name flashed on the screen, and before I could stop myself, I answered.

The days leading up to his departure were filled with tentative conversations, attempts to mend the widening rift between us. We met a few times, talking about everything and nothing, trying to recapture the ease that had once defined our relationship. But something had shifted—at least for me. Every moment with him felt loaded, significant. I wanted to go back to the simplicity we'd had before, but I couldn't shake the shock of what had happened. And Sawyer, though stable on the surface, couldn't hide his own frustration. My insecurities were driving a wedge between us, one neither of us knew how to bridge. I could see it in his eyes—he was unsure too. Every time he spoke, there was a slight hesitation, a pause that wasn't there before. Like he didn't know if he could fix this, if we could get back to what we'd had.

The night before he left for college, we lay in the grass in his backyard. The scent of late summer hung heavy in the air, that familiar mix of earth and leaves, signaling the slow approach of autumn. The grass beneath me felt cool, damp, pressing into my skin like a reminder of the chill that had settled between us.

Sawyer broke the silence first. "Josie, you know I love you, right?"

"I know." My voice came out soft, almost a whisper, as I traced the outline of his face in the dim light. "But how are we going to do this?"

"We'll make it work."

"But with Val at Penn State too . . ." I couldn't keep the bitterness out of my voice. I saw his face tighten, and my chest ached. I hated that she was still such a sore spot, but I couldn't ignore it.

He turned to me, his eyes glazing over at the prospect of beating this dead horse again. "Josie, we've talked about this. It's not going to be an issue."

But it was an issue. Her words at prom had lodged themselves in my mind like a shard of glass, impossible to remove. "Her words, Sawyer . . . at the prom. How can you say it's not an issue? 'Oh, and I hope your dress doesn't have too many buttons. Sawyer doesn't like trying to get those off.' You remember that?"

His hand hovered over mine for a second before he pulled it back, unsure of what to do. "She was trying to mess with your head, Josie. That's what she does. She wants to hurt you."

"And you *let* her!" The sound of my own voice startled even me, but I couldn't stop the hurt from pouring out.

"I didn't let her do anything!" He flinched, his eyes darting away from mine. "I ignored her. She doesn't matter!"

"She does matter!" My voice cracked, emotions flooding me. "She's obsessed with you, Sawyer. You've hooked up with her before, and she wants that again. I'm not a fool. Stop acting like this is nothing." My words were sharper than I intended, fueled by the jealousy and fear that had been gnawing at me since prom.

Sawyer's patience snapped, something I rarely saw from him. He sat up, running a hand through his hair in frustration. "Yes, I fucked around with Val, briefly! It's history, Josie. Why can't you see that? You're making this into something it's not." His voice cracked slightly, like he wasn't fully sure if it was nothing. He was starting to doubt himself.

I recoiled, his words slicing through me like a blade. "Am I? Or am I the only one seeing things clearly here?" My voice shook, but the anger bubbling inside me kept me going. "You *fucked around* with her."

Sawyer flinched, and the sight only fueled my rage. "Your words, Sawyer! She's always there—smiling at you, touching your arm, giving me shit. She does it right in front of me! What do you think she'll do when I'm not there?"

"You think I can't handle myself? That I'll just fall back into something with her because you're not there to babysit me?" His voice rose, disbelief and frustration spilling over.

"That's not what I said, Sawyer. I just don't trust her." My voice wavered, my anger teetering on the edge of heartbreak. I pressed the heels of my hands to my eyes, trying to keep it together. I hated feeling like this—so weak, so vulnerable. "And why are you mad at *me*? Like I'm the one who did this?"

Sawyer exhaled sharply. "I'm not mad at you. You have all of me. What happened with her—it was nothing. *Nothing* compared to what I feel for you. It kills me that you don't see that. If I could go back in time and change it, I would."

"How can I see that when you never defend me?" I said, my voice dropping to a whisper. "She said those things, and you just . . . stood there."

A flicker of guilt passed over his face. His anger seemed to soften, replaced by something else—remorse, maybe. "I thought ignoring her would show that she doesn't matter to me."

"To me, it just feels like *I* don't matter to you," I said quietly, the truth in my words hanging between us. The night air felt heavier now, charged with lingering fears and doubts.

Sawyer reached out, his hand closing over mine. "Josie, you mean everything to me, and we're going to make it through this. I promise you."

I nodded, but his words felt hollow, like they lacked the depth they once had. I forced a smile, trying to believe him, but something had changed. The Sawyer I once put on a pedestal had fallen, and I couldn't unsee it. The fact that he had been with Val—had touched her the way he had touched me—had taken him down a peg in my eyes, and I didn't know how to move past that.

"We'll be okay," he said, his voice gentle but firm, as though willing it to be true. "We have to be."

I nodded again, though doubt gnawed at me. *Could we really make it through this? Could I forget the way he'd stood there, silent, as Val taunted me? Could I trust him when part of me couldn't let go of the image of her wrapped around him, wanting him?*

As the silence stretched on, we lay back down, staring up at the stars. The vastness of the night sky mirrored the growing distance between us. The cool grass felt strange against my skin, while the stars above seemed too far away—untouchable, just like the warmth I used to feel between us. I felt small under the weight of it all, insignificant, like everything that had once been bright and easy between us had been eclipsed by doubt.

We lay side by side, but the space between us felt like miles.

Chapter 23

As we approach Miner's, we stop abruptly, searching for the source of the frantic voice calling our names. Beatrice comes jogging toward us, relief evident on her face. "There you are!"

My eyes dart around, panic seizing me. "Is Dermott okay? What's wrong?" Anxiety surges through me, my senses on high alert.

"Oh my God, yes! He's fine. I'm sorry, I didn't mean to scare you." She twists her hands nervously. "He's back at the shop helping me pack arrangements." She glances sheepishly at Sawyer. "But I need help. I have a bridal shower scheduled on Miner's back patio in an hour, and my delivery truck broke down. The arrangements are still at the shop, and I need a vehicle big enough to transport them." She looks at Sawyer with pleading eyes. "Could we use your truck? Please?"

Relief crashes over me, leaving my legs weak. After everything that has happened in my life, my mind immediately jumps to the worst. I try to shake it off as Beatrice continues. "Sawyer, can you bring your truck around to the shop? Josie, come with me to the back room."

In no time, Sawyer heads back to the stadium for his truck, and Beatrice and I hurry toward her floral shop. The sweet scent of fresh flowers envelops us as we enter, their vibrant colors brightening the cozy back room. "These are beautiful, Bea," I say, genuinely impressed by the floral arrangements filling the room.

Dermott appears, narrowing his eyes as he takes in my appearance. "Are you okay? You look stressed."

I wave him off. "I'm fine. Just another rough letter. I'll tell you about it later." I take a moment to look him over. "Why are you wearing an apron?"

A dramatic smile spreads across his face. "Looks good, doesn't it? I fit right in."

Beatrice giggles, shaking her head. "Not sure that's possible." She claps her hands, eager to get to work. "Let's get these ready for transport." She opens the back door wide just as Sawyer backs his truck up to the entrance.

We begin carefully loading the arrangements into the truck, making sure each one is secure. It feels good to focus on something other than the tension with Sawyer. The distraction is a much-needed reprieve for my heart and mind. As we work, a memory suddenly surfaces.

"Remember that time we tried to help you with your horticulture project?" I ask, breaking the silence. "We mixed up all the seedlings. Beatrice, you were ready to kill us."

Beatrice chuckles. "I'm still traumatized by that. We spent hours trying to figure out which plant was which."

Sawyer smiles, a genuine smile that reaches his eyes. The shared memory lightens the mood, bridging the gap between us, even if only for a moment. I find myself watching his face for a second longer than I should, and an unexpected memory flickers in my mind. I see Sawyer standing in the auditorium, clutching wildflowers for my mother, and I quickly look away.

Once everything is loaded, Beatrice issues her final instructions. "Okay, I have to get back inside and finish arranging another big order. Dermott can stay here and help me. You two take these to Miner's and set them up on the back patio."

Sawyer and I stand side by side, clearly uncomfortable with the plan. "I can stay in the shop, and you can go with Sawyer to Miner's," I suggest, hoping for a quick escape.

Beatrice raises an eyebrow, mockingly. "You can put together arrangements?"

I hesitate, knowing I'm defeated. "No. No, I have no idea how to do that."

"Exactly. Off you go! Call me if you need anything."

***

Beatrice and Dermott head back inside, leaving Sawyer and me with a truckload of flowers. We drive to Miner's in silence, awkwardness pressing down on us. When we arrive, the back patio and gazebo are already bustling with staff setting up. Heat lamps glow softly, casting the space in a warm, welcoming light.

"Wow, it's beautiful back here. I've been staying here and didn't even notice this place," I say, taking it all in. Another hidden gem in this little town I used to call home. I can feel Sawyer watching me as I take in the scene, my awe difficult to hide.

After a moment, we start unloading the flowers, carefully carrying them to their designated spots. The air is filled with the sweet scent of the blooms and the faint murmur of busy preparations. The patio is a vibrant tapestry of fall colors—deep oranges, rich reds, and golden yellows. The late-afternoon light catches on each flower, making the scene glow with warmth.

Sawyer and I fall into a rhythm. I place a centerpiece on one of the tables, adjusting it until it's perfectly centered. Across from me, Sawyer is doing the same, his brow furrowed in concentration. When our eyes meet, he gives me a small, almost shy smile, and for a brief moment, the years between us seem to melt away.

After the centerpieces are in place, we move on to the floral swags. We drape them over the railings and around the gazebo, the greenery adding a touch of natural elegance. As I reach up to secure a particularly stubborn swag, my fingers brush against Sawyer's. A jolt of electricity shoots through me, and I quickly pull my hand back, hoping he doesn't notice the flush creeping up my cheeks.

"Here, let me help with that," Sawyer says softly. He takes the swag from my hands, our fingers brushing again. This time, neither of us pulls away immediately. We linger for a moment, the contact sending a mix of emotions through me—familiarity, longing, and something that feels almost like hope. But I shut it down quickly, knowing that wherever I find hope, I usually find pain.

"Thanks," I murmur, stepping back to give him space. I watch as he secures the swag, his movements precise and confident. It's a side of him I haven't seen in years, and it stirs something deep inside me.

We continue working, the tasks keeping us busy but not so busy that we can't steal glances at each other. We hang delicate flower crowns on the backs of the chairs, their soft petals adding a whimsical touch to the setting. As I adjust one of the crowns, I notice Sawyer doing the same, his fingers gentle as he handles the fragile blooms.

When it's time to scatter the petals along the walkway, we work side by side, our hands occasionally brushing as we reach into the basket. Each touch sends a spark through me, a reminder of the connection we once had. The walkway soon fills with a trail of petals, their colors vibrant against the dark wood.

At one point, I look up and catch Sawyer watching me. There's a tenderness in his eyes, an admiration that makes my heart skip a beat. His gaze lingers, as if he's seeing me for the first time all over again, and it makes my pulse quicken.

"What?" I ask, trying to sound casual despite the flutter in my chest.

He shakes his head, a small smile playing on his lips. "Nothing. Just . . . you're somehow more beautiful than I remember." I feel warmth spread through me at his words. "And I remember you as the most beautiful girl I ever saw."

"Are you sure you haven't been smoking some of those flowers?" I say, nodding toward the centerpieces and laughing, defaulting to my classic avoidance technique. But inside, the old butterflies stir in my stomach, clattering around.

Finally, we step back to admire our work. The patio looks stunning, a testament to our efforts and the beauty of Beatrice's flowers. The sun casts a golden glow over everything, making the fall colors even more vibrant.

Sawyer turns to me, a smirk playing on his lips. "You know, if you ever find yourself out of a job, you might have a future in flowers."

I laugh. "Ha! Maybe I could drop them off, but putting them together? Definitely not my thing." I glance at the gorgeous colors in front of me and feel a sense of pride in Beatrice's work. "Damn, Beatrice is good."

"She sure is." We stand there, taking it all in. The earlier tension seems to dissipate, and then I hear a light chuckle come from Sawyer. "Do you remember the last time someone asked us to help set up for a party?"

I bring my hand to my mouth as the memory floods back. "Oh my God, your poor uncle," I say, laughing. "Your mom volunteered us, and we ended up being the only ones there to set everything up."

Sawyer shakes his head, chuckling. "Yeah, Uncle Lou had no idea what he was getting into. We tried putting up decorations, and half of them ended up in the lake."

"And your aunt tried to chase down the floating lanterns in the rowboat," I add, grinning.

"And Aunt Marietta fell out of the boat!" Sawyer exclaims, his laughter echoing mine.

"Oh my God, it was a disaster!" I'm practically crying with laughter. "We tried to save her, but she swam out on her own—and we somehow ended up covered in mud, soaking wet."

"And then we tried making it up to them by setting up the dessert table," Sawyer says, shaking his head.

In unison, we say, "The raccoons!"

"Those damn raccoons ate everything," Sawyer says, smiling. "They never asked me to help with anything again."

We laugh, the kind of laugh that lifts a heavy heart. But as the laughter fades, nostalgia casts a shadow.

"I loved that lake. I loved that house. I loved everything about that place," I say, a wistful note creeping into my voice. "Do you still visit there?"

"Uncle Lou and Aunt Marietta moved to Florida a few years ago. They sold the house."

"Oh," I say, trying to mask the sadness I have no right to feel. The house wasn't mine—but the memories are. So the sharp pang of its loss still stings. "Everyone around here moves to Florida."

"The winters still suck, so a lot of people leave." He smiles. "I remember we used to drive up there all the time, just to sit on the dock. You loved Maple Lake."

"It was heaven," I agree. "The most peaceful place I'd ever been. And it was only ten minutes away."

We stand there, lost in the shared memory. The laughter has lifted the mood, but an undercurrent still lingers, a quiet reminder of everything left hanging between us. "I could sit there for hours. I miss feeling like that—just . . . being. Those were some of the best times. Watching the sunset, listening to the water. It felt like the whole world disappeared. I felt safe." I pause, remembering those times. I never realized they would end. "I used to dream about that place when I was away."

"You did?"

I nod, my voice distant. "I'd picture us there, on the dock, with the water lapping at our feet and the sky turning shades of orange and pink."

Sawyer's gaze softens even more, his eyes filled with a mixture of sadness and longing. When I catch his expression, I blush, realizing how much I've revealed.

"Sorry. I don't know why I rambled like that—"

"I think about that place. That *time*. More than you know," Sawyer admits suddenly.

I see the sincerity in his eyes, and it stirs something deep within me. But before I can respond, I notice Mrs. Miner bustling around the patio, directing employees with an air of authority despite her age. Her presence breaks the moment, reminding us that the time to deliver Sarge's letter has arrived.

Chapter 24

Then

Sawyer and I sat on the edge of the dock at his uncle's house on Maple Lake, our feet dangling just above the still, reflective water. It was early fall, and Sawyer was home for the weekend from college. I didn't think he would've come home so soon if it weren't for the uncertainty between us before he left. The autumn leaves—brilliant reds, oranges, and yellows—floated gently down, creating a colorful blanket on the lake's surface. The air was crisp and cool, filled with the distant hint of woodsmoke.

"It's so beautiful here," I said softly, not wanting to shatter the peace. "This is my favorite place."

Sawyer nodded, his gaze fixed on the horizon where the sun was beginning to set. "I know what you mean. It's like time stands still here. No matter how crazy things get, this place always brings me back."

I turned to look at him, studying his familiar profile—his strong jawline, the slight scruff of his beard, the way his eyes always warmed when they found mine. "Yeah, me too," I said quietly. "It feels like everything's changing so fast. Sometimes I worry about losing . . . this." I gestured toward the lake, but my voice carried the weight of what I really meant—us.

Sawyer turned to me, his eyes serious, the easy smile from moments ago gone. "You know you never have to worry about losing me, right?"

I wanted to believe him. I knew he meant it, but deep down, I couldn't shake the feeling that something was shifting. Still, the earnestness in his eyes comforted me enough to push that feeling aside—for now.

"What do you see for our future, Sawyer?" I asked, my voice barely above a whisper as I twisted a strand of hair around my finger, nervous for his answer.

He took a deep breath, steadying himself. "I see us finishing school, finding jobs," he said, putting his arm around me and pulling me close. "That's the boring part. But I see so much happiness, Josie. Laughter. All of it."

I felt his words stir something deep inside me, something I hadn't even realized was sleeping.

"We'll build something beautiful, just for us. A home, a family. And I want you to visit me at Penn State soon. I miss you," he added, his voice almost pleading.

I looked away, my fingers tracing the edge of the dock as I tried to swallow the lump rising in my throat. His words were so full, so heavy, and they settled in me like stones.

"Is that what you want?" he asked, his voice gentle, but with an urgency that made my heart clench.

"Yes," I replied, my voice cracking.

"Then why do you look like I just told you I want to lock you in a prison for eternity?"

I laughed, a shaky sound that barely masked my anxiety. "No. No. I want the same things so much it hurts. I'm just scared."

Sawyer's brows knit together in concern. "Why?"

"Because of my mom. My family." Sawyer waited patiently while I paused to gather my words. "I haven't had a great example. I love my parents. I know it sounds crazy, but I wouldn't want to have another mom and dad. It's just—I don't want to repeat the life I've grown up in. I don't want to have kids and do to them what my mom and dad have done to me. I'm afraid. I'm afraid I'll turn out like them. Like her." The tears spilled over as the words escaped. "I don't want to do to you what she's done to my dad."

"Josie." The pain and sympathy in his voice cut through my defenses like a blade.

"Doesn't that scare you? That I'll ruin your life?"

He pulled me even closer, resting his chin on top of my head. "No, Josie. It doesn't scare me. Because I know you. I know your heart. And I know you're nothing like your mom."

I let out a shaky breath, leaning into his embrace. "But what if I am? What if I end up hurting you?"

Sawyer gently lifted my chin, making me look into his eyes. "We're in this forever, Josie O. So as much as it sucks, we're going to hurt each other at some point. But not like that. Not like what your mom has done to your family. Not like what my dad has done to mine. We'll make our own life, our own family, and we'll do it better. We'll do it together." His words wrapped around me like a warm blanket, soothing my fears. "And if, in some wild alternate universe, you start drinking and can't stop, I'll go to the ends of the earth with you to get help and hold your hand until you come back to me."

And with those words, I crumbled. I stumbled and fell so much deeper in love than I ever thought possible. I thought we had lost each other after the prom and the widening gap between us, but now it felt like I was free-falling back into the beauty that was Sawyer and me, with no end in sight. We stayed there, wrapped in each other's arms, as the sun set and the stars began to appear, painting the sky with a thousand points of light—yet nothing seemed brighter than the future I was beginning to see with him.

"Since we're placing orders for things in our future, I have a request," I said, staring wide-eyed into his eyes, my heart pounding with excitement and hope.

"I'll give it to you," he said without a moment's hesitation.

A laugh bubbled out of me. "You don't even know what it is!"

"What is it?" he asked, his eyes sparkling with curiosity and affection.

"When I grow up, I want to live here on Maple Lake with you—and our kids," I said, my voice filled with a dreamy certainty. "Is that silly? Am I supposed to want to run a company and be a high-powered executive?"

Sawyer kissed me gently on the nose. "That's a good plan," he said, his voice warm and tender. "You can be all those things, here with me, and our kids if that's what you want."

"Is that what you want?"

"You are what I want."

"And a dog," I added, feeling the joy of planning our future together.

"What?"

"I want a dog too."

"It has to be a cool dog. Not one of those little ones that look like rats," he teased, his eyes dancing with mischief.

My hands flew to my chest in mock horror. "Don't talk about Princess like that!"

Sawyer groaned dramatically and gently tackled me backward on the dock, his laughter mingling with mine as we tumbled into a playful heap. "What will I do with you, Josie O?" he murmured, his voice filled with love and wonder. He didn't wait for an answer. "I know what I'll do."

"What?" I whispered.

"I'll marry you someday."

***

Sawyer kept asking me to visit him at Penn State, and I pretended to be only mildly interested in seeing the campus, making vague plans for the future. What he didn't know was that Beatrice, Jason, and I, with some meticulous planning, had organized a surprise visit. Beatrice and I would drive down together, stay at a hotel near the campus, and surprise Sawyer right before the football game. The days leading up to my visit crawled by with excruciating slowness. I kept imagining the excitement of seeing Sawyer, of watching his face light up when he saw me, and it kept me going through the tough days at home.

When the weekend finally arrived, Beatrice and I packed her car, queued up our playlists, and hit the highway with the windows down, the autumn air crisp and invigorating. We checked into a small hotel with views of the rolling Pennsylvania hills—nothing fancy, but perfect for our plan. After freshening up and donning our Penn State gear, we headed to the campus. The buzz of game day filled the air. Students and families dressed in blue and white swarmed the grounds, their excitement contagious.

The Penn State campus was alive with energy. The aroma of grilled burgers wafted through the air as parking lots transformed into a carnival of blue and white. Fans laughed and cheered, spirits high in anticipation of the game. Beatrice and I could barely contain our excitement as we wove through the crowd, my heart pounding with each step closer to the tailgate where Jason said he and Sawyer would be.

Rounding a group of rowdy students tossing a football, we spotted Jason's setup. My stomach flipped with nervous excitement. Beatrice squeezed my hand, her grin as wide as mine.

"Ready?" she whispered.

"Ready!" I replied, trying to steady my trembling hands.

We approached quietly, slipping through clusters of laughing fans and families. Jason caught my eye first, his expression turning to mock surprise as he played along with the plan. He gave a subtle nod toward Sawyer, who was laughing at something a friend had said, completely oblivious to my approach.

I cleared my throat and mustered my most dramatic, high-pitched Valley girl impression.

"Like, oh my gawd! Isn't that the super cute new catcher?" I squealed. "Can I, like, have your autograph and maybe marry you?"

Sawyer paused for a split second. Without turning around, he tossed over his shoulder, "I'm flattered, but I'm taken." He turned back to his friend, chuckling.

My mouth fell open at his unwitting dismissal, and Beatrice suppressed a laugh. Ready for round two, I put on an exaggerated pout and stepped closer.

"But, like, are you sure you're really taken? Because I heard from Becky, who heard from Chad, that you're totally single and ready to mingle! And I'm ready to catch some balls." I poked him lightly in the back.

This time, Sawyer turned around, eyes wide with alarm, ready to confront his overly enthusiastic admirer. Beatrice was laughing hysterically, barely able to breathe at the ridiculousness of the scene.

Sawyer's expression shifted from shock to confusion and then to elation in an instant.

"Josie! Holy shit!" He wrapped his arms around me, lifting me off the ground. My legs wrapped around his waist as he held me close, our faces inches apart, both of us smiling.

"You're here. I can't believe you're here."

"I'm here," I confirmed, my heart pounding with excitement. Our lips met, and the whoops and hollers from his friends faded as we were lost in our own world—my favorite place to be.

Eventually, he gently set me down, resting his forehead against mine, his arm still around my waist.

"I can't believe you surprised me," he grinned.

"And I can't believe you didn't recognize your number one fan," I teased, poking his side gently.

"Wait. Are you really ready to catch some balls? Because I can arrange that," he teased, mock seriousness in his tone.

I grabbed his sides, squeezing because I knew he'd squirm. We laughed, smiled, kissed, and intertwined hands in glorious moments of affection. It was easily the best time of my life.

His eyes traveled over me from head to toe. "Look at you," he said, smiling as he gently turned me around. "Like you were born to be a Nittany Lion."

I looked down at my outfit—jeans, as usual, paired with a blue-and-white Penn State football top.

"I have to play the part," I replied with a grin.

Sawyer introduced me to his friends, who were all eager to meet the girl they'd heard so much about. His introduction felt like a spotlight turning on me. His friends—grouped around a makeshift grill—welcomed me with enthusiastic cheers.

"The famous Josie!" one of them exclaimed, offering a high five as I approached.

Suddenly, the group burst into song—not just any song, but a raucous, off-key rendition of the Outfield's Your Love. Their enthusiastic abandon turned the melody into more of a joyful shout, and I couldn't help but laugh when they emphasized the opening line, clearly inspired by my name. It was the kind of nostalgic anthem everyone seemed to know by heart, and their energy was contagious.

Their voices echoed across the parking lot, drawing laughter and a few curious stares from other tailgaters. Beatrice and I were doubled over, clinging to each other for support as tears of laughter streamed down our faces.

As their spirited serenade wound down, I wiped the tears from my cheeks, still breathless from laughing. The joy bubbling up inside me was intoxicating, and for the first time in a while, I felt truly light. But then, as my eyes drifted over the small crowd of onlookers, the air shifted. Among them, standing slightly apart with a look that could curdle milk, was Val.

She was impossible to miss—her arms crossed over her chest, lips curled in a smug, knowing smile that seemed to mock everything about this moment. Her bleached hair fell in loose waves around her shoulders, but instead of blending in, she looked sharp, predatory, like she was stalking her prey. Our eyes met, and for a brief, bitter second, I thought I saw her smirk widen. She didn't need to say a word—her mere presence was enough to send a chill crawling down my spine.

Val rolled her eyes dramatically, and with a deliberate flick of her hair, she turned and slunk back into the crowd, her hips swaying like she was the queen of her own twisted world. I swallowed hard, willing the sudden tightness in my chest to ease. It was just Val, I told myself. Just Val being Val—poisoning the air with her existence. But the knot in my stomach wasn't so easy to shake.

Her being here, so close to Sawyer, was an awful reminder that she would always be lurking on the edge of my life, waiting for her chance.

Sawyer's gaze was on me now, his eyes filled with a question I didn't want to answer. He must've seen Val too, must've noticed the way my body tensed. I forced a smile, squeezed his hand, trying to convey that everything was fine, even though a part of me felt like I was crumbling from the inside out.

His hand tightened around mine, calming me, as if to say, I'm here. You're not alone. But no amount of reassurance could erase the truth—Val wasn't going anywhere. She'd always be there, lingering in the shadows of our lives, like a ghost that refused to rest.

Sensing my unease, Sawyer leaned in, his voice low and determined.

"I'll say something to her, Josie. She won't do this to us again."

I shook my head, gripping his hand tighter, desperate to hold on to the peace of the moment and grateful that he didn't want to ignore the elephant in the room as he'd done before.

"No, don't bait her. That's what she wants. Please, let's just have fun today."

His jaw tightened for a second, but then he nodded, pulling me closer. Val hadn't said anything outright since I'd been here. Confronting her would only give her more power, and I wasn't going to let her ruin this day for us. Not again.

Sawyer guided me to the cornhole boards set up nearby. The game started with friendly competition but quickly escalated as more of Sawyer's friends joined in, each hilariously competitive. As I took my turn, tossing the beanbag with more enthusiasm than accuracy, Sawyer cheered from the sidelines.

"That's it, Josie O! Aim for the hole, not the barbecue!" His laughter was contagious, and even I had to laugh at my dismal throw that went wildly off course.

The afternoon drifted into evening, the sky tinting with the colors of sunset as we joined the crowd heading toward the stadium. The energy was electric, and by the time we found our seats, the excitement was contagious. I took a moment to savor the sense of belonging, of being part of this lively, joyful setting. I felt welcomed and at home in a way I hadn't expected. This felt real—a glimpse of the future I could see with Sawyer, here at Penn State.

***

After the game, we decided to grab some food at a nearby diner. The smell of coffee and fried food filled the air as we slid into a large booth. Laughter and chatter dominated the table, the camaraderie palpable. Beatrice mentioned she wanted to go to a party with some friends from Maplewood, and Jason had agreed to keep an eye on her. Knowing I wasn't interested in a party, she suggested Sawyer stay with me for the night, an idea Sawyer eagerly agreed to.

We reached the hotel, our pace slowing as we approached the entrance. The lobby was dimly lit and so quiet that I wondered if my heartbeat was loud enough to hear. Sawyer's hand tightened around mine, a silent communication of his own anticipation. Something was about to change—we both knew it. He led me to the elevator, and as the doors closed, shutting us off from the world, I saw the flicker of a smile play across his lips.

"Alone at last," he whispered, his voice a soft rumble that sent a shiver down my spine. The elevator crawled to our floor, the tension between us building with every passing moment. We leaned into each other, and when the doors finally opened, we hurried down the hallway to my room. The keycard swipe sounded impossibly loud in the quiet.

In the hotel room, the soft glow from the lamps bathed Sawyer's face in a warm light. He stepped closer, his eyes searching mine. I could see the flicker of uncertainty in his expression, like he was waiting for me to change my mind. His hand hovered over my cheek for a second before he finally cupped my face, his thumb brushing gently over my skin.

"Are you sure?" His voice was softer now, not quite steady. I could feel the tremble in his fingers, the way his breath seemed to catch in his throat.

I pulled him closer, reassuring him as much as myself. But even then, I could sense the hesitation in him—the way his hand gripped mine a little tighter, the way his eyes flickered with something I couldn't quite place. He wanted this, I knew he did, but I could tell he was afraid I didn't.

"I'm ready." My eyes were wide, searching his.

"Josie, are you sure?" he asked, a quiver in his voice, the concern in his eyes sincere.

I threaded my fingers through his hair, pulling him down to me. "I've never been more sure about anything," I murmured.

"Oh, thank God," he whispered, smiling just before our lips met.

The kiss was gentle, full of the months we'd spent missing one another and the years we'd spent truly knowing each other. Everything else faded away as we found comfort in simply being together. Every touch and quiet word felt like a promise, a reminder of the bond we had. We shared whispered "I love yous" and, in the stillness of the night, began a new chapter in our story.

That night became one of my most cherished memories. Later, as we lay side by side, the world outside seemed impossibly far away. Sawyer's hand brushed lightly along my arm, the quiet closeness a comfort all its own.

"I love you so much," he murmured, his voice soft in the dim room.

My fingers traced his face, down his neck, across his collarbone. I stared into his deep, soulful eyes.

"I don't even know how to describe how much I love you, Sawyer."

He chuckled softly. "You just did."

"Well, I can keep describing it if you need clarification." Our noses nearly touched as we laughed together in the dark.

He kissed my forehead softly. "I remember the first time I saw you. It felt like someone flicked a switch in my chest. At Maple's Ice Cream Shoppe my freshman year of high school."

"How do you remember that?"

"Don't you?"

"Of course I do."

"You were sitting with your legs crossed, almost like you were trying to make yourself smaller, with a little cup of ice cream in your hands. Your hair was tied up in a messy bun, and you looked up at me with those eyes. Something happened inside me."

"Sawyer," I whispered in disbelief.

"And then I did whatever it took to be around you. I signed up for the damn Turkey Trot because I overheard Beatrice say you were volunteering, and then I didn't even get to talk to you. I'd call Sarge and ask if I could cut his grass or shovel his snow just to be near you."

My eyes widened, disbelief flickering through me—how could my life, so messy and flawed, hold a moment this extraordinary? His words weren't just beautiful; they carried a raw, unguarded love that still surprised me. I still wasn't sure I really deserved this.

"I watched you at the baseball field that day," I blurted, not wanting him to be alone in his revelations. "Before I ever saw you at the ice cream shop. You took your mask off, and in that moment, it was like I'd been asleep my whole life and had just woken up."

Sawyer's gaze softened, and he cupped my face gently, brushing a thumb across my cheek. "Then I guess we woke each other up, Josie."

Overwhelmed by emotion, I touched his face, tracing his features. His hand covered mine, pressing it gently to his cheek.

"I'm sorry we're in a hotel and not somewhere more special. You deserve the best."

"Sawyer, anywhere with you is special. We could be in a dumpster and I'd be happy." I winced. "Well, maybe a dumpster wouldn't be ideal for the first time, but you know what I mean."

We laughed, kissed, and cuddled, finally drifting off to sleep, entwined and content, so hopeful for the future—naïve to what it would bring.

Chapter 25

We approach Mrs. Miner, who is directing a young waiter with the precision of a drill sergeant, her voice firm as she instructs him on properly setting up the dessert table.

Sawyer, with a mischievous glint in his eye, chimes in, "We know a thing or two about setting up a dessert table, Mrs. Miner." I gasp in surprise, then burst into laughter. "You don't have any raccoons around, do you?"

Mrs. Miner turns to us with a raised eyebrow, clearly unimpressed by our interruption. Her expression relaxes slightly as she takes in our earnest faces. I quickly try to recover the moment before it slips away.

"Hello, Mrs. Miner. We're so sorry to bother you. We know you're busy, but we were wondering if we could steal a moment of your time."

"Josie, is everything okay with your accommodation?"

"Oh yes! Yes, of course!" I reply, my voice a bit too eager.

Her eyes dart to Sawyer, trying to figure out what we could possibly want with her.

"We're actually here to deliver something to you—from Sarge," Sawyer says gently.

Mrs. Miner's eyes widen, curiosity and a hint of sadness flickering across her face. "From Sarge?" she echoes, her voice quivering.

I reach into my purse and carefully pull out the letter. As I hand it to her, Mrs. Miner's hands tremble slightly. Her eyes mist over as she recognizes the familiar handwriting. "RP," she murmurs with a faint, bittersweet smile.

The busy patio fades into the background, the noise and activity becoming a distant hum. "Come inside for a moment, will you?" She turns and leads us into the inn, the door creaking softly as it closes behind us, shutting out the world outside.

Sawyer stays close to me, his shoulder brushing against mine as we follow Mrs. Miner through the dimly lit hallway. The scent of old wood and lavender permeates the air, so different from the bustling energy outside. We turn a corner and find ourselves in a small, cozy sitting room filled with antique furniture. Soft light from a nearby lamp dances gently on the walls. This must be Mrs. Miner's private living quarters.

In the corner of the room, I notice her brother standing by the window, lost in thought as he gazes outside. He seems completely unaware of our presence, absorbed in his own world. I catch Sawyer's eye and nod subtly toward Mrs. Miner's brother. Sawyer lifts his eyebrows in acknowledgment, understanding the unspoken message.

Mrs. Miner gestures for us to sit down in a pair of overstuffed armchairs near the fireplace. Sawyer's hand lingers on the back of my chair, his presence comforting. As we settle in, Mrs. Miner sits opposite us, the letter clutched in her hands.

She looks at the letter again. "RP," she murmurs, the initials bringing a mix of emotions to her face. She looks up at us. "Now, tell me, how did you come to receive this letter?"

Sawyer and I exchange a glance. *Why isn't she tearing the letter open to hear what her long-lost love has to say from beyond the grave?*

"Well," Sawyer begins, "it seems Sarge decided to send us on a scavenger hunt of sorts."

"A scavenger hunt?" Mrs. Miner repeats, her brow furrowing.

I lean forward. "That's right, Mrs. Miner. Sarge's sister gave me a letter at the funeral home, and she gave one to Sawyer too. Those letters sent us to the baseball field, where we discovered we were on a scavenger hunt—together."

I glance at Sawyer, who is smiling at me as I speak. His smile encourages me to continue. "And then we were sent to the ice cream shop, and then the football field, and now here."

Mrs. Miner takes a deep breath and leans back slightly. "And what did these letters say?"

Sawyer and I exchange another look, searching for the right words. "Nothing and everything," I begin. "He talked about his past, the places that were special to him, and the lessons he learned—but it sounds like he had some heavy regrets." I smile weakly. "I'm sorry, Mrs. Miner. It's clear you two had a pretty intense history."

Sawyer carries on for me. "We saw your initials engraved together on a tree at the baseball field. He really drove home that he regretted not putting his roots down."

I swallow hard, the enormity of this moment sinking into me. Before the emotion can silence me, I find my voice. "Mrs. Miner, he seemed to think that he made decisions about his life based on what other people thought. And when he sent us to Maple's Ice Cream Shoppe, we saw a picture of you and Sarge. It made us wonder if there was some sort of competition between Sarge and your husband." I clear my throat awkwardly, fearing I've gone too far. "You looked so happy in that photo, by the way."

Mrs. Miner laughs softly. "I know exactly the photo you're talking about. I have a copy myself."

"He talked about how the paths we dodge can haunt us more than the ones we take," Sawyer says, his voice growing more thoughtful, his gaze lingering on me with a depth that makes my stomach flip.

A wistful smile crosses Mrs. Miner's lips. "Yes—I would say Sarge regretted the path he chose, but he thought he was doing the right thing."

Sawyer and I both sit quietly for a moment, thinking Mrs. Miner is about to share the details of their story, but she doesn't. She just looks at us and nods, bidding us to carry on.

"And at the football field," I start, "he guided us to the bleachers where he said goodbye to you before Vietnam changed everything. He alluded to leaving himself there too. The thing that shocks me the most—and this whole thing is pretty shocking," I say, throwing my hands in the air dramatically, "is how he keeps saying he wasn't brave! Can you believe that?" I feel Sarge's words pressing on my heart and once again catch Sawyer directing a sweet smile my way before stepping in.

"He said it takes courage to see past the obvious, to question what you think you know," Sawyer finishes, his eyes meeting mine.

Mrs. Miner looks down at the letter, her fingers tracing the edges. "I suppose he wanted to say something important. Something he couldn't say while he was alive."

My curiosity is still piqued. "Mrs. Miner, what's your maiden name?"

"Patterson. I left that name behind when I was very young."

"Would you mind telling us about it? Sarge really got us invested in your lives."

"Oh, I'd love to. I never miss a chance to talk about Martin." She takes a deep breath. "I married Martin Miner when I was very young." Mrs. Miner smiles as she reaches into a drawer in the table beside her, pulling out a copy of the picture framed at the ice cream shop. She glances at it briefly before resting it on her lap.

"He was the love of my life, my rock, my everything. We met at a dance in the old town hall. I remember him standing across the room, looking so handsome and confident. When he finally asked me to dance, I knew my life would never be the same."

She pauses, her eyes misting over with the memories. "We were inseparable from that night on. He was kind, funny, and had a way of making me feel like the most special person in the world. We dreamed of building a life together, and part of that dream was this inn. We bought it just after we got married, a place where we could create our own little slice of heaven. Martin had some health issues. Nothing major, but it was enough to keep him out of the draft. We thought we got lucky. Imagine that."

Her fingers gently trace the edges of the photo. "But life had other plans. Martin fell seriously ill shortly after we bought the inn. It was sudden and unexpected—aggressive cancer. By the time we found out, it was too late. He fought bravely, but he passed away within a year. It was the hardest thing I've ever faced, other than having to carry on without him, of course."

Tears slip down her cheeks, but she remains resolute. "I couldn't bear to let go of Miner's. It was our dream, our legacy. So I stayed. I ran it in his memory, pouring all my love and dedication into keeping it alive. I never loved anyone the way I loved Martin. He was my one and only, and without him, I couldn't move on."

She looks up at us, her eyes clear and determined. "I'm not afraid to die because I know I'll see him again. Every day here at Miner's, I feel his presence, his love. It's what has kept me going all these years. And when my time comes, I'll be ready to be with him again."

Sawyer and I are silent. My heart breaks for this woman before me, sharing the most poignant story of lost love. But Mrs. Miner's story leaves more questions than answers.

"But what about Sarge?" I ask, my curiosity burning.

She smiles fondly. "Sarge was a good friend. I, of course, knew him best as William. He was a delight to be around. But when he came back from Vietnam, he had choices to make, and looking back, he made the choices he thought he had to at the time. There was a lot of pain, and that pain kept him from coming around here. I suspect it haunted him throughout his life."

Mrs. Miner laughs at our dumbfounded expressions, then places the letter—unopened—on the table in front of her. Sawyer and I exchange bewildered looks.

Finally, Sawyer speaks the words on the tip of my tongue. "Aren't you going to open that?"

She shakes her head. "It's not my letter to open." She places the copy of the photo from the ice cream shop on the table, facing us. Sawyer leans forward to pick up the photo.

"Holy shit," he murmurs, realization dawning on his face.

Chapter 26

Then

Sawyer and I parted on a high note after my surprise visit, but things went downhill fast when he returned for Christmas break. I knew he was getting a ride home with someone from Maplewood, a kid a year or two older than him. It never even crossed my mind who else might be in the car.

When he texted that he was on his way, I decided to surprise him by being at his house when he arrived. I got there early and sat at the kitchen table, sipping hot chocolate while chatting with his mom. The warmth of the cocoa and our familiar conversation felt comforting. Over the time Sawyer and I had been together, his mom had become like the maternal figure I'd always longed for, filling the void left by my own mother, whose absence gnawed at me constantly.

"I'm going to start dinner. You can help," she said, pulling out pots and pans.

"Okay, full disclosure—I'm terrible in the kitchen," I said with a nervous laugh, hoping to mask just how true that was.

She glanced at me with a knowing smile. "So, who does all the cooking in your house? Mom or Dad?"

I hesitated, her question catching me off guard. Neither, really. When my mom was well, she cooked, but it was rare—fleeting moments of normalcy that never lasted. How could I admit the truth? That most nights, dinner was whatever I could pull together—a sandwich, a bowl of cereal, something easy and lonely.

The contrast between Sawyer's warm, bustling kitchen and my own hit me like a gust of cold air, sharp and cutting.

Before I could answer, she passed by me, squeezing my arm gently. "It's a good thing Johnny can cook. He'll take care of you," she said softly, as if sensing my discomfort.

I smiled. The idea of Sawyer taking care of me, of being part of his family, was more than just comforting—it gave me hope. This wasn't just a relationship. This was safety, warmth, the home I never really had.

We laughed and continued making dinner, but soon I heard a car pull up outside, followed by cheerful voices. My heart leaped with excitement. I rushed to the front door, a grin already spreading across my face.

The car door opened, and my smile fell as Val stepped out and held the door for Sawyer. She glanced at me, her smirk sinister and satisfied, relishing my expression.

"Thanks for letting me squeeze in next to you, Sawyer. I know it was a tight ride!" she said, her voice dripping with a taunting edge.

Sawyer climbed out, his eyes immediately finding mine, guilt flickering there. I could feel the sting of it, even though he hadn't said a word. Seeing her with him—it felt like a betrayal.

As Val slid back into the car, she leaned out of the window. "Don't forget to call me!" she added casually, her words aimed at him, but her gaze darted toward me for just a second longer than necessary.

Sawyer's head snapped around, his expression a mix of disbelief and frustration, as if he couldn't believe she'd actually said it. When he turned back to me, worry flickered in his eyes—he wasn't going to call her, but he was afraid I might think otherwise.

Val waved in my direction. "Merry Christmas, Josie!" she said, her tone drenched with false cheer as the car rolled away.

Sawyer, his duffel bag slung over his shoulder, stepped forward, looking like he was about to say something, his lips already parting for an apology. But it was too late. The damage was already done.

"I've got to go," I said, my voice cold and brittle. "I don't have time for your bullshit excuses."

I saw him flinch. My words were sharp, but not sharp enough to cut through the anger and hurt rising inside me. This wasn't just about Val anymore. It was about Sawyer's constant disregard for my feelings—about him allowing her presence to tear at mine, again and again. Every time she was near, it felt like he was saying my pain didn't matter, that I didn't matter.

I turned to leave, my steps heavy, but then his mom stepped onto the porch, her face lighting up at the sight of her son.

"Johnny boy!" she called, her voice filled with joy. She looked at me with a warm smile. "You're staying for dinner, Josie."

Her words were like a knife twisting in my chest. I wasn't just walking away from Sawyer—I was walking away from them. This family that had started to feel like my own. This home where I had found comfort. If I lost him, I lost all of it.

I forced a smile that felt brittle. "Thanks, but I've got to get to the Christmas Market tonight. I'll catch up with you later." The words came out steadier than I expected, the lie slipping past my lips with practiced ease.

Turning away, I quickened my pace, my footsteps crunching against the icy sidewalk. Each step felt like an act of defiance against the invisible thread that still pulled me toward Sawyer. I could feel his gaze on my back, heavy and unrelenting, but I didn't dare look over my shoulder.

Beneath the anger, there was a deep fear clawing at me—a fear that in freeing myself from the mess Val had created, I would need to lose Sawyer too.

***

By the time I was setting up the stand at the Christmas Market later that evening, my emotions were still raw. The festive atmosphere did little to lift my spirits. As I arranged the baked goods, my mind replayed the scene with Val over and over. Val always seemed to get the best of me. Whether it was pushing me against a locker, calling my mom a drunk, humiliating me at prom, and now—this. She had a knack for finding my weakest points and squeezing them.

Tight ride—my ass, I internally scoffed.

Each time I placed a cookie or cupcake on the table, the weight of Val's words and actions pressed down harder on me. What frustrated me even more was the nagging feeling that I was just a jealous little high school girlfriend clinging to my popular college boyfriend. But it wasn't just jealousy eating at me. It was the deep sense of disrespect. I felt like the person I cared about most didn't consider my feelings about the person who had bullied and demeaned me relentlessly for years to be relevant.

Yes, I felt disrespected. But more than that, I struggled to respect someone who wouldn't defend me by simply finding another ride home. So no, I wasn't worried about Sawyer cheating on me. I was worried that I had become like all those other desperate girlfriends fawning over someone who didn't care about them in public the same way they pretended to in private. I felt embarrassed. I felt shame. Both familiar feelings. It was a harsh realization, and it cut deep.

As I stood there at the market, my thoughts tangled in a web of hurt and frustration, I knew that something had to change. I couldn't continue to feel like this, constantly undermined and unvalued. But I had promised Mrs. Larson, the owner of the bakery, that I'd help her out tonight, and I wasn't going to let Val be the cause of me breaking a promise. I wasn't going to let Sawyer make me break this promise either. So I held my head up and got to work.

I was setting up the baked goods in their portable cases and making sure we had the boxes and bags to accompany the orders when Mrs. Larson appeared behind me. "I brought you some help, Josie. This is my nephew, Ricky."

I turned around, and there stood Ricky McGrath, my date who had ditched me at the ninth grade dance, with a wide smile on his face. Ricky was different from Sawyer in many ways. He was shorter, with a clean-cut, preppy look, blond hair neatly styled, and an air of polished confidence. He struck me as the type of guy who had politics in his future. Despite the differences, Ricky was undeniably charming and handsome in his own right.

"Hey, Josie!" Ricky greeted me warmly, his smile genuine. We hadn't left things on bad terms back then. I wasn't exactly heartbroken by our short-lived date, too wrapped up in my crush on Sawyer at the time to care much. "When my aunt told me you were working and needed some help, I was happy to volunteer."

We exchanged a friendly hug. "It's so good to see you!" I said, stepping back to take in how much he'd changed since freshman year.

"It's good to see you too," Ricky replied, his enthusiasm infectious. "So, where do we start?"

We got to work, arranging the pastries and cookies and chatting easily. Ricky's presence was a welcome distraction. We fell into a comfortable rhythm, serving customers and making small talk. Ricky's friendly demeanor and easy smile put everyone at ease, and I found myself relaxing a bit, despite the lingering hurt from earlier.

Ricky was charming and charismatic for sure. Where Sawyer had a more subtle sense of humor, Ricky was more flamboyant and intentional with his brand of comedy. I was glad for the reprieve, considering my mood had been so horrible before he'd arrived, but my laughter was more like an audience member at a comedy show. He was definitely an actor, and I was enjoying the performance.

"You know, I heard this crazy story. Want to hear it?" Ricky asked, a mischievous glint in his eye.

"Sure," I replied, intrigued.

"So this guy asked this beautiful girl to a dance freshman year and she was crazy enough to accept. Then, right before the dance, the guy had a brain-eating amoeba take over his mind, planted there by some cracked-out aliens, and somehow he ended up leaving with the wrong girl!" His mouth dropped open in a dramatic show of shock and horror. "Can you believe that?"

I burst into laughter. "Holy shit. That sounds wild and strikingly familiar, Ricky. Minus the aliens and brain-eating amoeba."

"Hand to God—all true," he said, holding up his hand in a mock solemn oath.

"Better be careful with that 'Hand to God' business. It's like Pinocchio, except instead of your nose growing, Sister Honor is suspended from the sky and lands in front of you."

With that, Ricky made a show of hiding behind the table and screeching, "Not Sister Honor! Take it all, Sister! All the baked goods you want! Just leave me in peace!"

I was buckled over laughing at the ridiculousness of it all, barely able to catch a breath. Ricky stood up, laughing along with me. Onlookers would have thought they were missing a lot of fun not being on the inside of our little baked goods stand.

Just as I was catching my breath, I saw Sawyer approaching the stall. His eyes immediately narrowed as he saw me laughing with Ricky. He walked up to us, his gaze shifting between Ricky and me.

"Josie," Sawyer said, his voice tight, and the laughter between Ricky and me died down.

"Are you here to buy something?" I asked, glaring at him pointedly.

Sawyer's eyes went to Ricky again, who gave him a polite nod. I sighed. "Sawyer, this is an old friend of mine, Ricky McGrath. This is Sawyer."

"Her boyfriend," Sawyer added, and I rolled my eyes. He was marking his territory, and it felt as cheesy as it looked and sounded.

Ricky, the ever-polite gentleman, reached out his hand to Sawyer, who shook it. "Nice to meet you. I went to Holy Redeemer with Josie a few years ago."

"Ricky McGrath," Sawyer repeated, and I knew he recognized the name as the boy I'd gone to the dance with years before.

Lucky for Ricky, a customer asked for some help, so he took the opportunity to move away.

"Can I talk to you for a second?" Sawyer asked.

"Now is not a good time. I'm working," I replied, my voice tense.

"Do you have a break coming up? I really want to talk to you. I don't like the way we left things," he persisted.

"Sawyer, our time to talk was when you got home—but that didn't happen, did it? So, no. I'm not following you around like your little bitch and running when you call. I don't have time to talk. I'm working," I shot back, my frustration boiling over.

Ricky came up behind me and reached for a dessert I was blocking. He placed his hand on my shoulder and reached around me. Sawyer's eyes caught on his hand, and I felt the energy change around us.

Sawyer's jaw clenched, his eyes darkening with jealousy. "Josie, we need to talk—now."

I stepped back from Ricky. "Sawyer, who the hell do you think you're talking to right now? I'm trying to do my job here."

Ricky, sensing the awkwardness, quickly finished helping the customer and stepped back. "Hey, it looks like you two need to chat. I can handle things here for a bit, Josie."

I sighed, knowing I couldn't avoid the conversation any longer. "Fine. Five minutes, Sawyer."

We moved a few steps away from the stall, and I crossed my arms, waiting for him to speak. "What's going on with you and that guy?" he demanded.

I felt a surge of anger rise up inside me. "Seriously, Sawyer? After everything I've put up with when it comes to Val, you're going to get jealous over Ricky?"

Sawyer looked taken aback. "This isn't about Val."

"It's exactly about Val!" I shot back. "I've had to deal with her being around you, making snide comments, always trying to get between us. And now you're jealous because Ricky is here, helping out at the Christmas Market?"

"It wasn't my car, Josie! What was I supposed to do? I can't kick her out of a car that's not mine."

"Get another ride, Sawyer. There are like twenty kids from Maplewood who go to Penn State. Jason is driving home tomorrow! You could have gone with him!"

"I didn't want to wait until tomorrow to see you."

I pointed my finger at him. "No. Don't you do that. Don't you try to turn this around. When did you become this way? When did you turn into this guy, Sawyer?" I paused, searching his eyes. "Were you even going to tell me she was in the car if I didn't see her myself?"

He didn't say anything and then ran his hand through his hair. I felt something break inside of me. That was my answer. I stepped back, feeling like I had been slapped. "Oh my God," I said, the realization that he was fine lying to me washing over me.

"Josie, why is this such a big deal?"

"Why is this such a big deal? Sawyer, she fucking tortures me. You have the nerve to come here and get all jealous boyfriend because I'm working a dessert stand with a boy I went to a school dance with when I was fourteen! A boy, I might add, I never even kissed. And you don't understand why I'm pissed that a girl you not only messed around with but who throws it in my face every single chance she gets, a girl who threw me up against a locker, who called me a deranged leprechaun, and threw my mother's alcoholism in my face in front of a bunch of kids—you don't understand how that would wreck me?" My face twisted in shock and pain as the truth fully settled on me. "I'm done, Sawyer. I am done with Val. I am done with being treated like shit. I am done with *you*."

"What?" Sawyer seemed stunned, still catching up from the agony I'd described, not quite registering the finality of my words.

"I said I'm done."

"C'mon, Josie." Sawyer reached for me, and I took another step back.

His hand hovered in the air for a second, and something flickered in his eyes—confusion, maybe regret—but he didn't move. "Josie, if I had known it would upset you this much, I would've done things differently."

I threw my hands up. "Are you seriously going to pretend you didn't know this would upset me?" My voice trembled, despite the resolve building inside me. "Because I think you did get it. You just didn't care enough to do anything about it."

His mouth opened, but no words came out. For a second, it looked like he wanted to say something—maybe to defend himself, maybe to apologize—but he couldn't. And in that moment, I saw the realization dawn on him. The hurt he had caused was deeper than he could fix with an easy excuse.

I took a deep breath, blinking back the sting of tears. "Sawyer, if I have to explain to you why this matters to me—then I've misunderstood this entire relationship from the start. My mistake was thinking I could count on you to defend me—but I realize now I need to defend myself."

He stood there, stunned, his hand dropping to his side. "Josie, please. Don't do this."

"I can't keep doing this, Sawyer. You don't understand what it feels like to have someone like Val in your life. And if you can't see why that's a problem, then I can't keep pretending that everything's okay."

He opened his mouth to argue, but I held up my hand to stop him. "No more excuses. No more lies."

"I love you, Josie. Please let's talk about this. We can get past this."

I turned away, feeling the decision settle on my shoulders, but stopped short and turned back to face him. "Sawyer, I've grown up with the shittiest example of love, and maybe I never really knew what love was—but I do know what it's not."

He flinched, and for a second, his eyes dropped to the ground. The regret I had wanted him to feel—finally, it seemed to hit him. But it was too late.

I walked back to the stall, my heart heavy but my resolve firm. Ricky looked up as I approached. "Are you okay?"

I took a deep breath, forced a smile, and lied, "Everything's fine." But my words felt hollow, like an echo fading into the night.

As I set up the next batch of pastries, I couldn't shake the mix of emotions swirling inside me—relief that I had stood up for myself, sadness at what I had just ended, and a strange sense of emptiness. For so long, I had wrapped my heart around Sawyer. Letting go left me with a hole I hadn't expected. But somewhere deep inside, beneath the pain, I knew this was right. I wasn't going to fall apart.

Not this time.

Chapter 27

Now

Mrs. Miner glances toward the window, where her brother stands, lost in his own world. "Rupert, it seems you have some mail," she calls out.

Sawyer and I turn our heads in unison, following her gaze. The man at the window turns to face us, and the realization strikes me like a thunderclap. My breath catches as the full weight of the revelation settles over me. He's the man from the photo—the one Sarge left behind.

I can hardly believe it, and from the look on Sawyer's face, he's feeling the same shock. The air thickens with the gravity of what we've just discovered, and I suddenly feel like we're standing on sacred ground.

Mrs. Miner reaches into a drawer, her eyes twinkling with a knowing smile. She winks at me as she places another letter on the table. "Sarge's sister left this at the desk earlier today," she says softly. "Seems she was sent on a mission of her own."

Sawyer and I exchange a look of disbelief, our understanding deepening. This was no simple scavenger hunt—it was a carefully orchestrated journey meant to unravel truths we didn't even know existed.

Mrs. Miner excuses herself with a gentle nod, leaving us alone with Rupert, who approaches slowly. His eyes are filled with curiosity, tinged with trepidation.

We stand, and I hand him the letter, my fingers trembling slightly. His hand brushes against mine—surprisingly warm. "It's from Sarge," I whisper, as though speaking too loudly might shatter the moment.

Rupert's breath catches in his throat. "William?" His voice cracks, and hearing him say Sarge's real name feels intimate in a way that makes my chest tighten.

He opens the letter with deliberate care, like someone unwrapping an old wound. As he reads, emotions ripple across his face—first, a faint smile, then a soft laugh, and finally, tears that spill over, uncontainable. His shoulders shake with silent sobs, and he clutches the letter to his chest as though it's the last thread connecting him to a long-lost part of himself.

We watch in reverent silence. It feels too personal, like we're intruding on something sacred, but we can't look away. Rupert's reaction is a testament to the power of Sarge's words—words that somehow reach across time and space, binding two people who had been forced apart.

Sawyer shoots me a look but he doesn't say a word. I nod in return. We both understand now—this journey was more than a nostalgic trip down memory lane. Sarge had planned it meticulously, leaving no stone unturned.

Finally, Rupert looks up, tears still glistening in his eyes, and walks toward us, the letter still pressed to his chest. "Thank you," he says, his voice trembling with emotion. "Thank you for bringing William back to me."

Before we can respond, he turns and leaves, disappearing down the hallway, clutching the letter like a lifeline.

We stand in stunned silence, the room suddenly feeling too small for the enormity of what we've just uncovered. I'm expecting Sawyer to say something, to cut through the tension, but instead, he's silent. He's still staring at the door where Rupert just exited. His brow is wrinkled, and there's a tightness in his mouth I recognize.

"What are you thinking?" I ask.

Sawyer shakes his head slightly, as if trying to clear a fog. "It's just . . . I never really knew him." His voice is strained. "I thought I did. I mean, I grew up hearing his stories, thinking I had him figured out. But this—" He pauses, running a hand through his hair, his fingers tangling for a moment before falling limply to his side. "Sarge never talked about this. Never mentioned Rupert or anything close to it."

I feel a pang in my chest as I watch Sawyer. The regret is written all over his face, twisting his features in a way that's painfully familiar. He's grappling with how much he never knew about the man who shaped so much of his life. I recognize it because I feel the same way—the realization reflected in my own heart.

I reach for his hand, feeling the stiffness in his grip ease as I squeeze gently. "Maybe that's what he wanted. For us to figure out the questions we never knew we should've been asking."

Sawyer contemplates for a moment before quoting a part of one of Sarge's letters: "The deepest answers are often hiding in plain sight." He shakes his head. "I wish he'd told us," Sawyer murmurs. "Maybe we could've been there for him, been what he needed."

"Maybe he didn't know if he'd be accepted."

Sawyer scrubs his hand down his face, and I realize it's not just confusion he's feeling—it's despair. "No," he murmurs. "He knew us. He knew our hearts. I wish he'd just told me. I don't know . . . it feels like I missed something important. I should've asked more questions, been more curious about his past. All this time, and I never really asked."

"I don't think it's that simple," I say softly. "I think he was scared—scared he wouldn't be seen the same way anymore."

Sawyer looks crushed. "But we would have, Josie. We would've stood by him. We loved him, and he knew that. Dammit, I hope he knew that."

"He did know that, Sawyer. He did." I rush to comfort him, but his words catch me off guard—not because of the frustration in his voice, but because of how naturally he includes me in this, as if I haven't been gone all these years. For the first time, there's no reminder of my absence. It's as though he's forgotten I was ever away, as if I've always belonged in this with him.

"But," I say, my voice quivering, "it's not about us. It's about him. This is why he didn't feel brave," I whisper, remembering the letters. "Damn. I kinda wish I could read Rupert's letter."

I feel a rush of emotions—shock, empathy, sadness. But beneath it all, there's something else: a quiet, aching understanding. Sarge spent years carrying a secret, keeping a part of himself hidden, not because he didn't trust us, but because he didn't trust himself to be loved completely.

Feeling Sawyer beside me, I can't help but think about us. About what we've been through. The secrets we've kept, the unspoken hurts, the things we've been afraid to admit to each other. Is that what Sarge was trying to show us? That you can't fully love someone without being honest? That hiding parts of yourself only leads to regret?

As we turn to leave, I spot the last sealed letter on the table and reach for it. My fingers brush over the familiar handwriting. The words scrawled on the outside catch both our eyes, and my heart stumbles as I read them aloud:

Open at your park bench.

Chapter 28

Then

When I got home from the Christmas Market, I turned off my phone and collapsed onto my bed, tears streaming down my face as I cried for most of the night. Ricky had offered to drive me home after the market, but I'd politely declined, glancing in the direction of Sawyer. I decided to walk, knowing Sawyer was following me at a distance, making sure I got home, but I couldn't face him, so I pretended not to notice.

I woke up the next morning after a fitful sleep, feeling completely drained, both physically and emotionally. My chest felt tight, as if my heart were being squeezed by an invisible hand, each beat sending a fresh stab of pain through me. The agony of the breakup was unbearable, a raw and unrelenting ache that seemed to permeate every fiber of my being.

My mind churned with relentless thoughts, swinging wildly between doubt and conviction. Had I done the right thing by breaking up with Sawyer? The memories of our happiest moments together—his laugh, his touch, the way he made me feel seen and loved—clashed against the bitter reality of Val's relentless torment and Sawyer's failure to protect me from it. One moment, I felt justified and strong for standing up for myself; the next, I was consumed by the fear that I had thrown away something precious out of hurt and anger.

I needed to talk to Beatrice, but there was someone else I needed to talk to more. The weight of the breakup hung heavy on my shoulders as I made my way to Sarge's house that morning. He was the one adult I knew I could turn to for advice. His wisdom and straightforward nature had guided me through many rough patches in my life, and I needed his perspective now more than ever.

The early-morning air was crisp, the snow crunching under my boots as I walked the familiar path to Sarge's front porch. I took a deep breath and knocked on the door.

"Josie, come on in," Sarge's gruff voice called out from inside.

I pushed the door open and stepped into the cozy warmth of his living room. The smell of woodsmoke from the fireplace filled the air, and I immediately felt a bit more at ease. Sarge was moving around his cozy kitchen, making coffee, when he looked up at me.

"Oh boy," he said, seeing my puffy eyes already telling my story. "Sit down, kid. Tell me what's going on." As I took off my coat and boots and settled on the old worn couch, Sarge brought me a cup of coffee.

He sat across from me and waited until I was ready to talk. "I broke up with Sawyer," I finally blurted out.

Sarge leaned back in his chair, his expression thoughtful. "What happened?"

I took a deep breath and recounted the events, from seeing Val in the car to the argument at the Christmas Market. As I spoke, tears filled my eyes, but I forced them back, determined to stay strong.

When I finished, Sarge was silent for a moment, his eyes fixed on me with understanding and concern. Finally, he spoke. "Sounds like you've been carrying a heavy load, Josie. Val's been a thorn in your side for a long time."

I nodded, feeling the validation of his words. "I just couldn't take it anymore, Sarge. I feel like Sawyer is making a fool out of me. He doesn't seem like the same Sawyer anymore."

Sarge sighed, rubbing his chin thoughtfully. "You're right to stand up for yourself, Josie. Sawyer's a good kid, but he's got a lot to learn, and he's blind to what's right in front of him."

I nodded, taking in his sage advice.

"But this is more than what's right in front of you, isn't it?" Sarge continued, his voice gentle but probing.

I nodded again, the tears spilling over. "I just—I've spent my whole life having my feelings discarded by the people who supposedly care about me. That's not the life I'm trying to build. And I keep telling Sawyer over and over again how Val treats me. He sees it with his own eyes, and I guess he just decided it's not important."

Sarge's eyes were filled with understanding. "That's a tough road you've walked, Josie. Your parents haven't made things easy on you. And you're damn right to want something different, something better. You listen here. You don't let anyone, not even Sawyer, make you feel less than you are. And believe me—if he really loves you—he wouldn't want you to let him get away with that."

I hastily wiped my tears. "So what should I do?"

Sarge was quiet for a moment. There was something in his expression—something distant, a flicker of a memory I couldn't grasp, but I could see the sadness in his face.

"You know," Sarge added quietly, his eyes drifting toward the fire, "I wasn't always brave enough to fight for what mattered. I took the easy way out more times than I'd like to admit. Letting things slide, hoping they'd get better on their own . . . I thought it was easier. But sometimes, the easy way costs you more in the end. I'd hate to see our Sawyer go down that road. It's a painful one. So, honey, I can't tell you what to do about Sawyer, but I'll tell you what you can do about yourself. Focus on you, Josie," Sarge advised. "Take this time to understand what you need and what makes you happy. But don't throw the baby out with the bathwater."

I laughed through my tears. "God, Sarge, you have some weird sayings."

He chuckled. "I picked up a lot through the years."

"How do you know all this stuff?"

"Oh, you'd be surprised, honey. I've made many mistakes in life, and I learned the hard way." I frowned, hearing something in his tone that didn't fit the Sarge I knew. He was the strongest person I had ever met.

"Not you, Sarge."

He chuckled softly, a sadness in his eyes that I didn't fully understand. "Let's just say I know someone who has been where you are, Josie. And I don't want to see you suffer the same way."

I stared at him, trying to connect the dots, but I couldn't quite piece together his past with the man I knew. Still, his words resonated.

He laughed, seeing my bewilderment, but I sensed there was no humor to it. "You're stronger than you think, kid. Don't forget that. And don't be afraid to fight for what you deserve. Love is worth fighting for, but it's got to be the right kind of love—the kind that lifts you up, not the kind that drags you down. And if you find that kind of love—don't you dare let it go."

I took a deep breath, absorbing his words. "Thank you, Sarge."

"You're welcome, honey. Now let's drink this coffee and start the day over."

***

It was shaping up to be a truly awful Christmas. Aside from the breakup with Sawyer, my mother's drinking had reached frightening new levels. A trip to detox or the psych ward seemed increasingly inevitable.

I was feeling sorry for myself, and I knew it. Last year with Sawyer had been the first Christmas where I didn't feel terribly lonely. My Christmases had always been sad affairs. My mother would be drunk, and my father would play the martyr, petting her and trying to keep her drunkenness from escalating into rage. She'd lament and wail about how much she missed Ireland, while my father tried to placate her. It was worse when I was younger. I'd hear all the kids at school talk about their winter plans with their big happy families, and I'd sit on the couch, eating cereal and watching Christmas movies. There was always a ham or turkey frozen in the freezer, bought with the best of intentions by my mother before the alcohol stole her away from me again. Losing Sawyer meant I lost the warmth of his family too.

God bless Sarge, though. He asked if I wanted to go to the VFW Christmas party with him, but I laughed and politely declined. He was probably relieved when he saw the sad sack I had become over the past week.

Just as I poured myself a bowl of Coco Crunch and settled in front of the TV, with my mother drunk and shouting upstairs, I heard a knock at the door. I jumped, nearly spilling the cereal, and my eyes went to the staircase, hoping my mother wasn't disturbed. If these were Christmas carolers and they upset the beast upstairs, they'd be in for the fright of their lives.

I made my way to the window and peered out, shocked to see Sawyer standing there. He knew it was never a good idea to come to my house with my mother's unpredictable behavior.

I pulled on a coat and opened the door, meeting him outside on the porch.

"Sawyer, what are you doing here?" I whispered urgently, glancing back at the house.

"I'm here to pick you up, Josie," he said, his breath visible in the cold night air. I caught him glancing in the window and knew he saw my bowl of cereal sitting on the coffee table. "To bring you to my house for Christmas dinner."

"Are you crazy? Sawyer, why would you bring me to Christmas at your house? I'm not your girlfriend." Saying the words out loud felt like glass lodged in my throat.

His face twisted like the words physically hurt him. "Don't say that. Please, don't say that. This isn't over between us. Josie, our lives together are just starting."

He was dressed for Christmas dinner, but he looked worn out. His shirt was slightly wrinkled under his open coat, and his red-rimmed eyes suggested he hadn't slept. The sight of him like this, clearly affected by everything, tugged at my heartstrings. I could see the toll our breakup had taken on him, and it mirrored my own exhaustion.

Sawyer took a deep breath, his eyes earnest. "You were right about everything, Josie. I didn't think about how much Val being around would hurt you, and I'm sorry. I am so sorry. It seems obvious now, and I feel so stupid and insensitive. God, I'm so sorry, Josie."

I looked at him, trying to measure his sincerity. Seeing him standing there, looking so shattered and worn, made it harder to keep my walls up. He wasn't just saying words; he was visibly affected, and that softened something inside me. But it didn't change the hurt I'd felt, and I didn't know if I could trust him anymore.

Before I could respond, the front door creaked open, and my mother's slurred voice echoed from inside. "Josie, who's at the door?"

I turned quickly, panic clawing at my chest. "Christmas carolers, Mom, but they're gone. Go back to bed." The words were barely out of my mouth before regret hit me like a punch. I squeezed my eyes shut, every nerve in my body tensing.

I held my breath, as if somehow that would keep the moment frozen—this fragile second before the inevitable fallout. My chest burned, but I didn't dare exhale. I knew better. I was always hypervigilant, always on edge, scanning for anything that might set her off. But I'd slipped. One tiny, distracted moment, and I knew I was about to pay for it.

And worse—Sawyer would see it all.

"Don't you tell me to go back to bed, you thankless little bitch!" I flinched at her words, the sting of her venomous tone cutting deep and the embarrassment of Sawyer hearing them. I braced myself for her to stumble out onto the porch, but I heard my dad catching her just before she made it outside. There was a struggle, but he seemed to pull her away from the door. I pushed Sawyer farther down the porch toward the steps, never taking my eyes off the front door, preparing for an ashtray or a mug to be thrown at my head.

"You little rotten bitch! I'll show you. You are a waste! You no-good, selfish bitch!" she roared drunkenly. "I won't waste my breath on the likes of you!" I could hear my dad pleading with her as my mother's hateful words spewed from inside the house.

I looked back at Sawyer, ashamed by what he was hearing. His eyes widened as the truth of my life settled over him. He'd heard the stories before, the ones I'd carefully edited to sound less damning. But words could never measure up to the reality. Sawyer was living it now, and the harsh truth was, what he'd witnessed tonight was barely a glimpse of the worst of it.

When our eyes met, the silence between us spoke louder than any words—carrying everything he wasn't saying and everything I wished he couldn't see.

"I'm sorry about that," I whispered.

Sawyer's hand shot out, pulling me into him, and he wrapped his arms around me tightly. "Come with me," he said, his voice firm yet gentle.

I pulled back slightly, looking up at him, confusion and desperation warring inside me. "Sawyer, it's okay. This is nothing."

His jaw clenched, and I could see how much he hated those words. "Josie, this isn't *nothing*. Don't downplay it."

"Please just go," I begged, my voice barely a whisper, desperate to protect him from what he might hear next. The sound of something shattering inside the house made me jump, and his arms tightened around me instinctively.

"Listen to me, Josie," he said, his voice cracking under the weight of his emotion. "I'm not leaving without you."

I looked down at myself, a shaky laugh escaping before I could stop it. "Sawyer, I'm literally wearing shorts and a T-shirt under this coat. I'm not going anywhere."

He cupped my face gently, his touch grounding me even as chaos swirled around us. "We'll figure it out. Your wardrobe, Christmas dinner, us—everything. We can figure it out together. I love you. Just come with me."

Tears blurred my vision as I stepped back, breaking free from his grasp. "You don't get it, Sawyer. I could go with you tonight, but I'd still have to come back here tomorrow. I have to take care of them." I gestured toward the house, where the shouting seemed to grow louder by the second. "My life, my struggles—they don't just disappear because you're not living them. If it's not Val bullying me, it's my own mother. And the men who say they care about me? They leave me to drown." My voice cracked, the truth spilling out in a way I hadn't meant to share. "But you've never had to live that, Sawyer."

He froze, the weight of my words hitting him like a punch. He dropped his gaze, dragging in a shaky breath, his shoulders rising and falling as he processed what I'd said. "You're right," he said finally, his voice breaking slightly. "Holy shit, Josie, I never—I didn't see it like that. God, I didn't see you like that."

His hands clenched at his sides, and I watched as he seemed to pull strength from somewhere deep inside. When he looked back at me, his jaw was set, his eyes resolute. "You're right, I haven't lived it. And I've been blind to what you've been going through, blind to what I should have been doing. But that stops now. I want to understand. I want to be there for you, no matter how messy or hard it gets." His voice grew steadier, his stance firmer. "I've been an idiot for not seeing it sooner, but I'm here now. I'm going to handle this. Let me take care of this."

I stared at him, stunned. "Sawyer," I said softly, shaking my head, "I never asked you to take care of this."

"What?"

"I never wanted you to take care of this," I said, motioning to the house behind me. "*This* is my life. I only ever wanted you to understand me. I wanted what mattered to me to matter to you. I wanted to feel like we were on the same team." My voice grew firmer, and I stepped back. "But I never needed you to fix it. And not to sound harsh, but if you can't do something as simple as cutting off Val—then how could you ever handle this?"

The sound of glass shattering inside punctuated my words, and I saw him flinch as if the noise physically struck him. His face was etched with agony, his eyes pleading with me to take it all back.

"Josie," he whispered, his voice trembling, "I love you. Please don't go back in there."

"Sawyer, *in there* is where I live." I shook my head, stepping back, my heart splintering in my chest. "I'm sorry. I have to go back inside."

Then, I turned and walked back into the house, closing the door on Sawyer as he stood helpless on my porch. The sounds of my parents' chaos swallowed me whole the moment the latch clicked.

It didn't feel like a victory—not with my mother's screams echoing through the walls, not as I carefully stepped over shards of broken glass—but I had made a choice. I had chosen myself. And for the first time in a long time, that was enough.

<h1 style="text-align: center">Chapter 29</h1>

Now

As much as I wanted to run straight to the park and tear open Sarge's letter, something held us back. So Sawyer and I agreed to meet at the bench later. I think we both needed space—to let the shock of Sarge's bombshell settle, to absorb what it all meant.

Later that evening, I make my way to the park, my heart feeling heavier with every step. When I spot Sawyer sitting on our bench, his back to me beneath the large maple tree, a wave of emotion crashes over me, twisting me inside out. For a moment, I freeze, watching him in the dimming light, an image that feels too familiar and yet too distant.

This was our place. At least, it used to be. A place that once belonged to a different version of us—a version that seems so far away now. It isn't that we grew apart. It's that, one day, everything between us started to feel like an illusion. And once I saw our relationship through that funhouse lens, I couldn't unsee it.

But seeing Sawyer's silhouette now, framed against the backdrop of our old bench, is like stepping through a portal back to a time when everything between us felt pure, untouched by the trauma of the world. My heart clenches with a mix of nostalgia and pain, as if the air between us is filled with the ghosts of who we once were.

I notice his familiar pose—head in hands, lost in thought. It's how he's always grappled with the world, wrestling with whatever's inside him. That used to be my cue to step in, to help pull him out of his own head. But now, I hesitate.

When he finally looks up and sees me, his smile is small, hesitant, like he's not sure he's allowed to give it to me. But it's there. And it wrecks me. I take a shaky step closer, and before I can second-guess it, his hand reaches out—warm, steady. He doesn't say a word. He just wraps his fingers around mine and gently pulls me down beside him.

It's such a small thing, something we've done a thousand times before. But right now, it feels monumental, like the universe just shifted slightly. Like Sawyer isn't just looking at me—he's seeing me. And worse, I'm seeing him.

And in this quiet, fragile moment, it feels like Sawyer is happening to me all over again.

"Are you okay?" I ask, searching his face for some answer, some sign.

"Yeah . . . I just feel bad for Sarge," Sawyer says, his voice low. It cracks slightly on the last word, like it's too heavy for him to carry alone.

Bad for Sarge? That doesn't even begin to cover it. I feel like my chest might explode from all the things I'm feeling at once—grief, rage, frustration. But mostly, anger. At a world that made someone as brave as Sarge believe he couldn't live his truth. Sarge wasn't afraid of anything, so what kind of hell would make him keep a secret like this?

Sawyer keeps going, like he can't stop himself. "I can't imagine . . ." He hesitates, his hand raking through his hair. "I can't imagine how lonely he must've felt. All that history with someone, and they've been right here all along. Just a few blocks away." He lets out a breath, his eyes flicking to me for a second before dropping again. "Writing him a letter on his deathbed . . . That's not just pain. That's torture. But . . . I get it. I know what it's like to hurt."

"Me too." The words slip out before I can catch them. They're so soft I'm not sure I said them out loud—until his eyes snap to mine.

I look away immediately. His gaze is too much. It feels like he's pulling pieces of me apart, examining them under a microscope.

"It's all starting to make sense," I say, mostly to myself, just to fill the silence.

"What is?" he asks, leaning in like he's afraid to miss anything.

I pause, my mind racing through all the conversations I've had with Rupert. "The way Rupert talks. He's always so cryptic, but it's obvious now—he was thinking about Sarge. About what they went through. He told me once that facing danger is one thing, but facing yourself is something else entirely." I laugh bitterly, shaking my head. "He wasn't just talking about Sarge, though. He was talking about me, too."

Sawyer leans back, his hand scrubbing over his face. For a moment, he doesn't say anything, and I almost regret opening my mouth. But then he looks at me again, and there's something in his eyes—something determined.

"Well," he says, his voice quieter now, "maybe this letter will tell us what we need to know about Sarge. And maybe . . . we can finally stop avoiding what we need to say to each other. Maybe it's time we face our own shit."

I blink, stunned by the honesty in his words. He says it like it's the easiest thing in the world. Like he hasn't just cracked me open. Like so much of my suffering wasn't directly linked to him.

I nod because I can't bring myself to speak. My hands are shaking as I reach into my pocket and pull out the letter. The paper feels like it could crumble in my grip, and for a second, I think maybe I should let it. But then I hear Sawyer shift closer.

When his shoulder brushes mine, something steadies inside me.

I unfold the letter carefully, the sound of the paper breaking the quiet. The autumn air wraps around us, and I begin to read aloud.

***

Hey kids,

Well, here we are. If you're reading this, it means you made it through the wild-goose chase I set up. You earned this. I owe you both a story—the real one. You've been patient, and now it's time you knew everything.

Rupert and I fell in love a long time ago, in a world that wasn't kind to men like us. We had to hide who we were, hide what we felt. Back then, being gay wasn't just frowned upon—it was dangerous. You could lose everything for loving the wrong person. We lived in fear, constantly looking over our shoulders. But Rupert—he had it harder than I did.

People always knew Rupert was different. They judged him, ridiculed him, beat him up more times than I can count. I used to promise him I'd make them pay, that I'd show them one day. But they didn't know about me. I hid myself too well. I told Rupert I was protecting him by staying in the shadows, but I wasn't. The truth is, I was protecting myself. Rupert was the brave one. Every day, he faced their cruelty while I stayed silent.

Then the draft came, and I was sent to Vietnam. Rupert didn't go because of a lung condition. Before I left, we made a promise—when I came back, we'd run away to New York City, where maybe we could finally be ourselves. That promise kept me going through a lot of dark nights.

Vietnam . . . it changed me in ways I'm still reckoning with. I was a medic, patched up men with one hand while shooting with the other. I saw more death than I care to remember. Hell, I thought I was going to die out there more times than I could tell you. But every time I thought the end was coming, I'd close my eyes and picture Rupert. I'd imagine us in a little apartment in New York City, having coffee together in the morning. Just that simple thought—us sitting there, quiet, drinking coffee—got me through the worst of it. When everything else was chaos, that dream of a peaceful life with Rupert was my anchor.

Funny how a little thing like that can carry you through a war.

But when I came home, the world hadn't changed. People were still as cruel as ever, and Rupert was taking the worst of it. He was still himself—still brave—and I was still hiding. I convinced myself the best thing I could do was walk away, to protect him from the pain of being with me. So I let him think I didn't love him anymore. I let him believe I abandoned him, when the truth is, I was just scared. And angry. And traumatized. And I needed Rupert more than ever, but I didn't even know who I was anymore.

I could face death in Vietnam, but I couldn't face the world's judgment. And by the time I stopped caring what people thought, I was too scared to ask Rupert for another chance. So I stayed silent. I let fear steal my future with him. He thought I didn't love him, but the truth is, I loved him every damn day of my life, and I finally told him that in the letter you brought him. Too bad I couldn't give it to him myself.

Years after I came back from the war, I read an interview with Johnny Cash. They asked him what he thought paradise was, and he said, "This morning, with her, having coffee." He meant June. And I remember thinking, that's it—that's paradise. Just sitting with the person you love, sharing the little moments. That's what I wanted with Rupert. That's what I dreamed of when I thought I wouldn't make it back. And hearing Johnny Cash put it into words . . . well, it hit me hard. It was like a punch to the gut, reminding me of what I had lost. What I had let slip through my fingers because of fear.

That's the thing about love—it's not in the grand gestures or the big promises. It's in the small, everyday moments. Those quiet mornings over coffee, the shared silence, the simple knowing that someone is there beside you. I let the world take that from me, but I don't want it to take it from you.

Fear will always be there, lurking in the shadows, trying to convince you to hide. But don't let it steal your chance at happiness like it did mine. Don't wait for life to pass you by. Don't wait until it's too late to say what matters, to do what matters. Paradise isn't some far-off dream—it's the little moments, the ones you fight for every day.

Thank you for bringing light into this old heart of mine. I've seen a lot of things in my time, but nothing has meant more to me than watching the two of you become the people you are. I am so proud of you both. Now, keep making me proud.

Catch you later,

Sarge

PS: Josie girl, don't throw the baby out with the bathwater.

Chapter 30

Then

Sawyer and I didn't get back together after I left him on the porch that night. But we didn't completely lose contact either. Despite everything, Sawyer kept trying to mend what we had broken, refusing to let me slip away entirely. He'd text me, call, even send emails when I didn't respond to anything else, but I never gave him more than polite replies. He wanted to fix what had shattered between us, to go back to how things were, but I couldn't.

Prom was supposed to be our night. He was supposed to be my date. That had always been the plan. Even after we broke up, he still asked if we could go together, and for a while, I let myself imagine that we might. But his baseball schedule got in the way. He was playing an away series in Iowa, flying out Thursday, back on Sunday. There wasn't anything either of us could do. It wasn't like I had the energy to care, anyway. Sawyer seemed devastated, like missing prom was just another nail in the coffin of whatever future we might've had. But I couldn't bring myself to feel the same.

Three different guys asked me to prom after word spread that Sawyer and I were finished. I turned them all down. I had no interest in pretending I cared about a night that was supposed to be special when everything else in my life felt like it was crumbling. I thought about skipping it entirely, but Beatrice wouldn't let that happen. "You're going," she insisted, dragging me to the mall to find a dress. "You only get one senior prom, Josie. You're not letting it pass you by just because all this shit is hitting the fan."

So, once again, my mother—sober, with the best intentions—wanted to help me pick out my dress. But I wasn't investing my energy in her sobriety anymore. Last year's prom had been a disaster, and the wounds from that night still hadn't healed. My mother had let me down in ways that lingered, and I couldn't shake the feeling that something would go wrong again. I couldn't summon the excitement I was supposed to feel. I had recently received my acceptance letter to Penn State, but even that felt distant, as if I couldn't quite picture a future where things got better. Everything seemed too heavy.

I tossed my dress and accessories into a bag, my movements mechanical and detached. Slinging the bag over my shoulder, I headed toward the door, ready to leave for Beatrice's to get dressed. "I'm going! See you later!" I called out, not really expecting anyone to respond. It had become a habit, an automatic gesture. As my hand touched the knob, I was surprised to hear my mother's voice drifting in from the kitchen.

"Josie, are you—are you leaving already?" she asked, her voice carrying a note of uncertainty, maybe guilt.

I turned to my mom, not sure how to respond. I had almost forgotten to account for her in my plans. "Oh, hi. Yeah—I'm heading out." I glanced out the window, where I saw Beatrice's car idling on the sidewalk.

"To the prom?" she asked, her eyes searching mine.

"Yes—that's tonight." It felt strange to have this conversation with my mom when all my friends' moms were readying their houses for pictures, helping their daughters primp for one of the biggest events of their lives. We talked about it like it was a minor event, an afterthought.

"Are you getting your hair and makeup done again?" she offered, trying to connect, but I didn't want to think about the last time I got myself done up for a big event.

I shook my head. "No—I'm just going to do it myself."

"I can give you money for it if you want to go," she said, a hint of desperation in her voice. I tried to contain my wince, but I'm not sure I succeeded. The last time she paid for my hair, she took it back by tearing my updo out before Sawyer's prom. Even my bitterness felt numb, so I let it go.

"No. No. It's okay. It's really not a big deal. I don't even want to go, to be honest." I was telling the truth but also trying to brush off the significance of an event she should have been part of—but wasn't. Even if it wasn't my fault she was excluded.

"So I won't see you all dressed up?" she asked, her shoulders slumping slightly. It shouldn't have made my heart twist, to see her disappointment, but it did. My mom was two different people, and somehow I couldn't hold the sins of my drunk mother against the sober and guilty one in front of me.

"Not this time," I replied, my tone distant. We both knew the time for that had passed.

"Okay, well then, have fun. Be careful. I love you," she said softly, her words hanging in the air.

"I love you too," I responded automatically, turning away quickly, trying to get out of the house as fast as I could, never looking back.

***

Beatrice's after-party was a cozy affair, the living room bathed in the soft glow of fairy lights. The air buzzed with the lingering excitement of prom, and her parents had thoughtfully prepared snacks and drinks, creating a warm, welcoming atmosphere. Laughter rippled through the room as everyone relived moments from the night—awkward dances, almost-kisses, inside jokes. But it all felt distant to me, like I was watching from behind a thick pane of glass. I smiled when I was supposed to, nodded at the right moments, but I didn't feel any of it.

It should've been fun. It should've been special. But instead, all I felt was empty. The dress I had chosen with so little enthusiasm felt like a costume, something I was wearing to play a part I didn't believe in. I looked around at the faces of my classmates, all of them gleaming with the afterglow of the night, and I felt like an outsider in my own life.

I couldn't help but think about how it was supposed to go. Sawyer and I were supposed to be at prom together. We were supposed to be making memories—dancing, laughing, maybe sneaking off for a quiet moment under the stars. But everything had unraveled, and now there was just this gaping hole where something beautiful could have been. I checked my phone out of habit, half expecting a message from him, something that would bridge the distance between us. But there was nothing, just a missed call from my dad.

I sighed and stepped outside into the cool night air, wrapping my arms around myself as I called him back. The weight of it all—Sawyer, my family, my mother's drinking—pressed down on me like a heavy blanket, smothering what little spark I had left.

"Josie." My dad's voice was stressed and urgent, and instantly my heart sank.

Of course. I threw my head back, staring at the sky, knowing damn well what was happening. "What's wrong?"

"She's very bad, Josie. I don't know where she got it, but she's very bad. I can't handle her on my own."

I couldn't believe it. On prom night. Again. My dad was calling me to come home and deal with my drunk mother, who had once again broken her stretch of sobriety. And this excuse—*I don't know where she got it*—was getting old. He knew exactly where she got it. He was always the one to give it to her. My frustration mixed with a kind of bitter resignation. After everything, I was still surprised. How could I still be surprised?

"Are you serious right now?" I asked, my voice sharp, barely containing the anger.

He started crying. "Josie, please! She's out of control," he begged.

I felt my heart harden. It was always like this. I had been doing this for years, being the one to step in and fix things, put out fires that weren't mine. And here he was, asking again, not even pretending to understand how much it hurt. "Dad, I'm at Beatrice's. It's prom night. I can't come home," I said, my voice steady, leaving no room for negotiation.

"Josie, you don't understand. She needs you," he insisted, his voice rising with panic. The familiar guilt he had instilled in me since I was a child twisted in my chest, but this time, the anger pushed it aside.

I closed my eyes, my breath trembling as the words left my lips. "No, Dad. You don't understand. She doesn't need me. She needs rehab. She's needed it for years, and you've always made excuses. You've both made excuses. And it's me who's had to pay the price. I'm the one who has to put everything on hold, take care of her while she tears me apart. I'm the one she screams at, throws things at. And you watch. *You watch.* You've never stepped in to protect me." My voice cracked, but I pushed on. "I'm done, Dad. I'm not coming home."

"Josie." His voice took on that stern tone, the one that used to make me fold when I was younger. "Come home now, or I'm coming to get you."

For a moment, I almost wavered. The years of conditioning were hard to break. But this time, something inside me refused to bend. "Call the cops if you can't handle her," I said, my voice cold. "I'm not coming home."

The silence on the other end felt like a void opening between us. My father, so used to controlling the situation, didn't know how to respond to this version of me. I hung up, cutting him off when he started pleading again.

I stood there, the phone still in my hand, trembling. *I did it. I said no.* The weight of the years spent sacrificing myself for them threatened to crush me, but underneath that, there was something new—a flicker of relief. I didn't have to do this anymore. I don't have to be their savior.

The line I had drawn felt fragile, like it could shatter at any moment. But it was there. For the first time, I had put myself first. The thought was terrifying and exhilarating all at once. My mind raced with uncertainty. *What would happen when I went home tomorrow? How would they react?* The fear gnawed at me, but it was mixed with something else: the knowledge that, for tonight, I had chosen me.

I took a deep breath, walking back into the party. I wasn't sure what tomorrow would bring—probably more of the same. But for now, I was free.

Chapter 31

Now

I sit on the park bench next to Sawyer, clutching Sarge's letter like it's the only thing tethering me to this moment. The tears come hard, unstoppable, and I don't even try to hold them back. At some point, I lean forward, my head dropping between my knees as I gasp for air between relentless sobs. My body shakes, raw and unguarded, but for once, I don't care that Sawyer is here, seeing me like this—completely undone.

His arm slips around me, steady and warm, pulling me closer. He doesn't speak at first, just holds me tight like he's trying to keep the pieces of me from scattering in the wind. His hand moves in slow circles on my back, comforting in a way that only makes me cry harder.

And I'm not even crying for me. Or for Sarge. I'm crying for Rupert—for a man who spent his life feeling unwanted, unloved, only to discover too late that he'd been chosen all along. And now he'll never get to feel it.

"I'm here, Josie," Sawyer whispers, his voice low and steady, a lifeline in the chaos. "I've got you. I'm not going anywhere."

His words hit me like a wave, and the sobs wrack my chest harder. I feel his pain, too—he's hurting, I can hear it in his voice—but he doesn't ask me to stop, doesn't try to fix it. He just holds on, anchoring me when I feel like I'm being swept away.

Eventually, the tears slow, leaving me breathless and hollow. My chest aches from crying, but the release feels like air after drowning. And because my emotions are ridiculous and uncontrollable, I let out this awkward half-laugh. It's ugly, somewhere between a gasp and a hiccup, but it surprises me.

Sawyer chuckles softly, his hand still on my back. "What's funny?"

I shake my head, wiping my face with the back of my sleeve. "This. Me. Crying my guts out in a park, then laughing like a lunatic. It's just . . . a lot."

He leans back slightly, enough to look at me. "You're human, Josie. That's allowed."

Despite everything, I laugh again—a real laugh this time, soft but genuine. And just like that, the tension breaks. For a moment, I let myself rest in the quiet, his steady presence reminding me of how it used to feel, back when I believed I could count on him to catch me every time I fell.

But the thoughts keep circling back to Sarge. To Rupert. To the cruel irony of it all. How can someone nearly give their life for this country, only to return to a world that refused to accept him? A world that demanded so much but couldn't give him the one thing he deserved—a simple, peaceful life with the person he loved.

It's unbearable. Unforgivable. And it stays lodged in my chest like a weight I'm not sure I'll ever be able to set down.

"He was scared," I say, my throat tightening again. "He let fear take everything from him. Rupert . . . all they wanted was a simple life together, and he couldn't let himself have that." I glance down at the letter, running my fingers over the words. "He could face war, but not this."

Sawyer stays quiet, letting me sit with that for a moment. The wind rustles the leaves of the big maple tree above us, and the silence stretches between us.

"Simple doesn't mean easy," he says at last, his voice low, hesitant. He shifts slightly beside me. "Do you think we're any better?"

I turn to him, frowning. "What do you mean?"

He leans forward, elbows on his knees, his eyes locked on mine. "I mean, we've been running in circles around this for years, Josie. What we wanted a long time ago . . . it shouldn't have been so hard, right? But here we are." He pauses, his voice softening. "We need to talk about it, don't we?"

I swallow hard, pulling back slightly. I know he's right—we've needed to talk for years. But what good would it do? Even if we unpacked every bit of pain, untangled every knot of hurt, it wouldn't change anything. I can't live here, and Sawyer can't live there. We have no future. Only the past.

"Where would we even start?" I ask quietly.

Sawyer reaches out, brushing a strand of hair from my face, the simple gesture disarming me. "Wherever you want," he says softly.

I sigh, the weight of his words pressing on my chest. I'm not sure what's worse—keeping everything bottled up or letting it spill out. But as I stare at him, I realize I'm too tired to keep carrying this alone.

"Well . . . I never got over it when you—" My voice falters, and I force myself to keep going. "When you left me. I guess a part of me understood, even if I didn't want to admit it. I was a mess, Sawyer. After everything with my parents, I was unraveling. Hell, I was unraveling before that."

I gesture toward him, my voice trembling. "You were young, had everything going for you—school, baseball. You were the all-American boy with a bright future. And I was . . . drowning. I felt like something you'd find under a rock in the garden."

His expression twists, and I see the hurt flicker in his eyes, but I push forward.

"As much as I hated it, I understood why you didn't want to be with me. I was a mess. But what I couldn't understand . . ." My voice cracks, and I take a shaky breath. "What I couldn't forgive was how you did it. Who you did it with."

His jaw tightens, and I can see the words settling over him, the truth hitting like a sucker punch.

I press on, the dam breaking. "You can end a relationship without setting the other person on fire, Sawyer. And you burned me. You scorched the earth. And the worst part is . . . the man sitting beside me now? You're so much like the Sawyer I fell in love with. And I can't make sense of that."

He leans forward, his hands clasped in front of him, and for a moment, I think he's going to apologize. But then he lets out this low, frustrated growl, his jaw clenched so tight I swear I can hear his teeth grinding.

"Did you just growl at me?" I ask, stunned.

Sawyer stands abruptly, pacing a few steps toward the tree and back, his movements restless. I lean back on the bench, watching him in disbelief.

"You're angry with me right now?"

He stops, turning to face me, his eyes blazing with a mix of pain and frustration. "Angry? Josie, what did I do to make you think I didn't care about you? That I didn't want to be with you?" His voice shakes, raw with emotion. "It's all I ever wanted. You're all I ever wanted."

I stare at him, dumbfounded, as he runs a hand through his hair, his frustration spilling out in every word. "Maybe I wasn't perfect, but I didn't think I left any doubt that I loved you. Not back then, not now. And I can't believe you thought I didn't care."

Not now? The world around me starts to blur, and I blink, hoping it's just my eyes drying out from all the tears. But I know what's happening. The edges of my vision shimmer, like I'm looking through a warped piece of glass.

The image of Val, the flash of her smile—cruel and taunting—hits me like a slap. It's sudden, uninvited, and too vivid to ignore. My vision blurs, and there she is again, lurking at the edges of my mind. I shake my head, trying to push her away, but the memory refuses to leave, hovering like a shadow. Her triumphant look as I stumbled out of the room all those years ago. I shake my head again, an attempt to dispel the unwelcome memories.

Not here. Not now. Not on this bench where we shared so much. I don't want her haunting this place too.

Sawyer paces relentlessly, and I fight to steady my breath. My heart pounds erratically, the familiar prelude to an anxiety attack. *Name three things you can see,* I tell myself. *Focus. Breathe.*

Three things.

Sawyer. Tree. Bench.

Name three things.

Sawyer. Bed. Val.

The stark image of Val, naked and smirking atop my equally bare boyfriend, invades my thoughts. Her head propped up by her hand, that taunting smile directed at me.

"Shit," I mumble to myself, dropping my head into my hands. I try to focus, but the shimmering intensifies, transforming into a kaleidoscope of colors that dance and twist before me. It's like someone smeared paint across my field of vision, bright and disorienting. I close my eyes, but it's no use. The dull ache already forms behind my eyes, ready to explode into a full-blown headache.

"You left me, Josie! I was so worried about you, I thought I was going to die. I literally thought my heart was going to stop. I quit baseball. I left school. I tried to find you! Nothing mattered without you." His voice sounds so far away, as if in a tunnel or underwater. I hear him say he quit baseball and left school, but the words feel out of order.

Sawyer's voice cuts through the thickening air, desperate and pleading. "Just tell me why! Why didn't you come back? What did I do?"

Cold sweat beads on my forehead, my vision narrowing as panic wraps its icy grip around me. Yet, I find the strength to respond, my voice laced with pain. "Goddammit, Sawyer! I did come back!" I lift my gaze from my shoes, meeting his eyes, the same confusion shadowing his face as it had the day before. "I came back to surprise you for your birthday, but I was the one who ended up with the surprise."

Sawyer's complexion drains, and he steps back, like he too is coming to a painful realization. My voice cracks, fueled by a volatile blend of anger and despair as I stand. Stepping closer, I place my trembling hands on his chest. "So fuck you and your feelings, Sawyer!" I push him forcefully, and he staggers back, his face ashen, eyes wide with shock.

"Josie! No! Listen to me, please!" Sawyer's plea reaches me, sounding distant, muffled as though coming through a thick fog. I turn away, my vision clouded with tears, my heart pounding in my ears, my brain feeling like it's swelling in my head. I can barely see in front of me.

"I swear, Josie, I'm begging you. Let me explain!" His voice is raw with emotion. "That night . . . it was the worst of my life. I tried calling, emailing, anything to reach you, to explain. I didn't know you were there, but I was trying to find you—to tell you—"

I reach a trash can just in time, my stomach revolting against the turmoil, the haunting images pushing me to the brink. As I retch, Sawyer is suddenly there, one hand gently holding back my hair, the other comforting me. Too weak to push him away and unsure if I'm even standing, I sag against the bin.

A sharp pain lances through my temple, the migraine taking me hostage. I clutch at my head, a groan escaping as the intense throbbing begins to take hold. This is a bad one.

"Are you okay?" Sawyer's voice, softer now and tinged with concern, is right by my ear, and I realize I'm leaning into him for stability.

I try to form the words, to tell Sawyer what's happening, but my tongue feels heavy, my thoughts sluggish. "Sawyer," I manage to croak, my voice barely above a whisper, "migraine . . . need to get back to Miner's."

"No way, Josie. I'm not leaving you alone like this." He pauses. "Beatrice's house is the closest. Come on, I'll help you."

I want to protest, to insist I can make it back on my own, but the pain is overwhelming. Defeated, I let him guide me, his arm firmly supporting my shaking body. The short walk to his truck feels like an eternity, each step pounding in rhythm with the throbbing in my head.

Sawyer rummages through the back seat and pulls out a soft, worn T-shirt. "Here, let's cover your eyes with this," he suggests gently, holding the fabric open. "It'll help keep the light out and maybe ease the migraine a bit."

Grateful for the respite, I lean forward as he drapes the T-shirt gently over my face, covering my eyes. The immediate darkness brings a small relief from the relentless pounding in my head. Guided by Sawyer's careful hands, I settle into the passenger seat, the world around me dimmed to nothing but shadows and muffled sounds.

As Sawyer slides behind the wheel of his truck, he hesitates. "Josie, I think we should head to the hospital instead."

"No, just a dark room, please."

He must have texted Beatrice, because when we reach her door, she is already there waiting. She and Sawyer lead me to the living room and gently lower me onto the couch. Beatrice hurries off and returns with a cool, damp cloth, placing it tenderly on my forehead. "Just relax, Josie. You're safe here," she murmurs soothingly.

The cool cloth begins to ease the edge of the pain. I close my eyes, focusing on my breathing, trying to let the migraine wash over me without completely drowning in it. Beatrice's voice is a soft murmur in the background as she speaks to Sawyer, but I can't make out the words. I hear another voice, but the fatigue prevents me from even caring who it is. All I can do is let the darkness pull me under, hoping that when I resurface, the pain will be gone.

As I drift into a restless, pain-filled sleep, one thought lingers in my mind: *The other voice is Jason's.*

Chapter 32

Then

The morning light filtered softly through the curtains as I stirred awake at Beatrice's house. For a brief, fleeting moment, there was peace—like I was still in a dream. The warmth of the covers and the distant memory of last night's prom lingered like a whisper in the back of my mind. But something felt . . . off. Beatrice's bed was already empty, and the house was too quiet, the kind of quiet that wasn't comforting.

Anxiety stirred in my chest—heavy and suffocating. My first thought was of my dad. I had turned off my phone last night to avoid him, but now the silence weighed heavily. Was he okay? Was she okay? I pictured my mom spiraling, her drunk and incoherent words echoing in my mind. I imagined my dad trying, in vain, to manage her on his own. But there was something more—something deeper gnawing at me.

I reached around for my phone, but it wasn't next to me. I had left it in the living room the night before. Still, the idea of turning it on felt like inviting chaos back into my life.

Voices drifted in from the hallway—Beatrice and someone else, their murmurs low and serious. I tried to shake the unease creeping up my spine as I slipped out of bed and pulled on my jeans. Maybe it was nothing. Maybe it was everything.

That gnawing sensation deepened.

I heard the soft creak of the door opening, and Beatrice appeared in the doorway. One look at her and my heart plummeted. Her face was pale, her eyes red-rimmed like she'd been crying. She wasn't saying anything, but her expression was screaming. Something was wrong. Something was really wrong.

"Josie," Beatrice said, her voice rough and cracked.

"What's going on?" I glanced past her, toward the hallway, half expecting my mother to be standing there, drunk and furious.

Beatrice's mom stepped in behind her, her face just as stricken. "Come to the kitchen, sweetheart. There's something we need to tell you."

I stared at Mrs. Knight, the room spinning slightly. My mind raced to fill the silence. *Is it Mom? Did she fall?* I braced myself for the worst. It had to be her, didn't it? Or was it Dad? Had she hurt him this time?

"Is Sawyer okay?" The question escaped my lips before I could even think. My heart beat wildly, irrationally clinging to the hope that at least he was safe.

Mrs. Knight's face softened, though it didn't ease the tension in her shoulders. "He's fine, honey," she said gently. But that didn't settle the knot twisting in my gut. Everything in the room felt wrong, like the walls were closing in around me, squeezing the air out.

I followed them down the hall, feeling like I was floating—disconnected. The cold floor under my feet didn't register. My legs felt leaden. *Something's happened. What is it?* The slow-motion dread clawed at me, but I couldn't make sense of it.

When we stepped into the kitchen, the first thing I saw was Mr. Knight, sitting at the table, staring into his hands. His face was drawn, pale, like the weight of the world had crashed into him. And then I noticed the man sitting across from him, back turned to me, his shoulders hunched.

I blinked, and my breath caught. That was a figure I'd recognize anywhere.

"Sarge?" I said softly, but he didn't turn at first. It was as if he couldn't. And that—*that* was the moment everything inside me shattered.

Sarge slowly stood and turned to face me. The second our eyes met, the air in the room changed—heavier, colder. His face was etched with pain, his eyes filled with a sorrow I had never seen in him before. My legs weakened. The Sarge I knew, the strong, stable presence in my life, looked like he was about to break. It didn't make sense. Why would *he* be here? And then it hit me.

Something terrible had happened.

My stomach dropped, the dread I had been fighting slamming into me with full force. I felt dizzy, lightheaded, like the ground beneath me was giving way. Sarge wasn't here for just any reason. He was here because my life was about to be torn apart.

*****

Even though I knew, somewhere in the deep recesses of my soul, that Sarge's presence here could not be good, I smiled when I saw him. It was automatic—a small, reflexive smile at seeing the person who had always been my anchor. Sarge meant safety. For just a second, the chaos receded because he was here. But that second flickered and died almost as soon as it came. There was something horribly wrong. My mind snagged on his expression.

I had never seen Sarge like this—never seen him *crushed*. His face was hollowed out with a pain I couldn't comprehend. And then, just as quickly, my body reacted. A tightening gripped my chest, spreading out until my limbs felt impossibly heavy. My ears buzzed, a strange ringing that seemed to drown out the world.

His lips moved, but I couldn't understand at first. The words weren't real. They couldn't be. "Fire . . . all gone . . . mom and dad . . . gone."

The floor seemed to tilt under my feet, but somehow I stayed standing. *What's all gone?* The thought drifted through my mind, but my mouth wouldn't work. Everything around me blurred, leaving just me and Sarge in a bubble of terror. His voice was distorted, like I was hearing him from underwater.

"What's all gone?" I mumbled. But my voice sounded far away, like it wasn't mine. Everything slowed. I couldn't focus. The edges of my vision began to blur, and I felt dizzy, like I might pass out. My chest tightened further, until each breath was a struggle. I wasn't here. This wasn't happening.

His words came in fragments, detached from reality. "Fire . . . all gone . . . mom and dad . . ." Each repetition tore into me, as if my body was being pummeled with blows I couldn't see.

The room spun, but I couldn't stop trembling. My hands shook so violently, I didn't notice at first how I'd gripped the edge of the counter, knuckles white. Mrs. Knight was saying something, but it sounded muffled, far away. Like she was speaking from the other side of a wall. I watched her lips move, but the meaning didn't register.

Sarge was moving closer, his voice strained with sorrow, but I couldn't hear anything but the roaring in my ears. His eyes searched mine for some kind of response, but I was slipping—slipping into a place where nothing could touch me, where this wasn't happening.

"Sit down, Josie," I heard him say, or maybe I didn't. I felt hands on my arms, lowering me into a chair. But my mind was somewhere else, replaying last night—prom, the laughter, the temporary escape.

"I need my phone," I muttered, my fingers suddenly patting down my pockets, searching frantically. "My phone. My phone." It was the only thing keeping me tethered. I can call Dad. *I can fix this. I just need my phone.*

Sarge knelt in front of me, blocking my view of the room. His face was inches from mine, but his eyes—his eyes were filled with devastation. And still, I couldn't register it. I couldn't face it.

"Josie . . ." he whispered, his voice strained. I couldn't even hear it clearly. I shook my head, twisting to look for the phone. I needed to call Dad. I needed to hear his voice tell me everything was okay. What was the last thing I said to him?

I'm not coming home.

"Where is my phone?" I screamed, not recognizing the sound of my own voice. My body jerked as if to stand, but Sarge's hands held me firm, grounding me. My voice echoed in the room, breaking through the layers of numbness, and in the distance, I heard Beatrice crying, a sound that finally hit me like a punch to the gut.

But no—there is still time. There has to be time to fix this.

Sarge's grip on my shoulders tightened, pulling me back down. "Josie, listen to me. You can't fix this. You can't." His voice cracked.

Was I thinking out loud?

A sob rose in my throat, primitive and untamed. I doubled over, pressing my forehead into his chest as reality came crashing down.

This was real. This was happening.

Sarge's arms tightened around me, his voice barely audible over my crying. "I'm sorry. I'm so, so sorry." His voice wavered, and that's when I broke. I couldn't breathe, couldn't see, couldn't think beyond the overwhelming weight of those words.

"My phone," I whimpered again, not because I thought it would change anything, but because it was the only thing my mind could cling to.

"Who can we call for you, honey?" Sarge whispered, trying to break through the spiral of my thoughts.

I blinked through the tears, my gaze darting toward Beatrice, Mrs. Knight, anyone. *Who can I call? Who do I even have left?*

Finally, I looked back at Sarge, my voice shaky but clear. "You. You and Beatrice. You and Beatrice and Sawyer are all I have left."

And that realization—that hollow truth—seared me more than fire.

Chapter 33

Now

I open my eyes with a start and sit up too quickly, the throb on one side of my head immediately punishing the sudden movement. The room spins for a moment before settling. I'm in Beatrice's room again—Beatrice's new room. The once-familiar floral wallpaper is gone, replaced by cool, muted gray walls. The old patchwork quilt that used to cover her bed, the one I clung to that night fifteen years ago, has been replaced with crisp white bedding, modern and minimalistic. It's strange. The room is different, yet the pain of that memory—waking up here after prom, finding out my parents were gone—still lingers in the air. Everything has changed, and yet, somehow, it hasn't.

I take a slow, deep breath, trying to compose myself. The migraine's dull throb still lingers at the edge of my vision, not as fierce as it was, but a reminder that my body hasn't yet fully recovered. Every muscle feels tight, as if I've been gritting my teeth for hours. I ease myself back against the headboard, careful not to make any sudden moves. My body feels as though it's been wrung out, the physical exhaustion matching the emotional storm that's been brewing inside me.

On the bedside table, I notice a glass of water and my prescription migraine medication. Next to them is a small note in Beatrice's familiar handwriting.

Drink this, rest. Dermott brought your medicine. I'm here if you need anything.

—B

The simplicity of the message, the unspoken care behind those words, eases the tightness in my chest.

Before I can even begin to untangle it all, the sheer gravity of everything crashes over me. The travel. The festival. The beers. The unresolved friction with Sawyer. And then there's Sarge's letter—the revelation that left me breathless and reeling. It's all a chaotic storm in my mind, leaving me drained and shattered. And, as usual, I've done what I always do—neglected myself entirely. So now I'm here, sprawled out on Beatrice's bed, feeling like I've been completely flattened by life.

Hearing a noise, I turn to see the door opening gently. Beatrice peeks in, her brow furrowed slightly, but her lips curve into a tentative smile when she sees me sitting up. I try not to picture her as she opened this same door fifteen years ago. "Hey, you're awake," she says softly, stepping inside. "How do you feel?"

"Oh, Bea," I groan. "I'm so sorry. I'm so embarrassed."

She comes over and sits next to me on the bed. "Oh my God. Stop being embarrassed! You poor thing. When did you start getting migraines?"

I reach over, take my medicine, and follow it with a few gulps of water. "After the fire."

"Ah. I see." Beatrice nods knowingly, her eyes filled with sadness.

"But this one was bad. It's my fault," I say, trying to find humor in my own stupidity. "I've been eating crap, not sleeping. The emotions, the travel, beers at the festival, a little Sawyer, Sarge's earth-shattering revelation, and a healthy dose of PTSD—and here I am." I laugh, throwing my hands up playfully in the air, then squeeze my eyes shut at the dull remainder of the pain. "Is Dermott okay?"

"He's fine. He's actually out in the living room. Sawyer picked him up this morning at Miner's."

"This morning? How long have I been here?"

"Since last night."

I sigh, the reality of how much time has passed sinking in. "Oh my God." My voice is tinged with disbelief. I glance around the room again, a bit more aware this time. "Did I . . . um, make a complete fool of myself?"

Beatrice gives my hand a reassuring squeeze. "It's not like you went out on a bender and were doing keg stands in the woods, Josie. You got a migraine. Go easy on yourself. You were out like a light, and Sawyer carried you in here, made sure you were comfortable. He was really worried. Like helicopter-mom worried—but Dermott knew it was a migraine."

The mention of Sawyer's concern warms me but also reignites a spark of anxiety about everything we've left unfinished. I shift uncomfortably, the bed creaking slightly under my movement.

Beatrice sighs. "He told me a little bit about your argument. There's more to it, as you can probably imagine. You guys have a lot to sort out, huh?" Her tone is gentle, probing without pushing too hard.

I nod, afraid I'm being pulled into something far bigger than I can handle.

She smiles then. "You have another visitor when you're ready."

The look on my face must betray my anxiety, because she speaks quickly. "It's just Jason. I called him the other day, and he caught a flight."

"Jason's here? I thought I heard his voice."

"Yeah, he got here yesterday."

Jason. His name pulls me from the fog, and suddenly memories start to swirl. Jason was always there for me, not just in that annoying, brotherly way, but in a protective way that anchored me when everything else was falling apart. I vaguely remember his voice over the phone when I was in Ireland after the fire, his usual mischief replaced with an agony that I had never heard from him before. If he could have willed me to feel better, I know he would have. He would have given me years off his own life if it meant taking away even a fraction of my pain.

And now with Jason here, knowing I have Dermott, Beatrice, and even Sawyer, something just clicks into place. It's like the last piece of a puzzle I've been missing all these years. The only one missing is Sarge. And then I feel guilty for not needing my parents to complete my circle.

"He's in the kitchen with Dermott," Beatrice continues. "Sawyer left for a bit, but he's been texting me every five minutes to check on you." She rolls her eyes dramatically, and I can't help but laugh. "If you're feeling well enough, you can take a shower. You know where the bathroom is. Dermott brought your stuff from Miner's. Or you can stay here and rest. It's totally up to you. We just want you to feel well."

I nod, smiling weakly. "A shower sounds good. I'll meet you guys in the kitchen when I'm done."

***

The hot water feels like a balm to my weary body. I let it wash over me, soothing the lingering pain and washing away the remnants of the migraine. I take my time, letting the steam envelop me, giving myself a moment of peace.

As I step out of the shower, the steam clings to the air, and I wrap myself in a towel. I wipe the mirror clean, revealing my reflection. For the first time in what feels like ages, I recognize the person staring back at me. The last time I stood in this house, in this room, I was a broken teenager. Now, I'm something else—not broken, though silver scars run through me, but more whole in ways that matter. There's a bit more clarity in my eyes, a sense of calm replacing the anxiety I've carried for days. I quickly dress in the clothes Dermott brought from the inn and stack the bracelets on my wrist like armor, the familiar feeling grounding me, offering a small but much-needed comfort.

When I'm ready, I make my way to the kitchen. Laughter and conversation spill into the hallway, a welcome reprieve from the chaos of my thoughts. I pause in the doorway, taking in the scene: Jason sits at the table with Dermott, both of them looking up as I enter, while Beatrice stands by the stove, brewing a fresh pot of coffee. It feels warm, familiar. But there's an absence, a space left unfilled. My heart beats unbidden to the rhythm of a name.

Sawyer. Sawyer. Sawyer.

Jason stands up, a warm smile spreading across his face as he opens his arms to me. "Welcome home, Josie."

The words hit me somewhere deep. *Home.*

It's something I've been chasing for so long—since that night when everything burned down and I lost more than I could put into words. Maybe even before that. And now, as I walk with a smile into Jason's arms, in Beatrice's kitchen, I wonder if there was ever a home for me. I've tried to re-create it in other places, with other people, but nothing ever felt right. But how do you re-create something that never really existed?

Maybe . . . you don't.

Chapter 34

Then

The next few days, or perhaps weeks, passed in a disorienting haze. Time seemed to lose its meaning, stretching and compressing in ways I couldn't grasp. I felt detached from my own body, as if I were floating above, watching the world move around me. But beneath the numbness, something darker simmered. A tight knot of anger tangled inside me, kept at bay only by the overwhelming fatigue. I couldn't afford to feel it—not yet.

The house was gone, completely razed to the ground. Nothing spared. My parents were dead. I kept replaying the details in my mind, picking at the fragments like a wound that refused to heal. The fire started because my mother passed out with a lit cigarette—something I'd feared my whole life. I had been hypervigilant about it, running water over her ashtrays since I was tall enough to reach the faucet. But the one time I didn't, my whole world turned to ashes. I should've felt sadness, maybe pity, but all I could summon was anger—at her carelessness, her selfishness, the way she always dragged us down with her. Her charred remains were found by the front door. My dad too. He'd almost managed to get them out before being overtaken. He died a martyr after all.

The guilt was crushing. But beneath the guilt was rage, hot and festering. *Why was it always me? Why was I the one who had to save them? Why couldn't they save themselves, just once?* These questions haunted me, a relentless reminder of my failure. No matter how angry I felt, the guilt always won, wrapping around me like chains, dragging me down. I didn't even need sleep for nightmares to come. I'd imagine their final moments—see my dad struggling to breathe, trying to get my mother out—and I would begin to choke, my breath turning shallow as if I were suffocating too. I imagined him calling my name, pleading for the help I'd always given, begging me to save them—like I always had. I saw their faces in those final moments, realizing I wasn't coming home—and it scorched me from the inside out.

Aunt Fiona arrived to take me back to Ireland, her presence threading both comfort and sorrow into the room. There was no funeral in Maplewood—just the swift departure orchestrated by Aunt Fiona, who swooped in like a force of nature, handling everything with quiet precision. She seemed to know exactly what to do while I floundered in confusion, her efficiency both a relief and a frustration. She took charge, made the decisions, and whisked me away before I could even begin to process what had happened.

I insisted we drive by what was left of my house on the way to the airport, though I wasn't sure why. Maybe I thought seeing it one last time would bring some kind of closure, but when we got there, I didn't even look. My eyes were fixed on Sarge, standing on his porch, watching me leave. He didn't wave. Neither did I. He just stood there, and all I could do was stare back at him through the car window. I wanted to be grateful for everything he'd done, for how much he'd been there. But mostly, I just felt . . . tired. Too tired to feel anything at all.

Everything felt like a haze, a heavy fog of sorrow and confusion. Sawyer scrambled to get back from his away series, desperately trying to reach me before I left, but he wasn't fast enough. I was so numb I didn't even think to wait. It didn't matter. Nothing mattered. The people who had once meant everything—Sawyer, Beatrice, Jason, Sarge—felt like distant echoes, their voices unable to break through the wall I'd built around myself. I was like a corpse loaded onto the plane—in total shock. Maplewood, with all its memories, receded into the distance as I flew toward an uncertain future.

In Ireland, days blended together in a monotonous blur. Aunt Fiona did her best to draw me out, to encourage me to talk, but I was a hollow shell. Her kindness should have felt like a lifeline, but instead it felt suffocating, like I was drowning in her attempts to make things better. Dermott hovered too—always there, never leaving my side. They both wanted to help, but I was beyond help. The grief and guilt clung to me, shadows that refused to dissipate. I spent countless hours gazing at the Irish countryside, wondering if I would ever feel whole again. It was beautiful. All of it. The rolling green hills, the misty mornings. But it might as well have been a prison, locking me in my own mind. I couldn't feel anything but the emptiness.

A month later, we had a Mass for my parents in their home village in Ireland. The small church was filled with relatives and neighbors, some people I hadn't seen in years. Their condolences washed over me, their faces a swirl of unfamiliar familiarity. They whispered kind words, offered warm hands, but I couldn't make sense of any of it. I moved through the rituals on autopilot, my mind circling the same unanswerable questions.

The prayers, the ceremonies—they felt hollow, like reciting lines in a play where nothing could change the ending. My parents were gone. No amount of hymns or rosaries could fix what was broken. No rite could bring them back or erase the anger and guilt lodged deep inside me. I stood there like a shadow of myself, surrounded by people who cared but couldn't reach me. They didn't understand. No one could.

***

I missed the last week of school, didn't walk across the stage at graduation. Everything I had worked for felt like it was slipping through my fingers. My acceptance to Penn State was deferred for a year. "To heal," they said. "To get better." But how do you heal from something that feels endless? What did "better" even mean when everything felt broken?

In the early-morning hours, when it all became too much, I would wander the fields around my aunt's house like a ghost, like a banshee caught in her own endless wail. The air was thick with fog, and the damp grass pulled at my feet, trying to root me to the earth. I walked because there was nothing else to do. No sense of direction, no goal—just the steady rhythm of my feet, like a heartbeat.

Aunt Fiona would watch me from the window, her figure blurred in the distance, but she never stepped outside. Maybe she knew there was no pulling me back, not yet. Her hands always clasped together like she was praying for me as I wandered, hoping movement would keep me from falling apart completely. It didn't. But I kept walking anyway.

Then Dermott started following me. He never said a word, just fell into step beside me. He was there, but also not. Maybe I was dreaming him, conjuring him from the fog like everything else. His presence was a weight, something I could sense, but I never turned to look. It was enough to know someone was there, even if it didn't feel real. Everything felt unreal—like I was floating, trapped in some half-world where time barely moved, and I couldn't find a way out. The ground pulled at me, and the fog wrapped around me, trying to drag me down.

At some point, the anger I'd carried toward my parents began to loosen its grip. The better times—the happy times—started to resurface. In their deaths, I was finally recalling the moments I wished I could have held onto when they were alive. But back then, those moments had always been overshadowed by the chaos and agony of my mother's addiction.

Now, as I walked, I could almost feel her hands rubbing my back the way she had when I was a child. I'd crawl into bed with her, and she'd soothe me with one hand while reading the *Irish American* newspaper with the other. I remembered the day she marched into St. Mary's, ready to take on the nuns because one of the boys had been picking on me. She'd left triumphant, and that boy never bothered me again.

I'd spent years defending myself from my mom in her worst moments, but when she was at her best, she defended me fiercely. Those times did exist. I could see them now, in a way I hadn't before—now that they were gone forever.

There were Christmas mornings when I was little, mornings filled with magic. My parents would sit side by side, smiling as I tore into my gifts. They must have shared a love once—a love that made those mornings possible. But I hadn't saved them. Which meant I'd destroyed any chance of those moments ever happening again, and I hated myself for it.

Eventually, the fog lifted—just enough to let me breathe. But I wasn't better. I wasn't anywhere close to better. I had simply learned how to exist in a world that felt out of focus. That was when I started calling Sawyer. His voice on the other end of the line became my anchor, something steady and familiar in a life that no longer made sense.

Sawyer's voice was soothing, like the echo of a place I used to belong. He wanted so badly to pull me back—to him, to the life we thought we were building together. I wanted it too. I even convinced myself I needed it. But looking back now, I can see how far gone I really was. I wasn't healing. I was slipping, breaking apart in ways neither of us could fully grasp. I was shattered, and he couldn't see it any more than I could.

Sawyer thought he could fix me, thought bringing me back would make everything right again. But the girl he loved was gone, lost in the fire too—something neither of us wanted to admit. We were holding on to a dream, believing we could force it into reality if we just tried hard enough.

I kept reaching back, grasping for the version of us that had existed before, searching for the moment everything started to go wrong, like I could rewind time and hit some kind of reset button. But the truth was, we were on shaky ground long before everything burned. I was slipping, and I knew it, but I couldn't stop myself. The cracks were there, growing wider every day, and I was terrified of what would happen when I finally broke apart.

Each call with Sawyer felt like it was happening in some other world, like I was watching it from a distance. We talked, but it didn't feel like us. His voice was the same, but nothing else was. We clung to memories, to plans we used to make, to dreams we were too afraid to say out loud now. I wasn't the girl he remembered, and I was scared he'd see that. I didn't want him to see how far I'd fallen. I was afraid he'd figure out that I was going crazy.

But it didn't matter. I kept calling. Because even though I knew deep down that it was all slipping away, that everything was broken, I needed to believe that somehow he could make it better. That going back to him would bring back something I'd lost. I was chasing a shadow, and I didn't even know it.

But, the idea of Sawyer felt like the only real thing left. We made plans for him to come to Ireland, and I made plans to visit him at Penn State. I held on to that, fragile as it was, like it was the only thing keeping me from disappearing completely.

But the more I wandered those fields, the more restless I became. I was running, trying to outrun something I couldn't even name. Grief clung to me like the fog, seeping into my bones, suffocating me. But I couldn't stop walking, running, reaching for something—anything—that would make it go away.

That's when I decided I couldn't wait anymore. I had to go to Sawyer. I told myself I'd only be gone a week, just one week for his birthday, and everything would feel real again.

"Are you sure it's not too soon?" Aunt Fiona asked, her voice soft, concern woven into her words.

"I'm only going for a week," I said, my words tumbling out too fast to leave room for questions. "It's his birthday. I'll be ok. I promise."

She didn't believe me. "You've been through a lot, love. You need time to heal, to process all of this. I worry that going back now . . . it might be too much."

Uncle Sean was quieter, but one afternoon, while we watched the fields, he said, "You know, you don't have to run back so soon, Josie. If the fella loves you like you say, he can come here."

I laughed, hollow and unconvincing. "Oh, he will. But I need to go to him. Just for a week." The words didn't feel like mine. I wasn't even sure I believed them. I shoved the doubts down, buried them in the fog.

When I told Dermott, he didn't argue, but his face said everything. "I'll come with you," he said, resigned. "My ma'll have my head if I let you go alone."

"I'll be fine," I told him, though part of me was grateful. The truth was, I didn't think I was fine at all.

"It's a surprise," I added, forcing a smile. "Sawyer doesn't even know I'm coming."

Dermott raised an eyebrow. "A surprise, huh? Sure that's a good idea?"

I shrugged, ignoring the gnawing pit in my stomach. "It'll be fine. He'll be happy to see me."

The plane ride felt endless, like I was floating through some otherworldly desert—vast, empty, terrifying. I stared out the window, but I wasn't really seeing anything. My mind was unraveling, and no matter how hard I tried, I couldn't stop it. A voice whispered that I was making a mistake, but I couldn't be hearing voices, could I? I pushed it away.

But it was too late. I was flying toward something I couldn't stop. Toward my own undoing.

<h1 style="text-align:center">Chapter 35</h1>

Now

Beatrice, Dermott, Jason, and I gather around the kitchen table, the comforting aroma of freshly brewed coffee mingling with the scent of warm cinnamon rolls. Our conversation ebbs and flows, a mix of lighthearted banter and poignant reflections on recent events. Jason, ever the comedian, lightens the mood with his quick wit and jokes. He cracks one now and everyone chuckles, but I catch the briefest flicker in his eyes, like his mind is somewhere else.

As we talk, I notice the way Jason's smile doesn't quite reach his eyes, how his laugh is a little too short. His hand taps against his mug, his foot jittering lightly under the table. It's subtle—so subtle that I almost convince myself I'm imagining it. But when I mention something from the past few days, his gaze flickers toward me, sharp for just a second, before he masks it with another joke.

Even as he keeps up the banter, I can feel something lurking beneath his usual playful demeanor. It's there, just under the surface—a seriousness that feels out of place, a tension coiled like a spring.

After brunch, Jason gives me a meaningful look, his humor dropping completely for the first time all morning. "Josie, can I steal you for a few minutes? There's something we need to talk about."

Jason leads me out back to Beatrice's deck. It's quintessential Beatrice—her domain, a place of peace and creativity. The space is a picturesque haven adorned with a stunning array of fall mums in vibrant shades of orange, red, and yellow. The rich hues of the flowers contrast beautifully with the deep-green ivy that climbs the wooden trellis, creating a tapestry of autumn colors.

"God, she makes my dead little flowerpot on my windowsill in Dublin look worse than it is."

Jason laughs. "I'll admit it. She's really good at what she does." We move to sit on the oversized patio furniture. I shift some pillows out of the way and settle in.

"We need to talk about Sawyer."

"Jason," I say, a warning note in my voice.

"Just give me a second, Josie." He leans toward me, his eyes—usually full of playful spark—so serious now they hold me in place. "You have to hear this."

"Hear what?" I whisper, suddenly feeling afraid, like something is going to tilt my already shaky axis.

"Sawyer doesn't remember that night, Josie. But I do." His words hang in the air, heavy with the weight of revelation. Jason takes a deep breath, his expression earnest. "I thought I saw you that night. I thought I was seeing things. But when Beatrice called a few days ago and told me what was going on—she mentioned something about you coming back for Sawyer's birthday, but none of us knew about it." He leans back. "That's when it hit me. I did see you, didn't I?"

"I mean—I was there." My pounding heart makes it difficult to think. "But I didn't see you." An image of his car speeding up to the curb of their college house flashes in my mind. My hand comes up to cover my mouth as I realize it was Jason.

Jason leans forward again. "Then tell me, Josie—what did you see?"

Chapter 36

Then

Though I was still healing from emotional wounds, the idea of surprising Sawyer outweighed any lingering pain. When Dermott and I landed at the airport, we didn't go to Maplewood. Instead, we headed straight to Penn State.

Stepping out of the taxi, my heart raced as I touched the claddagh necklace around my neck. With a single backpack slung over my shoulder, I smiled at Dermott, who gave me an encouraging nod as I led him toward Sawyer's off-campus house. The jovial sounds of a party drifted through the open windows—music and laughter spilling into the night air. I smiled to myself, imagining it was a birthday celebration for him. The thrill of the moment bubbled inside me, momentarily eclipsing the heavy shadows of the past months.

As we approached the door, something shifted inside me. A flicker of doubt surfaced, brief but sharp, like a static charge. *What if he's not as happy to see me as I expect?* The thought was gone almost as quickly as it came, but it left a faint ripple of unease behind. I shook it off, telling myself I was being ridiculous. *This was Sawyer—my Sawyer. Of course, he'll be thrilled to see me.*

Still, a small knot twisted in my stomach, a quiet warning I refused to acknowledge. I pushed it aside, focusing instead on the image of his smile when he opened the door and saw me standing there.

I pushed the door open and stepped inside, the noise of the party enveloping me. Steep stairs led up to the second floor where Sawyer and Jason lived, so Dermott and I followed the noise. The apartment was packed with people I didn't recognize, but I didn't care. I was here for Sawyer. I wove through the crowd, my eyes searching for his familiar face.

"Hey, have you seen Sawyer?" I asked a group near the kitchen, but they barely glanced at me. My excitement faltered for a moment, but I pushed on, moving deeper into the living space. My heart was pounding harder now, a mix of excitement and that flutter of unease.

The music thumped in my ears, the bass vibrating through the floor. I approached another group. "Have you seen Sawyer?" The girls assessed me and smirked, then ignored me completely. It was only then I realized I wasn't dressed for a party. I had just traveled for most of the day. Sensing my nervousness, Dermott turned on his charm and moved to another cluster of people, helping in the search.

My heart started racing—not just with eagerness to see Sawyer, but with a sudden wave of nerves. *Where is he? Why haven't I seen him yet?* I shook the thought off again, telling myself he was probably just in another room, maybe getting drinks or caught up in a conversation. *Everything will be fine.* But as I moved through the crowded space, the knot in my stomach tightened.

"Do you know where Sawyer is?" I asked again, louder this time. Someone smirked and nodded toward a closed door down the hall. My heart leaped. I indicated to Dermott that I'd found him, and he nodded me off, continuing to chat with a few girls, his Irish accent charming them into a fit of giggles. I smiled, took a deep breath, adjusted my backpack, and made my way to the door, my pulse quickening with each step.

But as I reached for the handle, that flicker of doubt returned, stronger this time. *What if . . .* I paused, my hand hovering over the doorknob. *No, don't be ridiculous, Josie. He's waiting for you. He'll be so happy to see you.* Still, my fingers felt heavy as I twisted the knob and pushed the door open.

The sight that greeted me made my blood run cold.

Sawyer and Val lay tangled together on the bed, completely naked. Val's elbow rested casually on Sawyer's chest like she belonged there, her posture relaxed, victorious. When her head turned and she saw me standing in the doorway, shock flickered across her face for only a split second before it melted into a smug, taunting smirk that made my stomach churn.

I stopped breathing. The world tilted, and I felt like I was spiraling into nothingness. The excitement, the joy—everything drained out of me, leaving behind a hollow, icy dread. My lungs felt constricted, each breath shallow and sharp, as if the very air had turned toxic. My heart, which had been hammering with anticipation just moments ago, now pounded with a dull, relentless ache, every beat reverberating through me like a cruel echo of what I was seeing.

Val's smirk deepened, her eyes gleaming with malice. "Whoops," she purred, her voice dripping with mockery. "Looks like you walked in at the wrong time, Josie."

The sound of her voice jolted me out of my paralysis, the cruel satisfaction in her tone igniting a spark of anger amidst the suffocating betrayal. I wanted to scream, to demand an explanation, but the words caught in my throat.

Why isn't he saying anything? His silence was deafening. Like prom. Like the day of the Christmas Market. He was just watching me, letting me drown. The last thread of hope inside me snapped.

I didn't wait for him to move or speak. His stillness felt like the final betrayal. Before I even realized it, I was running—my feet pounding down the hallway toward the stairs. Faces blurred past me, their startled voices drowned out by the roaring in my ears.

Hot tears stung my eyes, spilling freely as my chest heaved with sobs that clawed their way up my throat. My legs burned as I took the stairs two at a time, my backpack thudding against me with each frantic step.

Bursting out of the house, I was momentarily blinded by the glare of headlights as a car screeched to a halt at the curb. I stumbled back, gasping, my breath ragged and uneven, my lungs burning like they couldn't keep up. I didn't know where I was going; I just knew I had to get away.

For a fleeting moment, I thought I might hear footsteps behind me—Sawyer, finally chasing after me. But there was nothing. Only silence. Only me.

My hand flew to my neck, gripping the chain that held the claddagh charm. With one sharp tug, it snapped free, the metal biting into my palm. Tears spilled over as I stared at it for a second longer than I wanted to, then hurled it onto the sidewalk with a broken sob.

I ran, and then I ran harder, the cold air slicing against my skin, my tears blurring everything around me. The pavement stretched endlessly beneath my feet, and my legs felt like they might give out, but I couldn't stop. I couldn't let the reality of what I'd just seen catch up to me. My chest burned, my stomach churned, and nausea clawed its way up my throat.

Somewhere in the chaos of my thoughts, I remembered Dermott—waiting for me, probably confused and worried. I slowed, turning back to find him, but before I could take another step, he was there.

His arms wrapped around me just as my knees buckled. I collapsed against him, my sobs tearing through the icy night. The weight of it all—what I'd seen, what I'd felt—crashed down like a wave, dragging me under. Dermott held me steady, his voice soft and soothing, though I barely registered the words. All I could do was cry, the shattered pieces of my world spilling out with every gasping breath.

I don't remember much about the rest of the night. Dermott and I took a Greyhound bus to Philadelphia, his calm voice pulling me through the haze of my despair. I clung to him like a lifeline. He didn't berate me or say, "I told you so." What I had seen—what I had lost—pressed on me relentlessly, suffocating and inescapable. The memories of Sawyer, the plans we'd made, the future we'd dreamed of—all of it lay in ruins. The betrayal wasn't just a wound; it was a gaping void that swallowed everything I thought I knew.

The last thing I murmured before falling asleep on the bus was, "He never even tried to follow me."

When we landed in Ireland, sorrow anchored in my chest, I made a vow. I would never step foot in Maplewood again.

Part Two

Chapter 37

Now

I avert my eyes from Jason as I recount the story, my voice trembling with the agony of the memories. When I finally finish, I lift my gaze. Jason's face is etched with pain and understanding.

"I wish I didn't remember that night as well as I do," he says, his voice low. "It was Sawyer's birthday. We were at some shitty underage college bar, and then Val showed up. None of us wanted her there, least of all Sawyer. She was going on about you, trying to show him pictures, claiming you had a boyfriend. It was desperate. Scary, even." Jason's expression hardens. "Sawyer finally lost it. Told her off in front of everyone. It was brutal, but she deserved every word. She left furious."

Jason exhales deeply, his voice tinged with regret. "I thought that was the end of it. I left Sawyer with the guys and went to the bar, but when I looked back, something felt off. He looked... off, like he was getting drunk way too fast. That's when I saw her again—Val—hanging off him."

I stiffen, nausea rising in my stomach.

"A fight broke out near the bar, and I got stuck on the other side of the room. By the time I made it back, Sawyer was gone. The guys were laughing, saying he left with Val, that she'd 'get him home safely.'" Jason's voice drips with disgust.

My breath catches, a tidal wave of anger and sorrow washing over me.

"I rushed back to the apartment, knowing something wasn't right. That's when I thought I saw you, but I blew it off. I just wanted to get inside and find Sawyer." He pauses, the memory visibly weighing on him. His jaw tightens, and for a moment, he looks away, like he's trying to find the strength to continue.

"When I got there, Sawyer was passed out in the bedroom. Val was on top of him, Josie. I had to get her off him." His voice cracks, and he looks away briefly, collecting himself. "She wasn't embarrassed—she was pissed. Like it was his fault he couldn't... you know. He was completely out of it, Josie. Nothing happened. I got there in time, I swear."

I don't realize I'm shaking until Jason grips my hand. "You were right about her, Josie. All along. None of us knew how far she would go, but you did."

Tears spill over as his words sink in. For years, I had clung to the image of Sawyer and Val together, let it define my pain, my choices. But I never even looked at him that night. Never really saw him.

"Sawyer. Is he—is he okay?" Sobs rack my body, the guilt and sorrow overwhelming me. "Does he know?"

Jason nods. "I told him the next morning. But not about seeing you. I honestly forgot about that part. I assumed it was some other girl who looked like you."

"I could have stopped her, Jason. I was there and I—I ran away."

"No. Do not go there. This was out of your control." He shakes his head, his grip tightening around my hand. "I went through the same guilt for a while, Josie. I shouldn't have gone back to the bar. I should have paid more attention. But the truth is, we had no idea this would happen."

I shake my head, trying to process it all. "But . . . Is Sawyer *okay*?" I ask again, not able to get past the worry of what this has done to him.

"He's okay, Josie." Jason takes a deep breath, and the knot of anger and pain in my chest loosens just a little. "But the thing that broke him most was that he lost you and didn't know why. He was just so worried about you."

I bury my head in my hands and cry. I lost so much time. Years. Years spent believing in a version of events that never happened. The betrayal, the agony, the heartbreak—all of it based on a lie.

And then the sorrow begins to shift. The tears don't stop, but beneath them, rage starts to bubble. The betrayal wasn't Sawyer's. It was Val's. She didn't just take everything from me—she took more from him. Did she get away with it? Did she ever pay for what she did?

I stand abruptly, my breath coming in sharp, uneven bursts. "Where is she? I'm going to kill her."

The words spill out of me before I can even think. My whole body trembles with the force of it, my anger surging hot and unrelenting. My fists clench, my nails digging into my palms, but I barely feel it. My vision narrows, tunneling on one single thought: *she doesn't deserve to get away with this.*

Jason's hand envelops mine, warm and steady. "Josie, calm down. She's not worth it. She's already paid the price."

"How?" I cry, frustration and rage surging through me. "How did she pay the price?"

"People didn't know all the details, but there was enough going around to make her a pariah."

"A *pariah*?" I scoff, my voice shaking with fury. "Jason, she's a predator!"

Jason stands, his face shadowed with something I can't quite place—pain, determination, guilt. "Josie, listen to me. I know how much this hurts, but you have to let it go. She's not worth destroying yourself over."

His words hit me like a slap. I take a step back, my voice trembling but sharp. "What if it were me, Jason? What if some guy did that to me?"

The question lands heavy between us. Jason's jaw tightens, his gaze falling to the ground for a moment before snapping back to mine.

"You know Sawyer and I would kill him," he says quietly. "If Beatrice didn't get to him first." He reaches for my hand again, gripping tightly, grounding me even as I feel like I might shatter. "But that's exactly why we can't let her win, Josie. She's already taken enough. Don't let her take any more from you."

I shake my head. "I can't just let this go, Jason. You don't understand."

The back patio door slides open, and I hear footsteps. When I look up, Beatrice and Dermott are there, their faces soft with concern. Beatrice settles on the bench beside me while Dermott kneels in front of me, his hands wrapping around mine like they're trying to hold me together.

"You knew?" I whisper, my voice cracking as I look at Dermott.

His expression is full of regret. "Beatrice just told me, love."

My eyes dart to her.

"I tried to tell you at the Bar and Grill," she says, her voice low. "But it felt too heavy, Josie. I didn't want to make it worse. And I didn't know everything. So I called Jason. I thought he'd know what to do. And that's when I got the whole truth."

Jason nods from where he stands. "I flew out the second I knew. I was the one who was there. I wanted to be the one to tell you."

I look between them, the truth settling over me. "Thank you," I whisper, the words fragile.

But there's only one person I need right now. "Where is Sawyer?"

Beatrice shifts, her hand brushing my arm gently. "He's still off work for the next few days. Said he had some time saved up and decided to take it."

"Okay, so where is he?"

Jason straightens. "He's home, Josie." He pauses, letting the words land before reaching out a hand to me. "Come on. I'll take you to him."

Chapter 38

Jason and I continue the conversation as we drive, our voices mingling with the hum of the engine. I ask him more questions about that night. He tells me he believes Val slipped something into Sawyer's drink, but it couldn't be proven.

"Sawyer was too embarrassed to talk about it, let alone pursue anything. I got him to go to campus counseling, but . . ." Jason trails off. "As far as I know, he went, but we never really spoke about it again."

"And you don't know where she is now?"

Jason hesitates, his fingers tapping restlessly against the steering wheel. "I really don't know, Josie." He sighs, glancing at me out of the corner of his eye. "I'm not sure if digging into this is going to help. Val's poison. Always was. Chasing her down won't heal what's broken."

As we drive, the familiar scenery of Maplewood slips past, each landmark brushing against memories that hover just out of reach. But those memories keep getting shoved aside. All I can think about is Sawyer—how he must have felt that night. If it had been me, I would have needed him. The realization that Sawyer needed me and I wasn't there twists like a knife in my gut, leaving a fresh ache I can't ignore.

After a few moments of quiet, I sit up straighter as we turn onto a familiar road. The trees thin out, revealing glimpses of the shimmering water beyond. "Are we going to Maple Lake right now?" I ask, my voice tinged with childlike excitement I haven't felt in years.

A grin spreads across Jason's face, but he stays silent. As we pull into Uncle Lou's driveway, a familiar excitement wells up, warm and uncontainable, just like it used to. The sight of the lake fills me with a mix of joy and nostalgia, a brief reprieve from the tension gnawing at my insides. But then confusion creeps in. "Sawyer told me Uncle Lou sold this place?"

Jason parks the car and turns to look at me. "He did. To his nephew."

I blink, trying to process this new information. "He did?"

Jason smiles and looks over my shoulder. "Go on. You'll want to see this for yourself."

I follow his eyes and see Sawyer in the distance, his back to us, sitting on the edge of the dock, the late-afternoon sun casting a golden glow on the water around him. I inhale sharply.

"Go on," Jason says again, this time more softly. "I'm going to head out."

I turn back to Jason, feeling a swell of uncertainty rise in my chest. "You're not coming with me?"

He chuckles, shaking his head. "Nope. This is all you, Josie."

I unbuckle, lean over the console, and give Jason a quick hug before stepping out of the car.

***

My feet carry me toward Sawyer before I even have time to think. The dock stretches out before me, each creak of the wooden planks under my feet like an echo of the heavy silence that lingers between us. The last time I saw him, we were fighting—raw words tumbling out between sharp breaths and fiery emotions that neither of us could fully untangle. And now, after learning the truth about that night, I feel like I should know what to say. But the truth doesn't change the way we left things.

The cool breeze from the lake brushes against me, causing goosebumps to prickle along my arms. I take a breath, steadying myself, my eyes on Sawyer as he sits at the edge of the dock, completely unaware of my presence. He's still, staring out at the water, lost in his own thoughts. For a moment, I just watch him.

And something inside me cracks.

I try to push it back. To shove it into that dark, hidden corner of my mind where it's lived for so long. But it won't stay there. It bursts out, spilling over me like a tidal wave I can't stop. It's too much—too big, too overwhelming.

Because it's him.

Sitting there, looking like he doesn't know he still owns every piece of me.

I thought I let go. God, I tried to let go. I spent years convincing myself I had. That I could move on. That I *had* moved on. But now? Now, with him right in front of me, I feel it all. Every piece of him I loved. Every piece of me I lost.

The way he sits, his broad shoulders slightly hunched, the way his hair falls messily against his forehead—it's all so achingly familiar, and it breaks my heart and fills it up at the same time.

The soft creak of the wood beneath my feet gives me away.

Sawyer hears me, and his head whips around, his body tensing as he cranes his neck to see who's behind him. His expression shifts between surprise, confusion, and something deeper as he stands, a little too quickly.

"Josie? How did you—?" His words falter as he starts to move toward me, his gaze traveling over me like he's still trying to make sense of my sudden appearance. "How's your head? Are you okay?"

His concern tugs at my heart, a reminder of how much he's always cared, no matter what's happened between us. I nod, trying to smile, but my stomach twists with all the things we've never said. "I'm fine. Completely fine," I say, though the words feel heavy in my mouth, like I'm trying too hard to convince both of us. "Thank you for taking me to Bea last night. I really appreciate it."

Sawyer watches me for a moment, his eyes narrowing slightly in suspicion. He used to be able to read me, to see through the walls I built up around myself, and I know he can sense that there's more going on beneath the surface. But he doesn't push. Not yet.

I take a deep breath, the fresh scent of the lake filling my lungs, and for a moment, I let myself be still. "It's just as beautiful as I remember," I breathe as my eyes take in the familiar landscape. The lake, the trees, the golden light filtering through the branches. "This is heaven," I murmur, my voice barely louder than a whisper. "I'm glad this place is still in your life. I was sad when I thought someone else owned it."

I don't mean for it to sound like an accusation, but I suppose it does. He turns his head slightly, and I catch the way his shoulders tense before he finally looks at me. There's something in his eyes that I can't quite place—something old, something familiar, and it hits me how much I've missed this. How much I've missed him.

"I bought it a few years ago," Sawyer says quietly, turning back to the water. His voice is calm, but the simplicity of his statement carries something that feels impossible to ignore. "You once told me it was your dream to live here, so I bought it in case you ever decided to come back."

The air seems to still around us, his words landing like a stone sinking deep into the water, creating ripples I wasn't prepared for. I blink, caught off guard by the bluntness of his admission, by the fact that he's saying it like it's nothing, like it's not breaking my heart all over again.

"I wanted you to have a home," he adds, and when he looks back at me, there's an innocence in his gaze that I haven't seen in years. It throws me, leaves me standing there, speechless.

I'm frozen as I try to process what he just said. The world around us seems to fade, leaving just the two of us and the quiet hum of the lake. Sawyer nods, his gaze drifting back to the horizon, as if my silence is an answer in itself. "I know," he says softly, his voice laced with a sadness I hadn't expected. "It seems crazy now."

"How many years ago?" I ask.

He turns to me slowly, his brow furrowing as though the question doesn't quite make sense. "What?"

"How many years ago did you buy it?" I clarify, desperately needing to understand. He couldn't have bought this place while he was in college. Uncle Lou wouldn't just hand this property over to him, not without a reason, not without Sawyer working for it.

He searches my face, as if trying to gauge why this matters so much, why I'm pushing. His stare lingers for a second longer before he looks back out at the water. "Four."

"*Four?*" I repeat, my shock evident.

"Four years ago, Josie," he says, his voice soft but firm, like it's a fact he's been living with for too long.

Four years. I let the words settle, the pressure of them sinking deeper into my chest. He bought this place four years ago—eleven years after I disappeared. My heart aches, overwhelmed by the realization. Even after all that time, Sawyer still bought this place, held on to it . . . for me.

I'm about to reach for him, my fingers twitching with the need to touch him, hold him, to give in to the pull that has never truly faded. But before I can, he speaks, his voice low and steady, as though he's been rehearsing this moment in his mind for days.

"I don't want you here, Josie."

The words hit me like a punch, and for a second, I can't breathe. I don't respond. I just stand there, trying to absorb what he's saying, waiting—desperately hoping—for him to take it back, to say something, anything, that could explain why. My hands still ache to reach for him, to stop him from slipping away, but I can't move.

He turns to look at me then, and the sorrow on his face is so raw, so real, it almost knocks me off balance. "I've been torturing myself for years, trying to make sense of what happened. I kept thinking, if you came back, if I could just see you, maybe I'd be able to figure it out. Maybe I could fix what I did wrong."

I open my mouth to tell him he didn't do anything wrong, to tell him I'm sorry, but he keeps talking.

"But I couldn't figure it out, Josie. I couldn't. And I have been so tired." His voice breaks on the last word, and he exhales like he's been holding everything inside for far too long. "I deserved a chance to explain."

It's not just exhaustion in his eyes—it's defeat. He's giving up, and the realization leaves me frozen. I thought this was the moment we'd finally talk, find a way to forgive each other for what we never did wrong. But he's already made his decision. We'll never get the closure we're desperate for.

And I feel like I'm losing him all over again.

I step forward then. "I was there the night of your birthday. I walked in on Val trying to—trying to—"

He shakes his head and steps back, like he wants me to stop. "I put that together at the park. You said something about surprising me for my birthday, but you were the one who got the surprise." He stands quietly for a second, then starts to move past me to leave the dock, but I reach out and grab his hand, holding it. He turns, and we are just inches apart. He's looking at me with an intensity I remember from years before.

"Sawyer, I am so sorry," I whisper, barely able to push past the lump in my throat.

His expression changes to something colder. "It's okay. It's water under the bridge." I flinch at my words being thrown back at me. He pulls himself from my grip and starts to walk away. "You can take my truck back to town. Keys are in the ignition. I'll get it later."

I watch him, my mouth hanging open, and my vision begins to cloud again. I suddenly feel the urge to run. I need to get out of here. I'm overexposed and raw and I feel a panic attack barreling toward me like a freight train. Just as I'm about to start my anxiety-alleviating techniques—and run for the road because I am not taking his fucking truck—the old familiar white-hot rage surges inside me and pins me in place.

No. This is not the way it ends.

"I crossed an ocean, Sawyer," I snap, my voice trembling with fury, "my heart in pieces the whole way, just to see you on your birthday. I barely slept, barely ate—everything was a blur because all I could think about was surprising you. And when I got to you, when I was right *there* . . ." My voice breaks, and I swallow hard, forcing myself to push back the horrifying images in my mind. "I walked in and saw her. And she *laughed* at me, Sawyer. She laughed in my face."

Sawyer freezes, his back still turned to me, but I know he's listening. His shoulders tense, his hands clenched at his sides.

"I am sorry," I continue, my voice rising. "I am *so* sorry, but I cannot blame myself for this. I have blamed myself for everything my entire life—but *this*?" My breath is unsteady, and the anger wells up inside me again, intense and blinding. "This is not my fault. So you can walk away from me, and I will walk away too, and we can finally put an end to this agonizing chapter of our lives—but I refuse to take the blame for this, and you should too. This was her fault, Sawyer. Not ours."

The silence that follows is deafening. I watch his back, waiting, hoping for some kind of response, my heart hammering in my chest. Sawyer spins toward me, his eyes blazing with fury. He starts walking back, closing the distance between us with a primitive, unsettled energy.

"I tried calling you," he begins, his voice filled with frustration. "Your aunt told me you weren't there. I tried over and over and over again, and I couldn't find you. Why wouldn't you give me a chance to explain? How could you just leave me like that?" We stand toe to toe now, the tension between us so palpable it feels like a live wire. He runs his fingers through his hair, exasperation clear in his movements. "Why couldn't you at least fucking yell at me, scream at me, tell me to go to hell if you thought I was with her? Why would you just disappear?"

His words hit me like waves crashing against the shore, relentless and unyielding. But I can't look away. I can't tear my eyes from him, even though the words I need to say feel like they're choking me. Why is it always this hard? To peel back the layers, to take my heart—raw, vulnerable—and hand it over to the one person I want to trust with it the most?

But deep down, I know it's pointless. This road doesn't lead anywhere. Loving Sawyer as fiercely as I do isn't just a risk; it's a gamble with my sanity. That thought terrifies me more than anything.

Because the truth is, I don't trust myself. I don't trust that I'm strong enough, whole enough, to survive losing him again. And if I break this time, I don't know if I'll ever be able to put myself back together.

I stumble over my words, trying to find a way to speak, but barely able to squeak out a sound. It's not that I don't want to tell him—I just don't know how.

How do I say it?

Here I am, standing in front of him, heart in pieces, hoping he'll love me the way I've always loved him. But it doesn't matter, does it? Because no matter how much I want it, there's no reality—no world—where this could ever work.

How do I tell him that I want him to love me, even though I'm convinced I'm too broken for anyone to love? That I'm terrified if he gets too close, he'll see it too—that he'll realize I'm not what he wants after all. And yet, even knowing that, there's still a selfish part of me that craves it, that wants him to want me anyway.

But if he doesn't? Or worse—if he does, and it only makes this more impossible?

It might destroy me.

How do I find the words to tell Sawyer that? How do I even begin? It doesn't even make sense. None of it does. But here I am, standing in front of him, wishing I could figure it out anyway.

The stakes are so high, and I'm terrified to admit that I can't just quit while I'm ahead. Did my parents do this to me? Was it the fire? Was it Val? When did I become so full of doubt, so afraid of my own feelings?

But I also know I'm strong. I've stood through storms that should've torn me apart. Gale-force winds have blown over me, and still, I've held my ground. But even the strongest can't weather everything. Even the sturdiest oak loses its leaves. Sometimes it loses its branches. And sometimes, no matter how strong it stands, someone decides to cut it down anyway.

My resolve falters for just a moment, and my eyes drift toward the road. I could leave. I could protect myself from the risk of falling apart again. It's the easiest option—to run. But the truth is, I've survived too much to run now. I've weathered storms that would have shattered others, and maybe that's why I'm so scared. Because I know the cost. But I also know my strength.

And I need to tell him.

Sawyer catches my eyes as they drift toward the road, and I see the anger flare in his. It's more than just frustration—there's a raw, seething hurt behind it, the kind that comes from someone who's been pushed too far, too many times. He's fed up, broken, and devastated, and it's all spilling out now, no matter how much he might have loved me once.

"Go, Josie. Leave," he snaps, his voice low but trembling with emotion.

"No."

"Go! Leave! I want you to leave! I don't want you here!" His voice cracks as he practically shouts the words, but I can hear the pain beneath his fury. He's trying to push me away, to protect himself.

"No."

Sawyer's chest heaves with the agony of everything he's been holding back. His hands clench into fists at his sides, and his voice drops to a hoarse whisper. "Do you think I want to keep doing this? Do you think I want to keep getting my heart ripped out every time you pull away? I'm so damn tired, Josie. I have nothing left inside me." His eyes are brimming with tears, a mix of anger and despair, and I know he means it. He's ready to let me go, even if it kills him. "Please just go!"

"I said NO!" I stomp my foot on the dock like a petulant child, but that's exactly how I feel—cornered, forced to reveal a piece of my past I've kept buried for so long.

"I completely cracked up, Sawyer! I was put away for so goddamn long I didn't even know who I was when I got out. Is that what you want to hear? You want the truth? Well—there it is! I went absolutely batshit crazy."

The words tear out of me, raw and painful. I wince at my own admission, cursing into the sky as the vulnerability slices through the armor I've built around myself. I wanted to say it, to tell him everything, but it still feels like a knife slicing into my soul.

He stumbles back, just slightly, but enough for me to catch it. We both fall silent. The sound of the water lapping back and forth and the creak of the dock is all that remains. His face shifts from fury to something softer—something broken. And I realize that we've both been holding on to so much pain that it's strangling us.

Sawyer takes in a shuddering breath. "I couldn't find you."

"Yeah—well, that makes both of us." My voice cracks on the last word, the bitterness and sorrow tangled in my throat.

The pain etched into Sawyer's face is almost unbearable. His red-rimmed eyes glisten with a sorrow so raw it cuts through me. He holds my gaze, and I can't look away, even though it hurts to see him like this.

"Tell me," he whispers, his voice breaking. And I know I owe him that much.

I drop my gaze to my hands, unable to meet his eyes. The memories of that night still sting, wounds that have only just begun to scab over. "Something inside me . . . broke back then," I begin, my voice barely audible. "I see it now, but I didn't recognize it at the time. My parents had just died, and I was already in a dark place. Seeing you . . . with her . . . it was like the final straw, and—"

I stop, the enormity of what I'm about to say bearing down on me. I can't breathe. I force myself to exhale, and then inhale again. "I know now that this was not your fault. But when I went back to Ireland after seeing you and Val, I wasn't just heartbroken, Sawyer. I was shattered. I wasn't in any state of mind for a visit in the first place. I hadn't dealt with my parents' deaths. I blamed myself, convinced that if I had gone home when my dad asked me to, I could have saved them. The guilt consumed me, and I started hating myself for surviving when they didn't. I was already on the edge, and I didn't even realize it."

Sawyer's expression shatters me. His devastation is raw and unfiltered, and for a second, I hate myself for putting it there. But he doesn't interrupt, doesn't look away, even as his eyes glisten.

"I need you to know I don't blame you for my breakdown," I say again, my voice trembling under the pressure of everything I'm laying bare. "I never did—not even when I thought . . . when I believed you and Val . . ."

The words catch in my throat, but I push through, feeling a strange, bittersweet relief in finally letting them out. "I lost so many years, Sawyer. I cut off all my hair. I started cutting myself." I jangle the bracelets on my wrist, the ones I've used to hide the scars, the evidence of those darkest days. "I thought maybe I could carve the pain out of me, start over somehow, but nothing worked. And when nothing worked . . . I didn't want to keep going."

My voice breaks, and the crack feels like it's splitting me open. His face twists, a mixture of horror and heartbreak that mirrors the way I feel inside.

"Dermott found me," I whisper, my gaze dropping to the dock. "I ended up in the hospital for a long time."

The words hang in the air between us, and I struggle to breathe through the tightness in my chest. "Recovery wasn't a straight line. It took years, and honestly, I don't think it's something you ever fully recover from. But I work on it, every single day. And I don't always get it right." I try to laugh, but it's a hollow sound, a shadow of humor. "By the time I felt like I could even stand on my own again, years had passed. I was embarrassed. Ashamed. I thought it would be easier to just fade away, to become a ghost. I hoped everyone had moved on, forgotten about me. It seemed easier than facing the possibility that everyone, especially Beatrice," I say, choking on her name, the guilt strangling me, "hated me for disappearing after everything they'd done for me."

I blink back tears, forcing myself to push forward. "I was so ashamed. And I kept thinking . . . what if you knew I went crazy? What if you hated me too?"

I finally risk another glance at him, and the look on his face nearly undoes me. His eyes are full of regret, glistening with tears he's barely holding back. When he speaks, his voice is soft and raw, breaking with the weight of his words.

"Josie O'Driscoll, there was not a moment—not one single moment in fifteen years—that you left my head or my heart." His voice cracks, but he keeps going, his gaze never leaving mine. "I'm so sorry."

I open my mouth to say something, anything, but he doesn't give me the chance. His words come tumbling out, as if he's afraid he won't be able to say them if he stops.

"I didn't know. I didn't know what you were going through—not really. I should have. I should've paid attention. I should've been there. But Josie, you have to believe me—if I'd known, if I'd understood even half of it . . . God, I would've been there. I wouldn't have given up trying to find you. I would've done anything to help you."

His voice is trembling now, filled with a mixture of guilt and anguish that mirrors my own. "You think I would've hated you? I could never hate you. Do you know what killed me the most all these years? Thinking I lost you because I wasn't enough. Thinking I failed you. And now you're standing here, telling me everything you've carried, and I hate myself for not seeing it, for not knowing how much pain you were in. For not finding you."

I shake my head, wanting to rid him of his guilt. "No, Josie. Don't you dare take this on yourself. What you went through? That's not something anyone should have to carry alone. I should've been there, and I wasn't. And I'm so damn sorry for that."

Tears spill down my cheeks, and I swipe at them uselessly. His voice softens, the raw edges giving way to something steadier, something almost pleading.

"You talk about being ashamed, about thinking you'd gone crazy, but Josie, look at me." He waits until I do, his gaze locking onto mine with a fierce intensity. "You didn't go crazy. You were in pain, and you survived it. You survived it, Josie. Do you know how strong that makes you? How incredible you are?"

I want to argue, to tell him he doesn't understand, but the words won't come. And maybe it's because, for the first time, a part of me wants to believe him.

"I'm so sorry, Josie. I'm so, so sorry."

"It's ok. It's not your fault. We were just kids," I murmur, almost to myself.

Sawyer shakes his head sharply. "We were never just kids, Josie."

His intensity catches me off guard, but before I can respond, his expression shifts. "Sarge. How did he find you? Why the hell didn't he tell me?"

I knew this moment would come, but that doesn't make it any easier. I owe him the truth, even if I don't have all the answers.

"Sarge always knew where I was. He stayed in touch with my aunt, but I didn't talk to him for years—not at first. I think he didn't want you to know . . . not when I was in such a dark place." I hesitate, forcing myself to keep going. "I don't think anyone thought I'd come out of it. And later, when I started to get better, I guess he didn't tell you because he thought it was too late—or maybe it was all part of his plan."

I try to laugh, thinking of the wild-goose chase Sarge had sent us on, but the sound is hollow. "We kept in touch, but I never asked about Maplewood or about you. I couldn't. I was terrified of revisiting the past, scared that I'd spiral again. I didn't want to go crazy. And he tried to talk to me, but I wouldn't let him."

I glance away, the shame still bubbling under the surface. "Yesterday, when you said you quit baseball and school . . . I wonder if Sarge was trying to protect you too. I'm so sorry, Sawyer. I'm sorry you lost those things because of me."

"No." His voice is firm, resolute. "No, Josie. I didn't lose anything because of you."

I look up, startled, as he shakes his head and blows out a breath.

"I never wanted those things. I mean—I loved baseball. Still do. But not in the way everyone thought I should." He pauses, his gaze locking onto mine. "What I wanted was you."

His words aren't loud, but they might as well be cymbals clanging in my ears. He turns back toward the water.

"We sat here once, talking about our future—marriage, kids, jobs. Maybe the world would call it simple or juvenile, but it wasn't to me. It was everything." He takes a deep breath, his voice steady and sure. "I grew up without a dad, without someone brave enough to stick around. And you grew up with parents who couldn't give you those so-called 'simple' things." He makes air quotes around the word, his tone tinged with frustration. "But that's the thing—there's nothing simple about it. The life I wanted with you wasn't small or boring. It was ours. I would've climbed any mountain with you, Josie. And yeah, I wanted to be a teacher and a coach. But I was scared to say it out loud because everyone kept pushing me to want more."

His eyes meet mine again, earnest and unflinching. "I quit baseball. Left the main campus. Finished school at a satellite campus, doing what I actually wanted to do. And I'm proud of that. But I never stopped wanting you."

His words land with a quiet finality, and for a moment, I'm too stunned to speak. The anger and regret that clouded his face moments ago are gone, replaced by something deeper—a bittersweet acceptance of what was and what might've been.

"I wish I had come to find you," he says softly. "I didn't know where to go or who to ask. And for a while . . . I thought you had a boyfriend."

The corner of his mouth quirks up in a small, sheepish smile, and I can't help but laugh through my tears.

"Oh, poor Dermott." I shake my head, wiping my face. "I don't know how I would've survived without him all these years."

Sawyer chuckles, the sound warm and familiar. "I'm glad you had him. And honestly? I never really believed you left me for someone else. I think I just convinced myself you did to make it easier to move on." His voice drops, his tone laced with quiet understanding. "Anger was easier than sadness."

I nod, a tear slipping down my cheek. Reaching out, I take his hand in mine, our fingers intertwining. His touch steadies me, but it also terrifies me. The connection feels as solid as the dock beneath our feet, yet I can't help but feel like I'm about to float away.

I know we're on the edge of something—of making a mistake. A mistake I shouldn't want. But I do. I want it with every fiber of my being.

Sawyer takes a step closer, his gaze locked on mine. "Josie," he whispers.

My heart pounds in my chest, each beat echoing in my ears. He raises his hand and gently cups my face, his thumb brushing away a tear that slips down my cheek. His touch is warm, filled with a fondness that seems to melt away every fear and doubt that has weighed me down for so long. As we stand there, our eyes locked, the world around us fades into the background, leaving just the two of us suspended in this moment.

"I live in a different country," I blurt out. The words hang there like a glaring neon sign, impossible to ignore.

His smile falters, just for a second, but he doesn't let go. Instead, he tightens his grip, like he's trying to keep me grounded. "You're not in a different country right now," he says softly, his voice steady, coaxing. His smile returns, tentative this time, like he's daring me to believe that right now is all that matters.

"No," I whisper, my lips curving into a weak smile. "I'm not."

But the truth—sharp and unrelenting—settles between us. A truth we can't ignore. This—whatever it is—is fleeting. Temporary. A fragile moment slipping through our fingers even as we hold on.

I could end it here. I could step back, close the door, and save us both the heartbreak. My fingers tremble, caught between the urge to pull away and the overwhelming need to stay.

Do I even want this?

The question twists inside me, clawing at my chest. And even as my pulse races, even as fear threatens to swallow me whole, I already know the answer.

Yes.

I want this. I want him. I need Sawyer more than I've ever needed anything in my life.

His hand slides down to my waist, pulling me gently toward him. "If we start this, it'll only end the same way, won't it? With both of us broken." His voice is soft, but there's something deeper in it—a sadness, a resignation. His eyes meet mine, searching not just for permission but for something more. Maybe a different answer. One I can't give.

"We live on different continents," I murmur, the words feeling like a wall between us. It's the truth. No matter how much we want each other, the gap between us is bigger than oceans and visas.

I was born in Ireland and came to the U.S. as a child. My parents and I were legal residents with green cards, but we never became citizens. I always planned to apply for citizenship, and so did my parents, but we never got around to it. When I went back to Ireland and didn't return, I essentially abandoned my legal status in the U.S. It's not as simple as deciding to stay awhile and figure things out. And Sawyer can't just move to Ireland and become a teacher either—it doesn't work that way.

Sawyer's grip on me tightens and he rests his forehead against mine. I can feel his breath, hot and shaky, like he's trying to hold back. "I know," he says, his voice barely above a whisper, but there's a tremor in it now—an unspoken pain. He pulls back slightly, his eyes locking on mine. His vulnerability is crushing me. His eyes glisten. "I've missed you for so damn long, Josie. I don't know if I can take it again."

He stops, like he's on the edge of saying something else but can't find the words. His lips hover inches from mine, and my heart races, as if it's trying to escape the fear and doubt clawing at my chest.

Then Sawyer leans back, just enough for our eyes to meet again. "I'm scared."

His voice is a near-whisper, but it shatters something inside me. I can see it all now—the pain he's been carrying, the fear that this could be our last chance. And it's the final push I need. I step forward, erasing the last bit of space between us. Lifting on my toes, I close the distance.

The kiss is soft, filled with a longing so deep I feel it in every inch of my skin. I hear a strangled sound escape from his chest. His lips move against mine, and the affection in his kiss wrecks me. It's careful, reverent, like he's memorizing the shape of my mouth, the feel of my skin, and I can't help but lean into him. His hand slides to the back of my neck, his fingers threading through my hair, while the other pulls me closer, as if he's afraid to let me go.

The tenderness between us slowly gives way to something more urgent, more desperate. It's as if we both realize that time is slipping through our fingers, that this connection—whatever it is—can't last. Not in the world we live in. My hands find their way to his hair, fingers tangling in the familiar auburn waves, pulling him closer, as if I can make up for all the lost time in this single moment.

Sawyer's hands travel down my back, the heat of his touch searing through my clothes, making me shiver with the intensity of our connection. His hands settle at the small of my back, pulling me firmly against him.

We are breathless, our kisses growing more intense, more searching. Each touch, each movement, is a desperate attempt to keep the other near. I can feel his heart pounding against my chest, mirroring the wild rhythm of my own. Our lips part only to gasp for breath, our heads gently leaning together, our eyes closed as we savor the closeness, the undeniable chemistry that has never truly faded.

It's in the stillness that it hits me: the taste of his kiss, the scent of his skin—it's all so achingly familiar. But this time, it's heavier, sharper, laced with promises we're both too afraid to speak aloud. And even if this can't last—if the world has other plans for us—it doesn't matter right now.

Because for the first time in fifteen years, I feel whole again.

"My Josie O," Sawyer murmurs.

Our lips meet again, a surge of electricity sparking between us, reigniting the passion we can't seem to extinguish. It feels like we're defying the years and distance that tore us apart, if only for a fleeting moment.

But just as the world narrows to only the two of us again, the shrill sound of his phone ringing in his pocket shatters the quiet of the lake and pierces through our dreamlike haze. Sawyer pulls back, his breath coming in sharp gasps. For a moment, neither of us moves, clinging to the last remnants of the moment before it all falls away.

"Shit." Sawyer scrubs a hand over his face, and we can't help but laugh at our misfortune. "I'm not answering that," he says with a wince.

My lips curve into a smile. "It's okay. You can answer it. Or at least make it stop ringing."

With a reluctant sigh, Sawyer pulls his phone from his pocket, glances at the screen, and answers. I try to catch my breath, though I don't really want to. All I want is Sawyer—right here, right now. I don't want to think about what comes next. I just want this moment.

His lips twitch with amusement. "Hold on. She's right here."

I blink, wide-eyed, as he hands his phone to me. "It's Dermott, calling from Beatrice's phone. I swear, I never understand a word that guy says."

I can't help but laugh, shaking my head as Sawyer disappears to give me a moment. Dermott's voice bursts through the line, his Irish lilt brimming with excitement. He's rambling about some eighties rock band Jason's obsessed with that's playing nearby tonight. Apparently, Dermott's itching to go.

I stifle a giggle, feeling that familiar mix of affection and exasperation. Dermott always knows how to check in—like my self-appointed crisis hotline.

"Just go and have fun," I say, doing my best to sound casual, even as my eyes scan the area for Sawyer. "Seriously, enjoy yourself."

There's a pause, then a chuckle from Dermott. "Sounds like you're enjoying yourself too, judging by that laugh."

I roll my eyes, grinning. "Bye, Dermott!"

Hanging up, I turn to find Sawyer sauntering back toward me, a tackle box in one hand and two fishing poles slung over his shoulder. His easy stride, his tousled hair—it's impossible not to think about how close we were moments ago.

"What do you think?" he asks, his smile disarming. "Want to try catching a couple of fish?"

"Fishing, huh?" I tease, glancing at the lake. "Is that your way of distracting me?"

Sawyer grins. "Maybe. Or maybe I just want an excuse to spend more time with you now that you don't hate me." His voice is soft, inviting.

"I never hated you," I say quietly.

He hands me a rod, and we walk to the edge of the dock as the sun dips lower. We sit down, legs dangling over the side, and he shows me how to bait the hook, just like he did years ago. His hands guide mine, their familiarity making my chest ache. It's comforting—just being here, together, without the trauma of the past pressing in.

"This reminds me of the first time I brought you fishing," Sawyer says, a nostalgic smile tugging at his lips.

I laugh. "*Fishing* is a bit of a stretch, don't you think? I caught that fish, and you told me to throw it back. But when I touched it, I got so grossed out I practically launched it across the lake like a football."

Sawyer chuckles, leaning closer. "You definitely took 'throw it back' to a whole new level."

I roll my eyes. "You didn't exactly prepare me for how slimy it would be."

His laughter is rich and warm. "I didn't realize I had to."

Our conversation flows easily, the playful banter thick with innuendo. Our hands brush occasionally as we adjust our rods, and every touch sends a jolt through me. The years apart have only intensified the pull between us, giving me the courage to ask him the question that's been on my mind.

"Sawyer, are you okay?"

He blinks, caught off guard. "What do you mean?"

"I mean . . . everything with Val. What happened."

His expression darkens, and he looks down at the fishing pole in his hands. "Honestly? It messed me up for a long time. I didn't want to talk about it, didn't want to think about it."

I watch him, feeling the gravity of his words. His voice is steady, but there's a rawness beneath it.

"I was ashamed," he continues quietly. "I felt like it was my fault, like I should've stopped her. But I couldn't remember anything, and that terrified me. I felt . . . weak. And then, you were gone. I was so afraid that something had happened to you. It all came crashing down at once."

I place my hand over his. "It wasn't your fault, Sawyer. You know that, right?"

He meets my gaze, his eyes heavy with years of pain. "Logically, yeah. But that doesn't make it easier to swallow. I still hate that I couldn't stop it." He pauses, a tremor in his voice. "If I had known you were there, watching . . . God, that would've been worse."

I lean in, squeezing his hand. "You didn't deserve any of it, Sawyer. Not from her. Not from me leaving. I'm sorry."

He looks at me, his eyes so open and warm. "I'm okay, Josie. I promise. And there's nothing for you to be sorry about. This whole thing was a twisted mess, but at least we've figured it out now and we don't have to live the rest of our lives never knowing what happened to each other."

He is right, but it is of little comfort now. "So, I take it Sarge didn't know about Val?"

Sawyer laughs, the sound lifting something heavy from my heart. "No! Jesus. Can you imagine the content of his letters if he knew about that shit?"

I can't help but laugh with him, the mental image of Sarge ranting with a cigarette dangling from his lips. "He'd have Lucky Strikes flying out of his ears."

Sawyer's laughter eases into a thoughtful smile. "But, now that I think about it, Sarge knew everything, didn't he? And his letters—" He pauses, his expression shifting as he leans closer. "They seem pretty hell-bent on getting us to talk. The way he wrote about the stories we tell ourselves not necessarily being true…" He trails off, his gaze meeting mine, his voice quieter now. "I bet he did know. And this was his way of trying to fix it."

His words sink in, and I nod, the realization settling quietly. "Wow." My voice is a whisper. "You're right."

For a moment, we just sit there, the air between us buzzing with something unspoken, something bigger than either of us. Sarge knew. Of course, he knew.

The fishing lines in the water become an afterthought, mere props to the charged energy building between us. As we reel them in, the banter flows easily, but with each glance and every brush of skin, the playful edge softens into something deeper, something electric. By the time the lines are stowed and the rods set aside, Sawyer turns to me, his eyes locking onto mine.

I toss him a cheeky smile. "We didn't catch anything."

He grins, slow and lopsided, the kind of grin that makes my chest ache. "I caught something."

I raise an eyebrow. "Oh yeah? What's that?"

His hand finds the small of my back, pulling me closer until I can feel the warmth of him. "You," he says softly. "And I'm not throwing you back."

A laugh bubbles out of me, light and a little breathless. "Well, aren't you the all-star catcher?"

"Best there is," he murmurs, and then his lips brush against mine, soft and tentative at first, like he's testing the waters.

But it doesn't stay soft for long. The kiss quickly shifts into something hungrier, something that feels like it's been waiting to happen for years. His hands grip my waist, pulling me firmly against him, grounding me even as my pulse races.

My fingers find their way to his hair, threading through the familiar waves, tugging just enough to draw a low sound from his throat that sends a shiver down my spine. I shift closer, my knees pressing into his sides as I straddle him. His hands slide up my back, steady and warm, anchoring me, and I lose myself completely in the moment, in him, in us.

"Sawyer," I whisper, breathless. His only response is a low, rumbling sound as his hands roam, exploring my body with an unmistakable hunger.

"We should—" he starts, but I silence him with another kiss, slower this time, savoring every moment.

I smile against his lips. "Let's go inside."

The walk from the dock to the house is a blur, our focus only on each other. The moment we're inside, the door barely shut, we're back at it—lips crashing together in a heated frenzy.

But as we stumble into the hallway, something catches my eye. I gently pull back, my lips brushing against his before breaking away.

"Wait," I whisper, breathless. "I want to see the house."

Sawyer pauses, a blend of surprise and amusement in his eyes. "The house?"

I nod, sliding out of his grasp but keeping one hand on his arm. We both know the dream he had when he bought this house won't come to pass, but I still want to see it.

He watches me carefully. With a small smile, he takes my hand and leads me through the hallway.

The house is beautiful, but it feels empty. The traces of Uncle Lou and Aunt Marietta are gone, leaving only blank walls and polished floors. It's like a canvas, waiting for something to fill it.

We move through the living room, the furniture sparse and minimal, like placeholders for what could be. I brush my fingers over the smooth surface of a table, feeling the emptiness that hangs in the air. There are no photos, no personal touches—just clean, open spaces that seem to highlight what's missing.

"It's beautiful," I say gently, trying to picture what it could be, what it might have been if things had been different. "But it feels . . . empty."

Sawyer nods, his expression thoughtful. "I know."

The kitchen is next, and it's the same—elegant but bare, with only the essentials in place. The countertops are clear, the open frame cabinets sparsely filled, like the house is waiting for someone to breathe life into it.

Finally, we reach the bedroom, and I pause at the doorway, taking in the sight of the space we're about to share. The bed is neatly made, the sheets crisp and inviting, but the space around it is stark, almost clinical. It's a beautiful room, but it feels more like a stage set, waiting for a story to unfold.

Sawyer steps closer, his hand finding the small of my back, a gentle, grounding touch. "I never brought anyone in here," he says softly, his voice low and thick with meaning.

His arms encircle me, pulling me close, and I let myself sink into him, his warmth wrapping around me like a safety net. Everything we've left unsaid hovers between us—the years, the silence, the ache of what could have been.

"Can I be *anyone*?" I whisper, a fragile echo from a lifetime ago.

His breath brushes against my hair as he presses a gentle kiss to the top of my head. "You're not just anyone, Josie," he murmurs, his voice steady but laced with a bittersweet honesty.

I look up at him, and without another word, he scoops me into his arms, carrying me to the bed. As he lays me down, I feel a tear slip down my cheek, not from sadness, but from the overwhelming emotion of being here with him. Sawyer's fingers brush lightly against my wrists, pausing as he gently removes the bangles I always wear. He turns my hands over, his gaze softening as he traces the faint scars with his fingertips. Without a word, he presses his lips to each mark, lingering there, as if trying to kiss away the pain I once felt, the pain that still lives deep inside.

His touch is delicate, reverent, as though he's afraid I might break under the weight of his love. But there's strength in the way he handles me too, an unspoken assurance that he's here, that he sees me—all of me—and loves me just the same. He runs his fingers gently through my hair, pushing it back from my face, his thumb brushing softly against my cheek as he leans in to kiss me again, slow and gentle, like he's savoring the moment.

His touch trails over the subtle changes time has etched into my body, tracing the curve of my back, the softness that wasn't there before. Fifteen years have changed us both, but from the way his hands move over me, it's clear he loves every change, as if they only deepen his affection. His lips brush the hollow of my throat, unhurried, savoring this rediscovery with a fondness that undoes me.

Every kiss, every touch, feels like a promise—a promise that no matter where life takes us after this, this moment will always be ours. In his arms, I don't just feel loved—I feel whole in a way I haven't in years. He holds me, not just my body, but all the fractured pieces of my heart, and in his embrace, I feel them slowly come together again.

Afterward, we lie tangled in each other's arms, the silence between us filled with the steady rhythm of our breathing. I rest my head on his chest, listening to the sound of his heartbeat, trying to memorize every detail—the warmth of his skin, the way his hand absently strokes my hair. It's peaceful, but the sadness hangs there, creeping in at the edges of this perfect moment.

"I wish . . ." I start, but my voice catches, and I can't bring myself to finish. I wish we had more time. I wish things were different. I wish I didn't have to leave.

Sawyer presses a kiss to my forehead, his grip tightening around me. "I know," he whispers softly, his voice a tender echo in the quiet darkness.

Neither of us says anything more. We both know that words won't change what's coming—that soon, I'll be on a plane back to Ireland, to the life I've built without him. But for now, we have this. We have tonight. And as I close my eyes and let myself fall asleep in his arms, I allow myself to believe, just for a little while, that this is enough.

Chapter 39

The next morning, sunlight filters through the curtains, casting a warm, golden glow across the room. I stretch lazily, savoring the warmth of Sawyer's body next to mine. He's still asleep, his arm draped over me protectively, his breathing soft and steady. I carefully slip out of bed, not wanting to wake him just yet, and pull on one of his T-shirts. It hangs loosely on me, smelling faintly of him, and I find myself smiling as I head to the kitchen to start the coffee.

As the rich aroma of brewing coffee fills the air, I hear the soft rustle of sheets from the bedroom. A moment later, Sawyer appears in the doorway, his auburn hair tousled, a sleepy smile on his face.

"Morning," he murmurs, his voice still husky from sleep. For a moment, I'm struck by how beautiful he looks in that unguarded state, the morning light catching the warmth in his eyes.

"Morning," I reply, handing him a mug with a playful wink. "Sleep well?"

"Best sleep I've had in ages," he says, wrapping an arm around my waist and pulling me close. "I could get used to this."

I laugh, but there's a pang in my heart, knowing this isn't a scene we can get used to.

"Are you hungry? I think I can manage some breakfast." I open the fridge and rummage around. "How about scrambled eggs and toast?"

"Sounds perfect," he says, kissing the top of my head. "But only if you let me help."

We move around the kitchen in a comfortable rhythm, bumping into each other playfully as we cook. Sawyer sneaks up behind me, pressing a kiss to my shoulder as I plate the eggs, and I can't help but smile at how natural this feels—like slipping into a life we never got to have. His words from yesterday echo in my mind:

I don't see why that so-called simple life couldn't have been an adventure for both of us.

I find some paper place mats tucked away in a drawer and set one on the small table by the window. The smell of coffee and breakfast fills the air, rich and comforting. We sit down at the table, our knees brushing under the wood. The kitchen feels different today. Warmer. Like the sunlight streaming through the window has found a way to soften all the edges that seemed so sharp yesterday.

As we sip our coffee, I notice how the moisture from our mugs leaves faint rings on the paper, overlapping and intertwining. It's a simple detail, but it feels like a mark of something shared, something more.

There's a cruel twist of fate in this, I think, *letting me live this dream, only to have to walk away from it.* We eat in a comfortable silence, the quiet of the morning making everything feel serene, but we playfully smirk at each other as we chew our food.

After breakfast, we carry our mugs out to the small porch and sit side by side, gazing out at the lake. The air is crisp and a sense of peace settles over me, as if, for this moment, everything is perfectly aligned. We talk a little about our lives, giving quick overviews, trying to condense fifteen years into a few moments. Sawyer tells me about coaching and how his love for the game has evolved. He loves finding raw talent, refining a player's skills, and building their confidence. I tell him about my job and some of my solo trips around Europe. I even mention my newfound love for soccer—now "football"—and he laughs in disbelief. We share long glances, and I can't help but wish this could last forever.

Sawyer leans back in his chair, his baseball cap now on his head with auburn tendrils peeking out, his coffee mug cradled in his hands as he looks out at the water.

"I could get used to this," he says again, softly, almost to himself.

"Yeah, me too," I reply, my voice just as quiet. I glance at him, our earlier conversation lingering between us. "Simple."

He grins, but there's sadness in his eyes. "So simple, and yet . . ."

I take a mental snapshot, storing it away, wanting to hold on to this moment forever, even as I fear the pain of carrying it with me. We sit like that for a while, sipping our coffee, both pretending this is the beginning of something and not the end.

"What do you say we stretch our legs? Go for a walk?" Sawyer asks, his voice light but his eyes holding something deeper. And I nod, grateful for the chance to steal a little more time with him, these moments precious and slipping away.

After I get dressed, we step into the crisp morning air. The smell of pine and lake water fills my lungs, grounding me as Sawyer grabs my hand without hesitation. We walk along the edge of the water, our steps naturally falling into rhythm. He tells me about his brother's kids, about how his nephew hit his first home run last month. I laugh when he describes his disastrous attempt at assembling a dollhouse for his niece last Christmas, and he grins like he's just happy to hear me laugh.

But even as I smile, the pain is there, deeper than I thought it could be. I picture the kind of dad Sawyer would be—patient, kind, loving—and it feels like the ache in my chest has no bottom. Like there's no limit to how much I can hurt.

I launch into a story about Dermott's relentless schemes to drag me into Dublin's nightlife, complete with exaggerated impressions of his "brilliant" plans and my disastrous attempts to keep up. "Let's just say the city was not ready for our impromptu Riverdance moves after a night of drinking," I add with a grin, watching as Sawyer's laugh comes easily, his eyes crinkling at the corners.

Then I shift to my short-lived farming phase, sharing how I offered to "help" Uncle Sean and ended up face-first in a muddy field within an hour. I can't stop myself from laughing as I describe my horrified reaction to witnessing the birth of a baby calf. "Movies lie, by the way. That was *not* a magical, Hallmark moment," I say, scrunching my nose for effect. "But I named her Daisy, and she forgave me for screaming when she arrived."

Sawyer's expression shifts with every word—amusement lighting up his face, curiosity sparking in his eyes, pride softening his features.

"Dermott's schemes, calves named Daisy, impromptu River-dance—sounds like you've been busy," he says, his voice warm with affection.

I shrug, biting back a smile. "At least I'm entertaining."

"More than that," he murmurs.

We pause by a cluster of rocks near the shore, and I hop onto one, wobbling as I try to keep my balance. The wind picks up, whipping my hair into my face, and I burst into laughter, unsteady but free. When I turn to Sawyer, he's watching me with a look that steals the air from my lungs. It's as if he's seeing sunlight for the first time, like he's trying to memorize me in this exact moment.

The time passes in fragments—Sawyer tossing a rock across the water, me leaning against his shoulder as we watch the ripples spread. Fingers entwining. Stolen kisses. It feels like we're racing the clock, trying to fit a lifetime into fleeting moments. At one point, I catch myself tracing the calluses on his palm, marveling at how something so rough can feel so achingly gentle.

But reality doesn't stay away forever. Eventually, Sawyer's phone starts buzzing, and the spell breaks. The day, the moments, begin to slip through my fingers. I know it's time to go. Time to leave this place, this fragile bubble of peace we've created for ourselves.

As we head back into the house, something catches my eye—the paper place mat still sitting on the kitchen table, the overlapping coffee rings faint but visible. The sight tugs at something deep inside me, a bittersweet reminder of how fleeting these moments are. But I push the feeling aside, focusing instead on what little time we have left.

The drive back to Miner's is quiet, the sound of the tires on the road the only thing breaking it. Both of us are lost in our thoughts, the reality of our impending separation hanging between us like a dark cloud. Each glance we exchange is laden with memories, and a deep sadness that words can't fully capture.

When we pull into the inn's driveway, Sawyer parks the car but doesn't move. His hand lingers on the steering wheel, knuckles white, but his eyes search mine, full of questions and longing.

"I don't want to leave you for a second," he murmurs.

"I know," I whisper, my chest aching. The thought of parting again, after everything, feels unbearable. There's a current in the air, like we're standing at the edge of something too big to navigate.

For a long moment, we sit in silence, the engine ticking softly in the background as the world outside continues on, indifferent to the storm inside the car. Finally, Sawyer's voice breaks through.

"I wish things were different, Josie." His words are simple but loaded with a kind of desperation. He reaches for my hand, and when his fingers entwine with mine, a shiver runs through me, like my body is trying to hold on to the feeling of him. "Is there a way? Any way at all?"

I drop my head. I want to answer him, to tell him yes, that there's always a way, but we both know that's not true. I close my eyes, exhaling a breath that feels heavier than it should.

"I wish we could go back," I whisper. "To the night we met. To that moment before everything got so complicated. I'd go through it all again—every heartbreak, every mistake—if it meant we could somehow come out of it together."

But we both know that going back in time is as impossible as finding a future together. There's no time machine that can rewrite the years, erase the scars. We never worried about paths forward when we were young. We believed in love conquering everything, thought we could live on air and dreams. But now, reality is far less forgiving. The weight of responsibility, of careers, of futures that don't align, presses down on us like a tidal wave. We can't survive on love alone, no matter how badly we want to.

I look into his eyes, and I see the same realization staring back at me. Beyond the practical pieces—work, geography, and money—there's the ghost of Maplewood. This town, as stitched into my heart as it is, feels like a graveyard for all the things I've lost. I don't say it out loud, but he reads it on my face. He knows how much this place haunts me, how fragile it made me. I've worked so hard on my anxiety, tackling it in small doses, surviving in the moment, but the truth is that I'm always just one step away from falling apart again. And I'm terrified that if I stay here, if I let myself breathe in this air for too long, the past will shatter me beyond repair.

"I'd follow you if I could," Sawyer says softly, his thumb brushing the back of my hand. "I hope you know that."

I believe him. His sincerity is clear, etched in the sadness in his eyes. But I also know he can't just abandon his life here—his house, his career, the roots he's planted. It's not that simple. We're at an impossible impasse, both of us standing on opposite shores, and there's no bridge long enough to close the distance between us. And we both know it.

I force a smile, blinking back the tears that burn at the corners of my eyes. "I know," I whisper, my voice trembling. "And that's what makes this so much harder."

I take a deep breath, willing the ache in my chest to quiet, if only for a moment. "I need to shower and pack so I can spend the rest of my time here with you, Beatrice, and Jason."

"Mostly me, though," he says, attempting a joke, but his voice is thin, and the sadness in his eyes gives him away.

"Mostly you," I say softly, the words carrying more weight than I intended. I lean in, flipping his baseball cap back so I can press my lips to his. The kiss is tender and bittersweet, a silent confession of all the things we can't bring ourselves to say.

It lingers, both of us holding on as if the kiss could freeze time, could keep us here, together, a little longer. But reality creeps in, and reluctantly, we pull apart.

His forehead rests against mine, his breath warm against my skin. "It's never going to be enough," he murmurs, and I can feel his heart breaking right alongside mine.

"I know," I whisper again, my voice barely audible. And in this moment, knowing is the hardest part.

"Okay, Josie, I'll be back later," he says softly, pushing a strand of hair behind my ear before kissing the tip of my nose. "I'll walk you to your room."

"Don't you dare!" I pull back, a small smile playing on my lips. "I'll drag you in like prey and never let you go."

We laugh, and Sawyer makes a show of trying to quickly unbuckle his seatbelt, but I step out of the car and close the door behind me. I blow him a kiss and then turn, jogging into Miner's, leaving another piece of me behind.

***

I step into the shower, hoping the water will wash away the whirlwind of thoughts spinning in my head. But even after I'm done, my mind won't quiet, and I find myself aimlessly shoving clothes into my suitcase. It's only when I come across the stack of letters from Sarge that I pause. I've held on to them since Sawyer and I read them, but I never had time to reflect on them until now.

Sitting on the edge of the bed, I inhale the faint scent of Lucky Strikes that clings to the paper. I unfold the first letter—the one addressed only to me. As I read, I can almost hear Sarge's voice, raspy yet tender, as his words leap from the page:

You were forged in flames.

A small smile tugs at my lips. Sarge always thought so highly of me. I knew I was lucky to have his admiration, but I don't think I ever realized just how much of a gift it truly was.

I run my fingers along the edges of the letter, feeling the coarse paper beneath my fingertips. He understood that more than just my parents were consumed by that fire. But he never saw me as broken or scarred. To him, I was a survivor, shaped by the heat, resilient against the odds. If Sarge were alive, he would remind me that I'll survive this too. Maybe it's time I start believing that myself.

There's a throbbing in my chest as I start to get ready for the evening, a quiet pull that I can't shake. I know what this night means. I know what it means to leave Sawyer behind, leave this version of my life behind. I've made a habit of leaving. But this . . . this feels different. Last time, I ran. This time, it feels like I'm being dragged away, piece by piece, leaving fragments of myself behind.

Later that evening, Dermott and I head to the back patio of Miner's, expecting Beatrice, Jason, and Sawyer to join us soon. But as we walk through the doors, I gasp at the sight before me. The space is transformed—strings of fairy lights and colorful lanterns cast a warm, inviting glow against the cool autumn evening. The crisp scent of fallen leaves mingles with the aroma of freshly grilled food. Beatrice has gone all out, setting a long table covered with a cozy plaid tablecloth, adorned with pumpkins, gourds, and vibrant fall flowers.

Dermott's eyes widen in surprise. "Well, Jesus! This is quite the send-off."

I meet Beatrice's gaze, and tears glisten in her eyes. "Bea, I don't deserve this. After everything I've put you through."

She waves me off, walking straight to me and grabbing my hands. "Stop it. No one deserves this more than you. You deserve so much more." Jason stands behind her, and my eyes automatically search for Sawyer, like no time has passed at all. He stands off to the side, a gentle smile on his lips, but there's a clear sadness in his eyes, and it takes every ounce of self-control not to launch myself into his arms.

I turn back to Beatrice, shaking my head. "You shouldn't be wasting all this on me."

Dermott wraps an arm around my shoulders. "How do you know this isn't for me? And we all know in that case it wouldn't be a waste at all!"

"Yes, Dermott. That has to be it," I say with a wry smile before turning my attention back to Beatrice, who seems to glow against the fairy lights. "You have a gift, my friend. Thank you for sharing it with me."

Beatrice pulls me into a tight hug, gently nudging Dermott aside. "You are still and will always be my best friend, Josie. No matter how far apart we are. This doesn't end here."

Dermott, never one to miss a moment, finds a way back into the conversation. "Listen, pet, we never got over the eighties in Ireland—thank God. So if you and Jason want to pop over, I know there's a good eighties night in the city."

Jason laughs, launching into a dramatic retelling of their escapades seeing Black Viper Fang the night before. "I figured Dermott's accent would attract the ladies, and I could ride the wave of his charm," Jason begins.

Dermott laughs. "I'll have you know my charm worked wonders. You could've ridden that wave all the way back to Maplewood."

"Dermott!" I exclaim, half laughing.

Jason scoffs. "Yes—if your type is a more mature woman smoking menthols in a dangerously stiff hairstyle that was clearly teased into a rat's nest of—of—of friggin' Aqua Net."

"Listen, mate, those ladies had stories of some epic nights with Black Viper Fang backstage."

"Yes—forty years ago. I was being polite and chatting with—" Jason pauses, trying to recall the name. "Renee?"

"Roxanne," Dermott corrects.

"Roxanne—yes—and she had to excuse herself to take her diabetes medication."

"Sure, anyone could have diabetes."

"Well, Roxanne *looked* like she had diabetes."

"Oh my God." Beatrice rolls her eyes dramatically. "Can we please eat before I lose my appetite?"

"You'd lose your appetite if you saw the lips tattooed on Renee's breast," Jason says.

"Roxanne's breast," Dermott corrects.

"I mean Roxanne's breast."

"Oh my God, Jason! Stop!" Beatrice gags.

I'm still laughing by the time we reach the table. But as I scan the scene, my smile fades slightly when I spot Sawyer lingering at the edge, like he's unsure of where to fit in. Beatrice, Jason, and Dermott are already deep into their usual banter, but Sawyer stands apart, watching, waiting.

It's strange how someone can feel so close and so far away at the same time. I've been keeping this distance between us for so long—afraid that if I let it collapse, everything I've buried would come rushing to the surface. There were so many moments we let slip by. So many things I should've said to him over the course of our scavenger hunt. Instead, I left. I argued. I ran, because it was easier than admitting I didn't know how to stay.

I've been clinging to what we once had, but maybe it's time to face the truth: we don't exist in that past anymore. I don't know how to stop loving him, though. And maybe that's why leaving him again feels like I'm ripping apart something that's already broken.

"Hey," I say, approaching him quietly.

"Hey, Josie O," he replies, his eyes soft and crinkling with tenderness.

"You're quiet tonight."

His shoulders are tense, his smile a little too soft, like it's trying to hold something back. When he finally speaks, his voice is low, almost cautious. "I don't know how to act," he admits, his brow furrowed as his eyes bore into mine.

I search his face, wanting to understand what's going on behind those tired eyes. "What do you mean?"

Sawyer lets out a small sigh, looking away for a moment before his gaze locks back on mine. "I don't know how to act like I'm okay with this—letting you go again." His voice cracks slightly, and I can see the vulnerability in his expression. "I thought . . . maybe I'd be ready, but I'm not. Not at all. Never will be."

He looks like he's standing on the edge of something he can't control, and I realize I'm the one pulling him back over that line. But I don't know how to stop. How do you let someone go when you're not even sure you should?

His voice lowers, his soul laid bare in a way that breaks my heart. "I want to sit next to you. I want to put my arm around you, be close to you . . . as close as I can, while I still have the chance."

For a moment, I can't find words. There's a longing in his voice that tugs at something deep inside me. I swallow past the lump in my throat and give him a small smile. "Then I guess you better hurry up and grab the seat next to me."

I reach for his hand, holding on tight as we walk back to the table together.

The humor and lightheartedness carry us through the night, helping to keep the looming sadness at arm's length. We eat, drink, and laugh, reminiscing about the past and filling each other in on the present. But there's palpable tension in the air, a silent agreement not to touch the subject of the future. I know deep down I can't pretend this is the beginning of many trips back to Maplewood. There are too many ghosts here, too much pain buried beneath the surface. I've become skilled at dodging the things that haunt me—or at least, I thought I had.

Even as the evening winds down, I catch myself smiling as I watch Sawyer and Dermott deep in conversation, their laughter mixing with the soft murmur of the night. It brings me a strange sense of peace, knowing that the loose ends of my own life—the ones I've left dangling for so long—are finally being tied up.

As the conversation shifts to more serious topics—Sarge, Rupert, and all they endured together—Sawyer edges closer, his arm draping over my shoulder with quiet assurance. His presence anchors me as we share our reflections on the scavenger hunt Sarge orchestrated. The warmth of his arm feels so natural, I can't help but wonder how I'll manage without him.

I notice the glances exchanged between Beatrice, Jason, and Dermott—the silent questions in their eyes as they try to piece together what happens next for us. They've seen how broken we've been without each other, and now, here we are, on the verge of parting again. I find myself worrying more about Sawyer than I do about myself.

When no one is looking, Beatrice catches my eye and mouths, *Put a pin in that*. I roll my eyes and smile, the familiar gesture lifting some of the tension.

My thoughts are interrupted by the sharp click of heels on the patio. I turn to see Mrs. Miner approaching.

"I'm sorry, Mrs. Miner. Are we being too loud?"

"No, no," she assures, waving off my concern. "I just wanted to stop by and say goodbye."

I stand to greet her, smiling, but she bypasses me and heads straight for Dermott. I catch Beatrice trying to hide her amusement. "Ah, Roberta!" Dermott exclaims, clasping her hands. "Thank you for everything."

"Oh, Dermott! I'm delighted to have met you. I'll be researching some tours for this upcoming summer and will be sure to connect with you before we arrive. I plan on bringing some extended family."

"That's lovely! We'd be delighted to have you!" Dermott beams, though I know my cousin well enough to sense his realization that maybe he shouldn't have tried so hard to secure his own room.

Mrs. Miner turns to me, her smile warm. "And, Josie, thank you."

She takes my hands in hers, her grip warm but trembling slightly, her gaze flicking briefly to Sawyer before settling on me. Her eyes are filled with something I can't quite place—gratitude, maybe, or even pity.

"If it weren't for you," she begins softly, her voice thick with emotion, "I don't know if William would have ever felt compelled to write to Rupert. He believed he was doing some kind of justice, punishing himself for their past. He thought that all those years apart dulled the longing in my poor brother's heart." She pauses, her expression twisting with something that feels like both sadness and relief. "But the truth is, William's self-inflicted wounds only deepened Rupert's pain."

Her hands squeeze mine, grounding me in the weight of her words. "Your presence, your journey... it gave him the courage to reach out. There's a lightness in Rupert now that wasn't there before. He's still a broken man and always will be, in this life," she adds, her voice catching, "but you and Sawyer have given him hope for the next one. For that, I'll never be able to thank you enough."

She leans in, wrapping me in a gentle hug that's as comforting as it is unexpected. When she pulls away, she turns to Sawyer and does the same, her hands lingering on his shoulders as she whispers something I can't hear.

And then she's gone, walking away with quiet purpose, leaving us both standing there, speechless. The truth of her words hangs in the air between us, impossible to ignore. I glance at Sawyer, but he's already looking at me, and in his eyes, I see the same overwhelming mix of emotions swirling inside me.

As the night winds down, each passing moment causes another crack in my heart to form. When Beatrice and Jason stand to leave, I can't hold back the tears. They flank me, wrapping their arms around me and promising this isn't goodbye. Jason is the first to walk away, his head bowed. Beatrice and I cling to each other, our grip so tight that nothing could pull us apart. But eventually, she breaks away, as if tearing off a Band-Aid, and rushes out as quickly as she can. Dermott shakes Sawyer's hand before telling me he'll see Beatrice and Jason out, leaving Sawyer and me alone.

Sawyer pulls me into his arms, wrapping me in a warmth that feels both familiar and heartbreaking. "My Josie O," he whispers into my ear, his breath tickling the side of my neck. "What am I supposed to do without you now?"

I cling to him tightly, his words sinking into my chest. I press my face against him, breathing him in like I'm trying to memorize every part of him—the scent of him, the feel of his arms around me—knowing that soon, it will be a memory I'll have to carry.

"I could kill Sarge for this!" I manage a laugh through my tears, pulling back just enough to look into his eyes, searching for the comfort I know I'll miss. That smile—the one that weakened my knees as a teenager and still does—spreads across his face, and I can't help but smile back, even through the anguish in my heart.

"Seeing you, Josie," he says softly, brushing a strand of hair away from my face, "being with you like this—it makes all the pain worth it." His voice cracks just a little, betraying the emotion he's holding back. "Are you sure I can't drive you to the airport?"

"No." I shake my head, knowing that watching him drive away from me at the airport would only make the goodbye harder. "That would just hurt more."

He sighs. "What time is your Uber?"

"Six a.m.," I whisper, my voice barely holding steady.

Sawyer leans in, his lips meeting mine in a soft, lingering kiss, as if he's trying to savor every second of it. He hovers there for a moment, his breath warm against my lips. "Josie O'Driscoll, if you think I'm not sleeping next to you tonight, then you've lost your marbles."

A soft laugh escapes me, though a dull pain settles deep inside me at the thought of how little time we have left. Without a word, I wrap my arms around him and guide him toward my room, holding on to the fleeting moment, unwilling to let go—not yet. Not tonight.

***

The sky is still dark when the alarm goes off, a sharp, unwelcome sound slicing through the quiet. I groan softly, feeling the weight of the morning settle in before I even open my eyes. My hand fumbles to silence the alarm, and for a brief second, I consider just staying here, cocooned in warmth with Sawyer, pretending the world outside doesn't exist.

But reality tugs at me. The Uber will be here soon, and leaving feels like an anchor pulling me under.

Next to me, Sawyer stirs, his arm still draped around my waist from the night before. His hold tightens slightly, as if, even in sleep, he knows what's coming and wants to keep me close for just a little longer. I turn to look at him. His eyes are closed, his face peaceful. For a moment, I let myself pretend we don't have to say goodbye—that this isn't the end.

Carefully, I slip out from under his arm, trying not to wake him just yet. I pull on the clothes I set aside last night and quietly make my way to the bathroom. My reflection in the mirror looks as exhausted as I feel. I splash cold water on my face, hoping it'll dislodge the pain from my chest, but it doesn't.

When I step back into the room, Sawyer is awake, sitting up in bed, his hair tousled, the sheet draped lazily across his lap. He watches me, his eyes soft but heavy with the same sadness I feel.

"I thought I could sneak out without waking you," I say with a weak smile.

"You're terrible at sneaking," he replies, his voice thick with sleep, but there's warmth there too, like he's trying to hold on to this moment for as long as he can. "And I know you'd never sneak away from me now."

I glance at the clock. My Uber will be here soon. I don't have much time. If I don't do this now, I never will.

"Sawyer, I need you to know something," I say, my voice trembling. The knot in my throat feels impossible to push past, but I have to try. "All the sadness I've had in life—it hit me out of nowhere. Like a freight train or a bomb. I never saw it coming, so I couldn't plan for it. I just... I just kept my eyes closed and crawled forward."

His brow furrows as he shifts closer, pulling me into his arms like he can protect me from my own memories. I let him. Just for a second. Just until I find the courage to keep going.

"My parents didn't survive the fire, Sawyer." My voice breaks, and I feel his arms tighten around me. "And neither did I."

His whole body stills. I feel his breath hitch against my hair, and I close my eyes, trying to find the strength to keep talking. "I've spent my whole life crawling. Inch by inch, like I was covered by a blanket of smoke, never knowing where I was headed. I kept my eyes closed, just hoping I'd find a door but never really believing I would."

"Josie," he whispers.

I pull back just enough to look at him. His eyes are glassy, his pain mirroring my own, but I need him to hear this. "You helped me find the door," I say, my voice cracking. "You helped me breathe again."

He takes a shuddering breath, his forehead dropping to mine as he holds me like he's afraid I'll disappear.

"I can see the future now, and without you, it's empty. It's going to hurt like hell, Sawyer, but at least I'm not crawling in the dark anymore. At least I'm not suffocating."

Tears spill from his eyes as he pulls me closer, his grip almost desperate. "This hurts like hell," I continue, my own tears falling freely now, "but I'm glad I came back. Because nothing was worse than thinking you chose her over me."

"Never," he chokes out, shaking his head vehemently. "Never, Josie. Not for one second."

"Please forgive me for ever thinking that," I whisper, my voice breaking.

"There is nothing to forgive," he says, his voice barely audible. "I swear to God, Josie, there is nothing to forgive."

I take a shaky breath, wiping at my tears, but they just keep coming. "And no matter where we are, no matter how old we get—even if it's a thousand years from now—I will always love you."

He exhales sharply, like my words are cutting him in half. But I have to say this. I have to.

"But..." My voice cracks. "And this is a big but."

"No." He shakes his head, his voice strained. "Don't do this."

"You have to listen," I say, trying to steady my breathing. "If you get a chance at happiness, take it. Don't live a lonely life because we didn't get our shot. Think of Sarge, Sawyer. Don't punish yourself the way he did."

Sawyer's face crumples as he shakes his head, his hands gripping mine like he's holding on to the last piece of us. "I can't promise that, Josie," he says, his voice breaking. "I don't want anyone else. It's always been you. Sarge wanted us to have our shot. Don't you get that?"

His words pierce me, filling the empty spaces I didn't even realize I had. But as much as I want to believe him, I know the truth. Love isn't always enough.

And as much as it hurts, I have to let him go.

"I know what Sarge wanted, but sometimes life doesn't work out the way people hope it will. And that's not anyone's fault. It's just . . . life."

He shakes his head, his eyes swimming with tears. "That's bullshit, Josie. Life doesn't just happen to us. We make choices. And I choose you."

Tears spill down my cheeks, and I pull my hand away from his, needing the space to breathe through the desperation building inside me. "Sawyer, what happens when this moment ends? What happens when I get on that plane and go back to a life we can't share?"

"I don't care about that," he says fiercely. "We'll figure it out. I'll come to you. I'll follow you anywhere, Josie. Just tell me what you want."

I close my eyes, the weight of his words pressing down on me. "What I want doesn't matter. We're not those kids anymore, dreaming about the future on a dock. I don't want to hold you back from the life you've built, the life you deserve. And I can't ask you to give up everything for me."

"You're not asking. I'm offering." His voice is low, desperate. "You think I care about anything more than you? Josie, my life doesn't mean anything if you're not in it."

The room feels too small, too charged, and I struggle to hold it together. "You say that now, but what about in a year? Or five? What if you wake up and realize you made a mistake? What if you regret me?"

"Never," he says, his voice breaking. "Never in a million years."

My heart aches at the conviction in his voice, but I know better. I know how life can twist and break promises, no matter how deeply they're felt. "Sawyer, you have to let me go. Please."

He stands abruptly, pacing the room like he can't bear to be still. "I can't do this, Josie. I can't pretend I'm okay with losing you again."

"You're not losing me," I say, my voice thick with emotion. "You never lost me, Sawyer. You're a part of me. You always will be. But we have to let this go before it destroys us."

He stops, turning to face me, and the devastation in his eyes almost undoes me. "I don't know how to do that," he whispers.

"Sawyer," I whisper, my voice cracking. "Please, just listen."

I pause, dragging air into my lungs like it might be the last breath I ever take. And maybe it is—because the words I'm about to say feel like they'll kill me. "This... all of this. It's a graveyard to me."

His chest rises and falls in uneven, jagged waves, and then he says it. The question I was hoping he wouldn't.

"Me too?"

His words drop into the pit of my stomach like a stone. I should say yes. I should tell him that he's a graveyard too. That he's a memory I need to bury, a ghost I need to let go of, even if it's the furthest thing from the truth. Because if that's what it takes to set him free—to give him the happiness he deserves, the kind of life where he builds a dollhouse for a little girl who calls him Daddy—then I'd do it. I'd break myself apart for him.

But the lie lodges in my throat.

I open my mouth. Close it again. Open it. I'm a broken record. A malfunctioning machine. But I don't have to say it.

Sawyer swallows, his Adam's apple bobbing. "Josie," he says, his voice so soft, so final, I know it's the end before he even finishes. "No one deserves happiness more than you. And if the only way you can find that is by leaving here and never looking back, then I won't stop you. I love you too much to stand in your way."

And even though he's giving me exactly what I asked for, exactly what I thought I needed, it feels like I've lost. I wanted him to let me go. I wanted this freedom. But now that it's here, I'm not sure what to do with it, because freedom without him feels a lot like a cage.

***

By the time we make our way to the lobby, Dermott is already there, his suitcase by the door. His usual energy is subdued.

"Ready for the final stretch?" Dermott asks, trying to lighten the mood. But his eyes give him away—this place has left its mark on him too.

I can't respond. I just stare at the ground, feeling the agony of leaving everything behind.

The Uber is idling as the first light of dawn creeps over the horizon, casting a soft glow over the inn. The driver gets out and begins loading our bags. Dermott shakes Sawyer's hand, clapping him on the back before sliding into the car, leaving Sawyer and me standing by the entrance.

For a few precious moments, we just look at each other, neither of us able to speak. I lock my gaze on his hazel eyes, trying to memorize every detail—the way they soften, the way they hold me like I'm the only thing that matters. I'll need that image to carry with me long after this moment.

Sawyer reaches up, brushing a tear from my cheek. His eyes are filled with love and resignation. "You do what you need to do," he whispers. "Live the life you deserve. And know that I'll always love you."

"I promise," I whisper, leaning in for one last, lingering kiss.

I step into the Uber, my heart shattering as the door closes behind me. I press my hand to the window, trying to hold on to him for just a moment longer. "I love you too," I whisper, hoping he can feel it, even if he can't hear me.

As the car pulls away, I keep my eyes on him, standing there on the steps of the inn, hands shoved deep in his pockets like they're the only thing holding him together. He grows smaller and smaller with each passing second, but the weight in my chest only gets heavier, like the distance between us is stretching a thread so taut it's bound to snap.

I tell myself to turn away, to stop looking, but I can't. I force my eyes to stay on him, even when he's just a blur, even when I can barely make out the shape of him against the gray of the morning sky.

Just as we round the corner, I glance up at the inn and see Rupert standing at the window. He places his hand on the glass, nodding at me with a knowing look. There's no smile, just a quiet understanding, a reflection of the pain of living with choices you can't undo—a reminder of the cost of silence, of what happens when love is denied, when two people who belong together let fear and time tear them apart. It's a warning, not a comfort. I am struck by the cruel realization that even knowing this truth doesn't mean I can rewrite the story, and I feel the agony of that cripple my spirit as we drive away.

Chapter 40

Every inch of the ocean as I fly back to Ireland feels like another needle piercing my heart. I thought I was dead before. I thought the grief had killed me, but there's no way a person could feel this sort of pain unless there's some life left in them. And this is a new kind of hell—one I haven't experienced before.

We land in Dublin, where rain lashes against my sorrow-soaked soul. I feel Dermott's eyes on me, but my voice is buried beneath the cinder block lodged in my chest. He doesn't get much conversation from me, but he seems to understand enough to let me be. The gray sky mirrors my mood, and I keep telling myself this is my only option, that I need to accept it and move on.

The weeks that follow are nothing short of torture. My heart aches with longing, but I tell myself to be practical. Beatrice and I exchange emails, but just as I did with Sarge, I avoid any conversation that involves Sawyer. I slip back into playing it safe, rearranging the bricks I've built around my heart. *This is good. This is safe.* Or so I tell myself.

I sit at my tiny kitchen table, sipping tea, staring out the rain-splattered window of my small flat in Dublin. It's nearly Thanksgiving in Maplewood. I imagine Mrs. Larson setting up the bakery for the Turkey Trot and Beatrice readying her flower shop for the Christmas season. Maplewood is approaching a season of togetherness, but here I am, alone, putting on my brave face.

Outside, the narrow streets of Stoneybatter glisten under the soft glow of streetlamps, the cobblestones slick with rain. Rows of colorful houses line the street, but their charm feels muted under the gray sky. A couple hurries by under a shared umbrella, their laughter barely audible through the glass. I wonder what their story is, what makes them laugh in the rain.

An image of Sawyer flits across my mind—us at Maple's Ice Cream Shoppe, him asking if I was happy, and me answering, "I'm not unhappy." But this—this feels like the true definition of unhappy. It feels unbearable. The couple under the umbrella seems happy, living their life, while I feel like an observer, not really a part of this world. I still haven't found home. Maybe I never will.

I rise from the table and walk over to my small bookshelf, where I've stored Sarge's letters in a little box. Carrying it back to the table, I sit and sip my tea, the rain still falling outside. I glance out the window again and notice a little girl walking hand in hand with her mother, her bright-yellow raincoat standing out against the dreary surroundings. They stop for a moment, the mother bending down to adjust the girl's hood, her face filled with tender affection. It reminds me of my own mother, of better days when she looked at me with that same love.

I wasn't much older than that little girl when I asked my dad what had gone wrong with my mother.

"Loneliness," he said.

"If she's so lonely, why don't we live in Ireland?" I asked, thinking it a simple solution. My dad gave me a look that suggested I was naïve. "She wouldn't give the neighbors back home the satisfaction," he said.

I didn't understand then, but now it makes sense. My mother had left Ireland with big dreams, and going back would have felt like admitting defeat. She chose to suffer, and somehow, I was bred to do the same.

Still looking out the window, I watch as a man joins the mother and daughter, holding a large umbrella. The little girl's face lights up, and she runs to him—her father—and he scoops her up into a joyful hug. My parents could have had that. I could have had that.

I open the box of letters, a little voice inside me whispering, *You could still have that.* My heart turns over like an engine coming to life, my body reacting to something my mind refuses to acknowledge.

I open Sarge's first letter, addressed only to me, and sip my tea again, glancing outside. The little family has gone, but across the street, an older man stumbles out of a pub. He lights a cigarette, and before the discomfort can rise in me—before the sight of the flame sets off any panic—the man exhales, and despite being two floors up and nowhere near his natural sightline, he looks straight into my window, straight into my eyes, straight into my soul.

There's a coldness that grips my heart. His eyes are haunted. I wonder what has happened to make them that way. Shivering, I look down, unseeing, at Sarge's letter, my hands trembling.

I built this life—every inch of it—from the ground up after I shattered into pieces. My apartment, my job, this city . . . it's the life I rebuilt. I clawed my way out of a breakdown, and I've invested everything I had left into becoming this version of myself. I can't just walk away from it. *Can I?*

Going back to Maplewood feels like stepping backward, like tearing down all the walls I've built around the person I used to be. And I can't show up there with nothing—no job, no place to live, my hands hanging empty. But it's more than that.

The pain Maplewood holds—it's suffocating. The memories of my parents, the fire, the empty space where Sarge should be but never will be again. How do I go back and face that? How do I walk through those streets, knowing every corner holds a piece of who I used to be before I fell apart?

But maybe that's not the whole story.

I've always told myself that Maplewood is sadness, that it's nothing but grief and loss. But if I'm honest, that's not all I see when I think of it. I see happiness too. I picture Larson's Bakery, the warm, comforting scent of cinnamon rolls wafting through the air and filling the street during the Turkey Trot. I see the diner, the football field on Friday nights, the baseball stand where kids line up for popcorn and slushies. I see Beatrice and Jason, and now Blossom & Briar. I see Maple Lake, the way the water glistens in the early-morning light when we used to go fishing. I see the raccoons rummaging through discarded desserts and the laughter that followed. And then I'm back again at Maple's Ice Cream Shoppe, where I answered Sawyer's question with a half-truth: "I'm not unhappy."

Maybe I was lying to myself. Because even now, part of me smiles when I think of those things. Even with all the hurt that's tangled up with Maplewood, it's not just a place of sadness. It never was. But I've let it become that because it was easier to shut it out—to close the door on all of it, the good and the bad.

I realize then, as I stare out at the rain-soaked streets of Dublin, that I've been doing what my mother did. Choosing to suffer. I built this life here, but it's a life of survival, not living. My mother stayed in Maplewood because she didn't want to face the defeat of returning to Ireland. I've been doing the same—pretending I'm better off far away, that going back would mean I've failed. But maybe staying here, alone, in a life I don't truly want, is the real failure.

The memories of Maplewood aren't just ghosts—they're roots. I squeeze my eyes shut and I see our bench under the giant maple tree. I see Sawyer.

Shivering, I open my eyes and look down at Sarge's letter, my hands trembling. My eyes fall on the final sentence, and the words hit me with the force of a truth I've been avoiding for too long.

Remember this, Josie girl—sometimes we put down our own roots. The choice is ours.

And then an image of Sawyer flits across my mind. *Life doesn't just happen to us. We make choices. And I choose you.*

The choice. The choice is ours. *The choice is mine.*

I push back from the table, my chair clattering to the floor behind me. I don't bother picking it up. I make my way to the bed, pulling out the suitcase I stored under it.

I need to go home.

Chapter 41

Snow falls softly as my plane lands in Philadelphia, dusting the city in a pristine white blanket. The cold air nips at my cheeks as I step outside, pulling my coat tighter. My heart aches to see Sawyer, but I know I can't make the same mistake as before. I need to face the mountains in my life alone—without Sawyer, Dermott, or even the memory of Sarge to lean on. If I want a future with him, I need to find my own strength first.

In the quiet of my hotel room, I resist the urge to call him. The snow outside feels like a clean slate, a moment of stillness before the journey ahead. Eventually, sleep finds me, a brief reprieve from the whirlwind inside.

The next morning, snow still falls as I pull my coat tighter around me and step into a diner in Harrington, desperate for coffee and closure. The place bustles with the morning rush. I take a deep breath, steadying myself, and scan the room.

My heart pounds as I approach the counter, the weight of what I'm about to do settling heavily on my shoulders. I glance around at the worn booths and absorb the hum of conversation. My eyes land on a figure behind the counter, her back turned as she fills a coffeepot. Sliding onto a stool, I wait.

The woman turns around, fills a cup of coffee, and slides it my way without a glance. "You ready to order?"

Val looks older, worn down by time and whatever demons she's been wrestling with. She looks up, clearly irritated by my silence—until recognition dawns. Her eyes widen, the color draining from her face.

"I'll just stick with coffee for now."

Her hands shake as she sets down the pot. "What are you doing here?" she whispers.

I shrug, arching an eyebrow. "Can't a girl order a coffee?" I stir in some creamer, my gaze locked on hers. "I seem to remember you saying something about going to nursing school?" I glance around the diner. "Didn't work out?"

Val shifts uncomfortably, her eyes darting around the room like she's looking for an escape. The clatter of dishes and the hum of chatter go on, oblivious to the battle unfolding at the counter. Her face tightens with anger.

I smile, slowly sipping from my cup. "Ah, there she is."

"You think you're better than me?" Her voice cracks, but she tries to sound sharp.

"I know I am," I say calmly, meeting her glare without flinching. "And not because you're a waitress. I'm better because you're a predator, Val. I thought you were just a sad, insecure girl lashing out. But no, you're worse than that. You're the scum of the earth—no better than the shit on the bottom of my shoe."

Her hands tremble as she glances over her shoulder, desperate, cornered. I lean in, lowering my voice. "Does your boss know? I could let them know. Don't think they'd want someone like you around the coffee." I watch as Val nervously glances at a tall, older man walking from table to table, greeting patrons with friendly words.

"You know, you might think you got away with it, Val, but secrets have a way of coming out." I pause, giving her time to realize I'm looking right at her boss. "Ooh. It looks like he's seeking customer feedback." I take another sip of coffee. "I've got plenty to share."

Her eyes flash with panic. "What do you want, Josie?" she snaps, wrapping her arms around herself like she's trying to hold herself together. "Haven't you done enough by ruining my life? Always taking what's mine?"

I laugh, the bitterness escaping like a bark. "My God, what is wrong with you? You ruined your life all on your own, Val."

Her face contorts with resentment, that same twisted expression I'd seen so many years ago. "You think you're perfect, don't you? Coming here to flaunt your perfect little life in front of me?"

That's when it hits me—she was jealous the whole time. I had no idea. I was so busy just trying to survive that I didn't see what she saw. What everyone saw. My thoughts drift back to Sawyer's words at prom, just moments before Val threw a stick of dynamite into our lives: *"This untouchable goddess. Strong, smart, wickedly funny—and don't get me started on how beautiful you are."*

"No, I'm not trying to flaunt my perfect life," I say, my voice steady, ice-cold. "I came here to tell you that even though I am better than you, I still would love nothing more than to see you taken down. And I plan on keeping a very close eye on you for the rest of your life so I can get that chance."

Her glare hardens, eyes blazing with hatred. "You don't know what my life's been like. You have no idea how much I've suffered."

"I don't need to know, and frankly, I don't care," I reply, my tone unyielding. "You made your choices, and now you're drowning in them. You can rot in this mess you've made, but don't think for a second you succeeded in keeping Sawyer and me apart."

Her eyes flash with that familiar spark of envy. "Fine, congratulations. You got your closure."

I lean in, my voice dangerously calm. "I don't need closure from you, Val. I just want to make it clear—if you come anywhere near Sawyer, me, or anyone I care about, I will ruin your pathetic existence. You were shamed out of school, out of Maplewood, but knowing you, you've been lurking, watching, waiting with those beady little eyes of yours. We all know how you operate."

Tears well up in her eyes, but I feel nothing. Not an ounce of sympathy.

I realize there's not much I can really do to her. Fifteen years have passed. No evidence. No witnesses. No proof. The statute of limitations has probably run its course, and even if it hadn't, dragging this mess into the open would do more harm than good—mostly for Sawyer.

The justice system won't help me here.

But the worst part isn't what Val did to me back then. It's what she could have done to him.

I think of Sawyer, his face when I saw him again after all those years, the quiet pain I never fully understood until now. Val's twisted need for control could have destroyed him. She could have taken everything from him—his future, his sense of safety, his ability to trust. She could have stripped away everything good in his life, and for that, I can't let her get away with it.

Not because of the bullying. Not even because of her attempts to get between Sawyer and me. But because of Sawyer. Because what she almost did—the attack she attempted—is something I can never forgive.

I take another sip of coffee. I'm not here for revenge, not in the traditional sense. I know there's no neat, tidy ending for people like Val. No courtrooms, no handcuffs. The only thing I have left to give her is the knowledge that I'll be watching her, always, waiting for her to slip. Because the truth is, people like Val never really change. They just learn how to hide better.

She'll never know peace, not while I'm breathing.

I lean in closer, savoring the moment, feeling the force of my own power for the first time. Val's eyes dart to her boss again, then back to me, her hands shaking. She knows, just like I do, that this confrontation—this cup of coffee—could ruin whatever little life she's built here. All it would take is one whisper. One carefully placed word. Her boss would toss her out like yesterday's trash.

But I don't even need to do that. Watching her squirm, seeing the fear in her eyes—that's enough. She can keep waiting for the other shoe to drop, knowing it could fall at any moment.

I smile slowly, letting her feel the gravity of my silence, and then I stand, tossing a few bills on the counter. "Come near us, and I will destroy you. Philadelphia won't be far enough for you to hide."

And just for fun, I add a nod to the darkest parts of my own path, dragging my skeletons out to dance in the sunshine. I swirl my fingers near my temple. "And I am fucking crazy, so don't test me."

As I walk toward the door, I can feel her eyes burning into my back, but they don't touch me anymore. I hear Sarge's words from years earlier, when he comforted me after my mom attacked me before Sawyer's prom: *"Don't give anyone the power to dim your light, especially not those who can't find their own."*

I lift my chin, glance back, and toss a wink in her direction. "I'd wish you luck in living with yourself, but honestly, I don't give a damn if you do."

The cold air stings my face as I step outside, the snow falling in quiet contrast to the storm raging inside that diner. And with each step, I feel lighter, finally free of the weight of Val, of the past. Ready to face whatever comes next. The road to Maplewood and Sawyer lies ahead, and I won't let Val steal another second of my life.

***

As I exit the bus station, I pause for a moment, taking in the familiar sights of Maplewood, now blanketed in thick snow. I'm lucky I got here at all. Just as we approached the exit on the highway, we learned all buses were being grounded for the rest of the night and likely tomorrow. I could not believe my luck as I watched my small town come into view, knowing I was so close to being stranded in Philadelphia. The town has a serene, almost magical quality under the white veil, and for a brief moment, peace washes over me. It's like being caught inside a perfect snow globe. But I'm on a mission, and I'll be damned if this snowstorm, however magical, stops me.

I walk through the familiar streets, quiet and deserted as the storm keeps everyone inside. I turn a corner and pause for a moment, gathering the strength to keep going. I am scared. I am shaking. I am sad. But I am *not* stopping. My heart pounds as I approach the part of Maplewood I deliberately avoided for fifteen years.

When I reach the site, the scarred earth where my childhood home once stood, my breath catches in my throat. The snow covers the ground, masking the pain and devastation beneath. Memories crash over me, overwhelming me with a wave of emotions I've kept buried for years. The house may be gone, reduced to ashes long ago, but the outline of the foundation is still visible beneath the snow. I stand there, staring at the remnants of my past, feeling the agony of fifteen years of grief and loss pressing down on me.

I take a few hesitant steps forward, my feet sinking into the snow. Tears well up in my eyes, blurring my vision. I drop to my knees, the cold seeping through my jeans, but I barely feel it. Placing my hands on the icy ground, I allow myself to cry. The sobs shake me, my body racked with the grief I've held back for so long. It's strange how easy it is to fool yourself into thinking you've healed just because you've ignored the wound.

"Mom, Dad," I whisper, my voice breaking. "I'm so sorry."

Even as I cry, the guilt clings to me, whispering that I should have been there. I should have been home. Maybe if I'd been with them that night, things would've been different. Maybe they'd still be alive. Maybe my mom would have eventually gotten sober, and my dad would have owned his own life. Maybe there were brighter days ahead, just there—around the corner. Maybe.

I've carried this with me for so long, pretending it didn't shape everything I've done since. The choices I made—where to live, how to love, what to avoid—they were all rooted in that guilt. And as much as I've wanted to let it go, I don't know if I ever truly can.

I cry not just for the loss of my parents but for the girl who has carried this burden for so long. For the guilt that's hollowed out parts of me I didn't even know were missing. I wasn't there when they died. *Did they think of me in those final moments? Did they have regrets? Did they call my name?* Those are questions I'll live with for the rest of my life. But I don't have to sentence myself to live in that moment anymore. I don't have to burn in that fire. I never deserved hell.

After what feels like an eternity, my sobs subside. I lift my head, wiping the tears from my face, and take a deep breath. My gaze shifts to the house next door—Sarge's house. I almost expect to see him on the porch, smoking his Lucky Strikes, ready with his gruff yet kind advice. I need it now. But the porch is empty, and the familiar ache in my chest swells. I can hear him somewhere in the recesses of my mind.

Josie girl, you don't quit just because it hurts. You keep going because it hurts. That's how you know you're still alive.

But he's not here, and the realization hits me hard—he's gone, and I have to accept that.

My body feels heavy, but there's a strange lightness in my soul. For years, I thought this was where my story ended, that everything of value was buried beneath the ashes here. But now, looking at it, I realize this isn't the end at all. It's just the beginning. I've been running from this place, from this grief, for so long that I forgot what it meant to stand still and face it.

Slowly, I stand, brushing the snow off my jeans. My legs are shaky, but my resolve is stronger than it's ever been. I've mourned, I've cried, and I've faced what I thought I couldn't. Now it's time to live. Time to move forward—not just because I have to, but because I want to.

I turn to leave, but not without one last glance at the scarred ground that holds the remnants of my past. It's a part of me, but it's not the whole story. Not anymore.

Lifting my head, I let the snowflakes kiss my cheeks, and for the first time in a long while, I smile through my tears.

***

I quicken my pace, my breath visible in the cold air, mingling with the falling snowflakes. The streets of my hometown, now blanketed in white, stretch out before me, guiding me toward Beatrice's Blossom & Briar. A flutter of nervousness settles in my belly as I notice the weather has shut down most of the shops in Maplewood. I can only hope Beatrice is still at her shop.

I exhale in relief when I see the light on inside. Pushing the door open, the bell chimes overhead, and the warmth of the floral shop envelops me. The vibrant arrangements decorating the space are stunning, showcasing Beatrice's extraordinary talent. Even now, in this moment of anticipation, I can't help but admire her work.

From the back room, I hear the sounds of someone shuffling around. "Be right there!" Beatrice calls out. "I'm actually getting ready to close up early—"

She stops short as she emerges from the back, her eyes widening in surprise. "Josie?" She freezes for a split second before a radiant smile spreads across her face like sunshine breaking through clouds. "Josie!" She runs the few steps toward me and throws herself into my arms. "You're here!" she cries.

She steps back to look at me, her expression suddenly changing. "Holy shit."

A sense of dread creeps over me. "Bea, what is it?"

Sensing my fear, she quickly smiles. "No, no, nothing bad. Just—holy shit." She lifts a finger, indicating for me to stay put, and pulls her phone from her back pocket. "Put a pin in that," she says before she speaks a command into her phone. "Call Sawyer."

I start to protest, but Beatrice places a finger over her lips, urging me to be quiet. She holds the phone to her ear.

"Hey. Where are you? . . . No, no, I'm fine. I just wanted to see how the roads are." There's a pause while Beatrice listens. Then she shakes her head and laughs softly. "The baseball field? Of course you are. Listen—do me a favor and stay there for five minutes. Just stay there, okay? . . . Bye. Oh, and, Sawyer, I know you're disappointed that your flight was canceled, but these things happen. I have a feeling that it will all work out." She disconnects the call and slips the phone back into her pocket.

My mouth drops open as I start to piece their conversation together.

She grabs my hands. "He's feeling sorry for himself at the baseball field since his flight to freaking *Ireland* was canceled due to the blizzard that's literally about to wreak havoc here in an hour."

I can't find my words, so I stand with my mouth open, frozen in disbelief.

"Go!" she says with a laugh, gently pushing me toward the door. "Go and hunker down with your man, and for the love of God, keep me in the loop on your surprises so I can make sure you don't land in a transcontinental mix-up!"

I hug her tightly. "I love you so friggin' much. I'll call you tomorrow." With that, I turn and run out the door, wheeling my bag behind me through the snow, feeling the thrum of my pulse in my ears as a giddy energy pushes me forward.

***

By the time the baseball field comes into view, I'm breathless, snowflakes tangled in my hair. I'm shivering and sweating at the same time, my feet numb, yet a thrill of excitement courses through me—Sawyer is close.

As I near the field, I drop my suitcase and quicken my pace, scanning for a glimpse of auburn amidst the falling snow. My heart sinks for a moment, fearing he might have left, but then I see him. He's leaning against the chain-link fence behind home plate, unaware of my presence. His eyes are closed, head tilted back, as if savoring the feel of snowflakes on his skin.

I pause, letting a memory wash over me—seeing him here, in this very place, years ago. Back then, watching the boy with auburn curls catch Jason's fastballs, something inside me stirred. I didn't understand it at the time. It was curiosity then, but now, standing here in the snow, I realize it was always more.

I reach up and touch the claddagh necklace around my neck and smile. Despite my hasty departure, Dermott was still my only call. He showed up just as I was about to leave for the airport. He pulled me in, hugging me tightly, and when he let me go, he dropped the gold claddagh necklace into my hand. I didn't notice when I tore it from my neck all those years ago, Dermott was right behind me. He'd picked it up, keeping it this entire time. He had the chain repaired a few days after we returned from Maplewood this last time. He said he figured I'd want it back.

I move toward the food stand, circling the field. Sawyer is so lost in thought that he doesn't notice me approaching. Spotting a patch of soft, fluffy snow, I can't resist—before I know it, a snowball is forming in my hand, and without hesitation, I launch it straight at Sawyer, my bangles jangling with the pitch.

The snowball explodes across his chest, a puff of white scattering into the air. For a heartbeat, everything stills—his eyes snap open, wide with shock, and he looks down at the snow dusting his coat.

He lifts his head, locking eyes with me.

For a second, he just stands there, staring at me like he's not sure I'm real. His lips part, a flicker of recognition flashing across his face. I watch as the shock fades, replaced by something warmer, something that makes my heart come alive in my chest.

"Nice catch, all-star!" I call out, my voice trembling with nerves and exhilaration.

I barely have time to register the smile tugging at the corners of his mouth before we're both moving—me, already running, and him, narrowing the gap between us with those long, purposeful strides. Sawyer leaps over the fence in one smooth motion. My smile widens as he draws closer.

When we're finally toe to toe, his hand comes up to gently lift my chin. "You're here," he says, his voice soft, in disbelief.

"I'm here."

"How?"

"Well, it wasn't easy," I say, glancing up at the sky before offering a cheeky smile. "But I like it here, and I didn't think it was fair to turn my back on the place. I've had some magical experiences in Maplewood. A wise man once told me not to throw the baby out with the bathwater."

Sawyer smiles. "That same guy told me that fortune favors the bold. Which is why I booked a ticket to Dublin two days ago. It was supposed to take off in an hour, but it got canceled."

We stare at each other, smiling.

"Why were you going to Dublin, Sawyer?" I whisper.

"To do what I should have done fifteen years ago. To find you. To tell you I love you and don't want to live without you." His expression is so gentle as his hand finds my hair. "To tell you that I'll be there for the worst of it. That I'll hold you together when you feel like you're breaking apart. Not because you're not strong enough—you are—but because I'm not. I'm not strong enough to exist without you, and I'm tired of pretending I am." He presses his forehead to mine, his eyes full of hope. "And to tell you that if you feel happier, safer, better in Ireland, then I'll find a way to be there with you too."

I can barely catch my breath. Here he is, the other part of me. I don't care how it sounds—strong, independent, capable of living alone—none of it matters. I wasn't designed for that. I was designed for Sawyer, and he was designed for me. He's home. Wherever he is, that's home.

"Sawyer, that wise man told me something else."

"Yeah?"

"Yep. He said sometimes we put down our own roots. The choice is ours." I reach up and touch the auburn curls peeking out from under his skully cap. "I choose Maplewood. I choose you."

Sawyer brings my hand to his chest, tucking it inside his coat. "I can feel your heart pounding," I whisper.

"Josie, I swear the only time I've felt my own heart in the last fifteen years is when you're near me."

With that, I pull his head down and press my lips to his. The cold of our skin, the wet snow, and the heat of our mouths create such an intense sensation that I gasp for breath, only to dive back in for more. We kiss until we're breathless, our bodies pressed together as if trying to close the gap of all the lost time.

Eventually, we pull back, hearts racing, his eyes locked on mine.

"Please tell me you didn't book a room at Miner's."

"Why would I do something silly like that when I live at Maple Lake with my boyfriend?" I laugh, then add with a playful grin, "Besides, I'm already halfway to becoming his green card wife." The words are light, but a flicker of self-consciousness washes over me. *What if he thinks that's crazy? What if he's not ready for that?*

"Oh thank God. Let's go home, Josie O," he says, grabbing my face and kissing me again until every doubt, every question, and every ghost from our past melts away with the snow.

Epilogue

Two years later

Sawyer

Snow dusts the windows of our home, falling gently outside, blanketing Maple Lake in a serene white. Inside, the house hums with life—warm, cozy, and bursting with the sounds of family. Christmas decorations are strung up everywhere, from the twinkling lights draped over the fireplace to the garland wrapped around the banister. The massive Christmas tree in the corner, adorned with ornaments Josie and I picked out together, nearly touches the ceiling.

I stand at the stove, stirring the pot of gravy, the rich aroma curling up to fill the kitchen. Mom is beside me, checking the oven, humming softly along with "Have Yourself a Merry Little Christmas" playing from Alexa. Her voice wavers off-key here and there, but it doesn't matter. It feels right. It feels perfect.

And damn, this perfection didn't come easy. It was fought for—every inch of it—and well earned.

"Your brother will be here soon with Tracy and the kids," she says, her gaze drifting toward the living room. It settles on Ken, her husband, crouched by the fireplace as he adds another log to the flames. Her expression is gentle, affection quietly spilling through.

Beatrice breezes in from the living room, grinning. "Jason just landed," she says, grabbing a cookie off the tray on the counter. "He's on his way from the airport, and get this—he's bringing a girl. Apparently, it's serious."

I raise an eyebrow. "Jason? Serious? Is she real?"

Beatrice laughs, giving me a playful punch. "All I know is, he's like a giddy schoolgirl. Might be fun to watch him squirm." She winks and heads back into the living room.

I'm still grinning as I glance across the room, but then I see her—and the air leaves my lungs like it always does.

Josie.

She's standing near the Christmas tree, one hand resting lightly on the back of the couch, the other gesturing as she talks to Aunt Marietta. Her head is tilted just so, her laughter soft and warm, and there's that glow in her eyes—the one that pulled me under the first time I saw her. The one that still makes me believe in things I thought I'd long since given up on.

God, she's so pretty.

Her auburn hair falls down her back in loose waves, catching the glow of the twinkling lights and turning it to fire. Her skin, porcelain and freckled in all the places I've kissed a hundred times, contrasts against the dark-green sweater she's wearing. It hugs her in all the right ways, bringing out the deep emerald of her eyes. Eyes that sparkle with something more than joy—something stronger, fiercer.

And as she moves, tucking a strand of hair behind her ear, I can't help but notice the way she makes those simple jeans look like a goddamn ballgown. Like nothing in the world could outshine her.

She glances over at me then, her lips curving into a soft smile, and it's like time slows. I'm brought back to our first Christmas together, when I gave her the claddagh necklace she still wears, and I told her I loved her. The music fades, the fire crackles in the background, and all I can think is, *How did I get so lucky?*

Because somehow, despite everything, she's still here. Still mine. And as long as I'm breathing, I'm never letting her go again.

It's her quiet strength, her bravery, her beauty inside and out, that undoes me. Two years ago, she was still running from her grief, unsure if she could ever stop. Now, she stands here, in this home we've made together, fearless. She's faced the darkest parts of herself and emerged stronger, more radiant than I ever imagined. Well—that's not entirely true. I've always known she was capable of anything.

It hasn't been easy. Just because we found our way back to each other doesn't mean the trauma didn't leave scars. She still carries those burdens—but she's learned how to breathe through them, to live with them without letting them define her. I'm in awe of her resilience.

"Hey, you okay?" Josie's voice pulls me out of my thoughts.

I blink, smiling at her. "Just admiring the view."

She rolls her eyes. "Cheeseball." But her grin is warm. "Everything smells amazing. You sure you don't need help?"

"We're good," I say, waving her off with the wooden spoon. "You just keep glowing over there."

She laughs, her cheeks flushing. "Well, if that isn't the politest way to keep me out of the kitchen before I ruin everything."

Her laugh—one I hear more and more—is one she's earned. Even when the past catches up with her, when memories try to pull her under, she stands tall. She's always working to be better, stronger, braver. I don't think she could be any better, and yet she always strives to be—for us. I see her grounding herself when she's anxious, counting her breaths, naming three things to stay present. And most times, I'm lucky enough to be one of those things—*Sawyer, William, Rupert.*

Aunt Fiona steps into the room, cradling a tiny bundle in her arms. Josie's face lights up as she takes William from her aunt, holding him close. Uncle Sean follows, holding Rupert, his calloused farmer's hands surprisingly gentle. I watch as Josie presses kisses to their foreheads, her whole world wrapped up in those moments, and I can't believe she ever doubted the kind of mother she would be.

When Josie came back, we couldn't get married fast enough. She was home by Thanksgiving, and by New Year's Eve, we were standing on the back patio of Miner's, surrounded by the warmth of close friends and heat lamps keeping the Pennsylvania cold at bay, exchanging the vows we always held in our hearts.

Sarge's Rupert, as we've come to call him since the boys were born, passed away not long after. It was as if Rupert finally was granted the long-desired permission to join his William. His sister found him sitting in a rocking chair on the porch of Miner's, a letter clutched to his chest, a smile on his face.

When we found out Josie was pregnant, her old fears crept back in. She worried that she'd repeat her mother's patterns, that she wouldn't know how to love our boys the way they deserved. But from the moment that test came back positive, she's been nothing short of a doting mother. Watching her with them, I know she was born for this. Her maternal instinct, the way she cares for people—it's a sight to behold.

Of course, we've had our struggles, but we faced them together. After the twins were born, Josie experienced severe postpartum anxiety. We had prepared ourselves for postpartum depression, given her history, but it wasn't sadness that took hold of her—it was fear. A fear so gripping, it consumed her. She had already lost so much, and the thought of losing our boys terrified her.

I installed cameras everywhere, giving her a sense of security. And when she insisted on putting up a fence around the house to keep the kids safely away from the lake, I didn't hesitate. The fence is so big I can barely get through it myself some days, but if it brings her peace, it's a small price to pay for her happiness.

The front door bangs open, and Dermott stumbles in, carrying a bag of toys. He shakes the snow from his boots and grins. "Happy Christmas!" he booms, dropping the bag by the tree. "The twins are getting spoiled this year, whether you like it or not!"

Josie rolls her eyes. "Dermott, that's too much."

"Feck off, Josie!" Dermott smirks, plopping into a chair. "You can never overdo it on Christmas. And I'm only here for another week. These boys deserve the world." He winks at me, clearly pleased with himself. "Just call me Santa Claus."

Before I can reply, there's a commotion. Our big, goofy German shepherd comes barreling into the room, her tail wagging like a propeller. She makes a beeline for Dermott, who yelps in mock horror.

"Down, Princess!" I call out, laughing as the dog practically tackles him, sniffing at the bag of toys.

"Josie, for fuck's sake, I thought you wanted a small dog!" Dermott cries.

"Well, Sawyer gave me everything I wanted, so I let him pick the dog."

"Yeah, but did you know he chose a bloody horse!" Dermott grumbles, trying to fend her off, but he's amused too.

I shake my head, laughing, but my attention shifts when I catch Beatrice standing off to the side, her gaze lingering on Dermott. There's something soft in her expression, something I haven't seen before. And then, when she isn't looking, I notice he sneaks a glance in her direction too, his eyes following her as she busies herself near the tree.

As Josie rocks William, she catches my eye, her smile full of love. I walk over, wrapping an arm around her waist and pressing a kiss to her temple. She nods toward Beatrice and Dermott and winks. "Put a pin in that."

I raise my eyebrows, and Uncle Sean hands me Rupert. As I hold him, warmth floods through me, his tiny body warm and soft against my chest. I shift him gently, cradling him as his little fingers grasp at my sweater. His eyes flutter closed, and I feel the steady rise and fall of his breath. It's incredible, really, how much life can change in just two years. How much love can fill the spaces where grief once lived. Rupert stirs in my arms, his small face scrunching in a way that makes me smile. *Life is fragile,* I think, *but it's also relentless, always pushing forward, always giving us more reasons to keep going.*

I glance at the wall near the tree, where a framed place mat hangs next to our wedding portrait. It's nothing fancy—just a simple place mat marked with coffee rings from the morning Josie and I thought we were over. I kept it, unable to throw it away, knowing it held more than just stains. When we came home, after that surprise at the baseball field, I showed it to her. It was the first thing we framed and hung on the wall together.

Above the rings, we've written the Johnny Cash quote Sarge shared in his last letter:

With her, this morning, having coffee.

That's what paradise is like, and now, standing here, I understand exactly what he meant. Paradise isn't some distant, perfect dream—it's here, in this house, on this snowy Christmas morning, with her, our boys, and family filling every corner with love.

Simple. Perfect.

As the smell of pine and cookies fills the air and Christmas music plays softly in the background, Beatrice glances at Dermott, her cheeks flushed. Dermott, blissfully unaware, is pulling dog toys from the bag, tossing them to Princess, who eagerly pounces after each one. And Josie looks up at me, as we hold our children, her green eyes sparkling, and I know—this is everything.

This is home.

Acknowledgements

The first book I ever wrote was in fifth grade. At the time, I was traveling back and forth to Ireland because my granny had fallen ill and, sadly, passed away. Fourteen weeks later, my granddad passed as well. During that time, I bought a little blank journal in a shop in County Kerry, Ireland, and poured a story into it. That story has, thankfully, never seen the light of day, but I still remember the joy of creating it. That joy has stayed with me ever since, and writing this book has brought it back to life in ways I never imagined.

I don't know if I can ever truly express how much I love these characters. Josie and Sawyer have become cherished parts of my life. Watching them grow, stumble, and find their way has been an unforgettable experience. Josie, in particular, emerged as her own force as I wrote her story. She took her own path, often surprising me along the way. When she left Sawyer on the porch on Christmas and walked back into her chaotic home, that was all Josie. I had intended for them to reconcile in that scene, but Josie had other plans. I was simply the go-between, and for that, I am grateful.

First and foremost, I want to thank my husband, Jake, the most steadfast and supportive figure in my life. While I've always claimed not to model my characters after real people (to protect the innocent—ha!), it's impossible to deny that my beautifully bald husband—who had stunning auburn hair before I came along—might have influenced Sawyer's character just a little. Jake, your unwavering encouragement and boundless belief in me inspire me every day. You never place limits on my dreams, no matter how wild they seem, and for that, I feel endlessly lucky. Thank you for being my partner in life, love, and every crazy idea I pursue.

To my children, Caitlin and Jack: There are moments when my dreams feel too far-fetched, and I catch myself thinking, "Who do you think you are?" when the itch to chase something big—like writing a book—takes hold. It's tempting to let those little doubts win. But then I think of you, and you remind me why I push forward. I want to face the big, scary things so you'll always believe you're capable of tackling even bigger, scarier things. You are my greatest inspiration, and everything I do, I do with you in mind.

While the characters in this book are fictional, I couldn't have written about the love of true, authentic friendship without the incredible, genuine friends in my life. Katie Cimino, we often find ourselves unfairly comparing other friendships to ours—because ours has set the bar so high. There's never been a moment when we weren't rooting for each other, pushing each other to be better, offering unwavering support, or sharing in both the tears and the celebrations. And, yep, we really are the funniest.

To my friends who were the first to read this book—Patty Jones, Katie Cimino, and Jennifer Heffron—thank you from the bottom of my heart. I was terrified to admit I had written a book, grappling with imposter syndrome, but your encouragement and belief in me gave me the confidence to keep going. I'll always be grateful for your kind words and enthusiasm.

Ryan Kavulich, your gift for seeing meaning beneath the surface and inspiring others has left a lasting impact on me. Your thoughtful encouragement came at exactly the right time, and I'm deeply thankful for it.

To my editor, Jessica Fogelman, whom I found through Reedsy—thank you from the bottom of my heart. Your sharp eye and meticulous attention to detail elevated this book to a level I couldn't have achieved alone. I am so grateful for your expertise and care.

To my parents, both Irish immigrants: I was so incredibly lucky to have you, and I miss you every single day. My parents didn't die, thank God, in the way Josie's did, but they both left me at different times, and very suddenly. The raw grief Josie felt in this story is something I could feel acutely. Though the circumstances could not have been more different, I berated myself for years for not being with them in their final moments and for not realizing what led to their deaths until it was too late. Writing about that grief—and the guilt—was deeply cathartic and a way to honor the love and loss I carry.

While Josie's parents in this book are not based on mine, their struggles and triumphs—especially as immigrants—shaped many of the paths I explored in this story. My parents gave me what Josie's could not: unwavering love, endless encouragement, and a deep sense of belonging. But even with that belonging, growing up as the child of immigrants with most of our family still in the motherland made finding roots a challenge. That endless search for home became a central part of Josie's journey because it has been part of mine as well.

I wish they were here to see this book completed. Although, knowing my mother, the kissing scenes would have made her nervous enough to douse me with Holy Water and have a few Masses said on my behalf. Their strength and resilience continue to inspire me, even now. They didn't just give me and my brother love and laughter—they gave us Ireland. They instilled in us a reverence for our heritage and culture, and because of them, I could so vividly picture Josie's walks through the fields, as we had walked those same fields ourselves. For all they gave me, and for the privilege of being their daughter, I will forever be grateful.

I would be remiss if I didn't thank my "found family." You know who you are. I can't possibly name you all—though I'll give a special nod to Nanny Rose, Adam D, Jen, and my whole crew. There are far too many of you to list, and I know you'd never be mad at me for leaving someone out (even if I'd worry about it endlessly). Just know that you've shaped my heart and my words more than you could ever imagine, and I'm forever grateful.

To the aspiring author: If I had listened to the talking heads and the chatter on social media, I never would have written this book—let alone published it. But here's the truth: the only way to write a book is to write. Everything else matters little or comes later. I wrote on my laptop and sometimes on a Google Doc on my phone. Whether it was a few seconds or a few hours, I made time. If I told myself I needed perfect conditions, I'd never have started.

I didn't write this book to get famous or make money. I wrote it because there was a story in my head that demanded to be told. After finishing it, I watched a few videos on how to self-publish, learned how to format book covers, listened to podcasts, and made it happen—because that's what I wanted to do.

Don't let anyone convince you it's impossible. If you have a story inside you, don't overthink it. Just start writing. If you want to do it, you absolutely can.

To my community: Holy cow! I often say that part of my cultural Irish Catholic upbringing includes that self-deprecating, humble-but-really-low-self-esteem syndrome that comes with Jesus, Mary, and all the saints. And let's be real—we can't take a compliment to save our lives! So the truth is, I wasn't sure I was even going to share that I wrote this novel. And then I did.

And to say I am mind-blown, grateful, moved, a little scared, but absolutely brimming with emotion for how so many people have supported me, uplifted me, and PREORDERED, would be the understatement of the century. I don't know how to react or properly show my gratitude. It felt like that Sally Field moment (often misquoted but so true): "You like me! You really like me!"

How do I even begin to thank everyone? I don't know that I deserve it—but it's not the writing of a book that has changed my life. It's the support I received from my community. I hope that, after reading, you are proud of what you supported. Thank you from the bottom of my heart.

And finally, to you, the reader—thank you for giving this story a place in your life. I hope it resonates with you and reminds you that nothing is insurmountable. Home isn't a place; it's something we carry within us, and the journey to find it is always worth taking.

About the author

Kitty Conway's love of storytelling began in childhood and led her to a career teaching literature and writing to middle and high school students. She holds a B.A. in English and an M.Ed. in Secondary English Education. Her debut novel, Where Old Ghosts Meet, reflects her fascination with themes of resilience, second chances, and confronting the past.

Raised in Pennsylvania, Kitty lives there with her husband, two children, and their dog. The daughter of Irish immigrants, she spent summers in Ireland, where the culture and landscapes deeply influence her writing.

Kitty creates stories that explore love, loss, and redemption, inspiring readers to reflect on their own journeys.